The Obst

Other Books by Ethel M. Dell

The Obstacle Race

Ethel M. Dell

ÆGYPAN PRESS

1921

The Obstacle Race
A publication of
ÆGYPAN PRESS

www.aegypan.com

I Dedicate This Book
To My Dear "Half-Sister,"
Mary,
With My Love

"So run, that ye may obtain."

— I Corinthians 9:24

Give me the ready brain and steadfast face
To dare the hazard and to run the race,
The high heart that no scathing word can stay
O'erleaping obstacles that bar the way,
The sportsman's soul that, failing at the end,
Can smile upon the victory of a friend,
And to my judges make this one protest, —
A poor performance but — I did my best!

PART I

Chapter I

BETTER THAN LONDON

A long, green wave ran up, gleaming like curved glass in the sunlight, and broke in a million sparkles against a shelf of shingle. Above the shingle rose the soft cliffs, clothed with scrubby grass and crowned with gorse.

"Columbus," said the stranger, "this is just the place for us."

Columbus wagged a cheery tail and expressed complete agreement. He was watching a small crab hurrying among the stones with a funny frown between his brows. He was not quite sure of the nature or capabilities of these creatures, and till he knew more he deemed it advisable to let them pass without interference. A canny Scot was Columbus, and it was very seldom indeed that anyone ever got the better of him. He was also a gentleman to the backbone, and no word his mistress uttered, however casual, ever passed unacknowledged by him. He always laughed when she laughed, however obscure the joke.

He smiled now, since she was obviously pleased, but without taking his sharp little eyes off the object of his interest. Suddenly the scuttling crab disappeared and he started up with a whine. In a moment he was scratching in the shingle in eager search, flinging showers of stones over his companion in the process.

She protested, seizing him by his wiry tail to make him desist. "Columbus! Don't! You're burying me alive! Do sit down and be sensible, or I'll never be wrecked on a desert island with you again!"

Columbus subsided, not very willingly, dropping with a grunt into the hole he had made. His mistress released him, and took out a gold cigarette case.

"I wonder what I shall do when I've finished these," she mused. "The simple life doesn't include luxuries of this sort. Only three left, Columbus! After that, your missis'll starve."

She lighted a cigarette with a faint pucker on her wide brow. Her eyes looked out over the empty, tumbling sea — grey eyes very level in their regard under black brows that were absolutely straight and inclined to be rather heavily accentuated.

"Yes, I wish I'd asked Muff for a few before I came away," was the outcome of her reflections. "By this time tomorrow I shan't have one left. Just think of that, my Christopher, and be thankful that you're just a dog to whom one rat tastes very like another!"

Columbus sneezed protestingly. Whatever his taste in rats, Cigarette smoke did not appeal to him. His mistress's fondness for it was her only failing in his eyes.

She went on reflectively, her eyes upon the sky-line. "I shall have to take in washing to eke out a modest living in cigarettes and chocolates. I can't subsist on Mr. Rickett's Woodbines, that's quite certain. I wonder if there's a pawnshop anywhere near."

Her voice was low and peculiarly soft; she uttered her words with something of a drawl. Her hands were clasped about her knees, delicate hands that yet looked capable. The lips that held the cigarette were delicately molded also, but they had considerable character.

"If I were Lady Joanna Farringmore, I suppose I should say something rather naughty in French, Columbus, to relieve my feelings. But you and I don't talk French, do we? And we have struck the worthy Lady Jo and all her crowd off our visiting-list for some time to come. I don't suppose any of them will miss us much, do you, old chap? They'll just go on round and round in the old eternal waltz and never realize that it leads to nowhere." She stretched out her arms suddenly towards the horizon; then turned and lay down by Columbus on the shingle. "Oh, I'm glad we've cut adrift, aren't you? Even without cigarettes, it's better than London."

Again Columbus signified his agreement by kissing her hair, in a rather gingerly fashion on account of the smoke; after which, as she seemed to have nothing further to say, he got up, shook himself, and trotted off to explore the crannies in the cliffs.

His mistress pillowed her dark head on her arm, and lay still, with the sea singing along the ridge of shingle below her. She finished her cigarette and seemed to doze. A brisk wind was blowing from the shore, but the beach itself was sheltered. The sunlight poured over her in a warm flood. It was a perfect day in May.

Suddenly a curious thing happened. A small stone from nowhere fell with a smart tap upon her uncovered head! She started, surprised into full consciousness, and looked around. The shore stretched empty behind her. There was no sign of life among the grass-grown cliffs, save where Columbus some little distance away was digging industriously at the root of a small bush. She searched the fringe of flaming gorse that overhung the top of the cliff immediately behind her, but quite in vain. Some sea gulls soared wailing overhead, but no other intruder appeared to disturb the solitude. She gave up the search and lay down again. Perhaps the wind had done it, though it did not seem very likely.

The tide was rising, and she would have to move soon in any case. She would enjoy another ten minutes of her delicious sun-bath ere she returned for the midday meal that Mrs. Rickett was preparing in the little thatched cottage next to the forge.

Again she stretched herself luxuriously. Yes, it was better than London; the soft splashing of waves was better than the laughter of a hundred voices, better than the roar of a thousand wheels, better than the voice of a million concerts . . . Again reverie merged into drowsy absence of thought. How exquisite the sunshine was. . .!

It fell upon her dark cheek this time with a sharp sting and bounced off on to her hand — a round black stone dropped from nowhere but with strangely accurate aim. She sprang up abruptly. This was getting beyond a joke.

Columbus was still rooting beneath the distant bush. Most certainly he was not the offender. Some boy was hiding somewhere among the humps and clefts that constituted the rough surface of the cliff. She picked up her walking-stick with a certain tightening of the lips. She would teach that boy a lesson if she caught him unawares.

Grimly she set her face to the cliff and to the narrow, winding passage by which she had descended to the shore. Her dreams were wholly scattered! Her cheek still smarted from the blow. She left the sea without a backward glance. She sent forth a shrill whistle to Columbus as she began to climb the slippery path of stones. She was convinced that it was from this that her assailant had gathered his weapons.

With springing steps she mounted, looking sharply to right and left as she did so! And in a moment, turning inwards from the sea, she caught sight of a movement among some straggling bushes a few yards to one side of the path.

Without an instant's hesitation she swung herself up the steep incline, climbing with a rapidity that swiftly cut off the landward line of retreat. She would give her assailant a fright for his pains if nothing better.

And then just as she reached the level, very sharply she stopped. It was as if a hand had caught her back. For suddenly there rose up before her a figure so strange that for a moment she felt almost like a scared child. It sprang from the bushes and stood facing her like an animal at bay — a short creature neither man nor boy, misshapen, grotesquely humped, possessing long thin arms of almost baboonlike proportions.

The head was sunken into the shoulders. It was flung back and the face upraised — and it was the face that made her pause, for it was the most pathetic sight she had ever looked upon. It was the face of a lad of two or three and twenty, but drawn in lines so painful, so hollowed, so piteous, that fear melted into compassion at the sight. The dark eyes that stared upwards had a frightened look mingled with a certain defiance. He stood barefooted on the edge of the cliff, clenching and unclenching his bony hands, with the air of a culprit awaiting sentence.

There was a decided pause before his victim spoke. She found some difficulty in grappling with the situation, but she had no intention of turning her back upon it. She felt it must be tackled with resolution.

After a moment she spoke, with as much sternness as she could muster, "Why did you throw those stones?"

He backed at the sound of her voice, and she had an instant of sickening fear, for there was a drop of twenty feet behind him on the shingle. But he must have seen her look, for he stopped himself on the brink, and stood there doggedly.

"Don't stand there!" she said quickly. "I'm not going to hurt you."

He lowered his head, and looked at her from under drawn brows. "Yes, you are," he said gruffly. "You're going to beat me with that stick."

The shrewdness of this surmise struck her as not without humor. She smiled, and, turning, flung the stick straight down to the path below. "Now!" she said.

He came forward, not very willingly, and stood within a couple of yards of her, still looking as if he expected some sort of chastisement.

She faced him, and the last of her fear departed. Though he was so terribly deformed that he looked like some dreadful beast reared on its hind legs there was that about the face, sullen though it was, that stirred her deepest feelings.

She did her best to conceal the fact, however. "Tell me why you threw those stones!" she said.

"Because I wanted to hit you," he returned with disconcerting promptitude.

She looked at him steadily. "How very unkind of you!" she said.

His eyes gleamed with a smoldering resentment. "No, it wasn't. I didn't want you there. Dicky is coming soon, and he likes it best when there is no one there."

She noticed that though there was scant courtesy in his speech, it was by no means the rough talk of the fisher-folk. It fired her curiosity. "And who is Dicky?" she said.

"Who are you?" he retorted rudely.

She smiled again. "You are not very polite, are you? But I don't mind telling you if you want to know. My name is Juliet Moore. Now tell me yours!"

He looked at her doubtfully. "Juliet is a name out of a book," he said.

She laughed, a low, soft laugh that woke an answering glimmer of amusement in his sullen face. "How clever of you to know that!" she said.

"No, I'm not clever." Tersely he contradicted her. "Old Swag at The Three Tuns says I'm the village idiot."

"What a horrid old man!" she exclaimed almost involuntarily.

He nodded his heavy head. "Yes, I knocked him down the other day, and kicked him for it. Dicky caned me afterwards, — I'm not supposed to go to The Three Tuns — but I was glad I'd done it all the same."

"Well, who is Dicky?" she asked again. Her interest was growing.

He glared at her with sudden suspicion. "What do you want to know for?"

"Because I think he must be rather a brave man," she said.

The suspicion vanished. His eyes shown. "Oh, Dicky isn't afraid of anything," he declared with pride. "He's my brother. He knows — heaps of things. He's a man."

"You are fond of him," said Juliet, with her friendly smile.

The boy's face lighted up. "He's the only person I love in the world," he said, "except Mrs. Rickett's baby."

"Mrs. Rickett's baby!" She checked a quick desire to laugh that caught her unawares. "You are fond of babies then?"

"No, I'm not. I like dogs. I don't like babies — except Mrs. Rickett's and he's such a jolly little cuss." He smiled over the words, and again she felt a deep compassion. Somehow his face seemed almost sadder when he smiled.

"I am staying with Mrs. Rickett," she said. "But I only came yesterday, and I haven't made the baby's acquaintance yet. I must get myself introduced. You haven't told me your name yet, you know. Mayn't I hear what it is? I've told you mine."

He looked at her with renewed suspicion. "Hasn't anybody told you about Me yet?" he said.

"No, of course not. Why, I don't know anybody except Mr. and Mrs. Rickett. And it's much more interesting to hear it from yourself."

"Is it?" He hesitated a little longer, but was finally disarmed by the kindness of her smile. "My name is Robin."

"Oh, that's a nice name," Juliet said. "And you live here? What do you do all day?"

"I don't know," he said vaguely. "I can mend fishing-nets, and I can help Dicky in the garden. And I look after Mrs. Rickett's baby sometimes when she's busy. What do you do?" suddenly resuming his attitude of suspicion.

She made a slight gesture of the hands. "Nothing at all worth doing, I am afraid," she said. "I can't mend nets. I don't garden. And I've never looked after a baby in my life."

He stared at her. "Where do you come from?" he asked curiously.

"From London." She met his curiosity with absolute candor. "And I'm tired of it. I'm very tired of it. So I've come here for a change. I'm going to like this much better."

"Better than London!" He gazed, incredulous.

"Oh, much better." Juliet spoke with absolute confidence. "Ah, here is Columbus! He likes it better too."

She turned to greet her companion who now came hastening up to view the new acquaintance.

He sniffed round Robin who bent awkwardly and laid a fondling hand upon him. "I like your dog," he said.

"That's right," said Juliet kindly. "We are both staying at the Ricketts', so when you come to see the baby, I hope you will come to see us too. I must go now, or I shall be late for lunch. Good-bye!"

The boy lifted himself again with a slow, ungainly movement, and raised a hand to his forehead in wholly unexpected salute.

She smiled and turned to depart, but he spoke again, arresting her. "I say!"

She looked back. "Yes? What is it?"

He shuffled his bare feet in the grass in embarrassment and murmured something she could not hear.

"What is it?" she said again, encouragingly, as if she were addressing a shy child.

He lifted his dark eyes to hers in sudden appeal. "I say," he said, with obvious effort, "if — if you meet Dicky, you — you won't tell him about — about —"

She checked the struggling words with a very kindly gesture. "Oh, no, of course not! I'm not that sort of person. But the next time you want to get rid of me, just come and tell me so, and I'll go away at once."

The gentleness of her speech uttered in that soft slow voice of hers had a curious effect upon her hearer. To her surprise, his eyes filled with tears.

"I shan't want to get rid of you! You're kind! I like you!" he blurted forth.

"Oh, thank you very much!" said Juliet, feeling oddly moved herself. "In that case, we are friends. Good-bye! Come and see me soon!"

She smiled upon him, and departed, picking up her stick from the path and turning to wave to him as she continued the ascent.

From the top of the cliff she looked back, and saw that he was still standing — a squat, fantastic figure like a goblin out of a fairy-tale — outlined against the shining sea behind him, a blot upon the blue.

Again she waved to him and he lifted one of his long arms and saluted her again in answer — stood at the salute till she turned away.

"Poor boy!" she murmured compassionately. "Poor ruined child! Columbus, we must be kind to him."

And Columbus looked up with knowing little eyes and wagged a smiling tail. He had taken to the lad himself.

Chapter II

SACRIFICE

"Lor' bless you!" said Mrs. Rickett. "There's some folks as thinks young Robin is the plague of the neighborhood, but there ain't no harm in the lad if he's let alone. It's when them little varmints of village boys, sets on to him and teases him as he ain't safe. But let him be, and he's as quiet as a lamb. O' course if they great hulking fools on the shore goes and takes him into The Three Tuns, you can't expect him to behave respectable. But as I always says, let him alone and there's no vice in him. Why, I've seen him go away into a corner and cry like a baby at a sharp word from his brother Dick. He sets such store by him."

"I noticed that," said Juliet. "In fact he told me that Dicky and your baby were the only two people in the world that he loved."

"Did he now? Well, did you ever?" Mrs. Rickett's weather-beaten countenance softened as it were in spite of itself. "He always did take to my Freddy, right from the very first. And Freddy's just the same. Soon as ever he catches sight of Robin, he's all in a fever like to get to him. Mr. Fielding from the Court, he were in here the other day and he see 'em together. 'Your baby's got funny taste, Mrs. Rickett,' he says and laughs. And I says to him, 'There's a many worse than poor young Robin, sir,' I says. 'And in our own village too.' You see, Mr. Fielding he's one of them gentlemen as likes to have the managing of other folks' affairs and he's always been on to Dick to have poor Robin put away. But Dick won't hear of it, and I don't blame him. For, as I say, there's no harm in the lad if he's treated proper, and he'd break his heart if they was to send him away. And he's that devoted to Dick too — well, there, it fair makes me cry sometimes to see him. He'll sit and wait for him by the hour together, like a dog he will."

"Was he born like that?" asked Juliet, as her informant paused for breath.

Mrs. Rickett pursed her lips. "Well, you see, miss, he were a twin, and he never did thrive from the very earliest. But he wasn't a hunchback, not like he is now, at first. The poor mother died when they was born, and p'raps it were a good thing, for she'd have grieved terrible if she could have seen what he were a-going to grow into. For she was a lady born and bred, married beneath her, you know. Nor she didn't have any such life of it either. He were a sea-captain — a funny, Frenchy-looking fellow with a frightful temper. He never come home for twelve years after Dick were born. She used to teach at the village school, and make her living that way. Very sweet in her ways she were. Everyone liked her. There's them as says Mr. Fielding was in love with her. He didn't marry, you know, till long after. She used to sing too, and such a pretty voice she'd got. I used to think she was like an angel when I was a child. And so she were. Whether she'd have married Mr. Fielding or not I don't know. There's some as thinks she would. They were very friendly together. And then, quite suddenlike, when everyone thought he'd been dead for years, her husband come home again. I'll never forget it if I lives to be a hundred. I was only a bit of a girl then. It's more'n twenty years ago, you know, miss. I were just tidying up a bit in the school-house after school were over, and she were looking at some copybooks, when suddenly he marched in at the door, and, 'Hullo, Olive!' he says. She got up, and she was as white as a sheet. She didn't say one word. And he just come up to her, and took hold of her and kissed her and kissed her. It was horrid to see him, fair turned me up," said Mrs. Rickett graphically. "And I'll never forget her face when he let her go. She looked as if she'd had her death blow. And so she had, miss. For she was never the same again. The man was a beast, as anyone could see, and he hadn't improved in them twelve years. He were a hard drinker, and he used to torment her to drink with him, used to knock young Dick about too, something cruel. Dick were only a lad of twelve, but he says to me once,

'I'll kill that man,' he says. 'I'll kill him.' Mr. Fielding he went abroad as soon as the husband turned up, and he didn't know what goings-on there were. There's some as says she made him go, and I shouldn't wonder but what there was something in it. For if ever any poor soul suffered martyrdom, it was that woman. I'll never forget the change in her, never as long as I live. She kept up for a long time, but she looked awful, and then at last when her time drew near she broke down and used to cry and cry when anyone spoke to her. O' course we all knew as she wouldn't get over it. Her spirit was quite broke, and when the babies came she hadn't a chance. It happened very quick at the last, and her husband weren't there. He were down at The Three Tuns, and when they went to fetch him he laughed in their faces and went on drinking. Oh, it was cruel." Mrs. Rickett wiped away some indignant tears. "Not as she wanted him — never even mentioned his name. She only asked for Dick, and he was with her just at the end. He was only a lad of thirteen, miss, but he was a man grown from that night on. She begged him to look after the babies, and he promised her he would. And then she just lay holding his hand till she died. He seemed dazedlike when they told him she were gone, and just went straight out without a word. No one ever saw young Dick break down after that. He's got a will like steel."

"And the horrible husband?" asked Juliet, now thoroughly interested in Mrs. Rickett's favorite tragedy.

"I were coming to him," said Mrs. Rickett, with obvious relish. "The husband stayed at The Three Tuns till closing time, then he went out roaring drunk, took the cliff-path by mistake, and went over the cliff in the dark. The tide was up, and he was drowned. And a great pity it didn't happen a little bit sooner, says I! The nasty coarse hulking brute! I'd have learned him a thing or two if he'd belonged to me." Again, vindictively, Mrs. Rickett wiped her eyes. "Believe me, miss, there's no martyrdom so bad as getting married to the wrong man. I've seen it once and again, and I knows."

"I quite agree with you," said Juliet. "But tell me some more! Who took the poor babies?"

"Oh, Mrs. Cross at the lodge took them. Mr. Fielding provided for 'em, and he helped young Dick along too. He's been very good to them always. He had young Jack trained, and now he's his chauffeur and making a very good living. The worst of Jack is, he ain't over steady, got too much of his father in him to please me. He's always after some girl — two or three at a time sometimes. No harm in the lad, I daresay. But he's wild, you know. Dick finds him rather a handful very often. Robin can't abide him, which perhaps isn't much to be wondered at, seeing as it was mostly Jack's fault that he is such a poor cripple. He was always sickly. It's often the way with twins, you know. All the strength goes to one. But he always had to do what Jack did as a little one, and Jack led him into all sorts of mischief, till one day when they were about ten they went off bird's-nesting along the cliffs High Shale Point way, and only Jack come back late at night to say his brother had gone over the cliff. Dick tore off with some of the chaps from the shore. It were dark and windy, and they all said it was no use, but Dick insisted upon going down the face of the cliff on a rope to find him. And find him at last he did on a ledge about a hundred feet down. He was so badly hurt that he thought he'd broke his back, and he didn't dare move him till morning, but just stayed there with him all night long. Oh, it was a dreadful business." A large tear splashed unchecked on to Mrs. Rickett's apron. "An ill-fated family, as you might say. They got 'em up in the morning o' course, but poor little Robin was very bad. He was on his back for nearly a year after, and then, when he began to get about again, them humps came and he grew crooked. Mr. Fielding were away at the time, hunting somewhere in the wilds of Africa, and when he came home he were shocked to see the lad. He had the very best doctors in the land to see him, but they all said there was nothing to be done. The spine had got twisted, or something of that nature, and he'd begun to have queer giddy fits too as made 'em say the brain were affected, which it really weren't, miss, for he's as sane as you or me, only simple you know, just a bit simple. They said, all of 'em, as how he'd never live to grow up. He'd get them abscies at the base of the skull, and they'd reach his brain and he'd go raving mad and die. And the squire — that's Mr. Fielding — was all for putting him away there and then. But Dick, he'd nursed him all through, and he wouldn't hear of it. 'The boy's mine,' he says, 'and I'm going to look after him.' Mr. Fielding was very cross with him, but that didn't make no difference. You see, Dick had got fond of him, and as for Robin, why, he just worshipped Dick. So there it was left, and Dick gave up all his prospects to keep the boy with him. He were reading for the law, you see, but he gave it all up and turned schoolmaster, so as he could live here and take care of young Robin."

"Turned schoolmaster!" Juliet repeated the words. "He's something of a scholar then!"

"Oh, no," said Mrs. Rickett. "It's only the village school, miss. Mr. Fielding got him the post. They're an unruly set of varmints here, but he keeps order among 'em. He's quite clever, as you might say, but no, he ain't a scholard. He goes in for games, you know, football and the like, tries to teach 'em to play like gentlemen, which he never will, for they're a low lot, them shore people, and that dirty! Well, he makes 'em bathe every day in the summer whether they likes it or whether they don't. Oh, he does his best to civilize 'em, and all them fisher chaps thinks a deal of him too. They've got a club in the village what Mr. Fielding built for 'em, and he goes along there and gives 'em musical evenings and jollies 'em generally. They'll do anything for him, bless you. But he tells 'em off pretty straight sometimes. They'll take it from him, you see, because they respects him."

"I thought the parson always did that sort of thing," said Juliet.

Mrs. Rickett uttered a brief, expressive snort. "He ain't much use — except for the church. He's old, you see, and he don't understand 'em. And he's scared at them chaps what works the lead mines over at High Shale. It's all in this parish, you know. And they are a horrid rough lot, a deal worse than the fisher-folk. But Dick he don't mind 'em. And he can do anything with 'em too, plays his banjo and sings and makes 'em laugh. The mines belong to the Farringmore family, you know — Lord Wilchester owns 'em. But he never comes near, and a' course the men gets discontented and difficult. And they're a nasty drinking lot too. Why, the manager — that's Mr. Ashcott — he's at his wit's end sometimes. But Dick — oh, Dick can always handle 'em, knows 'em inside and out, and their wives too. Yes, he's very clever is Dick. But he's thrown away in this place. It's a pity, you know. If it weren't for Robin, it's my belief that he'd be a great man. He's a born leader. But he's never had a chance, and it don't look like as if he ever will now, poor fellow!"

Mrs. Rickett ended mournfully and picked up Juliet's empty plate.

"How old is he?" asked Juliet.

"Oh, he's a lot past thirty now, getting too old to turn his hand to anything new. Mr. Fielding he's always on to him about it, but it don't make no difference. He'll never take up any other work while Robin lives. And Robin is stronger nor what he used to be, all thanks to Dick's care. He's just sacrificed everything to that boy, you know. It don't seem hardly right, do it?"

"I don't know," Juliet said slowly. "Some sacrifices are worth while."

Mrs. Rickett looked a little puzzled. There was something about this young lodger of hers that she could not quite fathom, but since she 'liked the looks of her' she did not regard this fact as a serious drawback.

"Well, there's some folks as thinks one way and some another," she conceded. "My husband always says as there's quite a lot of good in Robin if he's treated decent. He's often round here at the forge. That's how he come to get so fond of my Freddy. You ain't seen Freddy yet, miss. He's a bit shy like with strangers, but he soon gets over it."

"You must bring him in to see me," said Juliet.

Mrs. Rickett beamed. "I will, miss, I will. I'll bring him in with the pudding. P'raps if you was to give him a little bit he wouldn't be shy. He's very fond of gingerbread pudding."

"I wish I were!" sighed Juliet, as her landlady's portly form disappeared. "I shall certainly have to have a cigarette after it, and then there will only be one left! Oh, dear, why was I brought up among the flesh-pots?" She broke off with a sudden irresistible laugh, and rising went to the window. Someone was sauntering down the road on the other side of the high privet hedge. There came to her a whiff of cigarette-smoke wafted on the sea-breeze. She leaned forth, and at the gap by the gate caught a glimpse of a trim young man in blue serge wearing a white linen hat. She scarcely saw his face as he passed, but she had a fleeting vision of the cigarette.

"I wonder where you get them from," she murmured wistfully. "I believe I could get to like that brand, and they can't be as expensive as mine."

The door opened behind her, and she turned back smiling to greet the ginger pudding and Freddy.

Chapter III

MAGIC

*T*he scent of the gorse in the evening dew was as incense offered to the stars. To Juliet, wandering forth in the twilight after supper with Columbus, the exquisite fragrance was almost intoxicating. It seemed to drug the senses. She went along the path at the top of the cliff as one in a dream.

The sea was like a dream-sea also, silver under the stars, barely rippling against the shingle, immensely and mysteriously calm. She went on and on, scarcely feeling the ground beneath her feet, moving through an atmosphere of pure magic, all her pulses thrilling to the wonder of the night.

Suddenly, from somewhere not far distant among the gorse bushes, there came a sound. She stopped, and it seemed to her that all the world stopped with her to hear the first soft trill of a nightingale through the tender dusk. It went into silence, but it left her heart throbbing strangely. Surely — surely there was magic all around her! That bird-voice in the silence thrilled her through and through. She stood spellbound, waiting for the enchanted music to fill her soul. There followed a few liquid notes, and then there came a far-off, flutelike call, gradually swelling, gradually drawing nearer, so pure, so wild, so full of ecstasy, that she almost felt as if it were more than she could bear. It broke at last in a crystal shower of song, and she turned and looked out over the glittering sea and asked herself if it could be real. It was as if a spirit had called to her out of the summer night.

Then Columbus came careering along the path in fevered search of her, and quite suddenly, like the closing of a lid, the magic sounds vanished into a deep silence.

"Oh, Columbus!" his mistress murmured reproachfully. "You've stopped the music!"

Columbus responded by planting his paws against her, and giving her a vigorous push. There was decidedly more of common sense than poetry in his composition. The passion for exploring which had earned him his name was his main characteristic, and he wanted to get as far as possible before the time arrived to turn back.

She yielded to his persuasion, and walked on up the path with her face to the shimmering sea. For some reason she felt divinely happy, as if she had drunk of the wine of the gods. It had been so wonderful — that song of starlight and of Spring.

It was very warm, and she wore neither hat nor wrap. If she had come out in a bathing-dress, no one would have known, she reflected. But in this she was wrong, for presently, as she sauntered along, she became aware of a faint scent other than the wonderful cocoa-nut perfume of the gorse bushes — a scent that made her aware of the presence of another human being in that magic place.

She looked about for him with a faint smile on her lips, but the cliff-path ran empty before her, ascending in a series of fairly stiff climbs to the brow of High Shale Point. Columbus hurried along ahead of her as if he had made up his mind to reach the top at all costs. But Juliet had no intention of mounting to the summit of the frowning cliff that night. She had a vagrant desire to track that elusive scent, but even that, it seemed was not to be satisfied, and at length she stopped again and sent a summoning whistle after Columbus.

It was almost at the same moment that there came from behind her a sound that shattered all the fairy romance of the night at a blow. She turned sharply, and immediately, like a fiendish chorus, it came again spreading and echoing along the cliffs — the yelling of drunken laughter.

Several men were coming along the path that she had traveled. She saw them vaguely in the dimness a little way below her, and realized that her retreat in that direction was cut off. Swiftly she considered the position, for there was no time to be lost. To pursue the path would be to go farther and farther away from the village and civilization, but for the moment she saw no other course. On one hand the gorse bushes made a practically impenetrable rampart, and on the other the cliff overhung the shore which at that point was nearly two hundred feet below. From where she stood, no way of escape presented itself, and she turned in despair to follow the path a little farther. But as she did so, she heard another wild shout from behind her, and it flashed upon her with a stab of dismay that her light dress had betrayed her. She had been sighted by the intruders, and they were pursuing her. She heard the stamp and scuffle of running feet that were not too sure of their stability, and with the sound something very like panic entered into Juliet. Her heart jolted within her, and the impulse to flee like a hunted hare was for a second almost too urgent to be withstood. That she did withstand it was a matter for life-long thankfulness in her estimation. The temptation was great, but she did not spring from the stock that runs away. She pulled herself up sharply with burning cheeks, and deliberately turned and waited.

They came up the path, yelling like hounds on a scent, while she stood perfectly erect and motionless, facing them. There were five of them, hulking youths all inflamed by drink if not actually tipsy, and they came around her with shouts of idiotic laughter and incoherent joking, evidently taking her for a village girl.

She stood her ground with her back to the cliff-edge, not yielding an inch, contempt in every line. "Will you kindly go your way," she said, "and allow me to go mine?"

They responded with yells of derision, and one young man, emboldened by the jeers of his companions, came close to her and leered into her face of rigid disdain. "I'm damned if I won't have a kiss first!" he swore, and flung a rough arm about her.

Juliet moved then with the fierce suddenness of a wild thing trapped. She wrenched herself from him in furious disgust.

"You hound!" she began to say. But the word was never fully uttered, for as it sprang to her lips, it went into a desperate cry. The ground had given way beneath her feet, and she fell straight backwards over that awful edge. For the fraction of an instant she saw the stars in the deep blue sky above her, then, like the snap of a spring, they vanished into darkness . . .

It was a darkness that spread and spread like an endless sea, submerging all things. No light could penetrate it; only a few vague sounds and impressions somehow filtered through. And then — how it happened she had not the faintest notion — she was aware of someone lifting her out of the depth that had received her, and there came again to her nostrils that subtle aroma of cigarette-smoke that had mingled with the scent of the gorse. She came to herself gasping, but for some reason she dared not look up. That single glimpse of the wheeling universe seemed to have sealed her vision.

Then a voice spoke. "I say, do open your eyes, if you don't mind! You're really not dead. You've only had a tumble."

That voice awoke her quite effectually. The mixture of entreaty and common sense it contained strangely stirred her curiosity. She opened her eyes wide upon the speaker.

"Hullo!" she said faintly.

He was kneeling by her side, looking closely into her face, and the first thing that struck her was the extreme brightness of his eyes. They shone like black onyx.

He responded at once, his voice very low and rapid. "It's perfectly all right. You needn't be afraid. I was just in time to catch you. There's an easier way down close by, but you wouldn't see it in this light. Feeling better now? Like to sit up?"

She awoke to the fact that she was propped against his knee. She sat up, still gasping a little, but shrank as she realized the narrowness of the ledge upon which she was resting.

He thrust out a protecting arm in front of her. "It's all right. You're absolutely safe. Don't shiver like that! You couldn't go over if you tried. Don't look if it makes you giddy!"

She looked again into his face, and again was struck by the amazing keenness of his eyes.

"How did you get here?" she said.

"Oh, it's easy enough when you know the way. I was just coming to help you when you came over. You didn't hear me shout?"

"No. They were all making such a horrid noise." She suppressed a shudder. "Have they gone now?"

"Yes, the brutes! They scooted. I'm going after them directly."

"Oh, please don't!" she said hastily. "Not for the world! I don't want to be left alone here. I've had enough of it."

She tried to smile with the words, but it was rather a trembling attempt. He abandoned his intention at once.

"All right. It'll keep. Look here, shall I help you up? You'll feel better on the top."

"I think I had better stay here for a minute," Juliet said. "I — I'm afraid I shall make an idiot of myself if I don't."

"No, you won't. You'll be all right." He thrust an abrupt arm around her shoulders, gripping them hard to still her trembling. "Lean against me! I've got you quite safe."

She relaxed with a murmur of thanks. There was something intensely reassuring about that firm grip. She sat quite motionless for a space with closed eyes, gradually regaining her self-command.

In the end a snuffle and whine from above aroused her. She sat up with a start.

"Oh, Columbus! Don't let him fall over!"

Her companion laughed a little. "Let's get back to him then! Don't look down! Keep your face to the cliff! And remember I've got hold of you! You can't fall."

She struggled blindly to her feet, helped by his arm behind her; but, though she did not look down, she was seized immediately by an overwhelming giddiness that made her totter back against him.

"I'm dreadfully sorry," she said, almost in tears. "I can't help it. I'm an idiot."

He held her up with unfailing steadiness. "All right! All right!" he said. "Don't get frightened! Move along slowly with me! Keep your face to the cliff, and you'll come to some steps! That's the way! Yes, we've got to get round that jutting-out bit. It's perfectly safe. Keep your head! It's quite easy on the other side."

It might be perfectly safe for a practiced climber, but Juliet's heart was in her mouth when she reached the projecting corner of cliff where the ledge narrowed to a bare eighteen inches and the rock bulged outwards as if to push off all trespassers.

She came to a standstill, clinging desperately to the unyielding stone. "I can't possibly do it," she said helplessly.

"Yes, you can. You've got to." Quick as lightning came the words. "Go on and don't be silly! Of course you can do it! A child could."

He loosened her clutching fingers with the words, and pushed her onwards. She went, driven by a force such as she had never encountered before.

She heard the soft wash of the sea far below her above the sickening thudding of her heart as she crept forward round that terrible bend. She heard with an acuteness that made her marvel the long sweet note of the nightingale swelling among the bushes above. She also heard a watch ticking with amazing loudness close to her ear, and was aware of a very firm hand that grasped her shoulder, impelling her forward. There was no resisting that steady pressure. She crept on step by step because she could not do otherwise; and when she had rounded that awful corner at last and would fain have stopped to rest after the ordeal, she found that she must needs go on, for he would not suffer any pause.

He had followed her so closely that his hold upon her had never varied. There seemed to her to be something electric in the very touch of his fingers. She was fully conscious of the fact that she moved by a strength outside her own.

"Go on!" he said. "Go on! There's Columbus waiting for you. Can you see the steps? They're close here. They're a bit rough, I'm afraid. I made them myself. But you'll manage them."

She came to the steps. The path had widened somewhat, and the dreadful sense of sheer depth below her was less insistent. Nevertheless, the way was far from easy, the steps being little more than deep notches in the cliff. It slanted inwards here however, and she set herself to achieve the ascent with more assurance.

Her guide came immediately behind her. She felt his hand touch her at every step she took. Just at the last, realizing the nearness of the summit and safety, she tried to hasten, and in a moment slipped. He grabbed her instantly, but she could not recover her footing though she made a frantic effort to do so. She sprawled against the cliff, clutching madly at some tufts of grass and weed above her, while the man behind her gripped and held her there.

"Don't struggle!" he said. "You're all right. You won't fall. Let go of that stuff and hang on to me!"

"I can't!" she said. "I can't!"

"Let go of that stuff and hang on to me!" he said again, and the words were short and sharp. "Left hand first! Put your arm round my neck, and then get round and hang on with the other! It's only a few feet more. I can manage it."

They were the most definite instructions she had ever received in her life, and the most difficult to obey. She hung, clinging with both hands, still vainly seeking a foothold, desperately afraid to relinquish her hold and trust herself unreservedly to his single-handed strength. But, as he waited, it came to her that it was the only thing to do. With a gasp she freed one hand at length and reaching back as he held her she thrust it over his shoulder.

"Now the other hand, please!" he said.

She did not know how she did it. It was like loosing her grip upon life itself. Yet after a few seconds of torturing irresolution she obeyed him, abandoning her last hold and hanging to him in palpitating apprehension.

He put forth his full strength then. She felt the strain of his muscles as he gathered her up with one arm. With the other hand, had she but known it, he was grasping only the naked rock. Yet he moved as if absolutely sure of himself. He drew a deep hard breath, and began to mount.

It was only a few feet to the top as he had said, but the climb seemed to her unending. She was conscious throughout that his endurance was being put to the utmost test, and only by the most complete passivity could she help him.

But he never faltered, and finally — just when she had begun to wonder if this awful nightmare of danger could ever cease — she found herself set down upon the dewy grass that covered the top of the cliff. The scent of the gorse bushes came again to her and the far sweet call of the nightingale. And she realized that the danger was past and she was back once more in the magic region of her summer dreams from which she had been so rudely flung. She saw again the shimmering, wonderful sea and the ever-brightening stars. One of them hung, a golden globe of light like a beacon on the dim horizon.

Then Columbus came pushing and nuzzling against her, full of tender enquiries and congratulations; and something that she did not fully understand made her turn and clasp him closely with a sudden rush of tears. The danger was over, all over. And never till this moment had she realized how amazingly sweet was life.

Chapter IV

BROTHER DICK

She covered her emotion with the most Herculean efforts at gaiety. She laughed very shakily at the solicitude expressed by Columbus, and told him tremulously how absurd and ridiculous he was to make such a fuss about nothing.

After this, feeling a little better, she ventured a glance at her companion. He was on his feet and wiping his forehead — a man of medium height and no great breadth of shoulder, but evidently well knit and athletic. Becoming by some means aware of her attention, he put away his handkerchief and turned towards her. She saw his eyes gleam under black, mobile brows that seemed to denote a considerable sense of humor. The whole of his face held an astonishing amount of vitality, but the lips were straight and rather hard, so clean-cut as to be almost ascetic. He looked to her like a man who would suffer to the utmost, but never lose his self-control. And she thought she read a pride more than ordinary in the cast of his features — a man capable of practically anything save the asking or receiving of favors.

Then he spoke, and curiously all criticism vanished. "I had better introduce myself," he said. "I'm afraid I've been unpardonably rude. My name is Green."

Green! The word darted at her like an imp of mischief. The romantic dropped to the prosaic with a suddenness that provoked in her an almost irresistible desire to laugh.

She controlled it swiftly, but she was fully aware that she had not hidden it as she rose to her feet and offered her hand to her cavalier.

"How do you do, Mr. Green? My name is Moore — Miss Moore. Will you allow me to thank you for saving my life?"

Her voice throbbed a little; tears and laughter were almost equally near the surface at that moment. She was extremely disgusted with herself for her lack of composure.

Then again, as his hand grasped hers, she forgot to criticize. "I say, please don't!" he said. "I wouldn't have missed it for anything. It was jolly plucky of you to stand your ground with those hooligans from the mine."

"But I didn't stand my ground," she pointed out. "I went over. It was a most undignified proceeding, wasn't it?"

"No, it wasn't," he declared. "You did it awfully well. I wish I'd been nearer to you, but I couldn't possibly get up in time."

"Oh, I think you were more useful where you were," she said "thank you all the same. I must have gone clean to the bottom otherwise. I thought I had."

She caught back an involuntary shudder, and in a moment the hand that held hers closed unceremoniously and drew her further from the edge of the cliff.

"You are sure you are none the worse, now?" he said. "Not giddy or anything?"

"No, not anything," she said.

But she was glad of his hold nonetheless, and he seemed to know it, for he kept her hand firmly clasped.

"You must let me see you back," he said. "Where are you staying?"

"At Mrs. Rickett's," she told him. "The village smithy, you know."

"I know," he said. "Down at Little Shale, you mean. You've come some way, haven't you?"

"It was such a lovely night," she said, "and Columbus wanted a walk. I got led on, I didn't know I was likely to meet anyone."

"It's the short cut to High Shale," he said. "There is always the chance of meeting these fellows along here. You'd be safer going the other way."

"But I like the furze bushes and the nightingale," she said regretfully, "and the exquisite wildness of it. It is not nearly so nice the other way."

He laughed. "No, but it's safer. Come this way as much as you like in the morning, but go the other way at night!"

He turned with the words, and began to lead her down the path. She went with him as one who responds instinctively to a power unquestioned. The magic of the night was closing about her again. She heard the voice of the nightingale thrilling through the silence.

"This is the most wonderful place I have ever seen," she said at last in a tone of awe.

"Is it?" he said.

His lack of enthusiasm surprised her. "Don't you think so too?" she said. "Doesn't it seem wonderful to you?"

He glanced out to sea for a moment. "You see I live here," he said. "Yes, it's quite a beautiful place. But it isn't always like this. It's primitive. It can be savage. You wouldn't like it always."

"I'm thinking of settling down here all the same," said Juliet.

He stopped short in the path. "Are you really?"

She nodded with a smile. "You seem surprised. Why shouldn't I? Isn't there room for one more?"

"Oh, plenty of room," he said, and walked on again as abruptly as he had paused.

The path became wider and more level, and he relinquished her hand. "You won't stay," he said with conviction.

"I wonder," said Juliet.

"Of course you won't!" A hint of vehemence crept into his speech. "When the nightingales have left off singing, and the wild roses are over, you'll go."

"You seem very sure of that," said Juliet.

"Yes, I am sure." He spoke uncompromisingly, almost contemptuously, she thought.

"You evidently don't stay here because you like it," she said.

"My work is here," he returned noncommittally. She wondered a little, but something held her back from pursuing the matter. She walked several paces in silence. Then, "I wish I could find work here," she said, in her slow deep voice. "It would do me a lot of good."

"Would it?" He turned towards her. "But that isn't what you came for — not to find work, I mean?"

"Well, no — not primarily." She made the admission almost guiltily. "But I think everyone ought to be able to earn a livelihood, don't you?"

"It's safer certainly," he said. "But it isn't everyone that is qualified for it."

"No?" Her voice was whimsical. "And you think I shall seek in vain for any suitable niche here?"

"It depends upon what your capabilities are," he said.

"My capabilities!" She laughed, a soft, low laugh. "Columbus! What are my capabilities!"

They had reached a railing and a gate across the path leading down to the village. Columbus, waiting to go through, wriggled in a manner that expressed his entire ignorance on the subject. Juliet leaned against the gate with her face to the western sky.

"My capabilities!" she mused. "Let me see! What can I do?" She looked at her companion with a smile. "I am afraid I shall have to refer you to Lady Joanna Farringmore. She can tell you — exactly."

He made a slight movement of surprise. "You know the Farringmore family?"

She raised her brows a little. "Yes. Do you?"

"By hearsay only. Lord Wilchester owns the High Shale Mines. I have never met any of them." He spoke without enthusiasm.

"And never want to?" she suggested. "I quite understand. I am very tired of them myself just now — most especially of Lady Joanna. But perhaps it is rather bad taste to say so, as I have been brought up as her companion from childhood."

"And now you have left her?" he said.

"Yes I have left her. I have disapproved of her for some time," Juliet spoke thoughtfully. "She is very unconventional, you know. And I — well, at heart I fancy I must be rather a prude. Anyhow, I disapproved, more and more strongly, and at last I came away."

"That was rather brave of you," he commented.

"Oh, it wasn't much of a sacrifice. I've got a little money — enough to keep me from starvation; but not enough to buy me cigarettes — at least not the kind I like." Juliet's smile was one of friendly confidence. "I think it's about my only real vice, and I've never been used to inferior ones. Do you mind telling me where you get yours?"

He smiled back at her as he felt for his cigarette-case. "You had better try one and make sure you like them before you get any."

"Oh, I know I should like them," she said, "thank you very much. No, don't give me one! I feel as if I've begged for it. But just tell me where you get them, and if they're not too expensive I'll buy some to try."

He held the open cigarette-case in front of her. "Won't you honor me by accepting one?" he said.

She hesitated, and then in a moment very charmingly she yielded. "Thank you — Mr. Green. I seem to have accepted a good deal from you tonight. Thank you very much."

He made her a slight bow. "It has been my privilege to serve you," he said. "I hope I may have further opportunities of being of use. I can get you these cigarettes at any time if you like them. But they are not obtainable locally."

"Not!" Her face fell. "How disappointing!"

"Not from my point of view," he said. "There's no difficulty about it. I can get them for you if you will allow me."

He struck a match for her, and kindled a cigarette for himself also.

Juliet inhaled a deep breath. "They are lovely," she said. "I knew I should like them when you went past Mrs. Rickett's smoking one."

He looked at her with amusement. "When was that?"

"When I was waiting for that dreadful ginger pudding at lunch — I mean dinner." She paused. "No, that's horrid of me. Please consider it unsaid!"

"Why shouldn't you say it if you think it?" he asked.

"Because it's unkind. Mrs. Rickett is the soul of goodness. And I am going to learn to like her ginger pudding — and her dumplings — and everything that is hers."

"How heroic of you! I wonder if you will succeed."

"Of course I shall succeed," Juliet spoke with confidence as she turned to pass through the gate. "I am going to cultivate a contented mind here. And when I go back to Lady Jo — if I ever do — I shall be proof against anything."

He reached forward to open the gate. "I think you will probably go back long before the contented mind has begun to sprout," he said.

She laughed as she walked on down the path. "But it has begun already. I haven't felt so cheerful for a long time."

"That isn't real contentment," he pointed out. "It's your spirit of adventure enjoying itself. Wait till you begin to be bored!"

"How extremely analytical!" she remarked. "I am not going to be bored. My spirit of adventure is not at all an enterprising one. I assure you I didn't enjoy that tumble over the cliff in the least. I am a very quiet person by nature." She began to laugh. "You must have noticed I wasn't very intrepid in the face of danger. I seem to remember your telling me not to be silly."

"I hoped you had forgiven and forgotten that," he said.

"Neither one nor the other," she answered, checking her mirth. "I think you would have been absolutely justified in using even stronger language under the circumstances. You wouldn't have saved me if you hadn't been — very firm."

"Very brutal, you mean. No, I ought to have managed better. I will next time." He spoke with a smile, but there was a hint of seriousness in his words.

"When will that be?" said Juliet.

"I don't know. But I can make the way down much easier. The steps are a simple matter, and I have often thought a charge of gunpowder would improve that bit where the rock hangs over. If I hadn't wanted to keep the place to myself I should have done it long ago. It certainly is dangerous now to anyone who doesn't know."

Juliet came to a sudden halt in the path. "Oh, you are an engineer!" she said. "I hope you will not spoil your favorite aerie just because I may some day fall over into it again. The chance is a very remote one, I assure you. Now, please don't come any farther with me! It has only just dawned on me that your way probably lies in the direction of the mines. I shouldn't have let you come so far if I had realized it sooner."

He looked momentarily surprised. "But I do live in this direction," he said. "In any case, I hope you will allow me to see you safely back."

"But there is no need," she protested. "We are practically there. Do you really live this way?"

"Yes. Quite close to the worthy Mrs. Rickett too. I am not an engineer. I am the village schoolmaster."

He announced the fact with absolute directness. It was Juliet's turn to look surprised. She almost gasped.

"You — you!"

"Yes, I. Why not?" He met her look of astonishment with a smile. "Have I given you a shock?"

She recovered herself with an answering smile. "No, of course not. I might have guessed. I wonder I didn't."

"But how could you guess?" he questioned. "Have I the manners of a pedagogue?"

"No," she said again. "No, of course not. Only — I have been hearing a good deal about you today; not in your capacity of schoolmaster, but as — Brother Dick."

"Ah!" he said sharply, and just for a moment she thought he was either embarrassed or annoyed, but whatever the feeling he covered it instantly. "You have talked to my brother Robin?"

"Yes," she said. "He is the only person I have talked to besides Mrs. Rickett. We met on the shore."

"I hope he behaved himself," he said. "You weren't afraid of him, I hope."

"No; poor lad! Why should I be?" Juliet spoke very gently, very pitifully. "I have a feeling that Robin and I are going to be friends," she said.

"You are very good," he said, in a low voice. "He hasn't many friends, poor chap. But he's very faithful to those he's got. Most people are so revolted by his appearance that they never get any farther. And he's shy too — very naturally. How did he come to speak to you?"

She hesitated. "It was I who spoke first," she said, in a moment.

"Really! What made you do that?"

She hesitated again.

He looked at her with sudden attention. "He did something that made you speak. What was it, please?"

His tone was peremptory, almost curt, Juliet hesitated no longer.

"Do you mind if I don't answer that question?" she said.

"He will tell me if you don't," he returned, with a certain hardness that made her wonder if he were angered by her refusal.

"That wouldn't be fair of you," she said gently, "when I specially don't want you to know."

"You don't want me to know?" he said.

"I should tell you myself if I did," she pointed out.

"I see." He reflected for a moment; then: "Will you promise to tell me if he ever does it again?" he said.

Juliet laughed with a feeling of almost inordinate relief. "Yes, certainly. I know he never will."

"Then that's the end of that," he said.

"Thank you," said Juliet.

They had reached the road that turned up to the village, and the light from a large lamp some distance up the hill shone down upon them.

"That is where Mr. Fielding lives," said Green, as they walked towards it. "Those are his lodge-gates. No doubt you have heard of him too. He is the great man of the place. He owns it, in fact."

"Yes, I have heard of him," said Juliet. "Is he a nice man?"

He made an almost imperceptible movement of the shoulders. "I am very much indebted to him," he said.

"I see," said Juliet.

They reached the cottage-gate that led to the blacksmith's humble abode, and a smell of rank tobacco, floating forth, announced the fact that he was smoking his pipe in the porch.

Juliet paused and held out her hand. "Good-bye!" she said.

His grasp was strong and very steady. "Good-bye," he said, "I hope you'll find what you're looking for."

He stooped to pat Columbus, then opened the gate for her.

Instantly there was a stir in the porch as of some large animal awaking. "That you, Mr. Green?" called a deep bass voice. "Come in! Come in!"

But Green remained outside. "Not tonight, thanks," he called back. "I've got some work to do. Good-night!"

The gate closed behind her, and Juliet walked up the path with Columbus trotting sedately by her side. She heard her escort's departing footsteps as she went, and wondered when they would meet again.

Chapter V

THE GREAT MAN

*T*he church at Little Shale was very ancient and picturesque. It stood almost opposite to the lodge-gates of Shale Court, the abode of the great Mr. Fielding. Two cracked bells hung in its crumbling square tower, disturbing once a week the jackdaws that built in the ivy. Just once a week ever since the Dark Ages, was Juliet's reflection as she dutifully obeyed the somewhat querulous-sounding summons on the following day. She could not picture their ringing for any bridal festivity, though it seemed possible that they might sometimes toll for the dead.

Two incredibly old yew trees mounted guard on each side of the gate and another of immense size overhung the porch. The path was lined by grave-stones that all looked as if they were tottering to a fall.

An old clergyman in a cassock that was brown with age hurried past her as she walked up the path. She thought he matched his surroundings as he disappeared at a trot round the corner of the church. Then from behind her came the hoot of a motor-horn, and she glanced back to see a closed car that glittered at every angle swoop through the open gates and swerve round to the churchyard. She wanted to stop and see its occupants alight, but decorum prompted her to pass on, and she entered the church, which smelt of the mold of centuries, and paused inside.

It was a plain little place with plastered walls, and green glass windows, and one large square pew under the pulpit. The other pews were modern and very bare, occupied sparsely by villagers who all had their faces turned over their shoulders and were craning to watch the door.

No one looked at her, however, and Juliet, after brief hesitation, sat down in a chair close to the porch. The entrance of the Court party was evidently something of an event, and she determined to get a good view.

Footsteps came up the path, and on the very verge of the porch a voice spoke — a woman's voice, unmodulated, arrogant.

"Oh, really, Edward! I don't see why your village schoolmaster should be asked to lunch every Sunday, however immaculate he may be. I object on principle."

The words were scarcely uttered before the notes of the organ swelled suddenly through the church. Juliet sent a quick look towards it, and saw the black cropped head of the man in question as he sat at the instrument. It occupied one side of the chancel and a crowd of village children congregated in the side pews immediately outside and under the eye of the organist. Juliet felt an indignant flush rise in her cheeks. She was certain that that remark had been audible all over the church, and she resented it with almost unreasonable vehemence.

Then with a sweep of feathers and laces the speaker entered, and Juliet raised her eyes to regard her. She saw a young woman, delicate-looking, with a pretty, insolent face and expensive clothes, walk past, and was aware for a moment of a haughty stare that seemed to question her right to be there. Then her own attention passed to the man who entered in her wake.

He was tall, middle-aged, handsome in a somewhat ordinary style, but Juliet thought his mouth wore the most unpleasant expression she had ever seen. It was drawn down at the corners in a sneering curve, and a decided frown knitted his brows. He walked with the suggestion of a swagger, as if ready to challenge any who should dispute his right to the place and everyone in it.

His wife entered the great square pew, but he strode on to the chancel, tapped the organist unceremoniously on the shoulder and spoke to him.

Juliet watched the result with a curiosity she could not restrain. The black head turned sharply. She caught a momentary glimpse of Green's energetic profile as he spoke briefly and emphatically and immediately returned to his instrument. The squire marched back to his pew still frowning, and the voluntary continued. He played with assurance but somewhat mechanically, and she presently realized that he was keeping a sharp eye on the schoolchildren at the same time. The service was a lengthy one and they needed supervision. They fidgeted and whispered unceasingly. A lady whom she took to be the Vicar's daughter sat near them, but it was quite obvious that she had no control over them. During the sermon, which was a very sleepy affair, Green left the organ and went and sat amongst them.

Then indeed a profound quiet reigned and Juliet became so drowsy that it took her utmost resolution to stay awake. Most of the congregation slept unrestrainedly. It was certainly a hot morning, and the service very dull.

When it was over at last, she stepped out under the yew trees and wondered why she had not made her escape before. She was the first to leave the church, and wandering down the path through the hot, checkered sunlight she saw the shining car drawn up at the gate, and a young chauffeur waiting at the door. She glanced at him as she passed, and was surprised for a second to find him gazing at her with a curious intentness. He lowered his eyes the moment they met hers, and she passed on, wondering what there was about her to excite his interest.

Columbus was waiting with pathetic patience to be taken for a walk, and overpoweringly hot though it was she had not the heart to keep him any longer. But she could not face the full blaze of noon on the shore, and she turned back up the shady church lane with a vague memory of having seen a stile at the entrance of a wood somewhere along its winding length.

The church-goers had dispersed by that time, but at the gate of the schoolhouse which was a few yards above the church she saw a group of boys waiting clamorously, and just as she found her stile she saw Green come out dressed in flannels with a bath-towel round his neck. The boys swarmed all about him like a crowd of excited puppies, and Juliet turned into the wood with a smile. So he had refused the squire's invitation to luncheon! She was very glad of that.

The green glades of the wood received her; she wandered forward with a delightful sense of well-being. The thought of London came to her — the heat and the dust and the fumes of petrol — the chattering crowds under the parched trees — the kaleidoscopic glitter of fashion at its crudest and most amazing. She knew exactly what they were all doing at that precise moment. She visualized the shifting, restless feverish throng with a vividness that embraced every detail. And she turned her face up to the tree-tops and reveled in her solitude. Only last week she had been in that seething whirlpool, borne helplessly hither and thither like driftwood, caught here or flung there by any chance current. Only last week she had felt the sudden drawing of the vortex, sucking her down with appalling swiftness. Only last week! And today she was free. She had awakened to the danger almost at the eleventh hour, and she had escaped. Thank God she had escaped in time!

She suddenly wished that she had remembered to utter her thanksgiving during that very monotonous service instead of going to sleep. But somehow it seemed just as appropriate out here under the glorious beeches. She sat down on a mossy root and drank in the sweetness with a deep content. Columbus was busy trying to unearth a wood-louse that had eluded him in a tuft of grass. She watched him lazily.

He persevered for a long time, till in fact the tuft of grass was practically demolished, and then at last, failing in his quest, he relinquished the search, and with a deep sigh lay down by her side.

She laid a caressing hand upon him, and ruffled his grizzled hair. "I'd be lonely without you, Columbus," she said.

Columbus smiled at the compliment and snapped inconsequently at a fly. "I wish we had brought some lunch with us," remarked his mistress. "Then we needn't have gone back. Why didn't you think of it, Columbus?"

Columbus couldn't say really, but he wriggled his nose into the caressing hand and gave her to understand that lunch really didn't matter. Then very suddenly he extricated it again and uttered a growl that might have risen from the heart of a lion.

Juliet looked up. Someone was coming along the winding path through the wood. She grasped Columbus by the collar, for he had a disconcerting habit of barking round the legs of intruders if not wholly satisfied as to their respectability. The next moment a figure came in sight, and she recognized the squire.

He was walking quickly, impatiently, flicking to and fro with a stick as he came. The frown still drew his forehead, and she saw at a first glance that he was annoyed.

He did not see her at first, not in fact until he was close upon her. Then, as Columbus tactlessly repeated his growl, he started and his look fell upon her.

Juliet had had no intention of speaking, but his eyes held so direct a question that she found herself compelled to do so. "I hope we are not trespassing," she said.

He put his hand to his hat with a jerk. "You are not, madam," he said. "I am not so sure of the dog."

His voice was not unpleasant, but no smile accompanied his words. At close quarters she saw that he was older than she had at first believed him to be. He was well on in the fifties.

She drew Columbus nearer to her. "I won't let him hunt," she said.

"He will probably get shot if he does," remarked Mr. Fielding, and was gone without further ceremony.

Juliet put her arms around her favorite and kissed him between his pricked ears. "What a sweet man, Columbus!" she murmured. "I think we must cultivate him, don't you?"

She wondered why he was going back towards the church lane at that hour, for it was past one o'clock and time for her to be wending her own way back to the village. She gave him ample opportunity to clear the wood, however, before she moved. She was determined that she and Columbus would be more discreet next time.

Mrs. Rickett's midday meal was fixed for half-past-one. She was not looking forward to it with any great relish, for her prophetic soul warned her that it would not be of a very dainty order, but not for worlds would she have had the good woman know it. Besides, she had one cigarette left!

She got up when she judged it safe, and began to walk back. But, nearing the stile, the sound of voices made her pause. Two men were evidently standing there, and she realized with something like dismay that the way was blocked. She waited for a moment or two, then decided to put a bold face on it and pursue her course. Mrs. Rickett's dinner certainly would not improve by keeping.

She pressed on therefore, and as she drew nearer, she recognized the squire's voice, raised on a note of irritation.

"Oh, don't be a fool, my good fellow! I shouldn't ask you if I didn't really want you."

The answer came instantly, and though it sounded curt it had a ring of humor. "Thank you, sir. And I shouldn't refuse if I really wanted to come."

There was a second's silence; then the squire's voice again, loud and explosive: "Confound you then! Do the other thing!"

It was at this point that Juliet rounded a curve in the path and came within sight of the stile.

Green was standing facing her, and she saw his instant glance of recognition. Mr. Fielding had his back to her, and the younger man laid a hand upon his arm and drew him aside.

Fielding turned sharply. He looked her up and down with a resentful stare as she mounted the stile, and Juliet flushed in spite of the most determined composure.

Green came forward instantly and offered a hand to assist her. "Good morning, Miss Moore! Exploring in another direction today?" he said.

She took the proffered hand, feeling absurdly embarrassed by the squire's presence. Green was bareheaded, and his hair shone wet in the strong sunlight. His manner was absolutely easy and assured. She met his smiling look with an odd feeling of gratitude, as if he had ranged himself on her side against something formidable.

"I am afraid I haven't been very fortunate in my choice today either," she said somewhat ruefully, as she descended.

He laughed. "We all trespass in these woods. It's a time-honored custom, isn't it, Mr. Fielding? The pheasants are quite used to it."

Juliet did not glance in the squire's direction. She felt that she had done all that was necessary in that quarter, and that any further overture would but meet with a churlish response.

But to her astonishment he took the initiative. "I am afraid I wasn't too hospitable just now," he said. "It's this fellow's fault. Dick, it's up to you to apologize on my behalf."

Juliet looked at him then in amazement, and saw that the dour visage was actually smiling at her — such a smile as transformed it completely.

"If Miss Moore will permit me," said Mr. Green, with a bow, "I will introduce you to her. You will then be *en rapport* and in a position to apologize for yourself."

"Pedagogue!" said the squire.

And Juliet laughed for the first time. "If anyone apologizes it should be me," she said.

"I!" murmured Green. "With more apologies!"

The squire turned on him. "Green, I'll punch your head for you directly, you unspeakable pedant! What should you take him for, Miss Moore? A very high priest or a very low comedian?"

Juliet felt her breath somewhat taken away by this sudden admission to intimacy. She looked at Green whose dark eyes laughed straight back at her, and found it impossible to stand upon ceremony.

"I really don't know," she said. "I haven't had time to place him yet. But it's a little difficult to be quite impartial as he saved my life last night."

"What?" said the squire. "That sounds romantic. What made him do that?"

"Allow me!" interposed Green, pulling the bath-towel from his neck, and rapidly winding it into a noose. "It happened yesterday evening. I was having a quiet smoke in a favorite corner of mine on a ledge about twenty feet down High Shale Cliff where it begins to get steep, when

Miss Moore, attracted by the scent of my cigarette, — that's right, isn't it?" — he flung her an audacious challenge with uplifted brows — "when Miss Moore attracted as I say, by the alluring scent of my cigarette, fell over the edge and joined me. My gallantry consisted in detaining her there, after this somewhat abrupt introduction, that's all. Oh yes, and in bullying her afterwards to climb up again when she didn't want to. I was an awful brute last night, wasn't I? Really, I think it's uncommonly generous of you to have anything at all to say to me this morning, Miss Moore."

"So do I," said Mr. Fielding. "If it were possible to treat such a buffoon as you seriously, she wouldn't. I hope you are none the worse for the adventure, Miss Moore."

"No, really I am not," said Juliet. "And I am still feeling very grateful." She smiled at the squire. "Good-bye! I must be getting back to Mrs. Rickett's or the dumplings will be cold."

She whistled Columbus to her and departed, still wondering at the transformation which Green had wrought in the squire. It had not occurred to her that there could be anything really pleasant hidden behind that grim exterior. It was evident that the younger man knew how to hold his own. And again she was glad, quite unreasonably glad, that he had stuck to his refusal to lunch at the Court.

Chapter VI

THE VISITOR

"May I come and see you?" said Robin.

Juliet, seated under an apple tree in the tiny orchard that ran beside the road, looked up from her book and saw his thin face peering at her through the hedge. She smiled at him very kindly from under her flower-decked shelter.

"Of course!" she said. "Come in by all means!"

She expected him to go round to the gate, but he surprised her by going down on all fours and crawling through a gap in the privet. He looked like a monstrous baboon shuffling towards her. When through, he stood up again, a shaggy lock of hair falling across his forehead, and looked at her with eyes that seemed to burn in their deep hollows like distant lamps at night.

He stopped, several paces from her. "Sure you don't mind me?" he said.

"Quiet sure," said Juliet, with quiet sincerity. "I am very pleased to see you. Wait while I fetch another chair!"

She would have risen with the words, but he stopped her with a gesture almost violent. "No — no — no!" He nearly shouted the words. "Don't get up! Don't go! I don't want a chair."

Juliet remained seated. "Just as you like," she said, smiling at him. "But I don't think the grass is dry enough to sit on."

He looked contemptuous. "It won't hurt me. I hate chairs. I'll do as I like."

But he still stood, glowering at her uncertainly near the hedge.

"Come along then!" said Juliet kindly. "Come and sit down near me! Why not?"

He came slowly, and let himself down with awkward, lumbering movements by her side. His face was darkly sullen. "I don't see any harm in it," he grumbled, "if you don't mind."

"Of course I don't mind!" she said. "I am pleased. As you see, I have no other visitors."

He lifted his heavy eyes to hers. "You'd pack me off fast enough if you had."

"No, I shouldn't. Don't be silly, Robin!" She smiled down upon him. "You are going to stay and have tea with me, aren't you?"

He smiled rather doubtfully in answer. "I'd like to. I don't know if I can though."

"Why shouldn't you?" she questioned.

He folded his long arms about his knees, and murmured something unintelligible.

Juliet looked at her watch. "Mrs. Rickett has promised to bring it in another quarter-of-an-hour, and we will ask her to bring out Freddy too, shall we? You'll like that."

The boy's face brightened a little. He did not speak for a moment or two; then he reached forth a clawlike hand and tentatively fingered her dress. "I don't want Freddy — when I've got you," he muttered.

"Oh, don't you? How kind!" said Juliet.

Again his dark eyes lifted. "It's you that's kind," he said. "I've never

seen anyone like you before." His brow clouded again as he looked at
her. "You're quite as much a lady as Mrs. Fielding," he said. "But you
don't call me a 'hideous abortion'.."

"I should think not!" Juliet moved impulsively and laid her hand
upon his humped shoulder. "Don't listen to such things, Robin! Put
them out of your head! They are not true."

He rested his chin upon her hand, looking up at her dumbly. Her
heart stirred within her. The pathos of those eyes was more than she
could meet unmoved. Their protest made her think of an animal in
pain.

"It doesn't do to take things too seriously, Robin," she said gently.
"There are people in the world who will say unkind things of anybody.
It's just because they are thoughtless generally. It doesn't do to listen."

"No one ever said anything unkind about you," he said.

"Oh, didn't they?" Juliet smiled. "Do you know, Robin, I shouldn't
wonder if there are plenty of them saying unkind things about me this
very moment — that is, if they are thinking about me at all."

He glanced around him savagely. "Where? I'd like to hear 'em! I'd
Kill 'em!"

"No — no!" said Juliet, restraining him. "And it's no one here either.
But you've got to realize that it doesn't really matter what people say.
They'll always talk, you know. Everyone does. It's the way of the world,
and we can't get away from it."

Robin looked unconvinced. "I'd kill anyone who said anything bad
about you anyway," he said.

"I don't think you ought to talk like that," said Juliet, in her quiet
way.

"Why not?" His eyes suddenly glowered again.

But she answered him with absolute calmness. "Because if you mean
it, it's wrong — very wrong. And if you don't mean it, it's just foolish."

"Oh!" said Robin. He edged himself nearer to her. "I like you," he
said. "Talk some more! I like your voice."

"What shall I talk about?" she asked.

"Tell me about London!" he said.

"Oh, London! My dear boy, you'd hate London. It's all noise and
crowds and dust. The streets are crammed with cars and people and there
is never any peace. It's like a great wheel that is never still."

"What do the people do?" he asked.

"They just tear about from morning till night, and very often from
night till morning. Everyone is always trying to be first and to be a little
smarter than anyone else. They think they enjoy it." Juliet drew a sudden
hard breath. "But they really don't. It's such a whirl, such a strain, like

always running at top speed in a race and never getting there. Yes, it's just that — a sort of obstacle race, and the obstacles always getting higher and higher and higher." She stopped and uttered a deep slow sigh. "Well, I've done with it, Robin. I'm not going to get over anymore. I've dropped out. I'm going to grow old in comfort."

Robin was listening with deep interest. "Is that why you came here?" he said.

"Yes. I was tired out and rather scared. I got away just in time — only just in time."

Something in her voice, low though it was, made him draw nearer still, massively, protectively.

"Are you-hiding from someone?" he said.

"Oh, not exactly." She patted his shoulder gently. "No one would take the trouble to come and look for me," she said. "They're all much too busy with their own affairs."

His eyes sought hers again. "You're not frightened then anymore?"

She smiled at him. "No, not a bit. I've got over that, and I'm beginning to enjoy myself."

"Shall you stay here always?" he questioned.

"I don't know, Robin. I'm not going to look ahead. I'm just going to make the best of the present. Don't you think that's the best way?"

He made a wry face. "I suppose it is — if you don't know what's coming."

"But no one knows that," said Juliet.

He glanced at her. His fingers, clasped about his knees, tugged restlessly at each other. "I know what's going to happen to me," he said, after a moment. "I'm going to get into a row — with Dicky."

"Oh, is that it?" said Juliet. "I knew there was something the matter."

He nodded, and suddenly she saw his chin quiver. "I hate a row with Dicky," he said miserably.

Her heart went out to him, he looked so forlorn. "Why don't you go and tell him you're sorry?" she said gently.

"Not — sorry," articulated Robin, with a sniff.

The matter presented difficulties. Juliet tried to hedge. "What have you been doing?"

"Quarreling," said Robin.

"What! With Dick?"

"No." Again he glanced at her, and wiped a hasty hand across his eyes. "Dick!" he repeated, as if in derision at her colossal ignorance.

"Well, but who then?" she questioned. "That is — of course don't tell me if you'd rather not!"

"Don't mind," said Robin. "I'll tell you anything. It was — Jack." He suddenly turned to her fully with blazing eyes. "I — hate — Jack!" he said very emphatically.

"Jack! But who is Jack? Oh, I remember!" Juliet abruptly recalled the young chauffeur at the churchyard gate. "He is your other brother, isn't he? I'd forgotten him."

"He's — a beast!" said Robin. "I hate him."

His look challenged reproof. Juliet wisely made none. "Isn't he kind to you?" she said.

"It wasn't that!" blurted out Robin. "It — it — was what he said — about — about —" He suddenly stopped, closed his lips and sat savagely biting them.

"About what?" asked Juliet, bewildered.

Robin sat mute.

"I should forget it if I were you," she said sensibly. "People often do and say things they don't mean. It doesn't pay to be too sensitive. Let's forget it, shall we?"

"I can't," said Robin. "Dicky's angry." He paused, then continued with an effort. "He said I wasn't to come here, said — said he'd punish me if I did. He called me back, and I wouldn't go. He —" He suddenly broke off, and crept close to her like a frightened dog — "he's coming now!" he whispered.

The catch of the gate had clicked, and Columbus who had accepted Robin without question, bustled forward to investigate.

He came back almost immediately, wearing a satisfied look, and as he settled down again by Juliet's side, Green appeared on the path that led to the apple trees.

Robin pressed closer to Juliet. She could feel him trembling. Instinctively she laid her hand upon him as Green drew near.

"Have you come to see me or to look for Robin?" she said.

Green's look was enigmatical. It comprehended them both at a single glance. She wondered if he were really angry, but if so, he had himself under complete control.

"I have brought you a box of cigarettes to go on with, Miss Moore," he said, and produced his offering with a smile.

"How very kind of you!" said Juliet. She sat up with a quick flush of embarrassment. "How did you manage to get them so soon? You must have had them by you."

"I had," said Green. "But I can spare you these with pleasure. It's awful to be without a smoke, isn't it?"

Juliet smiled. "These will last me for ages. I am being very economical now. Please will you tell me how much they are?"

"Half-a-crown," he said.

"Oh, please!" she protested. "Let us be honest!"

"Exactly," he said. "It's all they cost me. I get them through a friend."

"But perhaps your friend wouldn't care for me to have them at that price," objected Juliet.

"Yes, he would. It's all right," Green dismissed the matter with an airiness that was curiously final. "Don't bother about paying me now, please! I'd rather have it later. Robin, get up!"

He addressed his young brother so suddenly and so peremptorily that Juliet was momentarily startled. Then very swiftly she intervened.

"Mr. Green, please, don't — be angry with Robin!"

His look flashed straight down to her. His eyes were still smiling, yet very strangely they compelled her own. He stooped unexpectedly after an instant's pause, lifted her hand with absolute gentleness away from the quivering Robin, and laid it in her lap.

"Get up, old chap!" he said. "And don't be an ass!"

There was no questioning the kindness of his voice. Robin lifted his head, stared a moment, then blundered to his feet. He stood awkwardly, as if unwilling to go but expecting to be dismissed.

"He is staying to tea with me," said Juliet.

"Oh, I think not," Green said. "Another time — if you are kind enough. Not today."

He spoke very decidedly. Robin, with his head hanging, turned away.

Green, with a brief gesture of farewell, turned to follow. But in that moment Juliet spoke in that full rich voice of hers that was all the more arresting because she did not raise it.

"Mr. Green, I want to speak to you."

He stopped at once. She thought she caught a glint of humor behind the courteous attention of his eyes.

"Forgive me for interfering!" she said. "But I must say it."

"Pray do!" said Green.

Yet she found some difficulty in continuing. It would have been easier if he had shown resentment, but quizzical tolerance was hard to meet.

She looked up at him doubtfully for a moment or two. Then, hesitatingly, she spoke. "Please — don't — punish Robin for coming here!"

She saw his brows go up in surprise. He was about to speak, but she went on with more than a touch of embarrassment. "Perhaps it sounds impertinent, but I believe I could help him in some ways, — if I had the chance. Anyhow, I should like to try. Please let him come and see me as often as he likes!"

"Really!" said Green, and stopped. The amusement had wholly gone out of his look. "I don't know what to say to you," he said in a moment.

"You are so awfully kind."

"No, I'm not indeed." Juliet's smile was oddly wistful. "I assure you I am selfish to the core. But there's something about Robin that goes straight to my heart. I should like to be kind to him — for my own sake. So don't — please — try to keep him out of my way!"

She spoke very earnestly, her eyes under their straight brows, looking directly into his, — honest eyes that no man could doubt.

Green stood facing her, his look as kind as her own. "Do you know, Miss Moore," he said, "I think this is about the kindest thing that has ever come into my experience?"

She made a slight gesture of protest. "Oh, but don't let us talk in superlatives!" she said. "Fetch Robin back, and both of you stay to tea!"

He shook his head. "Not today. I am very sorry. But he doesn't deserve it. He has been getting a bit out of hand lately. I can't pass it over."

Juliet leaned forward in her chair. Her eyes were suddenly very bright. "This once, Mr. Green!" she said.

He stiffened a little. "No," he said.

"You won't?"

"I can't."

Juliet's look went beyond him to the figure of Robin leaning disconsolately against a distant tree. She sat for several moments watching him, and Green still stood before her as if waiting to be dismissed.

"Poor boy!" she said softly at length, and turned again to the man in front of her. "Are you sure you understand him?"

"Yes," said Green.

"And you are not hard on him? You are never hard on him?"

"I have got to keep him in order," he said.

"Yes, yes, I know. A man would say that." Juliet's face was very pitiful. "Let him off sometimes!" she urged gently. "It won't do him any harm."

Green smiled abruptly. "A woman would say that," he commented.

She smiled in answer. "Yes, I think any woman would. Don't be hard on him, Mr. Green! He has been shedding tears over your wrath already."

"He came here in direct defiance of my orders," said Green.

"I know. He told me. Please never give him such orders again!"

"You are awfully kind," Green said again. "But really in this case, there was sufficient reason. Some people — most people — prefer him at a distance."

"I am not one of them," Juliet said.

"I see you are not. But I couldn't risk it. Besides, he was in a towering rage when he started. It isn't fair to inflict him on people — even on anyone as kind as yourself — in that state."

"I should never be afraid of him," Juliet said quietly. "I think I know — partly — what was the matter. Someone made a rather cruel remark about him, and someone else maliciously repeated it. Then he was angry — very angry — and lost his self-control, and I suppose more cruel things were said. And then he came here — he asked me — he actually asked me — if I was sure I didn't mind him!"

A deep light was shining in her eyes as she ended, and an answering gleam came into Green's as he met them.

"I know," he said, in a low voice. "It's infernally hard for him, poor chap! But it doesn't do to let him know we think so. As long as he lives, he's got to bear his burden."

"But it needn't be made heavier than it is," Juliet said. "No, it needn't. But it isn't everyone that sees it in that light. I'm glad you do anyway, and I'm grateful — on Robin's behalf. Good-bye!"

He lifted his hand again in a farewell salute, and turned away.

Juliet watched him go, watched keenly as he approached Robin, saw the boy's quick glance at him as he took him by the arm and led him to the gate. A few seconds later they passed her on the other side of the hedge evidently on their way to the shore, and she heard Robin's voice as they went by.

"I'm — sorry now, Dicky," he said.

She turned her head to catch his brother's answer, for it did not come immediately and she wondered a little at the delay.

Then, as they drew farther away, she heard Green say, "Why do you say that?"

"She told me to," said Robin.

She felt her color rise and heard Green laugh. They were almost out of earshot before he said, "All right, boy! I'll let you off this time. Don't do it again!"

She leaned back in her chair, and reopened her book. But she did not read for some time. Somehow she felt glad — quite unreasonably glad again — that Robin had been let off.

Chapter VII
THE OFFER

"Well, it ain't none of my business," said Mrs. Rickett, with a sniff. "Nor it ain't yours either. But did you ever know anyone as wore anything the likes of that before?"

She shook out for her husband's inspection a filmy garment that had the look of a baby's robe that had grown up, before spreading it on her kitchen table to iron.

"Ah!" said Rickett, ramming a finger into the bowl of his pipe. "What sort of a thing is that now?"

"What sort of a thing, man? Why, a night-dress — of course! What d'you think?" Mrs. Rickett chuckled at his ignorance. "And that flimsy — why I'm almost afraid to touch it. It's the quality, you see."

"Ah!" said the smith vaguely.

Mrs. Rickett tested the iron near her cheek. "And it's only the quality," she resumed, as she began to use it, "as wears such things as these. Why, I shouldn't wonder but what they came from Paris. They must have cost a mint of money."

"Ah!" said Rickett again.

"She's as nice-spoken a young lady as I've met," resumed his wife. "No pride about her, you know. She's just simple and friendly-like. Yet I'd like to see the man as'd take a liberty with her all the same."

Rickett pulled at his pipe with a grunt. When not at work, it was usually his rôle to sit and listen to his wife's chatter.

"She ain't been brought up in a convent," continued Mrs. Rickett. "That's plain to see. With all the gentle ways of her, she knows how to hold her own. Young Robin Green, he's gone just plumb moon-crazy over her, and it wouldn't surprise me" — Mrs. Rickett lowered her voice mysteriously — "but what some day Dick himself was to do the same."

"Ah!" said the smith.

"She's so taking, you know," said Mrs. Rickett, as if in extenuation of this outrageous surmise. "And there isn't anyone good enough for him about here. Of course there's the infant teacher — that Jarvis girl — she'd set her cap at him if she dared. But he wouldn't look at her. Young Jack's a deal more likely, if ever he does settle down — which I doubt. But Dick — he's different. He's — why if that ain't Mr. Fielding a-riding up the path! What ever do he want at this time of night? Go and see, George, do!"

George lumbered to his feet obediently. "Happen he's come to call on our young lady," he ventured, with a slow grin.

"Well, don't bring him in here!" commanded his wife. "Take him into the front room, while I put on a clean apron!" She hastened to shut the door upon her husband, then paused, listening intently, as Mr. Fielding's riding-whip rapped smartly on the door.

"Happen it is only the young lady he's after," she said to herself.

It was. In a moment, Mr. Fielding's voice, superior, slightly over bearing, made itself heard. "Good evening, Rickett! I think Miss Moore is lodging here. Is she in?"

"Good evening, sir!" said Rickett, and waited a moment for reflection. "She was in, but I can't say but what she may have gone out again with the dog."

"Well, find out, will you!" said Mr. Fielding. "Wait a minute! You'd better take my card."

Mrs. Rickett returned to her ironing. "What ever he be come for?" she murmured.

The Squires' horse stamped on the tiled path. It was eight o'clock, and he wanted to get home to his supper. The squire growled at him inarticulately, and there fell a silence.

The evening light spread golden over the apple trees in the orchard. Someone was wandering among the falling blossoms. He heard a low voice softly singing. He flung his leg over his horse's back abruptly and dropped to the ground.

The voice stopped immediately. The squire fastened his animal to the porch and turned. The next moment Columbus burst barking through the intervening hedge.

"Columbus! Columbus!" called Juliet's voice. "Come back at once!"

"May I come through?" said Mr. Fielding.

She arrived at the orchard-gate, flushed and apologetic. "Oh, pray do! Please excuse Columbus! He always speaks before he thinks."

She opened the gate with the words, and held out her hand.

She was aware of his eyes looking at her very searchingly as he took it. "I hope you don't mind a visitor at this hour," he said.

She smiled. "No. I am quite at liberty. Come and sit down!"

She led the way to a bench under the apple trees, and the squire tramped after her with jingling spurs.

"I'm afraid you'll think me very unconventional," he said, speaking with a sort of arrogant humility as she stopped.

"I like unconventional people best," said Juliet.

He dropped down on the seat. "Oh, do you? Then I needn't apologize any further. You've been here about a week, haven't you?"

"Yes," said Juliet.

His look dwelt upon the simple linen dress she wore. "You came from London?"

"Yes," she said again.

He began to frown and to pull restlessly at the lash of his riding-whip. "Do you think me impertinent for asking you questions?" he said.

"Not so far," said Juliet.

He uttered a brief laugh. "You're cautious. Listen, Miss Moore! I don't care a — I mean, it's nothing whatever to me where you've come from or why. What I really came to ask is — do you want a job?"

Juliet stiffened a little involuntarily. "What sort of a job?" she said.

His fingers tugged more and more vigorously at the leather. She realized quite suddenly that he was embarrassed, and at once her own embarrassment passed.

"Have you come to offer me a job?" she said. "How kind of you to think of it!"

"You don't know what it is yet," said Fielding, biting uncomfortably at his black moustache. "It may not appeal to you. Quite probably it won't. You've been a companion before — so Green tells me."

"Oh!" Juliet's straight brows gathered slightly. "Did Mr. Green tell you I was wanting a job?"

"No, he didn't. Green sticks to his own business and nothing will turn him from it." The squire suddenly lashed with his whip at the grass in front of him, causing Columbus to jump violently and turn a resentful eye upon him. "I'll tell you what passed if you want to know."

"Thank you," said Juliet simply.

She leaned forward after a moment and pulled Columbus to her side; fondling his pricked ears reassuringly.

"It was on Sunday," said Fielding. "My wife saw you in church. She took rather a fancy to you. I hope you don't object?"

"Why should I?" said Juliet.

"Exactly. Why should you? Well, after Green's introduction, when you had gone, I asked him if he knew anything about you. He said he had only made your acquaintance the day before, that you had told him that you had held the post of companion to someone, he didn't say who. And I wondered if possibly you might feel inclined to see how you got on with my wife in that capacity. She is not strong. She wants a companion."

Juliet's grey eyes gazed steadily before her as she listened. The evening light shone on her brown head, showing streaks of gold here and there. Her attitude was one of grave attention.

As he ended, she turned towards him, still caressing the dog at her feet.

"Wouldn't it be better," she said, "if Mrs. Fielding knew me before offering me such a post?"

The squire smiled at her abruptly. "No, I don't think so. It wouldn't be worth while unless you mean to consider it."

"Is that her point of view?" asked Juliet.

"No; it's mine. If she gets to know you and sets her heart on having you, and then you go and disappoint her — I shall be the sufferer," explained Fielding, with another cut at the grass in front of him.

It was Juliet's turn to smile. "But I can't — possibly — decide until we have met, can I?" she said.

"Does that mean you'll consider it?" asked the squire.

"I am considering it," said Juliet. "But please give me time! For I have only just begun."

"That's fair," he conceded. "How long will it take you?"

She began to laugh. There was something almost boyishly naïve about him, notwithstanding his obvious bad temper. "You haven't told me any details yet," she said.

"Oh, you mean money," he said. "I leave that to you. You can name your own terms."

"Thank you," said Juliet again. "That would naturally appeal to me very much. But as a matter of fact, I was not referring to money at that moment."

He gave her a keen look. "I didn't mean to offend you. Are you offended?"

She met his eyes quite squarely. "On second thoughts — no!"

"Why second thoughts?" he demanded.

Her color rose faintly. "Because I think second thoughts are — kinder."

Fielding turned suddenly crimson. "So I'm a cad and a bounder, am I?" he said furiously.

Juliet's eyes contemplated him without a hint of dismay. There was even behind their serenity the faint glint of a smile. "I think that is putting it rather strongly," she said. "But I really don't know you yet. I am not in a position to judge — even if I wished to do so."

Fielding sat for a moment or two quite rigid, as if on the verge of springing to his feet and leaving her. Then with amazing suddenness he broke into a laugh, and the tension was past.

"By Jove, I like you for that!" he said. "You did it jolly well. You've got pluck, and you know how to keep your temper. You'll have to forgive me, Miss Moore. We're going to be friends after this."

There was something very winning about this overture, and Juliet was not proof against it. He was evidently of those who consider that an apology condones any offence, and, though she was far from agreeing with him on this point, it was not in her to be churlish.

She smiled at him without speaking.

"Sure you're not angry with me?" urged the Squire.

She nodded. "Yes, quite sure. Won't you go on where you left off?"

"Where did I leave off?" He frowned. "Oh yes, you asked for details. Well, what do you want to know? My wife always breakfasts in bed, so she wouldn't want you before ten. But you'd live with us of course. I'd see that they made you comfortable."

"If my duties did not begin before ten, there would be no need for that," pointed out Juliet.

He looked at her in surprise. "Of course you'd live with us! You can't want to stay here!"

"But why not?" said Juliet. "They are very kind to me. I am very happy here."

"Oh, nonsense!" said the squire. "You couldn't do that. I believe you're afraid I want to make a slave of you."

"No, I am not afraid of that," said Juliet. "But go on, if you don't mind! What happens after ten o'clock?"

"Well, she opens her letters," said the squire. "Tells you what wants answering and how to answer it. P'raps you read the papers to her for a bit before she gets up, and so on."

"Does that take the whole morning?" asked Juliet.

"No. She's down about twelve. Sometimes she goes for a ride then, if she feels like it. Or she walks about the grounds, or drives out in the dog-cart. She's very keen on horses. Then either she goes out to lunch or someone lunches with us. And after that she's off in the car for a fifty-mile run — or a hundred if the mood takes her. She's never quiet — except when she's in bed. That's what I want you for. I want you to keep her quiet."

"Oh!" said Juliet.

This was shedding a new light upon the matter. She looked at him somewhat dubiously.

"Come! I know you can," he said. "You've been through the treadmill. You know all about it and it doesn't attract you. This infernal chase after excitement — it's like a spreading fever. There's no peace for anyone nowadays. I want you to stop it. You've got that sort of influence. I sensed it directly I saw you. You've got that priceless possession — a quiet spirit. She wouldn't go tearing over the country racing and gambling and then card-playing far into the night if you were there to pull her up. She'd be ashamed — with anyone like you looking on."

"Would she?" said Juliet. "I wonder. And how do you know that that sort of thing doesn't attract me?"

"Of course I know it. You carry it in your face. You're a woman — not a dancing marionette. You wouldn't despise a woman's duties because they interfered with pleasure. You were made in a different mold. Anyone can see that."

Juliet was smiling a little. "I can't claim to be anything very great," she said. "But certainly, I was never very fond of cards."

"Of course you weren't. You've too much sense to do anything to excess. Now look here, Miss Moore! You're coming, aren't you? You'll give the thing a trial. I promise you, you shan't be bullied or overworked. It's such an opportunity, for my wife really has taken a fancy to you. And she can be quite decent to anyone when she likes. You can bring the dog along," continued the squire. "You can have your own sitting room — your own maid, if you want one. You can come and go as you choose. No one will interfere with you. All I want you to do is to put the brake on my wife, make her take an interest in her home, make her take life seriously. She's not at all strong. She doesn't give herself a chance. Unless I fetch in a doctor and practically keep her in bed by main force she never gets any decent rest. Why, she's hardly ever in her room before two in the morning. It's almost a form of madness with her, this ceaseless round. I can't prevent it. I'm a busy man myself." He suddenly got to his feet with a jerk and stood looking down at her with somber eyes. "I'm a busy man," he repeated. "I have my ambitions, and I work for them. I work hard. But the one thing I want more than anything else on earth is a son to succeed me. And if I can't have that — there's nothing else that counts."

He spoke with bitter vehemence, beating restlessly against his heel with his whip. But Juliet still sat silent, looking out before her at the golden pink of the apple trees in the sunset light with grave quiet eyes.

He went on morosely, egotistically, "I don't know what I've done that I shouldn't have what practically every laborer on my estate has got. I may not have been absolutely impeccable in my youth. I've never yet met a man who was — with the single exception of Dick Green who hasn't much temptation to be anything else. But I've lived straight on the whole. I've played the game — or tried to. And yet — after five years of marriage — I'm still without an heir, and likely to remain so, as far as I can see. She says I'm mad on that point." He spoke resentfully. "But after all, it's what I married for. I don't see why I should be cheated out of the one thing I want most, do you?"

Juliet's eyes came up to his, slowly, somewhat reluctantly. "I'm afraid I haven't much sympathy with you," she said.

"You haven't?" he looked amazed.

"No." She paused a moment. "It was a pity you told me. You see, a woman doesn't care to be married — just for that."

"And what do you suppose she married me for?" he demanded indignantly. "Do you think she was in love with me — a man thirty years older than herself? Oh, I assure you, there were never any illusions on that score! I had a good deal to offer her, and she jumped at it."

Juliet gave a slight shiver, and abruptly his manner changed.

"I'm sorry. Put my foot in it again, have I? You'll have to forgive me, please. No, I shouldn't have told you. But you've got such a kind look about you — as if you'd understand."

She was touched in spite of herself. She got up quickly and faced him. "What I can't understand," she said, a ring of deep feeling in her voice, "is how anyone can possibly barter their happiness, their self-respect, all that is most worth having, for this world's goods, this world's ambitions, and expect to come out of it anything but losers. Oh, I know it's done every day. People fight and scramble — yes, and grovel in the mud — for what they think is gold; and when they've got it, it's only the basest alloy. Some of them never find it out. Others do — and break their hearts."

He stared at her. "You speak as one who knows."

"I do know," she said. "Since I've been here, had time to think, I've realized it more and more. This dreadful fight for front places, for prosperity — this rooted, individual selfishness — the hopeless materialism of it all — the ultimate ruin —." She broke off. "You'll take me for a street ranter if I go on. But it's rather piteous to see people straining and agonizing after what, after all, can never bring them any comfort."

"But that's just what I was saying," he protested.

Her frank eyes looked straight into his. "But you're doing it yourself all the same," she said. "You're playing for your own hand all the time and so you're a loser and always will be. It's the chief rule of the game." She smiled faintly. "Please forgive me for telling you so, but I've only just found it out for myself; so I had to tell someone."

"You're rather a wonderful young woman," said the squire, still staring.

She shook her head. "Oh, no, I'm not. I've just begun to use my brains, that's all. They're nothing at all out of the ordinary, really."

He laughed. "Well, you've given me a pretty straight one anyway. Have you got a home anywhere — any home people?"

"None that count," said Juliet.

"Been more or less of a looker-on all your life, eh?" he suggested.

"More or less," smiled Juliet.

He held out his hand to her abruptly. "Look here! You're coming, aren't you?"

"I don't know," said Juliet.

"Well, make up your mind quick!" He held her hand, looking at her. "What's the objection? Tell me?"

She freed her hand gently but with decision. "I can't tell you entirely. You must let me think. For one thing, I want more freedom of action than I should have as an inmate of your house. I want to come and go as I like. I've never really done that before, and I'm just beginning to enjoy it."

"That's a selfish reason," said the squire, with a sudden boyish grin at her.

She colored slightly. "No, it isn't — or not wholly."

"All right, it isn't. I unsay it. But that reason won't exist as far as you are concerned. You will come and go exactly as you like always. No one will question you."

"You're very kind," said Juliet.

He bowed to her ceremoniously. "That's the first really nice thing you have said to me. I must make a note of it. Now would you like my wife to call upon you? If so, I'll send her round tomorrow at twelve."

"If she would care to come," said Juliet.

"Of course she would. She shall come then — and you'll talk things over, and come to an understanding. That's settled, is it? Good-bye!"

He turned to go, pausing at the gate to throw her another smiling farewell. She had not thought that gloomy, black browed countenance could look so genial. There was something curiously elusive, almost haunting, about his smile.

"Columbus!" said Juliet. "I'm not sure that he's a very nice man, but there's something about him — something I can't quite place — that makes me wonder if I've met him somewhere before. Would you like to go and live at the Court, Columbus?"

Columbus leaned against her knee in sentimental silence. He evidently did not care where he went so long as he was with the object of his whole-souled devotion.

She stooped and kissed him between the eyes. "Dear doggie!" she murmured. "I wonder — are we happier — here?"

Chapter VIII

MRS. FIELDING

*W*hen the great high-powered car from Shale Court stopped at the gate of the blacksmith's cottage on the following morning Mrs. Rickett, who was feeding her young chicks in the yard outside the forge, was thrown into a state of wild agitation. Everyone in Little Shale stood in awe of the squire's wife.

She went nervously to enquire what was wanted, and met the chauffeur at the gate.

"It's all right, Mrs. Rickett. Don't fluster yourself!" he said. "It's Miss Moore we're after. Go and tell her, will you?"

Mrs. Rickett looked at the bold-eyed young man with disfavor. "Well, you're not expecting her to come out to you, are you?" she retorted tartly.

He smiled. "Yes, I rather think we are, Mrs. Fielding doesn't want to get out. Where is she?"

Mrs. Rickett drew in her breath. "But Miss Moore is a lady born!" she objected. "Haven't you got a card I can take her?"

Mrs. Rickett had lived among the gentry in her maiden days, and, as she was wont to assert, she knew what was what as well as anybody. She had, moreover, a vigorous dislike for young Jack Green the chauffeur who, notwithstanding his airs, — perhaps because of them, — occupied a much lower plane in her estimation than his brother the schoolmaster. But Jack was one of those people whom it is practically impossible to snub. He merely continued to smile.

"Well, you'd better let me go and find her if you won't," he said, "or madam will be getting impatient."

It was at this point that Juliet came upon the scene, walking up from the shore with her hair blowing in the breeze. She carried a towel and a bathing dress on her arm. Columbus trotted beside her, full of cheery self-importance.

She quickened her pace somewhat at sight of the car, and its occupant leaned forward with an imperious motion of the hand. Her pale face gleamed behind her veil.

"Miss Moore, I believe?" she said, in her slightly insolent tones.

Juliet came to the side of the car. The sun beat down upon her uncovered head. She smiled a welcome.

"How do you do? How kind of you to come and see me! I am sorry I wasn't here to receive you, but it was so glorious down on the shore that I stayed to dry my hair. Do come in!"

"Oh, I can't — really!" protested Mrs. Fielding. "I shall die if I don't get a little air. I thought perhaps you would like to come for a little spin with me. But I suppose that is out of the question."

"My hair is quite dry," said Juliet. "It won't take me long to put it up. I should like to come with you very much."

"I can't wait," said Mrs. Fielding plaintively. "This heat is so fearful — and the glare! I will go for a short round, and come back for you if you like."

"Thank you," said Juliet. "I can be ready in five minutes."

"I should be grilled by that time," declared Mrs. Fielding. "Jack, we will go round by the station and back by the church. It is only three miles. We can do that easily. In five minutes then, Miss Moore!"

"Look out for the schoolchildren!" exclaimed Juliet almost involuntarily. "They are sure to be all over the road."

"Oh, really!" said Mrs. Fielding, sinking back into the car, as it swooped away.

Juliet and Mrs. Rickett looked at one another.

"That young Jack Green fair riles me," remarked the latter. "I can't abide him. He's not a patch on his brother, and never will be. It's funny, you know, how members of a family vary. Now you couldn't have a more courteous and pleasant spoken gentleman than Dick. But this Jack, why, he hasn't even the beginnings of a gentleman in him."

Juliet's thoughts were more occupied with Mrs. Fielding at the moment, but she kept them to herself. "I may be late back, Mrs. Rickett," she said. "Let me have a cold lunch when I come in!"

"Oh, dearie me!" said Mrs. Rickett. "I do hope, miss, as young Jack'll drive careful when he's got you in the car."

Juliet hoped so too as she hastened within to prepare for the expedition. She did not feel any very keen zest for it, but, as she told Columbus, they need never go again if they didn't like it.

It was nearly ten minutes before the Fielding car reappeared, and they were both waiting at the garden-gate as it drew up.

"Yes, we were delayed," said Mrs. Fielding pettishly, "by those little fiends of children. I do think Mr. Green might teach them to keep to the side of the road. Pray get in, Miss Moore! Oh, do you want to bring your dog?"

"He is used to motoring," said Juliet. "Do you mind if he sits in front?"

Mrs. Fielding shrugged her shoulders to indicate that if was a matter of supreme indifference to her, and Columbus was duly installed by the driver's side. Juliet took her place beside Mrs. Fielding, and in a few seconds they were whirling up the road again, leaving clouds of dust in their wake.

"It's the only way one can breathe on a day like this," said Mrs. Fielding.

Juliet said nothing. She was watching the village children scatter like rabbits before their lightning rush.

In the schoolhouse garden she caught sight of a heavy, shambling figure, and waved a swift greeting as she flashed past.

"Oh, do you know that revolting youth?" said Mrs. Fielding. "He's half-witted as well as deformed. His brother!" with a nod towards her chauffeur's back. "He's a great trial to Jack, I believe. My husband has offered a hundred times to have him put into a home, but the other brother — Green, the schoolmaster — is absolutely pig-headed on the subject, and won't hear of it."

"Poor Robin!" said Juliet gently. "Yes, I know him. He is certainly not normal, but scarcely half-witted, do you think?"

Mrs. Fielding turned her head to bestow upon her a brief glance of surprise. "I said half-witted," she observed haughtily.

Juliet turned her head also, and gave her companion a straight and level look. "And I did not agree with you," she said quietly.

Mrs. Fielding uttered a laugh that had a girlish ring despite its insolence. "Have you said that to my husband yet?" she asked.

"Not quite that," said Juliet.

"Well, if you ever do, may I be there to hear!" she rejoined flippantly. "He's like a raging bull when he's crossed. I hear he came to see you yesterday."

"He did," said Juliet.

"Did he talk about me?" asked Mrs. Fielding.

"He told me that you were not very strong," said Juliet.

"And that I wanted someone to look after me — coerce me, when he wasn't there to do it himself. Was that it?"

"Surely you know better than that!" said Juliet.

"Oh, I know him awfully well," said Mrs. Fielding, with her reckless laugh. "Are you really thinking of coming to live with us?"

"You haven't asked me yet," said Juliet.

"Oh, that doesn't matter. You'll come if you think you will; and if you don't, nothing will induce you. But — let me tell you — my husband will be furious — with me — if you don't."

"Oh, surely not!" said Juliet.

"Yes, he is that sort. If he doesn't get what he wants, it's always someone else's fault — generally mine. I warn you — we have most frightful rows sometimes. He has only just begun to speak to me again since last Sunday. We quarreled that day over Green. You know Green — the schoolmaster — don't you?"

"Yes, I think I might call him a friend of mine," said Juliet, with a smile.

"Oh, really! I didn't know that," Mrs. Fielding's tone was suddenly extremely cold. "Hence your championship of Robin, I suppose?"

"No, I made friends with Robin separately. He is coming to tea with me today, or rather, we are going down to the shore with it. I love the shore in the evening."

"I wonder you care to mix with people like that," remarked Mrs. Fielding. "I think it is such a mistake to take them out of their own class. Green the schoolmaster is a constant visitor up at the Court, and I object to it very strongly. I cannot understand my husband's attitude in the matter."

"But he is a gentleman!" said Juliet.

"Who? Green? Oh yes, of sorts. I am glad to say his brother has no aspirations in that direction." Mrs. Fielding glanced again towards her chauffeur's unconscious back. "Or if he has, I don't get the benefit of them. As for Robin, he gives me the cold shudders every time I see him."

"Poor Robin!" said Juliet again. "I think he feels his deformity very much."

"Of course he does! He ought to be in a home among his own kind. It would be far better for everyone concerned. Frankly, the Green family exasperate me," declared Mrs. Fielding. "I can put up with Jack. He's such a smart, good-looking boy, and he can drive like the devil. But I've no use for the other two, and never shall have. I think Green's a humbug. Is he going to join your picnic-party on the shore?"

"He hasn't been invited," said Juliet.

"Oh, you won't find he needs much encouragement. As Dene Strange puts it, he is always hovering on the outside edge of every circle and ready to squeeze in at the very first opportunity."

"I should imagine my circle is hardly important enough to attract anyone in that way," remarked Juliet. "Strange is very caustic. I am not sure I like him much."

"Oh, I enjoy him," said Mrs. Fielding. "He is so brilliant. He always gets right there. You have never met him, I suppose?"

Juliet shook her head. "Not under that name, anyway. They say he is a barrister. But I haven't much sympathy with a man who hides behind a pseudonym, have you? It looks as if he hasn't the courage of his opinions."

"I shouldn't think anyone ever accused Dene Strange of lack of courage," said Mrs. Fielding. "I read all he writes. He is so intensely clever."

"Some people think he's a woman," said Juliet.

"Oh, I don't believe that. Neither do you. No woman ever had a brain like that. It's quite Napoleonic. I'd give a good deal to meet him."

"And be horribly disappointed," said Juliet.

"Why do you say that?"

"Because lions always are disappointing when they're hunted down. The ones that roar are quite insufferable, and the ones that don't are just banal."

Mrs. Fielding looked at her with interest for the first time. "You've seen a good deal of life," she remarked.

"Oh, no!" said Juliet lightly. "But enough to realize that the torch of genius burns best in dark places. Perhaps Strange is right after all — from his own point of view at least. That lion-hunting business is so revolting."

"You speak as one who knows," said Mrs. Fielding.

Juliet smiled. "I have watched from the outside edge, as Dene Strange puts it. I expect you have heard of the Farringmores, haven't you? I am distantly related to them. I was brought up with Lady Joanna. So I know a little of what London people call life."

"I saw you had been in society," said Mrs. Fielding half enviously.

"Yes, I have had five seasons — nearly six. And I never want another." Juliet spoke with great emphasis. "That's why I'm here now."

"I wonder you never married," said Mrs. Fielding.

"Do you?" Juliet spoke dreamily. They were running swiftly up a steep and stony road leading to High Shale Point. "Lady Jo used to wonder that. But I've never yet met a man who was willing to wait, and I couldn't do a thing like that in a hurry."

"You could if you were in love," said Mrs. Fielding.

"Yes, perhaps you're right. In that case, I have never been enough in love to take the leap." Juliet spoke with a half smile. Her eyes were fixed upon the top of the hill. "But anyhow Lady Jo couldn't talk, for she has just jilted Ivor Yardley the K. C. and gone to Paris to buy mourning."

"Good gracious!" exclaimed Mrs. Fielding. "Why, I saw the description of the wedding-dress in the paper the other day. It must have been a near thing."

"It was," said Juliet soberly. "They were to have been married today."

"And she broke it off! That must have taken some pluck!"

"But she didn't stay to face the music," Juliet pointed out. "That was what I hated in her. She ought to have stayed."

"Was she afraid of him then?"

"Afraid? Yes, she was afraid of him — and of everybody else. I know that perfectly well, though you would never get her to admit it. She was terrified in her heart — and so she bolted."

"Why didn't you go with her?" asked Mrs. Fielding.

Juliet made an odd gesture of the hands that was somehow passionate. "Why should I? I have disapproved of her for a long time. Now we have finally quarreled. She behaved so badly — so very badly. I don't want to meet her — or any of her set — again!"

Mrs. Fielding was silent for a moment. She had not expected that intensity. "Do you know, that doesn't sound like you somehow?" she said at length, speaking with just a hint of embarrassment.

"But how do you know what I am really like?" said Juliet. "Ah! There is the sea again — and the wonderful sky-line! Is he going to stop? Or are we going to plunge over the edge?"

She spoke with a little breathless laugh. They had reached the summit of the great headland, and it looked for the moment as if the car must leap over a sheer precipice into the clear green water far below. But even as she spoke, there came a check and a pause, and then they were standing still on a smooth stretch of grass not twenty feet from the edge.

The soft wind blew in their faces, and there was a glittering purity in the atmosphere that held Juliet spellbound. She breathed deeply, gazing far out over that sparkling sea of wonder.

"Oh, the magic of it!" she said. "The glorious freedom! It makes you feel — as if you had been born again."

Her companion watched her in silence, a certain curiosity in her look.

After many seconds Juliet turned round. "Thank you for bringing me here," she said. "It has done me good. I should like to stay here all day long."

Her eyes traveled along the line of cliff towards that distant spot that had been the scene of her night adventure, and slowly returned to dwell upon a long deep seam in the side of the hill.

"That's the lead mine," observed Mrs. Fielding. "It belongs to your aristocratic relatives, the Farringmores. They are pretty badly hated by the miners, I believe. But your friend Mr. Green is extremely popular with them. He rather likes to be a king among cobblers, I imagine."

"How nice of him!" said Juliet. "And where do the cobblers live?"

"You can't see it from here. It's just on the other side of the workings — a horribly squalid place. I never go near it. It's called High Shale, but it's very low really, right in a pocket of the hills, and very unhealthy. You can see the smoke hanging over there now. The cottages are wretched places, and the people who live in them — words fail! Ashcott, the agent and manager of the mines, says they are quite hopeless, and so they are. They are just like pigs in a sty."

"Poor dears!" said Juliet.

"Oh, they're horrors!" declared Mrs. Fielding. "They fling stones at the car if we go within half-a-mile of them. And they are such a drunken set. Go round the other way, Jack, — round by Fairharbor! Miss Moore will enjoy that."

"Thank you," said Juliet, with her friendly smile. "I am enjoying it very much."

They traveled forty miles before they ran back again into Little Shale, and the children were reassembling for afternoon school as they neared the Court gates.

"Put me down here!" Juliet said. "I can run down the hill. It isn't worth while coming those few yards and having to turn the car."

"I want you to lunch with me," said Mrs. Fielding.

"Oh, thank you very much. Not today. I really must get back. I've got to buy cakes for tea," laughed Juliet.

Mrs. Fielding stopped the car abruptly. "I'm not going to press you, or you'll never come near me again," she said. "I never press people to do what they obviously don't want to. Do you think you would hate living with me, Miss Moore? Or are you still giving the matter your consideration?"

There was a hint of wistfulness in the arrogant voice that somehow touched Juliet.

She sat silent for a moment; then: "If I might come to you for a week on trial," she said. "You won't pay me anything of course. I think we should know by that time if it were likely to answer or not."

"When will you come?" said Mrs. Fielding.

"Just when you like," said Juliet.

"Tomorrow?"

"Yes, tomorrow, if that suits you."

"And if you don't hate me at the end of a week you'll come for good."

Juliet laughed. "No, I won't say that. I'll leave you a way of escape too. We will see how it answers."

Mrs. Fielding held out her hand. "Good-bye! Next time you take your tea on the shore, I want to be the guest of honor."

"You shall be," said Juliet.

Chapter IX

THE INTRUDER

"Everyone to his taste," remarked Green. "But I'd rather be anything under the sun than Mrs. Fielding's paid companion." He glanced at Juliet with a smile as he spoke, but there was a certain earnestness in his speech that told her he meant what he said. He sat with his back to a rock, smoking a cigarette. His attitude was one of repose, but in the strong light his dark face showed a tenseness that did not wholly agree with it.

"Do you really think you'll like it?" he asked, as Juliet did not speak.

She also had a cigarette between her lips, and there was genuine relaxation in her fashion of lounging on the shingle.

"I really don't know," she said. "I've got to find out."

"Don't let them bully you!" said Green.

She smiled. "No, they won't do that, I think it is rather kind of them to take me without references, don't you?"

"No," said Green.

She turned and surveyed him with a gleam of amusement in her look. "You sound cross! Are you cross about anything?"

His eyes flashed down to hers with a suddenness almost startling. He did not speak for a moment, then again he smiled abruptly with his eyes still holding hers. "I believe I am," he said.

"I wonder why," said Juliet.

He laughed. "Yes, you do, don't you? Great impertinence on my part of course. It's nice of you to put it so mildly."

"I don't think you impertinent," said Juliet; "only rather silly."

"Oh, thanks!" said Green. "Kinder and kinder. Silly to be cross on your account, is that it? Well, it certainly sounds silly."

Juliet smiled. "No, silly to think I am not capable of taking care of myself."

"Oh!" said Green. "Well, I have some reason for thinking that, haven't I?"

"None whatever," said Juliet.

"All right. I haven't," he said, and looked away.

"You are cross!" ejaculated Juliet, and broke into a laugh.

Green smoked steadily for some seconds with his eyes upon the sea. A few yards below them Robin wandered barefooted along the shore, accompanied by Columbus who had bestowed a condescending species of friendship upon him.

Green's dark, alert face looked strangely swarthy against the rock behind him. His expression was one of open discontent.

"I hate to think of you turning into that woman's slave," he said abruptly. "To be quite honest, that was what brought me along today, intruding upon your picnic with Robin. I want to warn you, I've got to warn you."

"You have warned me," said Juliet.

"Without result," he said.

"No, not without result. I am very grateful to you, and I shall remember your warning."

"But you won't profit by it," Green's voice was moody.

"I think I shall," she said. "In any case, I am only going for a week on trial. That couldn't hurt anyone."

He did not look at her. "You're going out of the goodness of your heart," he said. "And — though you won't like it — you'll stay for the same reason."

"Oh, don't you think you are rather absurd?" said Juliet. "I am not at all that sort of person, I assure you."

"I think you are," said Green.

She laughed again. "Well I am told you are quite a frequent visitor there. Why do you go — if you don't like it?"

"That is different," he said. "I can hold my own — anyway with Mr. Fielding."

She lifted her brows. "And you think I can't?"

"I think you'll lead a dog's life," he said.

"Oh, I hope not. It won't be on a chain anyhow. I've provided against that."

"You'll hate it," Green said with conviction.

"I don't think I shall," she answered quietly. "If I do, I shall come away."

"It'll be too late then," he said.

"Too late!" Juliet's soft eyes opened wide. "What can you mean?"

He made a gesture which though half-restrained was yet vehement "It's a hostile atmosphere — a hateful atmosphere. She will poison you with her sneers and snobbery!"

A light began to break upon Juliet. She sat up very suddenly. "That sort of poison doesn't have any effect upon me," she said, and she spoke with a stateliness that brought the man's eyes swiftly down to her. "I am — sneer-proof."

"She won't sneer at you," said Green quickly.

With her eyes looking straight up to him, she laughed.

"Oh, I quite catch your meaning, Mr. Green. But — really I am not in the position of listening to sneers against my friends. Now will you be satisfied?"

He laughed also though still with a touch of restraint. "Yes, I feel better for that. You are so royal in your ways. I might have known I was safe there."

"'Loyal' is a better word I think," said Juliet quietly. "Why should a paid companion aspire to be any higher in the social scale than a village schoolmaster? Do you think occupation really makes any difference?"

"Theoretically — no!" said Green.

"Neither theoretically nor practically," said Juliet. "I detest snobbery, so do you. If you came to the Court to sweep the kitchen chimney, I should be just as pleased to see you. What a man does is nothing. How could it make any difference?"

"It couldn't — to you," said Green.

"Or to you?" said Juliet.

He laughed a little, his black brows working comically. "Madame, if I met you hawking stale fish for cat's meat in the public street, I couldn't venerate you more or adore you less. Whatever you do — is right."

"Good heavens!" said Juliet, and flushed in spite of herself. "What a magnificent compliment! It's a pity you are not wearing a slouch hat with an ostrich plume! You really need a plume to express that sort of sentiment properly."

"Yes, I know," said Green. "But — I imagine you are not attracted by plumes. In fact, you have just told me so. Proof positive of your royalty! It is only crowned heads that can afford to despise them nowadays."

"Mine isn't a crowned head," protested Juliet.

He looked at her searchingly. "Have you never been to Court?"

She snapped her fingers airily. "Of course! Dozens of times! Poor companions always go to Court. How often do you go!"

"As often as you admit me to your most gracious presence," he said.

She clapped her hands softly. "Why, that is even prettier than the stale fish one! Mr. Green, what can have happened to you?"

"I daren't tell you," he said.

A sudden silence fell upon the words. Juliet puffed the smoke from her cigarette, and watched it rise. "Well, don't spoil it, will you?" she said, as it vanished into air.

Green's hand suddenly gripped a handful of shingle and ground it forcibly. He did not speak for a second or two. Then: "No, I won't spoil it," he said, in a low voice.

A moment later he flung the stones abruptly from him and got up. "You're not going?" said Juliet.

"Yes, I've got work to do. Shall I take Robin with me?"

There was a dogged note in his voice. His eyes avoided hers.

Juliet rose slowly. "Never mind Robin! Walk a little way with me!" she said.

"I think I'd better go," said Green restlessly.

"Please!" said Juliet gently.

He turned beside her without a word. They went down the shingle to the edge of the sand and began to walk along the shore.

For many seconds they walked in silence. Juliet's eyes were fixed upon the mighty outline of High Shale Point that stood out like a fortress, dark, impregnable, against the calm of the evening sky. Her companion sauntered beside her, his hands behind him. He had thrown away his cigarette.

She spoke at length, slowly, with evident effort. "I want to tell you — something — about myself."

"Something I really don't know?" asked Green, his dark face flashing to a smile.

There was no answering smile on Juliet's face. "Yes, something you don't know," she said soberly. "It's just this. I have much more in common with Mrs. Fielding than you have any idea of. I have lived for pleasure practically all my life. I have scrambled for happiness with the rest of the world, and I haven't found it. It's only just lately that I've realized why. I read a book called The Valley of Dry Bones. Do you know it? But of course you do. It is by Dene Strange. I hate the man — if it is a man. And I hate his work — the bitter cynicism of it, the merciless exposure of humanity at its lowest and meanest. I don't know what his ideals are — if he has any. I think he is probably very wicked, but detestably — oh, damnably — clever. I burned the book I hated it so. But I felt — afterwards — as if I had been burned, seared by hot irons — ashamed — most cruelly ashamed." Juliet's voice sank almost to a whisper. "Because — life really is like that — one vast structure of selfishness — and in many ways I have helped to make it so."

She stopped. Green was looking at her attentively. He spoke at once with decision. "I know the book. I've read it. It's an exaggeration — probably intentional. It wasn't written — obviously — for the super-sensitive."

"Wasn't it?" Juliet's lips were quivering. "Well, it's been a positive nightmare to me. I haven't got over it yet."

"That's curious," he said. "I shouldn't have thought it could have touched you anywhere."

"That is because you have a totally wrong impression of me," she said. "That is what I am trying to put right. I am the sort of person that horrible book applies to, and I've fallen out with myself very badly in consequence, Mr. Green. I haven't told anyone but you, but — somehow — I feel as if you ought to know."

"Thank you," said Green. "But why?"

She met his eyes very steadily. "Because I'm trying to play the game now, and — I don't want you to have any illusions."

"You don't want me to make a fool of myself," he said. "Is that it?"

She colored very vividly, but she did not avoid his look. "I don't think there is much danger of that, is there?" she said.

He stood still suddenly and faced her. His eyes burned with an amazing brightness. "I don't know," he said, speaking emphatically and very rapidly. "It depends of course upon the point of view. But I'll tell you this. I'd give all I've got — and all I'm ever likely to get — to prevent you going to Shale Court as a companion."

"Oh, but aren't you unreasonable?" Juliet said.

"No, I'm not." He made a vigorous gesture of repudiation. "Presumptuous perhaps — but not unreasonable. I know too much of what goes on there. Miss Moore, I beseech you — think again! Don't go!"

She looked at him in perplexity. "But it wouldn't be fair to draw back now," she objected. "Besides —"

"Besides," he broke in almost fiercely, "you've got your living to make like the rest of us. Yes, I know — I know! You regard this as a Heaven-sent opportunity. It isn't. It's quite the reverse. If you were unhappy in London, you'll be a thousand times more so there. And — and I shan't be able to help you — shan't get anywhere near you there."

"It's very kind of you," began Juliet.

He cut her short again. "No, it isn't kind. You're the only woman of your station I have ever met who has deigned to treat me as an equal. It — it's a bit rash on your part, you know." He smiled at her abruptly, and something sent a queer sensation through her — a curious feeling of familiarity that held and yet eluded her. "And — as you see — I'm taking full advantage of it. I hope you won't think me an awful cad after this. I can't help it if you do. Miss Moore, forgive my asking, — are you really obliged to work for your living? Can't you — can't you wait a little?"

Juliet was looking at him with wonder in her soft eyes. His sudden vehemence was rather bewildering.

"I don't quite know," she said vaguely. "But I rather want to do something, you know."

"Oh, I know — I know," he said. "But you're not obliged to do this. Something else is bound to turn up. Or if it doesn't — if it doesn't —" He ground his heel deep into the yielding sand, and ended in a husky undertone. "My God! What wouldn't I give for the privilege of working for you?"

The words were uttered and beyond recall. He looked her straight in the face as he spoke them, but an instant later he turned and stared out over the wide, calm sea in a stillness that was somehow more forcible even than his low, half-strangled speech had been.

Juliet stood silent also, almost as if she were waiting for him to recover his balance. Her eyes also were gazing straight before her to that far mysterious sky-line. They were very grave and rather sad.

He broke the silence after many seconds. "You will never speak to me again after this."

"I hope I shall," she said gently.

He wheeled and faced her. "You're not angry then?"

She shook her head. "No."

His eyes flashed over her with amazing swiftness. "I almost wish you were," he said.

"But why?" she said.

"Because I should know then it mattered a little. Now I know it doesn't. I am just one of the many. Isn't that it? There are so many of us that one more or less doesn't count either way." He laughed ruefully. "Well, I won't repeat the offence. Even your patience must have its limits. Shall we go back?"

It was then that Juliet turned, moved by an impulse so strangely urgent that she could not pause to analyze it. She held out her hand to him, quickly, shyly, and as he gripped and held it, she spoke, her voice tremulous, breathless, barely coherent.

"I am not — offended. I am — very — very — deeply — honored. Only you — you — don't understand."

He kept her hand closely in his own. His grasp vibrated with electric force, but he had himself in check. "You are more generous than I deserve," he said, his voice sunk to a whisper. "Perhaps — some day — understanding will come. May I hope for that?"

She did not answer him, but for one intimate second her eyes looked straight into his. Then with a little, sobbing breath she slipped her hand free.

"We — are forgetting Robin," she said, with an effort.

He turned at once. "By George, yes! I'm afraid I had forgotten him," he said.

They walked back along the shore side by side.

PART II

Chapter I

THE WAND OF OFFICE

*R*obin was in disgrace. He crouched in a sulky heap in a far corner of the schoolroom, and glowered across the empty desks and benches at his elder brother who sat in the place of authority at his writing-table with a litter of untidy exercise-books in front of him. There was a long, thin cane also at his elbow that had the look of a somewhat sinister wand of office. He was correcting book after book with a species of forced patience, that was not without an element of exasperation.

The evening sunlight slanted through the leaded windows. They were open to their widest extent, but the place was oppressively close. There was a brooding sense of storm in the atmosphere. Suddenly, as if in some invisible fashion a set limit had been reached and passed, Richard Green lifted his head from his work. His keen eyes sent a flashing glance down the long, bare room.

"Robin!" he said.

Robin gave a violent start, and then a shuffling, reluctant movement as if prodded into action against his will.

"Get up and come here!" his brother said.

Robin, in the act of blundering to his feet, checked abruptly, as if arrested by something in the peremptory tone. "What for?" he asked, in a surly note.

"Get up," Green repeated, with grim insistence, "and come here!"

Robin grabbed at the end of the row of desks nearest to him and dragged himself slowly up. But there he hung irresolute. His heavy brows were drawn, but the eyes beneath had a frightened, hunted look. They glared at Green with a defiance so precarious that it was pathetic.

Green waited inexorably, magisterially, at his table. The sunlight had gone and the room was darkening. Very slowly Robin moved forward, dragging his feet along the bare boards. At the other end of the row of desks he halted. His eyes traveled swiftly between his brother's stern countenance and the wand of office that lay before him on the writing-table. He shivered.

"Come here!" Green said again.

He crept a little nearer like a guilty dog. His humped shoulders looked higher than usual. His eyes shone red.

Across the writing-table Green faced him. He spoke, very distinctly. "Why did you throw that stone at Mrs. Fielding's car?"

Robin was trembling from head to foot. He drew a quivering breath between his teeth, and stood silent.

"Tell me why!" Green insisted.

Robin locked his working hands together. Green waited.

"It — it — I didn't see — Mrs. Fielding," he blurted forth at last.

Green made a slight movement that might have indicated relief, but his tone was as uncompromising as before as he said, "That's not an answer to my question. I asked you why you did it."

Robin shrank from the curt directness of his speech. His defiance wilted visibly. "I — didn't mean to break the window, Dicky," he said, twisting and cracking his fingers in rising agitation.

"What did you mean to do?" said Green.

Robin stood silent again.

"Are you going to answer me?" Green said, after a pause.

Robin made a great effort. He parted his straining hands and rested them upon the table behind which Green sat. Standing so, he glowered down into his brother's grim face with something of menace in his own. "I'll tell you one thing, Dicky," he said, with stupendous effort. "I'm not going — to take a caning for it."

Green's eyebrows went up. He sat perfectly still, looking straight up into the heavy face above him. For several seconds a tense silence reigned.

Then: "Oh yes, you will," he said quietly. "You will take — whatever I decide to give you. Sit down there!" He indicated the end of the bench nearest to him. "I'll deal with you presently."

Robin did not stir. In the growing gloom of the room his eyes shone like the eyes of an animal, goaded and desperate. But the man before him showed neither surprise nor anger. His clean-cut lips were closed in a straight, unyielding line. For a full minute he looked at Robin and Robin looked at him.

Then he spoke. "I've only one treatment for this sort of thing — as you know. It isn't especially inspiring for either of us. I shouldn't qualify for it if I were you."

Robin had begun to shake again. The cold, clear words seemed to deprive him of the brief strength he had managed to muster. His eyes fell before the steady regard that was fixed upon him. With an incoherent murmur he turned aside, and dropped upon the end of the bench indicated, his trembling hands gripped hard between his knees, his attitude one of utter dejection.

Green went back to his correcting with a frown between his brows, and a deep silence fell.

Minutes passed. The room grew darker, the atmosphere more leaden. Pencil in hand, Green went over book after book and put them aside. Suddenly he looked across at the silent figure. The humped shoulders were heaving. Slow tears were falling upon the clasped hands. There was no sound of any sort. Green sat and watched, a kind of stern pity replacing the unyielding mastery of his look. He moved at length, was on the verge of speech, when something checked him. Footsteps fell beyond the open door, and in a moment a man's figure appeared entering through the gloom.

"Hullo, Dick!" a voice said. "You here? There's going to be the devil of a storm. Where's that scoundrel Robin?"

Robin stirred with a deep sound in his throat like the growl of an angry animal.

Richard Green rose with a sharp movement. "Jack! I want a word with you. Come outside!"

He passed Robin and went to the newcomer, gripping him quickly by the shoulder and turning him back by the way he had come.

Jack submitted to the imperative touch. He was taller and broader than his elder brother, but he lacked that subtle something — the distinction of bearing — which in Richard was very apparent.

"Well, Dick! What do you want?" he said. "I'm pretty mad, I can tell you. I hope you're going to thrash him well. Because if you don't, I shall."

Briefly and decidedly Dick made answer. "No, you won't. You'll not touch him. I shall do — whatever is necessary."

"Shall you?" said Jack. "Then why don't you shut him up in a wild-beast house? It's the only place he's fit for."

"Shut up, please!" Richard's tone was an odd mixture of tolerance and exasperation. "I'll manage this affair my own way. But I've got to know the truth of it first. What made him throw that stone? Have you been baiting him again?"

"I?" Jack squared his shoulders; a sneer crossed his good-looking face. "Oh, say I did it!" he drawled.

"Don't be an ass, Jack! Can't you see I want your help?" Richard spoke with insistence; his hand gripped his brother's arm.

Jack's sneer turned to a self-satisfied smile. "I'll help you hammer him if you like. There's nothing would please me better. Oh, all right, man! Don't be impatient! That's my funny bone when you've done with it. I don't mind telling you all about it if you want to know. He chucked that stone at me out of sheer damned vindictiveness. He meant to break my head, but he broke the window instead, and frightened Madam Fielding into fits. In her own park too! It's a bit thick, you know, that. I don't wonder that she came straight along to you to demand his blood. You'll have the old man down next; also the beautiful Miss Moore. It's getting beyond a joke, you know, Dick. You'll have to shut the beast up. You can't let him run amuck like this."

"Shut up!" Dick said again. In the unnatural light his face looked drawn and almost haggard. "I want to know why he did it. Can't you tell me?"

"Oh yes, I can tell you that. He's taken to haunting the place – the Court, mind you – to lie in wait for the fair Juliet. She's been too kind to him, unluckily for her, and now he dogs her footsteps whenever he gets a chance. I caught him this afternoon, right up by the house, and I ordered him off. You know the squire and madam both loathe the very sight of him, and small wonder. I do myself. So I told him what he was and where to go to, and I presume he thought he'd send me there first. There you have it all – cause and effect."

"Thank you," said Dick. He paused a moment looking speculatively at Jack's complacent face. "It was a pity you were so damned offensive, but I suppose it's the way you're made. You were the sole cause of the whole thing, and if there's any decency in you, you'll go and tell the squire so."

He spoke quickly, but with characteristic decision and wholly without excitement. Jack jumped, and threw back his head as if he had received a blow across the mouth. Swift temper sprang to his eyes.

"What the devil do you mean?" he demanded.

"Exactly what I have said," returned Dick briefly. "And perhaps a little more."

"Confound you!" blustered Jack. "And you expect me to go to the squire and tell him it was my fault, do you?"

"No. I don't expect it in the least." Dick almost laughed. "In fact, nothing would surprise me more. Thank you for telling me the truth. Do you mind clearing out now? I don't want you in here."

His curt, cold tones fell like ice on flame. Jack swore a muffled oath and turned away. There was no one in the world who possessed the power to humble him as did Dick, who with a few scorching words could make him writhe in impotent fury. For there was no gainsaying Dick. He was always unassailable in his justice, since in a fashion inexplicable but tacitly acknowledged by both he occupied a higher plane altogether. Ignore it as he might, deep in his inner soul Jack knew this man to be his master. He might, and sometimes did, resist his control, deny his authority; yet the power remained, and Dick knew how to exercise it if the need arose. They were seldom at open variance, but practically never in sympathy.

The fate of poor Robin had been a matter of disagreement between them ever since Jack had come to man's estate, but the issue did not rest with Jack. No power on earth could move Dick in that direction. Robin was his own peculiar property, and in this respect he permitted interference from none.

He left Jack now, and turned back into the schoolroom with deep lines between his brows, but implacable determination in his every movement, a determination that was directed against the poor cowering form that crouched still in the same position waiting for him.

Robin looked up at his coming, drawing himself together with a nervous contraction of the muscles like the mute shrinking of an abject dog.

Dick stopped in front of him. "So you're not going to take a caning!" he said.

There was no longer any rebellion in Robin's attitude. He dropped his eyes swiftly from his brother's face, saying no word. In the silence that followed, his hands began to work, straining ceaselessly against each other.

Dick waited for a few seconds. "Going on strike, are you?" he asked then, as Robin did not speak.

Robin shook his head dumbly.

"What does that mean?" Dick said.

Robin was silent. He was nearly dislocating his fingerjoints in his agitation.

Richard bent suddenly and laid a quieting hand upon him. "Robin, do you know you've got me into bad trouble?"

Robin gave a violent jerk, and in a moment stumbled to his feet. He did not look at his brother, but turned aside in his blundering pathetic fashion, and went to the littered writing-desk.

Dick's wand of office still lay among the scattered exercise-books. He pulled it out with a clumsy eagerness, tossing papers and books on the floor in his haste. He turned and went back to Dick, thrusting the cane towards him.

"There, Dicky!" he said, and stood breathing heavily and trembling.

Dick reached out and took the cane. The lines of his face were oddly softened. He stood for a moment looking at the boy, then very sharply he moved, bent, and snapped the thing across his knee.

"Oh, dash it, Robin!" he said. "You're getting too much for me."

He tossed the fragments from him, and went to pick up the books that Robin had scattered on the floor.

Robin came and groveled by his side, helping him. "You aren't angry, are you, Dicky?" he murmured anxiously.

"I ought to be," Dick said, as he sat down and began to straighten out the muddle in front of him.

Robin knelt up by his side. "Please don't be, Dicky!" he said very earnestly. "I won't ever do it again. I swear I won't."

Dick smiled somewhat wryly. "No. You'll probably think of some other devilry even worse." He put his arm round the humped shoulders with the words. "You'll forget — you always do — that it's I who have to pay."

Robin pressed against him, still doglike in his contrition. "Will it cost much?" he asked.

"Oh that! The window, you mean? Well, not so much as if you had broken Jack's head — as you intended."

There was some hint of returning grimness in Dick's voice. Robin made an ingratiating movement, leaning his rough head against his brother's arm.

Dick went on, ignoring the unspoken appeal. "You've got to stop it Robin. If you don't, there'll be trouble — worse trouble than you've had yet. You don't want to leave me, I suppose?"

"Leave you, Dicky?" Robin stared round in horror. "Leave you?" he repeated incredulously. "Go to prison, do you mean?"

Dick nodded. "Something like it."

"Dick!" Robin stared at him aghast. "But — you — you'd never let them — take me?"

"If you were to damage Jack — or anyone else — badly, I shouldn't be able to prevent it." Dick said rather wearily. "If it came to that — I shouldn't even try."

"Dick!" Robin gasped again, then passionately; "But I — I — I couldn't live — away from you! I'd — I'd kill myself!"

"No, you wouldn't. You wouldn't get the chance." Dick was staring straight before him down the room, as if he watched some evil vision against the darkness. "People aren't allowed to kill themselves in prison. If they try to do anything of that sort, they're tied down till they come to their senses. If they behave like brutes, they're treated as such, till at last they turn into that and nothing else. And then — God help them!"

A sudden hard shudder caught him. He shook it off impatiently, and turned to the quivering figure still kneeling in the circle of his arm.

He gripped it suddenly close. "That's the sort of hell these fiendish tempers of yours might end in," he said. "You've got to save yourself, my son. I can't save you."

Robin clung to him tensely, desperately. "You don't — want me to go, Dicky?" he whispered.

"Good God!" Richard said. "I'd rather see you dead!"

In the silence that followed, Robin turned with a curious groping movement, took the hand that pressed his shoulder, and pulled it over his eyes.

Chapter II

MIDSUMMER MADNESS

An ominous darkness brooded over all things as Green walked up the long avenue of Shale Court half-an-hour later. The storm had been long in, gathering, and he judged that he would yet have time to reach his destination before it broke. But it was nearer than he thought, and the first dull roar of its coming reached him soon after he had passed the gates. He shrugged his shoulders at the sound and hurried on, for he was in no mood to turn back. The business before him was one that could not be shirked, and the lines on his dark face showed unyielding determination as he went.

He was half-way up the drive when the first flash of lightning glimmered eerily across the heavy gloom. It was followed so swiftly by a burst of thunder that he realized that he had no time to spare if he hoped to escape the threatening deluge. He broke into a run, covering the ground with the ease of the practiced athlete, elbows at sides and head up, going at an even pace which he knew he could maintain to the finish without distress.

But he was not destined to run to a finish. As he rounded a bend that gave him a view of the house in the distance, he suddenly heard a voice call to him from the deep shadow of the trees, and checking sharply he discerned a dim figure coming towards him across the grassy ride that bordered the road.

He diverted his course without a moment's thought, and went to meet it.

"Ah, how kind of you!" said Juliet. "And there's going to be such a downpour in a minute."

"What is the matter?" he said, her hand in his.

She was smiling a difficult smile. "Nothing very much. Not enough to warrant my extreme selfishness in stopping you. I have given my foot a stupid twist, that's all, and it doesn't like walking."

"Take my arm!" said Green.

She took it, her white face still bravely smiling. "Thank you, Mr. Green."

"Lean hard!" he said.

She obeyed him, and he led her, limping, to the road, Columbus, the ever-faithful, trudging behind.

"It really is a shame," she said. "We shall both be drenched now."

He glanced at the threatening sky. "It may hold off for a bit yet. What were you doing?"

"I was coming to see you," she said.

"To see me!" His look came swiftly to her. "What about?"

"About Robin," she answered simply. "I wasn't in the car when it happened, but I heard all about it when Mrs. Fielding came in. Mr. Green, I hope you haven't been very hard on him."

Green was silent for a moment. "And you started straight off to come to the rescue?" he said then.

"Oh, I felt sure that he acted on impulse, not realizing. You can't judge him by ordinary standards. It isn't fair," pleaded Juliet. "There was probably some extenuating circumstance in the background — something we don't know about. I hope you haven't been very severe. You haven't, have you?"

Green began to smile. "You make me out an awful ogre," he said. "Is it my trade that does it? No, I haven't punished him at all. As you say, we must be fair, and I found he wasn't the person most to blame. Can you guess who was?"

"No," said Juliet.

"I thought not. Well, I have traced it to its source, and it lies — at your door."

"At mine!" ejaculated Juliet.

"At yours, yes. You've been too kind to him. It's just your way, isn't it? You spoil everybody." Again for an instant his look flashed over her.

"With the result that Robin, not hampered by convention as are the rest of us, lies in wait on forbidden ground for a glimpse of his divinity. Being caught and roundly abused for it by his brother Jack, he naturally took offence and trouble ensued. That is the whole story."

"Oh, dear," said Juliet. "But surely that was very unnecessary of your brother Jack. He might have made allowances."

"My brother Jack often does unnecessary things," said Green dryly. "And he never makes allowances for anyone but himself."

"And you have to bear the consequences!" Juliet's voice was quick with sympathy. "But that's too bad!"

"I'm used to it," said Green, and laughed. "How are you getting on? Enjoying life at the Court?"

Juliet smiled. "Do you know — I am rather? They have been very good to me."

"So far," said Green. "Are you still on probation?"

"The week is up tomorrow," she told him.

"And you're staying on — of course?"

She looked at him. "Don't you want me to stay on?"

"You know my sentiments," said Green.

A sudden vivid flash rent the gloom over them, and Juliet caught her breath. There followed a burst of thunder that seemed to shake the very foundation of the earth.

She tried to break into a hobbling run, but he held her back. "Better not. You'll only hurt yourself. It isn't raining yet. You're not nervous?"

She laughed a little, breathlessly. "I don't admit it. I should never dare to show the white feather in your presence. Oh, look at that!" She shrank in spite of herself as another intolerable flare darted across the sky.

"We're nearly in," said Green, but his words were drowned in such a volume of sound as made further speech impossible. He awoke to the fact that Juliet was clinging to his arm with both hands, and in a second his free hand was on the top of them holding them tightly.

The thunder rolled away, and a deeper darkness fell. Great drops of rain began to splash around them.

"Quick!" gasped Juliet. "We can't — possibly — reach the house now. There is an arbor — by the garden gate. Let's go there!"

He turned off the road on to a side-path that led to a shrubbery. The rush and roar of the coming rain was sweeping up from the sea. Juliet pressed forward.

Again a jagged line of light gleamed before them. Again the thunder crashed. They found the little gate and the arbor beyond.

"Thank goodness!" gasped Juliet.

She stumbled at the step of the summer-house, and he thrust an arm forward to catch her. He almost lifted her into shelter. The darkness within was complete. She leaned upon him, trembling.

"You're not hurt?" he said.

"No, not hurt, only — shaken — and — and — stupid," she answered, on the verge of tears.

His arm still held her. It closed about her, very surely, very steadily. He did not utter a word.

The rain swept down in a torrent, as if the skies had opened. Great hail-stones beat upon the laurels around them with tropical violence. The noise of the downpour seemed vaster, more overwhelming, even than the thunder.

Juliet was palpitating from head to foot. She leaned upon the supporting arm, her eyes closed against the leaping lightning, her two hands pressed hard upon her breast. Columbus crouched close to her, shivering.

And ever the man's arm drew her nearer, nearer, till she felt the strong beating of his heart. The storm raged on about them, but they two stood, as it were, alone, wrapped at its very center in a great silence. For minutes they neither moved nor spoke.

Slowly the turmoil abated. The downpour lessened. The storm passed. And Juliet stirred.

"How — disgraceful of me!" she murmured. "I'm not generally so foolish as this. But — it was so very violent."

"I know," he said. His hold slackened. He let her go. And then suddenly he stayed her. He took her hand, and bending pressed it closely, burningly, to his lips.

She stood motionless, suffering him. But in a moment, as he still held her, very gently she spoke. "Mr. Green, please — don't be so terribly in earnest! It's too soon. I warned you before. You haven't known me — long enough."

He stood up and faced her, her hand still in his. A light was growing behind the storm-clouds, revealing his dark clean-cut features, and the look half humorous, half-tense, that rested upon them.

"Yes, I know you warned me," he said rather jerkily. "I quite realize that it's my funeral — not yours. I shan't ask you to be chief mourner either. I've always considered that when a man makes a fool of himself over a woman it's up to him to bear the consequences without asking her to share them."

"But we're not talking of — funerals," said Juliet.

"Aren't we?" His hand tightened for a moment upon hers. "I thought we were. What is it then?"

She smiled at him with a whimsical sadness in the weird storm-light. "I think there are a good many names for it," she said. "I call it midsummer madness myself."

He made a quick gesture of protest. "Do you? Oh, I know a better name than that. But you don't want to hear it. I believe you are afraid of me. It sounds preposterous. But I believe you are."

Her hand stirred within his, but not as though seeking to escape. "No, I don't think so," she said, and in her voice was a sound as if laughter and tears were striving together for the mastery. "But I'm trying — so dreadfully hard — to be — discreet. I don't want you to let yourself go too far. It's so difficult — you don't know how difficult it is — to get back afterwards."

"Good heavens!" he said. "Don't you realize that I passed the turning-back stage long ago."

"Oh, I hope not!" she said quickly. "I hope not!"

"Then I am afraid you are doomed to disappointment," he said, with a touch of cynicism. "But I am sure you are far too sensible — discreet, I mean — to let that worry you. And anyway," he smiled abruptly, "I don't want you to be worried — just when you're having such a jolly time at the Court too."

"You're very sarcastic," said Juliet.

He laughed a little. "No. That's not me. It's only the armor in which I encase myself. I hope it doesn't offend you. I can always take it off. Only — I am not sure you'd like that any better."

He won his point. She smiled, though somewhat dubiously. And at length her hand gently freed itself from his.

"Well, I don't like hurting people," she said. "And I don't want to hurt you. You understand that, don't you?" There was pleading in her words.

"Yes, perfectly," he said.

She glanced at him, for his tone was baffling. "And you don't think me — quite heartless?"

He bent towards her. "No," he said, and though he smiled as in duty bound she caught a deep throb in his voice that pierced straight through her. "I love you all the better for it." Then, before she could find words to protest, "I say, I believe it's left off raining. Hadn't we better go while we can?"

She turned to look. A pale light was shining from the western sky. The storm was over. The raindrops glittered in the growing radiance. The whole earth seemed transformed. "Yes, let us go!" she said, and stepped down into a world of crystal clearness.

He followed her, his face uplifted to the scattering drops, moving with a free and faunlike spring that seemed to mark him as a being closely allied to Nature, curiously vital yet also curiously self-restrained.

She did not look at him again, but as they passed together through the wonderland which with every moment was growing to a more amazing brightness, she told herself that there was little of midsummer madness about this man's emotions. Jest as he might, she knew by instinct that he was vitally in earnest and she had a strange conviction that it was for the first time in his life. The certainty disquieted her. Had she fled from one danger to another — she who only asked for peace?

But she reassured herself with the thought that he had held her against his heart, and he had not sought to take her. That forbearance of his gave him a greatness in her eyes to which no other man had ever attained. And gradually a sense of security to which she was little accustomed came about her heart and comforted her. She had warned him. Surely he understood!

Chapter III

A DRAWN BATTLE

*A*lmost in silence they passed up through the dripping garden to the house side by side, Columbus trotting demurely behind. Juliet was still limping, but she would not accept support.

"I suppose you are going to beard the lion in his den," she said as they drew near.

"I suppose I am," said Green. "If you hear sounds of a serious fracas, perhaps you will come to the rescue."

"Not to yours," she said lightly. "You are more than capable of holding your own — anywhere."

He flashed her his sudden look. "Do you really think so? I assure you I am considered very small fry, indeed, in this household."

"That's very good for you," said Juliet.

They mounted to the terrace that bounded the south front of the house, and entered by a glass door that led into a conservatory. Here for a moment Juliet paused. Her grey eyes under their level brows met his with a friendly smile.

"I think I must leave you now, Mr. Green," she said, "and go and find Mrs. Fielding. I expect the squire is in his study."

His answering smile was as ready as her own, but there was a secret triumph about it that hers lacked. "Pray don't trouble any further on my account!" he said courteously. "I can find my own way."

She threw him a nod, cool and kindly, over her shoulder, and took him at his word. He watched her disappear into the room beyond, Columbus in close attendance; then for a few seconds his hands went up to his face, and he stood motionless, pressing his temples hard, feeling the blood surging at fever heat through his veins. How marvelous she was — and withal how gracious! How had he dared? Midsummer madness indeed! And yet she had suffered him — had even stooped to plead with him!

A great shaft of red sunlight burst suddenly through the heaped storm-clouds in the west. He turned and faced it, dazzled but strangely exultant. He felt as if his whole being had been plunged into the glowing flame. The wonder of it pulsed through and through him. As it were involuntarily, a prayer sprang to his lips.

"O God," he said, "make me worthy!"

Then he turned, as if the glory had become too much for him, and went into the house.

He had been well acquainted with the place from boyhood though since the squire's marriage he had ceased to enter it unannounced. Before his appointment to the village school, he had acted for a time as the squire's secretary; but it had never been more than a temporary arrangement and it had come to a speedy end when Mrs. Fielding became mistress of the Court. Between her and her husband's protégé, as she scornfully called him, there had always existed a very decided antipathy. She resented his presence in the house at any time, and though the squire made it abundantly clear that he would permit no open insolence on her part, she did not find it difficult to convey her feelings on the subject to the man himself. He accepted the situation with a shrug and a smile, and though he did not discontinue his visits on her account, they became less frequent than formerly; and now generally he came and went again without seeing her.

The room he entered was empty. He passed through it without a pause and found himself in the great entrance hall. He crossed this to a door on the other side and, knocking briefly, opened it without waiting for a reply.

"Hullo!" said the squire's voice. "You, is it? How did you get here? Were you caught in the storm?"

"No, sir, I took shelter." Green shut the door, and came forward.

Mr. Fielding was seated in a leather armchair with a newspaper. He looked at his visitor over it with anything but a favorable eye.

"What have you come for?" he said.

Green halted in front of him. "I've come to make a very humble apology," he said, "for my boy Robin's misdemeanor."

"Have you?" growled Fielding. He sat motionless, still looking up at Green from under heavily scowling brows. "Do you think I'm going to be satisfied with just an apology?"

"May I sit down, please?" said Green, pulling forward a chair.

"Oh yes, sit down! Sit down and argue!" said the squire irritably. "You're always ready with some plausible excuse for that half-witted young scoundrel. I'll tell you what it is, Dick. If you don't get rid of him after this, there'll be a split between us. I'm not going to countenance your infernal obstinacy any longer. The boy is unsafe and he must go."

Green sat, leaning forward, courteously attentive, his eyes unwavering fixed upon his patron's irate countenance.

He did not immediately reply to the mandate, and the squire's frown deepened. "You hear me, Dick?" he said.

Green nodded. "Yes, sir."

"Well?" Fielding's hand clenched upon the paper in exasperation.

Dick's eyes very bright, wholly undismayed, continued to meet his with unvarying steadiness. "I'm very sorry, sir," he said. "The answer is the same as usual. I can't."

"Won't — you mean!" There was a sound in the squire's voice like the muffled roar of an angry animal.

Dick's black brows traveled swiftly upward and came down again. "He's my boy, sir," he said. "I'll be responsible for all he does."

"But — damn it!" ejaculated the squire. "Making yourself responsible for a mad dog doesn't prevent his biting people, does it? He's become a public danger, I tell you. You've no right to let him loose on the neighborhood."

"No, no, sir!" Dick broke in quickly. "That's not a fair thing to say. The boy is as harmless as any of us if he isn't baited. I knew — I knew perfectly well — that there was a reason for what he did today. So there was. I'm not going into details. Besides, he was clearly in the wrong. But you may take it from me — he was provoked."

"Oh! Was he?" said the squire. "And who provoked him? Jack?"

Dick hesitated momentarily, then: "Yes, Jack," he said briefly. "He had some reason, but he's such a tactless ass. He blames Robin of course. Everyone always does."

"Except you," said the squire dryly. "Oh, and Miss Moore! She makes excuses for him at every turn."

"She would," said Dick simply.

"I don't know why," snapped Fielding. He suddenly laid a hand on the younger man's arm, gripping it mercilessly. "Look here, Richard! Do you want me to break you? Because that's what it's coming to. Do you hear? That's what it's coming to. You're getting near the end of your tether."

Dick's eyes flashed with swift comprehension over the angry face before him, and an answering flicker of anger sprang up in them for an instant; but he kept himself in hand.

"Get me kicked out, you mean?" he said coolly. "Yes, sir, no doubt you could if you tried hard enough. You're all powerful here, aren't you? What you say, goes."

"It does," said Fielding grimly. "And I don't care a damn what I do when my monkey's up. You know that, don't you?"

"Rather!" said Dick. And suddenly the resentment died out of his face, and he began to laugh. "All right, sir! Break me if you like! I'll come out on top somehow."

"Confound you! Do you think you can defy me?" fumed Fielding.

"I'm sure of it," said Dick. "I can defy the whole world if I choose. There is a certain portion of a man, you know, that can't be beat if he plays fair, however hard he's hammered. It's the rule of the game."

"Confound you!" the squire said again, and sprang fiercely to his feet. "Don't talk to me! You go too far. You always have. You behave as if — as if —"

"As if I were my own master," said Dick quietly. "Well, I am that, sir. It's the one thing in life I can lay claim to."

"And a lord of creation into the bargain, eh?" the squire flung at him, as he tramped to the end of the room.

Dick rose punctiliously and stood waiting, a man unimposing of height and build yet possessing that innate dignity which no adversity can impair. He said nothing, merely stood and watched the squire with half-comic resignation till he came tramping back.

Fielding's face as he turned was heavy with displeasure, but as his look fell upon the offender a sudden softening began to struggle with the deep lines about his mouth. It was like a gleam of sunshine on a dark day.

He went to Dick, and took him by the shoulder. "Confound you!"

he said for the third time. "You're just like your mother. Pig-headed as a mule, but —"

"Are mules pig-headed?" said Dick flippantly.

The squire shook him. "Be quiet, you prig! I won't be dictated to by you. Look here, Dick!" His voice changed abruptly. "I'm not ordering. I'm asking. That boy is a mill-stone round your neck. Let him go! He'll be happy enough. I'll see to that. Give him up like a dear chap! Then you'll be free — free to chuck this absurd, farcical existence you're leading now — free to make your own way in the world — free to marry and be happy." Dick made a slight movement under the hand that held him, but he did not attempt to speak. The squire went on. "You can't hope for any of those things under existing conditions. It wouldn't be fair to ask any woman to share your present life. It would be almost an insult with this infernal incubus hanging on you. Can't you see my point? Can't you sacrifice your damned obstinacy? You'd never regret it. You're ruining yourself, Dick. Chance after chance has gone by, and you've let 'em go. But you can't afford to go on. You're in your prime now, but let me tell you a man's prime doesn't last. A time will come when you'll realize it's too late to make a start, and you'll look back and curse the folly that induced you to saddle yourself with a burden too heavy for you to bear."

He paused. Dick was looking straight before him with a set, grim face that gave no indication of what was passing in his mind.

Again, more gently, the squire shook the shoulder under his hand. "I'm out to make you happy, Dick. Can't you see it? For your mother's sake — as well as your own. And there's a chance coming your way now — or I'm much mistaken — which it would be madness to miss. This Miss Moore — she's dropped from the skies, but she's charming, she's a lady, she's just the woman for you. What, Dick? Think so yourself, do you? No, it's all right, I'm not prying. But this is a chance you'll never get again. And you can't ask her, you can't have the face to ask her, as long as you keep that half-witted creature dangling after you. It wouldn't be right, man, even if she'd have you. Look the thing in the face, and you'll be the first to say so! It would be a hopeless handicap to any marriage — an insurmountable obstacle to happiness, hers as well as yours. Don't tell me you can't see it! You know it. You know you've no right to ask any woman to share a burden of that kind with you. It would be manifestly unfair — iniquitous. There! I've done. I've never spoken my mind to this extent before. I've hoped — I've always hoped — the wretched boy would die. But he hasn't. That sort never does. He'll live forever. And it's a damned shame that you should sacrifice yourself to him any longer. For heaven's sake let him go!"

He ceased to speak, and there fell a silence so tense, so electric, that it seemed as if it must mask something terrible. Dick's face was still immovable, but he had the look of a man who endures unutterable things. He had flinched once — and only once — during the squire's speech, and that was at the first mention of Juliet. But for the rest he had stood quite rigid, as he stood now, his lips tightly compressed, his eyes looking straight before him.

He came out of his silence at last with a movement so sudden that it was as if he flung aside some weight that threatened to overwhelm him. The arrested vitality flashed back into his face. He threw back his head with a smile, and looked the squire in the face.

"You haven't left me a leg to stand on, sir," he said. "But all the same — I stand. There's nothing more to be said except — may I pay for the window?"

Fielding's hand dropped from his shoulder. He flung round fiercely and tramped to the window, swearing inarticulately.

Dick's black brows went up again to a humorous angle. He pursed his lips, but he did not whistle.

"Do you realize that my wife might have been killed?" Fielding growled at last.

"Oh, quite," said Dick. "I'm glad she wasn't. Ought I to congratulate her?"

"Oh, don't be so damn funny!" Fielding jingled the money in his pocket irritably. "You won't laugh when I turn you out."

"I wonder," said Dick.

Fielding turned sharply round upon him. "You behave as if you don't care what I do," he said, an ugly scowl on his face. "Or perhaps you think I won't or can't — do it."

"No, sir," Dick spoke deliberately, and though he still smiled his eyes held the squire's with unmistakable determination. "I'm sure you can do it. I'm equally sure you won't. And I'm surest of all that I shouldn't care a damn if you did."

"You wouldn't care!" The squire looked furious for a moment, then he sneered. "Oh, wouldn't you, my friend? We shall see. You'd better go now — before I have you kicked out."

Dick's shoulders jerked with a swift tightening of the muscles. His eyes gleamed with a fierce light though his smile remained. "I'll lay you even odds," he said, "that if you want that done, you'll have to do it yourself."

"I'm equal to it!" flashed the squire. "You'd better not try me too far!"

"I won't try you at all, sir," Dick suddenly relaxed again. He went to him with a pacific hand held out. "Good-bye! I'm going — now."

Fielding looked at him, looked at the extended hand, paused for a long moment, finally took it.

"Don't want to quarrel with me, eh?" he said.

"Not without cause," said Dick.

Fielding gripped the firm, lithe hand, looking at him hard and straight. "You're very cussed," he said slowly. "I wish I'd had the up-bringing of you."

Dick laughed. "Well, you've meddled in my affairs as long as I can remember, sir. I don't know anyone who has had as much to do with me as you have."

"And precious little satisfaction I've got out of it," grumbled the squire. "You've always been a kicker." He broke off as a knock came at the door, and turned away with an impatient fling. "Who is it? Come in!"

The door opened. Juliet stood on the threshold. The evening light fell full upon her. She was dressed in cloudy grey that fell about her in soft folds. Her face was flushed, but quite serene.

"Mrs. Fielding wants to know if you have forgotten dinner," she said.

The squire's face changed magically. He smiled upon Juliet. "Come in, Miss Moore! You've met this pestilent pedagogue before, I think."

"Just once or twice," said Juliet, coming forward.

"How is the ankle?" said Green.

She smiled at him without embarrassment. "Oh, better, thank you. It was only a wrench."

"Hurt yourself?" questioned Fielding.

"No, no. It's really nothing. I slipped in the park and nearly sprained my ankle — just not quite," said Juliet. "And Mr. Green very kindly helped me into shelter before the storm broke."

"Did he?" said the squire and looked at Green searchingly. "Well, Mr. Green, you'd better stay and dine as you are here."

"You're very kind," Dick said. "I don't know whether I ought. I'm not dressed."

"Of course you ought!" said Fielding testily. "Come on and wash! Your clothes won't matter — we're alone. That is, if Miss Moore doesn't object to sitting down with blue serge."

"I have no objection whatever," said Juliet. She was looking from one to the other with a slightly puzzled expression.

"What is it?" said Fielding, pausing.

His look was kindly. Juliet laughed. "I don't know. I feel as I felt that day you caught me trespassing. Am I trespassing, I wonder?"

"No!" said Fielding and Green in one breath.

She swept them a deep Court courtesy.

"Thank you, gentlemen! With your leave I will now withdraw."

The squire was at the door. He bowed her out with ceremony, watched her cross the hall, then sharply turned his head. Green was watching her also, but, keen as the twist of a rapier in the hand of a practiced fencer, his eyes flashed to meet the squire's.

Fielding smiled grimly. He motioned him forward, gripped him by the arm, and drew him out of the ream. They mounted the shallow oak stairs side by side.

At the top in a tense whisper Fielding spoke. "Don't you be a fool, Richard! Don't you be a damn' fool!"

Dick's laugh had in it a note that was not of mirth. "All right, sir, I'll do my best," he said.

It was a drawn battle, and they both knew it. By tacit consent neither referred to the matter again.

Chapter IV

A POINT OF HONOUR

"How like my husband!" said Mrs. Fielding impatiently, fidgeting up and down the long drawing room with a fretful frown on her pretty face. "Why didn't you put a stop to it, Miss Moore? You might so easily have said that the storm had upset me and I wasn't equal to a visitor at the dinner-table tonight." She paused to look at herself in the gilded mirror above the mantelpiece. "I declare I look positively haggard. I've a good mind to go to bed. Only if I do —" she turned slowly and looked at Juliet — "if I do, he is sure to be brutal about it — unless you tell him you persuaded me."

Juliet, seated in a low chair, with a book on her lap, looked up with a gleam of humor in her eyes. "But I am afraid I haven't persuaded you," she said.

Mrs. Fielding shrugged her white shoulders impatiently. "Oh, of course not! You only persuade me to do a thing when you know that it is the one thing that I would rather die than do."

"Am I as bad as that?" said Juliet.

"Pretty nearly. You're coming to it. I know you are on his side all the time. He knows it too. He wouldn't tolerate you for a moment if you weren't."

"What a horrid accusation!" said Juliet, with a smile.

"The truth generally is horrid," said Mrs. Fielding. "How would you like to feel that everyone is against you?"

"I don't know. I expect I should find a way out somehow. I shouldn't quarrel," said Juliet. "Not with such odds as that!"

"How — discreet!" said Mrs. Fielding, with a sneer.

"Discretion is my watchword," smiled Juliet.

"And very wise too," said Green's voice in the doorway. "How do you do, Mrs. Fielding? As I can't dress, I've been sent down to try and make my peace with you for showing my face here at all. I hope you'll be lenient for once, for really I've had a thorough bullying for my sins."

He came forward with the words. His bearing was absolutely easy though neither he nor his hostess seemed to think of shaking hands.

She looked at him with a disdainful curve of the lips that could scarcely have been described as a smile of welcome. "I imagine it would take a good deal of that sort of thing to make much impression upon you, Mr. Green," she said.

Green's eyes began to shine. He glanced at Juliet. "Really I am much more inoffensive than you seem to think," he said. "I hope you are not going to repeat the dose. I was hoping to secure your forgiveness for what happened this afternoon. Believe me, no one regrets it more sincerely than I do."

Mrs. Fielding drew herself together with a gesture of distaste. "Oh, that! I have no desire whatever to discuss it with you. I have long regarded your half-witted brother as a disgrace to the neighborhood, and my opinion is scarcely likely to be modified by what happened this afternoon."

"How unfortunate!" said Green.

Again he glanced at Juliet. She lifted her eyes to his. "I am afraid I haven't taken my share of the blame," she said. "But I think you know that I am very sorry for Robin."

"You are always kind," he rejoined gravely.

"How could you be to blame, Miss Moore?" asked Mrs. Fielding.

Juliet turned towards her. "Because Robin and I are friends," she explained simply. "He came here to look for me, and Jack ordered him off. That was the origin of the trouble. And so —" she smiled — "Mr.

Green tells me it was my fault."

"He would," commented Mrs. Fielding.

She turned with the words as if Green's proximity were an offence to her, and walked away to the window at the further end of the room.

In the slightly strained pause that followed, Juliet bent to fondle Columbus who was sitting pressed against her and her book slid from her lap to the ground. Green stooped swiftly and picked it up.

"What is it? May I look?"

She held out her hand for it. "It is *Marionettes*, — Dene Strange's latest. Mrs. Fielding lent it to me."

He kept the book in his hand. "I thought you said you wouldn't read anymore of that man's stuff."

She knitted her brows a little. "Did I say so? I don't remember."

He looked down at her keenly. "You said you hated the man and his work."

She began to smile. "Well, I do — in certain moods. But I've got to read him all the same. Everyone does."

"Surely you don't follow the crowd!" he said.

She laughed — her sweet, low laugh. "Surely I do! I'm one of them."

He made a sharp gesture. "That's just what you are not. I say, Miss Moore, don't read this book! It won't do you any good, and it'll make you very angry. You'll call it cynical, insincere, cold-blooded. It will hurt your feelings horribly."

"I don't think so," said Juliet. "You forget, — I am no longer — a marionette. I have come to life."

Again she held out her hand for the book. He gave it to her reluctantly.

"Don't read it!" he said.

She shook her head, still smiling. "No, Mr. Green, I'm not going to let you censor my reading. I will tell you what I think of it next time we meet."

"Don't!" he said again very earnestly.

But Juliet would not yield. She stooped again over Columbus and fondled his ear.

Green stood looking down at her, his dark face somewhat grim, his eyes extremely bright.

"I believe he's cross with us, Christopher." murmured Juliet. "Never mind, old thing! We shall get over it if he doesn't. Being cross always hurts oneself the most. We're — never cross, are we, Christopher? We please ourselves and we please each other — always."

Columbus grunted appreciatively and leaned harder against her. He liked to be included in the conversation.

Green suddenly bent and pulled the other ear. "You're a jolly lucky chap, Columbus," he said. "I'll change places with you any day in the week."

Columbus smiled at him indulgently, and edged his nose onto his mistress's knee. He knew his position was secure.

"Don't you listen to him, Christopher!" said Juliet. "He wouldn't be in your place two minutes. If I dared to thwart him in anything, he'd turn and rend me."

"He wouldn't," said Green decidedly. "Anyone else — perhaps, but his mistress — never."

Columbus yawned. The topic did not interest him. But Juliet laughed again, and for a moment her eyes glanced upwards, meeting the man's look.

"Is that a promise?" she asked lightly.

"My word of honor," he said.

"How generous!" said Juliet. "And how rash!"

Mrs. Fielding looked round from the window and spoke fretfully. "The storm seems to have made it more oppressive than ever," she complained. "I believe it is coming up again."

"I hope not," said Green.

Juliet got up quietly and moved to join her — a tall woman of gracious outlines with the poise of a princess.

"You know all about everything," she said to him, in passing. "Come and read the weather for us!"

He followed her. They stood together at the open French window, looking out on to the stormy sunset.

"It isn't coming back," said Green, after a pause.

Mrs. Fielding gave him a brief, contemptuous glance. Juliet regarded him more openly, a glint of mockery in her eyes.

"You are sure to be right," she said.

He made her a bow. "Many thanks, Miss Moore! I think I am on this occasion at least. We shall have a fine day for the Graydown races tomorrow."

"Are you keen on racing?" asked Juliet.

He laughed. "I've no time for frivolities of that sort."

"You could make time if you wanted to," observed Mrs. Fielding. "You are free on Saturday."

"Am I?" said Green.

She challenged him in sudden exasperation. "Well, what do you do on your off days?"

He considered for a moment. "I'll tell you what I'm doing tomorrow, if you like," he said. "In the morning I hold a swimming class for all who care to attend. In the afternoon I've got a cricket match. And in the evening I'm running an open-air concert at High Shale with Ashcott."

"For those wretched miners!" exclaimed Mrs. Fielding.

He nodded. "Yes, and their wives and their babies. They are rather amusing shows sometimes. We use native talent of course. I believe you would be interested, Miss Moore."

"I am sure I should," said Juliet. "May I come to one some day?"

He faced her boldly. "Will you help at one — some day?"

"Oh, really!" broke in Mrs. Fielding. "That is too much. I am sure my husband would never agree to that."

"I don't know why he shouldn't," said Juliet gently. "But the point is — should I be any good?"

"You sing," said Green with confidence.

She smiled. "Who told you so?"

His brows worked humorously. "It's one of the things I know without being told. Would you be afraid to venture yourself in that rough crowd with only me to take care of you?"

"Not in the least," said Juliet.

"Thank you," he said. "You would certainly have no need to be. You would have an immense reception."

"I am quite sure my husband would never allow it," said Mrs. Fielding with a frown. "These High Shale people are so hopelessly disreputable — such a drunken, lawless lot."

"But not beyond redemption," said Green quickly, "if anyone takes the trouble."

She shrugged her shoulders. "There are not many people who have time to waste over them. In any case, the responsibility lies at Lord Wilchester's door — not ours."

"And as Lord Wilchester happens to be a rotter, they must go to the wall," remarked Green.

"Well, it is no business of ours," maintained Mrs. Fielding. "I always leave that sort of thing to the busybodies who enjoy it."

"What a good idea!" said Green. "Do you know I never thought of that?"

"Tell me about the cricket match!" Juliet said, intervening. "Who is playing?"

He gave her a glance of quizzical understanding. "Oh, that's a village affair too — Little Shale versus Fairharbor, most of them fisher-lads, all of them sports. I have the honor to be captain of the Little Shale team."

"You seem to be everything," she said.

"Jack of all trades!" sneered Mrs. Fielding.

Green laughed. "I was just going to say that."

"How original of you!" said Juliet. "Well, I hope you'll win."

"He is the sort of person who always comes out on top whether he wins or loses," said Fielding, striding up the long room at the moment. "You've not seen him play cricket yet, Miss Moore. He's a positive tornado on the cricket-ground. Tomorrow's Saturday, isn't it? Where are you playing, Dick?"

His good-humor was evidently fully restored. He slapped a hand on Dick's shoulder with the words. Mrs. Fielding's lips turned downwards at the action.

"We are playing the Fairharbor crowd, sir, on Lord Saltash's ground," said Green. "It's in Burchester Park. You know the place don't you? It's just above the town."

"Yes, yes, I know it. A fine place. Pity it doesn't belong to somebody decent," said the squire.

Mrs. Fielding laughed unpleasantly. "Dear me! More wicked lords?"

Her husband looked at her with his quick frown. "I thought everybody knew Saltash was a scoundrel. It's common talk that he's in Paris at this moment entertaining that worthless jade, Lady Joanna Farringmore."

Juliet gave a violent start at the words. For a moment her face flamed red, then went dead white — so white that she almost looked as if she would faint. Then, in a very low voice, "It may be common talk," she said, "but — I am quite sure — it isn't true."

"Good heavens!" exclaimed the squire. "My dear Miss Moore, pray forgive me! I forgot you knew her."

She smiled at him, still with that ashen face. "Yes, I know her. At least — I used to. And — she may have been heartless — I think she was; — but she wasn't — that."

"Not when you knew her perhaps," said Mrs. Fielding's scornful voice. She had no sympathy with people who regarded it as a duty to stand up for their unworthy friends. "But since you quarreled with her yourself on account of her disgraceful behavior you are scarcely in a position to defend her."

"No — I know," said Juliet, and she spoke nervously, painfully. "But — I must defend her on — a point of honor."

She did not look at Green. Yet instantly and very decidedly he entered the breach. "Quite so," he said. "We are all entitled to fair play — though we don't always get it when our backs are turned. I take off my hat to you, Miss Moore, for your loyalty to your friends."

She gave him a quick glance without speaking.

From the door the butler announced dinner, and they all turned.

"Miss Moore, I apologize," said the squire, and offered her his arm. She took it, her hand not very steady. "Please forget it!" she said.

He smiled at her kindly as he led her from the room, and began to speak of other things.

Green sauntered behind with his hostess. His eyes were extremely bright, and he made no attempt to make conversation as he went.

Chapter V

THE WAY TO HAPPINESS

*I*t was an unpleasant shock to Juliet on the following morning when she went to Mrs. Fielding's room after breakfast to find her lying in bed, pale and tear-stained, refusing morosely to partake of any nourishment whatever.

Juliet always breakfasted alone, for the squire was in the habit of taking his early ride first and coming in late for the meal. She usually took a morning paper up with her with which to regale the mistress of the house before she rose, but the first glance showed her that this attention would be wholly unwelcome today. Even the letters that had accompanied her breakfast tray were scattered unopened by her side.

"Why, what is the matter?" said Juliet.

"I've had – a wretched night," said Mrs. Fielding, and turned her face into the pillow with a sob.

Her maid glanced at Juliet with raised brows, and indicated the untouched breakfast with a shrug of helplessness.

Juliet came to the bedside. "What is it? Aren't you well?" she questioned.

"No, I'm wretched – miserable!" The words came muffled with sobs.

Juliet looked round. "All right, Cox. You can go. I will ring when you are wanted."

Cox went, leaving the despised breakfast behind her.

Juliet turned back to the bed, and found Mrs. Fielding weeping unrestrainedly. She bent over her, discarding all ceremony. "My dear girl, do stop!" she said. "What on earth is the matter? You won't get over it all day if you go on like this."

"Of course I shan't get over it!" sobbed Mrs. Fielding indignantly. "I never do. He knows that perfectly well. He knows — that when once I'm down — it takes me days — weeks — to get up again."

"Oh, dear!" said Juliet. "It's a quarrel, is it?"

Mrs. Fielding raised herself with a furious movement and thrust out a white arm on which the bruises of a fierce grip were mercilessly defined. "That's how — he — quarrels!" she said bitterly.

Juliet drew down the loose night-dress sleeve with a gentle but very decided hand. "Don't let anyone else see it!" she said. "And don't tell me anymore unless you're sure — quite sure — you want me to know!"

"Why shouldn't you know?" said Mrs. Fielding pettishly through her falling tears. "It's your fault in a way. At least it wouldn't have happened if you hadn't been here — you and that horrid little cad of a schoolmaster."

"Oh, don't put it like that!" said Juliet. "It's such a pity to offend everybody at once. You really mustn't cry anymore or you'll be ill. I'm sure it isn't worth that."

"I don't care if I die!" cried Mrs. Fielding, with a fresh burst of weeping. "I'm miserable — miserable! And nobody cares."

She flung herself down upon the pillow in such a paroxysm of hysterical sobbing that Juliet actually was alarmed. She stood beside her, impotent, unable to make herself heard, and wondering what to do. She had never before looked upon such an abandonment of distress as she now beheld, and since Mrs. Fielding was obviously beyond all reasoning or consolation she was powerless to cope with it. She could only stand and wait for the storm to spend itself.

It seemed, however, to increase rather than to abate, and she was beginning to contemplate recalling Cox to her assistance when to her astonishment the door suddenly opened, and Fielding himself appeared upon the threshold.

She turned sharply, her first impulse to keep him out, for he wore an ugly look. But in a moment she realized that the direction of affairs was not in her control. He came straight forward with a mastery that would brook no interference.

"Leave her to me!" he said, as he reached Juliet.

But at the first word his wife uttered so wild a shriek of alarm that Juliet turned back to her with the swift instinct to protect. In an instant Mrs. Fielding was clinging to her, clinging desperately, frantically, like a terrified child.

"Oh, don't go! Oh, don't leave me!" she gasped. "Juliet! Juliet! Stay — oh, stay!"

She could not refuse the appeal. It went straight to her heart. She put her arms about the quivering, convulsed form and held it close.

"I can't go!" she said hurriedly to the squire.

"Stay then!" he said curtly.

Then abruptly he stooped over the trembling, hysterical woman. "Vera," he said, "stop it at once! Do you hear me? Stop it!"

He did not raise his voice, but his words had a pitiless distinctness that seemed somehow more forcible than any violence. Vera Fielding shrank closer to Juliet's breast.

"Don't leave me! Don't leave me!" she moaned, still shaken from head to foot with great sobs she could not control.

"She won't go if you behave yourself," said the squire grimly. "But if you don't, I'm damned if I won't turn her out and deal with you myself."

"Don't be brutal!" breathed Juliet.

He gave her a swift, fierce look, but she met it unflinching and as swiftly it fell away from her. He took one of his wife's feverish, clutching hands and firmly held it.

"Now you listen to me!" he said. "I don't want to bully you but I can't and won't have this sort of thing. It's damnably unfair to everybody. So you pull yourself together and be quick about it!"

The trembling hand clenched in his grasp. "I hate you!" gasped Mrs. Fielding furiously. "Oh, how I hate you!"

The man's mouth took an ominous downward curve. "I've heard that before," he said. "Now that's enough. We're not going to have a scene in front of Miss Moore. If you can't control yourself, out she goes."

"She won't go," flashed back Mrs. Fielding. "She's on my side. Ask her if she isn't! She won't leave me to your tender mercies again. She knows what they are like."

"Hush!" Juliet said. "Don't you know there isn't a man living who can stand this? Be quiet, my dear, for heaven's sake! You're making the most hideous mistake of your life."

She spoke with most unwonted force, and again the squire's steely eyes shot upwards, regarding her piercingly. "You're quite right," he said briefly. "I won't stand it. I've stood too much already. Now, Vera, you behave yourself, and stop that crying — at once!"

There was that in his tone that quelled all rebellion. Vera shrank closer to Juliet, but she began to make some feeble efforts to subdue her wild distress. Fielding sat on the edge of the bed, her hand firmly in his, and waited. His expression was one of absolute and implacable determination. He looked so forbidding and so formidable that Juliet wondered a little at her own temerity in remaining. She decided then and there that a serious disagreement with the squire would be too great a tax upon any woman's strength, and she did not wonder that Vera's had broken down under it.

Suddenly he spoke. "Has she had any breakfast?"

"Not yet," said Juliet.

"Oh, don't!" implored Vera, with a shudder.

He got up and went to the untouched tray. Juliet watched him pour out some tea as she smoothed the tumbled hair back from his wife's forehead.

He came back with the cup in his hand. "Now," he said, "you are going to drink this."

She lifted scared eyes to his stern face. "Edward!" she whispered. "Don't — oh, don't look at me like that!"

He stooped over her, and put the cup to her lips. She drank, quivering, not daring to refuse. When she had finished he brought her bread and butter and fed her, mouthful by mouthful, while the tears ran silently down her face.

At last he turned again to Juliet. "Miss Moore, my wife will not object to your leaving us now."

It was a distinct command. But she hesitated to obey. Vera looked up at her piteously, saying no word. The squire frowned heavily, his eyes grimly, piercingly, upon Juliet.

She met his look with steady resolution. "Won't you leave her to rest for a little while?" she said. "I think she needs it."

"Very well," he said, and though he did not look like yielding she realized to her surprise that he had done so. He turned to the door. "I should like a word with you in the library," he said, as he reached it. "Please come to me there immediately!"

He was gone. Vera turned with a sob and clasped Juliet closely to her.

"He is going to send you away. I know he is," she wailed. "What shall I do? What shall I do?"

"Lie down!" said Juliet sensibly, releasing herself to settle the tumbled bedclothes. "Don't cry anymore! Just shut your eyes and lie still!"

She laid her down upon the pillow with the words as if she had been a child, smoothed the rumpled hair again, and after a moment bent and kissed the hot forehead.

"Oh, thank you!" murmured Mrs. Fielding. "I'm dreadfully unhappy, Juliet. I don't know what I shall do without you."

"Go to sleep!" said Juliet, tucking her up. "I'll come back presently.

Lie quite still till I do!"

She guessed that exhaustion would come to her aid in this particular as she drew the curtains close and turned away to face her own ordeal.

"Come back soon!" Vera called after her as she softly shut the door.

"Presently," Juliet said again.

She realized as she descended the stairs that her heart was beating uncomfortably hard, but she did not pause on that account. She wanted to face the squire while her spirit was still high.

She held her head up as she entered the library where he awaited her, but she knew within herself that it was bravado rather than fearlessness that enabled her to face him thus. And when he turned sharply from the window to meet her she was conscious of a moment of most undignified dread.

Whether her face betrayed her or not she never knew but she was aware in an instant of a change in his attitude. He came straight up to her, and suddenly her hand was in his and he was looking into her eyes with the gleam of a smile in his own.

"Come along!" he said. "Let's have it! I'm the biggest brute you ever came across, and you never want to set eyes on me again. Isn't that it?"

It was winningly spoken, restoring her self-confidence in a second. She shook her head in answer.

"No. I'm not in a position to judge, and I don't think I want to be. I have no real liking for meddling in other people's affairs."

"Very wise!" he commented. "But you won't have much choice if you decide to stay with us. Are you going to stay?"

"Are you going to keep me?" said Juliet.

"Certainly," he returned promptly. "I regard you as the most valuable member of the household at the present moment. Miss Moore, will you tell me something?"

"If I can," said Juliet.

"Where did you learn such a lot about men?" he said.

She colored a little at the question. "Well, I haven't lived with my eyes shut all this time," she said.

"You evidently haven't," he said. "Allow me to compliment you on your tact! Ninety-nine women out of a hundred would have taken the obvious course of siding with their own sex against the oppressor. Why didn't you, I wonder?"

"I'm not sure that I don't," she said, smiling faintly.

He pressed her hand and released it. "No, you don't. You've too much sense. You know as well as I do that she deserved all she got and more. You haven't always found her exactly easy to get on with yourself, I'll be bound."

"I don't think you are either of you that," Juliet said quietly.

He nodded. "Now it's coming! I thought it would. No, Miss Moore, I am not easy to get on with. I've had a rotten life all through, and it hasn't made me very pliable." He paused, looking at her under his black brows as if debating with himself as to how far he would take her into his confidence. "I've been cheated of the best from the very outset," he said, "cheated and thwarted at every turn. That sort of treatment may suit some people, but it hasn't made an archangel of me." He fell to pacing up and down the room, staring moodily at the floor, his hands behind him. "Life is such an infernal gamble at the best," he said; "but I never had a chance. It's been one damn thing after another. I've tripped at every hurdle. I suppose you never came a cropper in your life — don't know what it means."

"I think I do know what it means," Juliet said slowly. "I've looked on, you know. I've seen — a good many things."

"Just as you're looking on now, eh?" said the squire, grimly smiling. "Well, you profit by my experience — if you can! And if love ever comes your way, hang on to it, hang on to it for all you're worth, even if you drop everything else to do it! It's the gift of the gods, my dear, and if you throw it away once it'll never come your way again."

"No, I know," said Juliet. She rested her arm on the mantelpiece, gravely watching him. "I've noticed that."

"Noticed it, have you?" He flung her a look as he passed. "You've never been in love, that's certain, never seriously I mean, — never up to the neck."

"No, never so deep as that!" said Juliet.

He passed on to the end of the room, and came to a sudden stand before the window. "I — have!" he said, and his voice came with an odd jerkiness as if it covered some emotion that he could not wholly control. "I won't bore you with details. But I loved a woman once — I loved her madly. And she loved me. But — Fate — came between. She's dead now. Her troubles are over, and I'm not such a selfish brute as to want her back. Yet I sometimes think to myself — that if I'd married that woman — I'd have made her happy, and I'd have been a better man myself than I am today." He swung round restlessly, found her steady eyes upon him, and came back to her. "The fact of the matter is, Miss Moore," he said, "I was a skunk ever to marry at all — after that."

"It depends how you look at it," she said gently.

"Don't you look at it that way?" he said, regarding her curiously.

She hesitated momentarily. "Not entirely, no. The woman was dead and you were alone."

"I was — horribly alone," he said.

"I don't think it was wrong of you to marry," she said. "Only — you ought to love your wife."

"Ah!" he said. "I thought we agreed that love comes only once."

She shook her head. "Not quite that. Besides, there are many kinds of love." Again for a second she hesitated looking straight at him. "Shall I tell you something? I don't know whether I ought. It is almost like a breach of confidence — though it was never told to me."

"What is it?" he said imperatively.

She made a little gesture of yielding. "Yes, I will tell you. Mr. Fielding, you might make your wife love you — so dearly — if you cared to take the trouble."

"What?" he said.

Her eyes met his with a faint, faint smile. "Doesn't it seem absurd," she said, "that it should fall to me — a comparative stranger — to tell you this, when you have been together for so long? It is the truth. She is just as lonely and unhappy as you are. You could transform the whole world for her — if you only would."

"What! Give her her own way in everything?" he said. "Is that what you're advising?"

"No. I'm not advising anything. I am only just telling you the truth," said Juliet. "You could make her love you — if you tried."

He stared at her for some seconds as if trying to read some riddle in her countenance. "You are a very remarkable young woman," he said at last. "I wouldn't part with you for a king's ransom. So you think I might turn that very unreasonable hatred of hers into love, do you?"

"I am quite sure," said Juliet steadily.

"I wonder if I should like it if I did!" said the squire.

She laughed — a sudden, low laugh. "Yes. You would like it very much. It's the last and greatest obstacle between you and happiness. Once clear that, and —"

"Did you say happiness?" he broke in cynically.

"Yes, of course I did." Her look challenged him. "Once clear that and if you haven't got a straight run before you —" She paused, looking at him oddly, very intently, and finally stopped.

"Well?" he said. "Continue!"

She colored vividly under his eyes.

"I'm afraid I've lost my thread. It doesn't really matter. You know what I was going to say. The way to happiness does not lie in pleasing oneself. The self-seekers never get there."

He made her a courteous bow. "Thank you, fairy god-mother! I believe you are right. That may be why happiness is so shy a bird. We spread the net too openly. Well," he heaved a sigh, "we live and learn."

He turned to the table and took up his riding whip. "I suppose my wife will be in bed and sulk all day because I vetoed the Graydown Races."

"Oh, was that the trouble?" said Juliet.

He nodded gloomily. "I hate the set she consorts with at these shows. There are some of the Fairharbor set — impossible people! But they boast of being on nodding terms with that arch-bounder Lord Saltash, and so everything is forgiven them."

Juliet suddenly stood up very straight. "I think I ought to tell you," she said, "that I know Lord Saltash. I have lived with the Farringmore family, as you know. He is a friend of Lord Wilchester's."

The squire turned sharply. "I hope you're going to tell me also that you can't endure the man," he said.

She made a little gesture of negation. "I never say that of anybody. I don't feel I can afford to. Life has too many contradictions — too many chances. The person we most despise today may prove our most valuable defender tomorrow."

"Heaven forbid!" said the squire. "You wouldn't touch such pitch as that under any circumstances. Besides, what do you want in the way of defenders? You're safe enough where you are."

Juliet was smiling whimsically. "But who knows?" she said. "I may be dismissed in disgrace tomorrow."

"No," he said briefly. "That won't happen. Your position here is secure as long as you consent to fill it."

"How rash of you," she said.

"A matter of opinion!" said Fielding. "How would you like to go over and see the cricket at Fairharbor this afternoon?"

She gave him a quick look. "Oh, is that the alternative to the races?"

He frowned. "I have already told you the races are out of the question."

"I see," said Juliet thoughtfully. "Then I am afraid the cricket-match is also — unless Mrs. Fielding wants to go."

"I'll make her go," said squire.

"No! No! Don't make her do anything — please!" begged Juliet. "That is just the worst mistake you could possibly make. To be honest, I would rather — much — go to the open-air concert at High Shale this evening."

"Along with those rowdy miners?" growled the squire. "I see enough of them on the Bench. Green of course is cracked on that subject. He'd like to set the world in order if he could."

"I admire his enterprise," said Juliet.

He nodded. "So do I. He's cussed as a mule, but he's a goer. He's also a gentleman. Have you noticed that?"

She smiled. "Of course I have."

"And I can't get my wife to see it," said the squire. "Just because —
by his own idiotic choice — he occupies a humble position, she won't
allow him a single decent quality. She classes them all together, when
anyone can see — anyone with ordinary intelligence can see — that he is
of a totally different standing from those brothers of his. He is on
another plane altogether. It's self-evident. You see it at once."

"Yes," said Juliet.

He moved restlessly. "I would have placed him in his proper sphere
if he'd consented to it. But he wouldn't. It's a standing grievance between
us. That fellow Robin is a millstone round his neck. Miss Moore," he
turned on her suddenly, "you have a wonderful knack of making people
see reason. Couldn't you persuade him to let Robin go?"

"Oh no!" said Juliet quickly. "It's the very last thing I would attempt
to do."

"Really!" He looked at her in genuine astonishment.

Juliet flushed. "But of course!" she said. "They belong to each other.
How could Mr. Green possibly part with him? You wouldn't — surely —
think much of him if he did?"

"I think he's mad not to," declared the squire. "But," he smiled at
her, "I think it's uncommonly kind of you to take that view, all the
same. I'll take you to that concert tonight if you really want to go."

"Will you? How kind!" said Juliet, turning to go. "But you won't
mind if I consult Mrs. Fielding first? I must do that."

He opened the door for her. "You are not to spoil her now," he said.
"She's been spoilt all her life by everybody."

"Except by you," said Juliet daringly.

And with that parting shot she left him, swiftly traversing the hall to
the stairs without looking back.

The squire stood for some seconds looking after her. She had opposed
him at practically every point, and yet she had not offended him.

"A very remarkable young woman!" he said again to himself as she
passed out of his sight. "A very — gifted young woman! Ah, Dick, my
friend, she'd make a rare politician's wife." And then another thought
struck him and he began to laugh. "And she'll be equally charming as
the helpmeet of the village schoolmaster. Egad, we can't have everything,
but I think you've found your fate."

Chapter VI

RECONCILIATION

*T*he luncheon-gong rang through the house with a tremendous booming, and Vera Fielding, sitting limply in a chair by her open window, closed her eyes with drawn brows as if the sound were too much for her overwrought nerves. The tempest of three hours before had indeed left her spent and shaken, and an unacknowledged tincture of shame mingling with her exhaustion did not improve matters. She had wept away her fury, and a dull resentment sat heavily upon her. She had entered upon the second stage of the conflict which usually lasted for some days, — days during which complete silence reigned between her husband and herself until he either departed to town to end the tension or his wrath boiled up afresh cowing her into a bitter submission to his will which brought nothing but misery to them both.

The last deep notes of the gong died away, and Vera's eyes half-opened again. They dwelt restlessly upon the brilliant patch of garden visible under the lowered sun-blind. The splendor of the June world without served to increase the wretchedness of her mood by contrast. The sultry heat seemed to weigh her down. Life was one vast oppression and bondage. She was weary to the soul.

Juliet had gone down to aid Cox in the selection of something tempting for her luncheon. She had every intention of refusing it whatever it was. Who as miserable as she could bear to eat anything — unless forced to do so by brutal compulsion?

Her head throbbed painfully. Her nerves were stretched for the sound of her husband's step in the adjoining room. She wished she had told Juliet to lock the communicating door, though she hardly expected him to come in upon her a second time. Even his wrath had its limits. It seldom gathered to its full height twice in a day.

She was trying to comfort herself with this reflection when suddenly she heard him enter his room, and in a moment all her lassitude vanished in so violent an agitation that she found herself gasping for breath. Still she told herself that he would not come in. It had always been his habit to leave her severely alone after a battle. He would not come in! Surely he would not come in. And then the handle of the intervening door turned, and she sank back in her chair with a sick effort to appear indifferent.

She did not look at him as he came in. Only by the quick heaving of her breast which was utterly beyond control did she betray her knowledge of his presence. Her face was turned away from him. She stared down into the dazzling sunlight with eyes that saw nothing.

He came to her, halted beside her. And suddenly a warm sweet fragrance filled the air. She looked round in spite of herself and found a bunch of exquisite lilies-of-the-valley close to her cheek. She lifted her eyes with a great start.

"Edward!"

His face was red. He looked supremely ill at ease. He pushed the flowers under her nose. "Take 'em for heaven's sake!" he said irritably. "I hate the things myself."

She took them, too amazed for comment, and buried her face in their perfumed depths.

He stood beside her, impatiently clicking his fingers. There fell an uncomfortable silence, during which Vera gradually remembered her dignity and at length laid the flowers aside. Her agitation had subsided. She sat and waited noncommittally for the new situation to develop. Even in their engagement days he had never brought her flowers, and any overture from him after a quarrel was a thing unknown.

She waited therefore, not looking at him, and in a few moments, very awkwardly, with obvious reluctance, he spoke again.

"I don't think we want to keep this up any longer, do we? Seems a bit senseless, what? I'm ready to forget it if you are."

Again, she was taken by surprise, for his voice had a curious urgency that made her aware that he for one had certainly had enough of it, and there was that in her which leaped in swift response. But it was not to be expected of her that she should be willing to bury the hatchet at a moment's notice after the treatment she had received, and she checked the unaccountable impulse.

"There are some things that it is not easy to forget," she said coldly.

His demeanor changed in an instant. "Oh, all right," he said, "if you prefer to sulk!"

He swung upon his heel. In a moment he would have been gone; but in that moment the inner force that Vera had ignored suddenly sprang above every other emotion or consideration. She put out a quick hand and stayed him.

"I am not sulking! I never sulk! But I can't behave — all in a moment — as if nothing had happened. Edward!"

It was her voice that held pleading now, for he made as if he would leave her in spite of her detaining hold. She tightened her fingers on his arm.

"Edward, please!" she said.

He stopped. "Well?" he said gruffly. Then, as she said nothing further, he turned slowly and looked at her. Her head was bent. She was striving for self-control. Something in her attitude went straight to the man's heart. She looked so small, so forlorn, so pathetic in her struggle for dignity.

On a generous impulse he flung his own away. "Oh, come, my dear!" he said, and stooping took her into his arms. "I'm sorry. There!"

She clung to him then, clung closely, still battling to check the tears that she knew he disliked.

He kissed her forehead and patted her shoulder with a queer compunction that had never troubled him before in his dealings with her.

"There!" he said. "There! That's all right, isn't it? We shall have Miss Moore in directly. Where's your handkerchief?"

She found it and dried her eyes with her head against his shoulder. Then she lifted a still quivering face to his. "Edward, — I'm — just as sorry as you are," she said, with a catch in her voice.

He kissed her again, wondering a little at his own softened feelings. "All right, my girl. Let's forget it!" he said. "You have a good lunch and you'll feel better! What are they giving you? Champagne?"

"Oh no, of course not!"

"Well, why not? It's the very thing you want. Just the occasion. What? You sit still and I'll go and see about it!" He put her down among her cushions, but she clung to him still. "No, don't go for a minute!" she said, with a shaky smile. "It's so good to have you — kind to me for once."

"Good gracious!" he said, but half in jest. "Am I such a brute as all that?"

She pushed back her sleeve and mutely showed him the marks upon her arm.

He looked, and his brows drew together. "My doing?"

She nodded. "Last night — when — when I said — something you didn't like — about Mr. Green."

He scowled a moment longer, then abruptly stooped, took the white arm between his hands and kissed it. "I'll get a stick and beat you the next time," he said. "You remember that — and be decent to Green, see?"

The kiss belied the words, covering also a certain embarrassment which Vera was not slow to perceive. Because of it she found strength to abstain from further argument. He had undoubtedly conceded a good deal.

"I'll be decent to anyone," she said, "so long as you are decent to me."

"Hear, hear!" said the squire. "Now dry your eyes and be sensible! Miss Moore will go for me like mad if she finds you crying again. If we don't pull together we shall have that girl running the whole show before we are much older, and neither of us will ever dare even to contradict the other in her presence again. We shouldn't like that, should we?"

She laughed a little in spite of her wan countenance. "Oh, no, Edward. We mustn't risk that." Then, with a touch of anxiety, "It wasn't Miss Moore's idea that you should bring me flowers, was it?"

"No." The squire grinned at her suddenly. "The worthy Columbus was responsible for that. I found him routing in the lily-bed after snails or some such delicacy. He was so infernally busy he made me feel ashamed. So I went down on my knees and joined him, gathered the lot, — nearly killed myself over it, but that's an unimportant detail. Now for your champagne! You'll feel a different woman when you've had it."

He departed, leaving his wife looking after him with an odd wistfulness in her eyes. She was seeing him in a new light which made her feel strangely uncertain of herself also. Was it possible that all these years of misunderstanding, which she had regarded as inevitable, might have been avoided after all?

A quick sigh rose to her lips as again she took his flowers and held them against her face.

Chapter VII

THE SPELL

A wonderful summer evening followed the sultry day. The sun sank gloriously behind High Shale, and a soft breeze blew in from the sea.

On the slope of the hill behind the lighthouse and above the miners' village there stood an old thatched barn, and about this a knot of men and youths loitered, smoking and talking in a desultory, discontented fashion. On the other side of the barn a shrill cackling proclaimed the presence of some of the feminine portion of the community, and the occasional squall of a baby or a squeal of a bigger child testified to the fact that the greater part of the village population awaited the entertainment which Green contrived to give on the first Saturday of every month.

He had started these concerts two winters before down in the village of Little Shale, and they had originally been for men and boys only, but the women had grumbled so loudly at their exclusion that Green had very soon realized the necessity of extending a welcome to them also. So now they flocked in a body to his support, even threatening to crowd out the men in the winter evenings when he had to assemble his audience at the Village Club at Little Shale. But in the summer, as a concession to High Shale, he held his concerts, whenever feasible, up on the hill, and practically the whole of High Shale village came to them. Little Shale was also well represented, but he always felt that he was in closer touch with the miners on these occasions, when he met them on their own ground.

The two villages were apt to eye one another with scant sympathy, the fisher population of the one and the mining population of the other having little in common beyond the liquor which they uniformly sought at The Three Tuns by the shore. Green never permitted any bickering, and they were all alike in their respect for him, but a species of armed neutrality which was very far removed from comradeship existed between them. Fights at The Three Tuns were by no means of unusual occurrence and the miners of High Shale were invariably spoken of with wholesale contempt by the men along the shore.

But, thanks to Green's untiring efforts, they met on common ground at his concerts, and any member of the audience who dared to commit any breach of the peace on any of these occasions was summarily dealt with by Green himself. He knew how to keep his men in hand. There was not one of them who ever ventured to question his supremacy. He ruled them, not one of them could have said how. Ashcott, the manager of the mine, who battled in vain against the rising spirit of disorder and rebellion among them, was wont to describe his influence over them as black magic. Whatever its source it was certainly unique. None but Dick Green could spring from the platform, seize a delinquent by his collar or the scruff of his neck, and run him, practically unresisting, out of the assembly. His lightning decisions were never questioned. His language, which could be forcible upon occasion, never met with any retort. The men seemed to recognize instinctively that it was useless to stand up to him. He could have compelled them blindfold and with his hands behind him.

It was this quality in him, this dynamic force, restrained yet always somehow in action, that had affected Juliet so strangely in the beginning of their acquaintance. Like these rough miners and fisher-folk she could not have said wherein the attraction lay, but she recognized in him that inner fire called genius, and it drew her unaccountably, irresistibly. Whatever the sphere to which he had been born, he was a man created to lead, to overcome obstacles, to wrest victory from failure, — a man who possessed the rare combination of a highly sensitive temperament and a practically invincible courage — a man who could handle the great forces of life with the fearless certainty of the born conqueror.

Yes, he attracted her, undoubtedly he attracted her. He stirred her to an interest which she had believed herself too old, too jaded with the ways of the world, ever to feel again. But she did not want to yield to the attraction. She wanted to hold aloof for a space. She had come to this quiet corner of the world in search of peace. She wanted to avoid the problems of life, to get back her poise, to become an onlooker and no longer a competitor in the maddening race from which she had so lately withdrawn herself. She was willing to be interested, she already was deeply interested, but only as a spectator, so she told herself. She would not be drawn in against her will. She would stand aside and watch.

It was in this mood that she drove off with the squire on the way to the open-air concert on the High Shale bluff on that magic June evening. Mrs. Fielding was too weary after the many emotions of the day to accompany them, but they left her in a tranquil frame of mind, and the squire was in an unusually good humor. Though he had small liking for the High Shale village people, it pleased him that Juliet should take an interest in Green's enterprises, eccentric though they might be. And he considered that she deserved a treat after her diplomatic handling of a very difficult situation that morning.

"Might as well call and see if Dick would like a lift," he said, as they neared the gates. "We've got to pass his door. I'll send Jack in."

But when they stopped at the school-house gate, a humped, familiar figure was leaning upon it, and Jack flung an imperious question without descending.

The squire's face darkened at the sight. "Here's that unspeakable baboon Robin!" he growled.

Robin paid about as much attention to his brother's curt query as he might have bestowed upon the buzzing of a fly. His dark eyes below his shaggy thatch of hair were fixed, deeply shining, upon Juliet.

Jack muttered an impatient ejaculation under his breath and flung himself out of the car. Before Juliet could speak a word to intervene, he had given the gate on which Robin leant a push that sent the boy backwards with considerable force on the grass while he himself went up the path to the house at a run.

"Oh, what a shame!" said Juliet, a quick vibration of anger in her deep voice.

She leaned forward sharply to open the door and spring out, but in a second Fielding's hand caught hers, holding her back.

"No, no! Leave the young beggar alone! He's none the worse. He can pick himself up again. Ah, and here comes Dick! He'll manage him!"

Robin was indeed struggling to his feet with a furious bellowing that might have been heard on the shore. But Dick was quicker than he. He came down the path, as it seemed in a single bound. He took Robin by his swaying arms and steadied him. He spoke, quickly and decidedly, and the roaring protest died down to a snarling, sobbing sound like the crying of a wounded animal. Then, still holding him, Dick turned towards the car at the gate. And Juliet saw that he was white with passion. The fierce blaze of his eyes was a thing she would not soon forget.

He spoke with twitching lips. "No, sir. I'm not coming, thanks. I shall go on foot over the down. It's only a quarter of the distance that way." He drew Robin aside at the sound of Jack's approach behind him, but he did not look at him. And Robin became suddenly and terribly silent. He was quivering all over like a dog that is held back from his prey.

Jack gave him a look of contempt as he strode past and returned to his seat at the wheel. And Juliet awoke to the fact that like Robin she was trembling from head to foot.

The car shot forward. She saw the two figures no more. But the memory of Green's face went with her, its pallor, and the awfulness of his eyes — the red flame of his fury. Robin's unrestrained wrath was of small account beside it. She felt as if she had never seen anger before that moment.

She scarcely heard the squire's caustic remarks concerning Robin. She was as one who had touched a live wire, and her whole being tingled with the shock. The hot glitter of those onyx eyes had been to her as the sudden revelation of a destroying force, fettered indeed, but how appalling if once set free!

She looked forward with a curious dread to seeing him again. She wondered if the man who drove the car so recklessly had the faintest suspicion of the storm he had stirred up. But surely he knew Dick in all his moods! He had probably encountered it before. They sped on through the fragrant summer night, and she talked at random, hardly knowing what she said. If the squire noticed her preoccupation, he made no comment. He had conceived a great respect for Juliet.

They neared their destination at last, and Jack performed what the squire called his favorite circus-trick, racing the car to the top of the towering cliff and stopping dead at the edge of a great immensity of sea and stars.

Again Juliet drew a deep breath of sheer marveling delight, speaking no word, held spellbound by the wonder of the night.

"We needn't hurry," Fielding said. "They won't be starting yet."

So for a space they remained as though caught between earth and heaven, silently drinking in the splendor.

After a long pause she spoke. "Do you often come here?"

"Not now," he said. Then, as she glanced at him: "I used to in the days of my youth — the long past days."

And she knew by his tone, by the lingering of his words, that he had not always come alone.

She asked no more, and presently the jaunty notes of a banjo floating up the grassy slope told them that Green's entertainment had begun.

They left the car at the top of the rise, and walked down over the springy turf towards the old barn about which Dick's audience were collected. Two hurricane lamps and a rough deal table were all he had in the way of stage property. But she was yet to learn that this man relied upon surroundings and circumstances not at all. As she herself had said, possibly the torch of genius burned brightest in dark places, for it was certainly genius upon which she looked tonight.

He sat on the edge of the deal table with one leg crossed over his knee, his dark face thrown into strong relief, intent, eager, with a vitality that seemed to make it almost luminous. From the crowd that watched him there came not a sound. The thought crossed Juliet's mind that the instrument he played so cunningly might have been a harp from a fairy palace. For there was magic in the air. He played with a delicacy that seemed to wind itself in threads of gold about the inner fibers of the soul. They listened to him as men bewitched.

When the music ended, a great noise went up — shouts and whistles and cat-calls. They were wild for more. But Green knew the value of a reserve. He laughed away the *encores* with a careless "Presently!" and called a young miner to him for a song. The lad sang and Green accompanied, and again Juliet marveled at the amazing facility of his performance. He seemed to be able to adapt the instrument to every mood or tone. The boy's voice was rough and untrained, but it held a certain appeal and by sheer intuition — comradeship as it seemed — Green brought it home to the hearers. The man's unfailing responsiveness was a revelation to her. She believed it was the secret of his charm.

When the song was ended, a fisherman came forward and danced a hornpipe on the table, again to the thrumming of the banjo, without which nothing seemed complete. It was while this was in progress that a thickset, somewhat bullet-headed man came up and addressed the squire by name.

"We don't often see you here, Mr. Fielding."

The squire turned. "Hullo, Ashcott. Your lambs are in force tonight. How are they behaving themselves?"

"Pretty fair," said Ashcott. "They're getting the strike rot like the rest of the world. We shan't hold 'em forever. If any of the Farringmore lot turned up here, I wouldn't answer for 'em. Lord Wilchester talked of motoring down the other day, bringing friends if you please to see the mine, I warned him off — the damn' fool! Simply asking for trouble, as I told him. 'Well, what's the matter?' he said. 'What do they want?' 'They'd like houses instead of pigsties for one thing,' I said. And he laughed at that. 'Oh, let 'em go to the devil!' he said. 'I haven't got any money to spare for luxuries of that kind.' So far as that goes I believe he is hard up, but then look at the way they live! They'd need to be multi-millionaires to keep it up."

The man's speech was crude, even brutal, and the girl on Fielding's other side shivered a little and drew a pace away. It was very evident on which side his sympathies lay. There was more than a tinge of the street ranter in his utterance. She was glad that Fielding spared her an introduction.

She tried to turn her attention back to the entertainment, but the coarse words hung in her memory like an evil cloud. They recalled Green's brief condemnation of the previous evening. Evidently his point of view was the same. He regarded the whole social system as evil. Had not the squire told her that he wanted to reform the world?

The evening wore on, and with unfaltering resource Dick Green kept the interest of his audience from flagging. He chose his assistants with insight and skill, and every item on his program scored a success. His banjo was in almost continuous demand throughout, but finally, just at the end, he laid it aside.

He took something from his pocket; what it was Juliet could not see, but she caught the gleam of metal in the lamp-light, and in a moment a great buzz of pleasure spread through the crowd. And then it began — such music as she had never dreamed of — such music as surely was never fluted save from the pipes of Pan. A long, sweet, thrilling note like the call of a nightingale, starting far away, drawing swiftly nearer, nearer, till she felt as if it ended against her heart, and then all the joy of spring, of youth, of hope, poured forth in an amazing ecstasy of silver sound — showers of fairy notes like the dancing of tiny feet or the lightest patter of summer rain that ever fell upon opening leaves — and the gold-flecked sunshine that shimmered in the crystal dawning of a day newborn. Afterwards there came the sound of waterfalls and laughing streams and the calling of fairy voices, the tinkle of fairy laughter, and then the sea and shoaling water — shoaling water — breaking in a million sparkles over the rocks of an enchanted strand!

And it was to her alone that that wonder-music spoke. She and he were wandering alone together along that fairy shore where every sea-shell gleamed like pearl and every wave broke iridescent at their feet. The sun shone in the sky for them alone, and the caves were mystic palaces of delight that awaited their coming. And once it seemed to her that he drew her close, and she felt his kisses on her lips. . . .

Ah, surely this was the midsummer madness of which they had spoken! It was a vision that could not last, but the wonder of it — ah, the wonder of it! — she would carry forever in her heart.

It ended at length, but so softly, so tenderly, that, spellbound, she never knew when lingering sound became enduring silence. She awoke as it were from a long dream and knew that her heart was beating with a wild and poignant longing that was pain. Then there arose a great shouting, and instinctively she laid her hand on Fielding's arm and drew him away.

"Had enough?" he asked.

She nodded. Somehow for the moment she could find no words. She had a feeling as of unshed tears at her throat. Ah, what had moved him to play to her like that? And why did it hurt her so?

She moved back up the grassy slope still with that curious sense of pain. Something had happened to her, something had pierced her. By that strange and faunlike power of his he had reached out and touched her inmost soul, and she knew as she went away that she was changed. He had cast a glittering spell upon her, and nothing could ever be the same again.

After a space she spoke at random and Fielding made reply. With the instinct of self-defense she maintained some species of casual conversation during their stroll back to the waiting car, but she never had the vaguest recollection afterwards as to what passed between them.

She was thankful to be swooping back again through the summer night. An urgent desire for solitude was upon her. All her throbbing pulses cried out for it. Was it but yesterday — but yesterday that she had felt so safe? And now —

Later, alone in her room at the Court, she leaned from her open window seeking with an almost frantic intensity to recover the peace that had been hers. How had she lost it? She could not say. Was it the mere piping of a flute that had reft it from her? She wanted to laugh at herself, but could not. It was too absurd, too fantastic, for everyday, prosaic existence, that rhapsody of the starlight, but to her it had been pure magic. In it she had heard the call of a man's being, seeking hers, and by every hidden chord that had vibrated in answer she knew that he had not called in vain. That was the knowledge that pierced her — the knowledge that she was caught — against her will, — still wildly struggling for freedom — but caught.

It had happened so suddenly, so amazingly. Yesterday she had been free — only yesterday — Or stay! Perhaps even then the net had been about her feet, and he had known it. How otherwise had he spoken so intimately — dared so much?

She drew a long, deep breath, recalling his look, his touch, his voice. Ah! Midsummer madness indeed! But she could not stay to face it. She must go. The way was still open behind her. She would escape as she had come, a fugitive from the force that pursued her so relentlessly. She would not suffer herself to be made a captive. She would go.

Again she drew a long breath, but curiously it broke, as if a sharp spasm had gripped her heart. She stood, struggling with herself. And then suddenly she dropped upon her knees by the sill with her arms flung wide and her head with its cloudy mass of hair bowed low.

"O God! O God!" she whispered convulsively. "Save me from this! Help me to go — while I can! I am so tired — so tired!"

Chapter VIII

THE HONOURS OF WAR

Columbus was not accustomed to being awakened in the early June morning and taken for a scamper when the sun was still scarcely two hours up. He arose blinking at his mistress's behest, and but for her brisk urging he would have turned over again and slept. But Juliet was insistent.

"I'm going down to the shore, you old sleepy-head," she told him. "Don't you want to come?"

She herself had scarcely slept throughout the brief night, and a great yearning for the sunshine and the sea was upon her. The solitude of the beach drew her irresistibly. It was Sunday morning, and she knew that no one but herself would be up for hours. She had grown to love it so, the silence and the shining emptiness and the marvel of the sea. She could not remember any other place that had ever attracted her in the same way. It suited every mood.

There was a short cut across the park, and she and Columbus took it, hastening over the dewy grass till they reached a path that led to the cliffs and the shore. Only the larks above them and the laughing waves before, made music in this world of the early morning. The peacefulness of it was like a benediction.

"And before the Throne there was a sea of glass like unto crystal. . . ." She found herself murmuring the words, for in that morning purity it seemed to her that the very ground beneath her feet was holy. She was conscious of a throbbing desire to reach out to the Infinite, to bring her troubled spirit to the Divine waters of healing.

She reached the shingly shore, and went down over the stones to the waves breaking in the sunlight. Yes, she was tired — she was tired; but this was peace. The tears sprang to her eyes as she stood there. What a place to be happy in! But happiness was not for her.

After a space she turned and walked along the strand till she came to the spot where she and Columbus had first sat together and played at being wrecked on a desert island. And here she sat down and put her arms around her faithful companion and leaned her head against his rough coat.

"I wish it had been true, Columbus," she said. "We were so happy just alone."

He kissed her with all a dog's pure devotion, sensing trouble and seeking to comfort. As he had told her many a time before, her company was really all his soul desired. All other interests were mere distractions. She was the only thing that counted in his world.

His earnest assurances on this point had their effect. She sat up and smiled at him through her tears.

"Yes, I know, my Christopher," she said, and kissed him between the eyes. "But the difficulty now is, what are we going to do?"

Columbus pondered for a few seconds, and then suggested a crab-hunt.

"Excellent idea!" said Juliet, and let him go.

But she herself sat on in the early sunshine with her chin upon her hand for a long, long time.

The tide was coming in. The white-tipped waves broke in flashing foam that spread almost to her feet. The sparkle of it danced in her dreaming eyes, but it did not rouse her from her reverie.

Perhaps she was half asleep after the weary watching of the night, or perhaps she was only too tired to notice, but when a voice suddenly spoke behind her she started as if at an electric shock. She had almost begun to feel that she and Columbus were indeed marooned on this wide shore.

"Are you waiting for the sea to carry you away?" the voice said. "Because you won't have to wait much longer now."

She turned as she sat. She had heard no sound of approaching feet. The swish of the waves had covered all beside. She looked up at him with a feeling of utter helplessness. "You!" she said.

He turned behind her, slim, upright, intensely vital, in the morning light. She had an impression that he was dressed in loose flannels, and she saw a bath-towel hanging round his neck.

"You have been bathing," she said.

He laughed down at her, she saw the gleam of the white teeth in his dark face. "I say, what a good guess! You look shocked. Is it wrong to bathe on Sunday?"

And then quite naturally he stretched a hand to her and helped her to her feet.

"I've been watching you for a long time," he said. "I was only a dot in the ocean, so of course you didn't see me. I say, — tell me, — what's the matter?"

The question was so sudden that it caught her unawares. She found herself looking straight into the dark eyes and wondering at their steady kindliness. She knew instinctively that she looked into the eyes of a friend, and as a friend she spoke in answer.

"I have had rather a worrying night. I came out for a little fresh air. It was such a perfect morning."

"And you hoped you would have the place to yourself and be able to cry it off in comfort," he said. "I wouldn't have interfered for the world if I hadn't been afraid that you were going to drown yourself into the bargain. And I really couldn't bear that. There are limits, you know."

She laughed a little in spite of herself. "No, I have no intention of drowning myself. I am not so desperate as that."

He smiled at her whimsically. "It happens sometimes unintentionally. Let's climb up to the next shelf and sit down!"

Her hand was still in his. He kept it to help her up the tumbling stones to a higher ridge of shingle.

"Will this do?" he asked her. "May I stay for a bit? I'll be very good."

"You always are good," said Juliet, as she sat down.

"No? Really? You don't mean that? Well, it's awfully kind of you if you do, but it isn't true." He dropped down beside her and offered her his cigarette-case. "I can be — I have been — a perfect devil sometimes."

"Yes. I know," she said, as she chose a cigarette.

"Oh, you know that, do you? How do you know?" He was watching her closely, but as the faint color mounted to her face, his eyes fell. "No, don't tell me! It doesn't matter. Wait while I get you a match!"

He struck one and held it first for her and then for himself, his brown hand absolutely steady. Then he turned with a certain resolution and fixed his eyes upon the gleaming horizon.

"It was kind of you to come round to the sing-song last night," he said, after a pause. "I hope it wasn't that that made you sleep badly."

"I enjoyed it," said Juliet, ignoring the last remark. "Your performance was wonderful. I should think you are tired after it."

"That sort of thing doesn't tire me," he said. "There's no difficulty about it when it goes with a swing and everybody is out to make it a success. I shall get you to sing next time."

She shook her head. "I'm afraid not, Mr. Green."

"Why not?" He turned and looked at her again, his hand shading his eyes.

She hesitated.

"Do you mind telling me?" he said gently. "There is a reason of course?"

"Yes." Yet she smoked her cigarette in silence after the word as though there were nothing more to be said.

He sat motionless, still with his hand over his eyes. At last "Juliet," he said, his voice very low, "am I being — a nuisance to you?"

She looked at him swiftly. He had uttered the name so spontaneously that she wondered if he realized that he had made use of it.

He went on before she could find words to answer him. "I'm not a bounder. At least I hope not. But — yesterday — last night — I hadn't got such a firm hold on myself as usual. I began by being furiously angry — you remember the episode at the gate — and that weakened my self-control. Then — when I knew you were standing there listening — temptation came to me, and I hadn't the strength to resist. You knew, didn't you? You understood?"

She nodded mutely.

"Will you forgive me?" he said.

She was silent. How could she tell him what that wild passion of music had done to her?

He went on after a moment. "I hope you'll try anyway, because I never meant to offend you. Only somehow I felt possessed. I had to reach you — or die. But I didn't mean to hurt you. My dear, you do believe that, don't you? My love is more than a selfish craving. I can do without you. I will — since I must. But I shall go on loving you — all my life."

His voice was still very low, but it had steadied. He spoke with the strong purpose of a man secure in his own self-mastery. He loved her, but he made no demand upon her. He recognized that his love entitled him to no claim. He even asked her forgiveness for having revealed it to her.

And suddenly the hot tears welled again in Juliet's eyes. She could not speak in answer, but in a moment she stretched her hand to his.

He took it and held it close. "Don't cry!" he said gently. "I'm not worth it. I've been a fool — no, not a fool to love you, but a three times idiot to lose hold of myself like this. There! It's over. I'm not going to bother you anymore. And you're not going to let yourself be bothered. What? You're not going to run away because of me, are you? Promise me you won't!"

Her fingers closed upon his. It was almost involuntarily. "I don't think I ought to stay," she whispered.

"I knew that was it!" He bent towards her. "Juliet! I say, please, dear, please! If one of us must go, it must be I. But there is no need. Believe me, there is no need. I've got myself in hand. I won't come near you — I swear — if you don't wish it."

"But — suppose — suppose —" Her voice broke. She drew her hand free and covered her face. "Oh, it's all so hopeless!" she sobbed. "I ought to have managed — better."

"No, no!" In a flash his arm was round her, strong and ready; he drew her to rest against his shoulder. "There's nothing to cry about really — really! If you knew how I loathe myself for making you cry! But listen! Nobody knows. Nobody's going to know. What happened last night is between you and me alone. Only you had the key. It isn't going to make any difference in your life. You'll go on as you were before. You'll forget I ever dared to intrude on you. What, darling? What? Yes, you will forget. Of course you'll forget. I'll see to it that you do. I'll — I'll —"

"Oh, stop!" Juliet said, and suddenly her face was turned upwards on his shoulder, her forehead was against his neck. "You're making the biggest mistake of your life!"

"What?" he said, and fell abruptly silent and so tensely still that she thought even his heart must have been arrested on the word.

For a long, long second she also was motionless, rigidly pressed to him, then with an odd little fluttering sigh she began to withdraw herself from the encircling arm. "I've dropped my cigarette," she said.

"Juliet!" He stooped over her; his face was close to hers. "Am I mad? Or am I dreaming? Please make me understand! What is the mistake I have made?"

She did not look at him, but he saw that her tears were gone and she was faintly, tremulously smiling. "That cigarette —" she murmured. "It really isn't safe to leave it. I don't like — playing with fire."

He bent lower. "We've got to risk something," he said, and with a swiftness of decision that she had not expected he took her chin and turned her face fully upwards to his own.

The color rushed in vivid scarlet to her temples. She met his eyes for one fleeting second then closed her own with a gasp and a blind effort to escape that was instantly quelled. For he kissed her — he kissed her — pressing his lips to hers closely and ever more closely, as a man consumed with thirst draining the cup to the last precious drop.

When he let her go, she was burning, quivering, tingling from head to foot as if an electric current were coursing through and through her. And the citadel had fallen. She made no further attempt to keep him out.

But he did not kiss her a second time. He only held her against his heart. "Ah, Juliet — Juliet!" he said, and she felt the deep quiver of his words. "I've got you — now! You are mine."

She was panting, wordless, thankful to avail herself of the shelter he offered. She leaned against him for many seconds in palpitating silence.

For so long indeed was she silent that in the end misgiving pierced him and he felt for the downcast face. But in a moment she reached up and took his hand in hers, restraining him.

"Not again!" she whispered. "Please not again!"

"All right. I won't," he said. "Not yet anyhow. But speak to me! Tell me it's all right! You're not frightened?"

"I am — a little," she confessed.

"Not at me! Juliet!"

"No, not at you. At least," she laughed unsteadily. "I'm not quite sure. You — you — I think you must let me go for a minute — to get back my balance."

"Must I?" he said.

She lifted the hand she had taken and laid it against her cheek. "I've got — a good deal to say to you, Dick," she said. "You've taken me so completely by storm. Please be generous now! Please let me have — the honors of war!"

"My dear!" he said.

He let her go with the words, and she clasped her hands about her knees and looked out to sea. She was still trembling a little, but as he sat beside her in unbroken silence she grew gradually calmer, and presently she spoke without any apparent difficulty.

"You've taken a good deal for granted, Dick, haven't you? You don't know me very well."

"Don't I?" he said.

"No. You've been — dreadfully headlong all through." She smiled faintly, with a touch of sadness. "You've skipped all the usual preliminaries — which isn't always wise. Don't you teach your boys to look before they leap?"

"When there's time," he said. "But you know, dear, you gave the word for — the final plunge."

She nodded slowly once or twice. "Yes. But I didn't expect quite — quite — Well, never mind what I expected! The fact remains, we haven't known each other long enough. No, I know we can't go back now and begin again. But, Dick, I want you — and it's for your sake as much as for my own — I want you, please, to be very patient. Will you? May I count on that?"

He put out his hand to her and gently touched her shoulder. "Don't talk to me like a slave appealing to a sultan!" he said.

She made a little movement towards him, but she did not turn. "I don't want to hurt you," she said. "But I'm going to ask of you something that you won't like — at all."

"Well, what is it?" he said.

"I want you —" she paused, then turned and resolutely faced him —
"I want you to be — just friends with me again," she said.

His eyes looked straight into hers. "In public you mean?" he said.

"In private too," she answered.

"For how long?" Swiftly he asked the question, his eyes still holding
hers with a certain mastery of possession.

She made a slight gesture of pleading. "Until you know me better,"
she said.

His brows went up. "That's not a business proposition, is it? You
don't really expect me to agree to that. Now do you?"

"Ah! But you've got to understand," she said rather piteously. "I'm
not in the least the sort of woman you think I am. I'm not — Dick, I'm
not — a specially good woman."

She spoke the words with painful effort, her eyes wavered before his.
But in a moment, without hesitation, he had leapt to the rescue.

"My darling, don't tell me that! I can see what you are. I know! I
know! I don't want your own valuation. I won't listen to it. It's the one
point on which your opinion has no weight whatever with me. Please
don't say anymore about it! It's you that I love — just as you are. If you
were one atom less human, you wouldn't be you, and my love — our
love — might never have been."

She sighed. "It would have saved a lot of trouble if it hadn't, Dick."

"Don't be silly!" he said. "Is there anything else that matters half as
much?"

She was silent, but her look was dubious. He drew suddenly close to
her, and slipped his hand through her arm.

"Is there anything else that really matters at all, Juliet? Tell me! I've
got to know. Does — Robin matter?"

She started at the question. It was obviously unexpected. "No! Of
course not!" she said.

"Thank you," he said steadily. "I loved you for that before you said
it."

She laid her hand upon his and held it. "That's — one of the things
I love you for, Dick," she said, with eyes downcast. "You are so —
splendidly — loyal."

"Sweetheart!" he said softly. "There's no virtue in that."

Her brows were slightly drawn. "I think there is. Anyway it appeals
to me tremendously. You would stick to Robin — whatever the cost."

"Well, that, of course!" he said. "I flatter myself I am necessary to
Robin. But with Jack it is otherwise. I've kicked him out."

"Dick!" She looked at him in sharp amazement.

He smiled, a thin-lipped smile. "Yes. It had to be. I've put up with him long enough. I told him so last night."

"You — quarreled?" said Juliet.

"No. We didn't quarrel. I gave him his marching orders, that's all."

"But wasn't he very angry?"

"Oh, pshaw!" said Dick. "What of it?"

She was looking at him intently, for there was something merciless about his smile. "Do you always do that, I wonder," she said, "with the people who make you angry?"

"Do what?" he said.

"Kick them out." Her voice held a doubtful note.

He turned his hand upwards and clasped hers. "My darling, it was a perfectly just sentence. He deserved it. Also — though I admit I have only thought of this since — it's the best thing that could happen to him. He can make his own way in life. It's high time he did so. I didn't kick him out because I was angry with him either."

"But you were angry," she said. "You were nearly white-hot."

He laughed. "I kept my hands off him anyhow. But I can't be answerable for the consequences if anyone sets to work to bait Robin persistently. It's not fair to the boy — to either of us."

"Do you think Robin might do him a mischief?" she asked.

"I think — someone might," he answered grimly. "But never mind that now! You don't regard Robin as a just cause and impediment. What's the next obstacle? My profession?"

"No," she said instantly and emphatically. "I like that part of you. There's something rather quaint about it."

His quick smile flashed upon her. "Oh, thanks awfully! I'm glad I'm quaint. But I didn't know it was a quality that appealed to you. I've been laying even odds with myself that I'd make you have me in spite of it."

She colored a little. "It doesn't really count one way or the other with me, Dick, anymore than it would count with you if I hawked stale fish in the street for cat's meat. You see I haven't forgotten that pretty compliment of yours. But —"

"But?" he said, frowning whimsically. "We'll have the end of that sentence, please. It's the very thing I want to get at. What is the 'but'?"

She hesitated.

"Go on!" he commanded.

"Don't be a tyrant, Dick!" she said.

"My beautiful princess!" He touched her shoulder with his lips. "Then don't you — please — be a goose! Tell me — quick!"

"And if I can't tell you, Dick? If — if it's just an instinct that says, Wait? We've been too headlong as it is. I can't — I daren't — go on at this pace." She was almost tearful. "I must have a little breathing-space indeed. I came here for peace and quietness, as you know."

He broke into a sudden laugh. "So you did, dear. You were playing hide-and-seek with yourself, weren't you? I'll bet you never expected to find the other half of yourself in this remote corner, did you? Well, never mind! Don't cry sweetheart — anyhow till you've got a decent excuse. I don't want to rush you into anything against your will. Taken properly, I'm the meekest fellow in creation. But we must have things on a sensible footing. You see that, don't you?"

"If we could be just friends," she said.

"Well, I'm quite willing to be friends." He laughed into her eyes. "Why so distressful? Don't you like the prospect?"

She drew his hand down into her lap and held it between her own, looking gravely down at it. "Dick!" she said.

His smile passed. "Well, dear? What is it? You're not going to be afraid of me?"

She did not answer him. "I want you to leave me free a little longer," she said.

"But you are not free now," he said.

She threw him a brief, half-startled glance. "I don't mean that," she said rather haltingly. "I mean I want you — not to ask any promise of me — not to insist upon any bond between us — not to — not to — expect a formal engagement — until, — well, until —"

"Until you are ready to marry me," he suggested quietly.

A quick tremor went through her. "That won't be for a long time," she said.

"How long?" he said.

"I don't know. Dick. I haven't the least idea. I had almost made up my mind never to marry at all."

"Really?" he said. "Do you know, so had I. But I changed it the moment I met you. When did you change yours?"

She laughed, but without much mirth. "I'm not sure that —"

"No, don't you say that to me!" he interrupted. "It's not cricket. You are — quite sure, though you rather wish you weren't. Isn't that the position? Honestly now!"

"Honestly," she said, "I can't be engaged to you yet."

"All right," he said unexpectedly. "You needn't call it that if you don't want to. Facts are facts. We may not be engaged, but we are — permanently — attached. We'll leave it at that."

Again swiftly she glanced towards him. "No, but, Dick —"

"Yes, but, Juliet —" His hand moved suddenly, imprisoning both of hers. "You can't get away," he said, speaking very rapidly, "anymore than I can. If you put the whole world between us, we shall still belong to each other. That is irrevocable. It isn't your doing, and it isn't mine. It's a Power above and beyond us both. We can't help ourselves."

He spoke with fierce earnestness, a depth of concentration, that gripped her just as his music had gripped her the night before. She sat motionless, bound by the same spell that had bound her then. She did not want to meet his eyes, but they drew irresistibly. In the end she did so.

For a space not reckoned by time she surrendered herself to a mastery that would not be denied. She met the kindling flame of his worship, and was strangely awed and humbled thereby. She knew now beyond all question that this man was not as most men. He came to her with the first, untainted offering of his love. No other woman had been before her in that inner sanctuary which he now flung wide for her to enter. There was a purity, a primitive simplicity, about his passion which made her realize that very clearly. He was no boy. He had lived a life of hard self-discipline and had put his youth behind him long since. But he brought all the intensity of a boy's adoration to back his manhood's strength of purpose, and before it she was impotent and half-afraid. The men of her world had all been of a totally different mold. She was accustomed to cynicism and the half-mocking homage of jaded experience. But this was new, this was wonderful — a force that burned and dazzled her, yet which attracted her irresistibly nonetheless, thrilling her with a rapture that had never before entered her life. Whatever the risk, whatever the penalty, she was bound to go forward now.

She spoke at last, her eyes still held by his. "I think you are right. We can't help it. But oh. Dick, remember that — remember that — if ever there should come a time when you wish you had done — otherwise!"

"If ever I do what?" he said. "Do you mind saying that again?"

She shook her head. "But I'm not laughing. Dick. You've carried me out of my depth, and — I'm not a very good swimmer."

"All right, darling," he said. "Lean on me! I'll hold you up."

She clasped his hand tightly. "You will be patient?" she said.

He smiled into her anxious face. "As patient as patient" he said. "That, I take it, means I'm not to tell anybody, does it?"

She bent her head. "Yes, Dick."

"All right," he said. "I won't tell a soul without your consent. But —" he leaned nearer to her, speaking almost under his breath — "when I am alone with you, Juliet — I shall take you in my arms — and kiss you — as I have done today."

Again a swift tremor went through her. She looked at him no longer. "Oh, but not — not without my leave," she said.

"You will give me leave," he said.

She was silent for a space. He was drawing her two hands to him, and she tried to resist him. But in the end he had his way, and she yielded with a little laugh that sounded oddly passionate.

"I believe you could make me give you anything," she said.

"But you can't give me what is mine already," he made quiet answer, as he pressed the two trembling hands against his heart. "That is understood, isn't it? And when you are tired of working for your living, you will come to me and let me work for you."

"Perhaps," she said, with her head bent.

"Only perhaps?" he said.

His voice was deeply tender. He was trying to look into the veiled eyes.

"Only perhaps?" he said again.

She made a little movement as if she would free herself, but checked it on the instant. Then very slowly she lifted her face to his, but she did not meet his look. Her eyes were closed.

"Some day," she said with quivering lips, — "some day — I will."

He took her face between his hands, and held it so as if he waited for something. Then, after a moment, "Some day — wife of my heart!" he said very softly, and kissed the eyes that would not meet his own.

PART III

Chapter I

BIRDS OF A FEATHER

*T*he annual flower-show at Fairharbor was one of the chief events of the district, and entailed such a gathering of the County as Vera Fielding would not for worlds have missed. It also entailed the donning of beautiful garments which was an even greater attraction than the first.

She had not been well during the sultry weather that had prevailed throughout the early part of June, and Fielding had been considering the advisability of taking her away for a change. But though her energy for many of the amusements which she usually followed with zest had waned with the lassitude that hot weather had brought upon her, she had set her heart upon attending the flower-show, and, in obedience to the new policy which Juliet by every means in her power persuaded him to pursue, the squire had somewhat impatiently yielded the point. The show was to take place in the grounds of Burchester Park. It was an immense affair, and everyone of any importance was sure to attend.

Juliet herself would gladly have stayed away, but Mrs. Fielding, partly as a natural consequence of her poor health and chiefly from a selfish desire to feel herself an object of solicitude, would not hear of leaving her behind. As Dick had predicted, she had come to lean upon Juliet, and her dependence became every day more pronounced. At times she was even childishly exacting, and though Juliet still maintained her right to direct her own movements, she found her liberty considerably curtailed.

If she went down to the shore with Robin she usually met with a querulous, and sometimes tearful, reception on her return, and though she steadily refused to admit that there was any reason on Vera's part for assuming this attitude, it influenced her nonetheless. Moreover, Vera could be genuinely pathetic upon occasion, and there was no disputing the fact that she stood in need of care — such care as only a woman could give.

"I don't want a nurse," she would say plaintively. "I only want companionship and sympathy. Motoring is my only consolation, and I can't go motoring alone."

And then the squire would draw her aside and beg her to bear with Vera's whims as far as possible since loneliness depressed her and she was the only person he knew whose company did not either tire her out or irritate her beyond endurance. It was not an easy position, but Juliet filled it to the best of her ability and with no small self-sacrifice.

Yet in a sense it made her life the simpler, for she was still at that difficult stage when it is easier to stand still than to go forward. She saw Green when he came to the house, but they had not been alone together since the morning on the shore when her love had betrayed her. She had a feeling that he was biding his time. He had promised to be patient, and she knew he would keep his promise. Also, his time, like hers, was very fully occupied. Till the holidays came he would not have much liberty, and in her secret soul Juliet was thankful that this was so. For the present it was enough for her to hold this new joy close, close to her heart, to gaze upon it only in solitude, — a gift most precious upon which no other eyes might look. It was enough for her to feel the tight grasp of his hand when they met, to catch for an instant the quick gleam of understanding in his glance, the sudden flash of that smile which was for her alone. These things thrilled her with a gladness so strangely sweet that there were times when she marveled at herself, and sometimes, trembling, wondered if it could possibly last. For naught in life had ever before shone so golden as this perfect dream. The very atmosphere she breathed was subtly charged with its essence. She was absurdly, superbly happy.

"I believe this place suits you," the squire said to her once. "You look years younger than when you came."

She received the compliment with her low, soft laugh. "I am — years younger," she said.

He gave her a sharp look. "You are happy here? Not sorry you came?"

"Oh, not in the least sorry," said Juliet.

He nodded. "That's all right. You've done Vera a lot of good. She's getting almost docile. But as soon as this flower-show business is over, I want you to use all your influence to get her away. We'll go North and see if we can get a little strength into her." Again he looked at her shrewdly. "You won't mind coming too?"

"But of course not," said Juliet. "I shall love it."

He was on his way out of the room, but a sudden thought seemed to strike him and he lingered. "Shall I make Green come to the flower-show with us?" he asked.

"I shouldn't," said Juliet quietly. "He probably wouldn't have time, and certainly Mrs. Fielding wouldn't want him."

He frowned. "Would you like him?" he asked abruptly.

"I?" She met his look with a baffling smile. "Oh, don't ask him on my account! I am quite happy without a cavalier in attendance."

And Fielding went out, looking dissatisfied. But when the day arrived and they were on the point of departure he surprised them both by the sudden announcement that Green was to be picked up at the gates. It was a Saturday afternoon, and for once he was at liberty.

"Oh, really, Edward!" Mrs. Fielding protested. "Now you've spoilt everything!"

"On the contrary," smiled the squire. "I have merely completed the party."

"I'm sure Miss Moore doesn't want him!" she declared petulantly.

"I am afraid Miss Moore will have to put up with him nevertheless," said Fielding, unperturbed. "For he is coming."

"You always do your best to spoil my pleasure," Vera flung at him.

Juliet saw the squire's mouth take an ominous downward curve, but to her relief he kept his temper in check. He was driving the car himself which was an open one. Somewhat grimly he turned to Juliet. "I hope you have no objection to sharing the back-seat with Mr. Green?"

She felt her pulses give a swift leap at the question, but with a hasty effort she kept down her rising color. "Of course not!" she said.

He gave her a brief smile of approval. "Then you will sit in front with me, Vera. That is settled. Let us have no more argument!"

"It's too bad!" Vera declared stormily on the verge of indignant tears.

"My dear," he said, "don't be silly! Has it never occurred to you that I may like to have my wife to myself occasionally?"

It evidently had not, for Vera gave him a look of sheer amazement and yielded the point as if she had no breath left for further discussion.

He settled her in her place, and tucked the rug around her with more than usual care. As he finished, she leaned forward and touched his shoulder with a slightly uncertain smile.

He glanced up. "All right?"

"Quite, thank you," she said.

And Juliet in the back-seat drew a breath of relief. The squire was becoming quite an adept at the game.

They shot down the avenue at a speed that brought them very rapidly in sight of the gates. A figure was waiting there, and again Juliet was conscious of the hard beating of her heart. Then she knew that the car was stopping, and looked forth with an impersonal smile of welcome.

He came forward, greeted the squire and Mrs. Fielding, and in a moment was getting in beside her.

"Good afternoon, Miss Moore!" he said.

She gave him her hand and felt his fingers close with a springlike strength upon it, while his eyes laughed into hers. Then the car was in motion again, and he dropped into the seat.

"By Jove, this is a treat!" he said. "I had the greatest difficulty in the world to get away, made Ashcott take my place. It isn't a very important match, and he's a better bowler than I am anyway."

"Do you want any rug?" she said, still battling to keep back the overwhelming flush of gladness from her face.

He accepted her offer at once, and in a moment his hand had caught and imprisoned hers beneath its shelter.

She made a sharp movement to free herself, and the blush she had so valiantly resisted flamed over face and neck as she felt his hold tighten as sharply, and heard him laugh at her impotence. But he went on talking as though nothing had happened, considerately covering her agitation, and to her relief neither Fielding nor his wife looked round till it had subsided.

It was barely half-an-hour's run to Burchester Park which was thrown open to the public for the great occasion. The Castle also was open on that day, and visitors thronged thither from every quarter.

A long procession of conveyances stood outside the great iron gates of the Park, but the squire, owing to an acquaintanceship with Lord Saltash's bailiff, held a permit that enabled him to drive in. They went up the long avenue of firs that led to the great stone building, but ere they reached it the strains of a band told them that the flower-show was taking place in an open space on their right close to the entrance to the terraced gardens which occupied the southern slope in front of the house.

Fielding ran the car into a deep patch of shade beside the road, and stopped. "We had better get out here," he said.

Juliet's hand slipped free. Dick threw her a smile and jumped out.

"Will the car be all right?" he said, as he turned to help her down.

"Oh, right enough," the squire said. "There is no traffic along here."

"I am hoping to go into the house," said Vera. "But I suppose it will be crammed with people."

"We'll do the flower-show first anyhow," said Fielding.

He led the way with her, and it seemed quite natural to Juliet that Green should fall in beside her. It was a cloudless day, and she had an almost childish feeling of delight in its splendor. She was determined to enjoy herself to the utmost.

They entered the first sweltering tent and in the throng she felt again the touch of Dick's hand at he came behind. "We mustn't lose each other," he said, with a laugh.

The midsummer madness was upon her, and, without looking at him she squeezed the fingers that gripped her arm.

In a moment his voice spoke in her ear. "Look here! Let's get away! Let's get lost! It's the easiest thing in the world. We can't all hang together in this crowd."

This was quite evident. The great marquee was crammed with people, and already Fielding was piloting his wife to the opening at the other end.

"We must just look round," murmured Juliet, "for decency's sake."

"All right, my dear, look!" he said. "And when you've quite finished we'll go out by the way we came and explore the gardens."

She threw him a glance that expressed acquiescence and a certain mead of amused appreciation. For somehow Dick Green in his blue serge and straw hat managed to look smarter if less immaculate than any of the white-waistcoated band of local magnates around them. So — for decency's sake — she prowled round the tent with Dick at her shoulder, admiring everything she saw and forgetting as soon as she had admired. She told herself that it was a day of such supreme happiness as could not come twice in any lifetime, and because of it she lingered, refusing to hasten the moment for which Dick had made provision.

"Haven't you had enough of it?" he said, at last.

And she answered him with a quivering laugh. "No, not nearly. I'm spinning out every single second."

"Ah, but they won't wait," he said. "Come! I think we're safely lost now. Let us go!"

She turned obediently from a glorious spread of gloxinias, and he made a way for her through the buzzing crowd to the entrance. When Dick spoke with the voice of authority, it was her pleasure to submit.

She felt her pulses tingle as she followed him, to be alone with him again, to feel herself encompassed by the fiery magic of his love, to yield throbbing surrender to the mastery that would not be denied. Yet when he turned to her outside in the hot sunshine with the blaring band close at hand she almost shrank away, she almost voiced a pretext for continuing their unprofitable wandering through the stifling tents. For, strangely, though he smiled at her, there was about him in that moment a quality that went near to scaring her. Something untamed, something indomitable, looked out at her from his glittering eyes. It was almost like a challenge, as if he dared her to dispute his right.

"That's better," he said, drawing a deep breath. "Now we can get away."

"We shan't get away from the people," she said.

He threw a rapid glance around. "Yes, we shall — with any luck. Come along! I know the way. There's a little landing-stage place down by the lake. We'll go there. There may even be a boat handy — if the gods are kind."

The gods were kind. They skirted the terraced gardens, which were not open to the public, and plunged down a winding walk through a shrubbery that led somewhat sharply downwards, away from the noise and the crush into cool green depths of woodland through which at last there shone up at them the gleam of water.

Juliet was panting when at length her guide paused. "My darling, what a shame!" he said. "But hang on to me! There are some steps round the corner, and they may be slippery. We'll soon be down now, and there's not a soul anywhere. Look! There's a fairy barque waiting for us!"

She caught sight of a white skiff, lying in the water close to the bank. As he had predicted, the final descent was a decided scramble, but he held her up until the mossy bank was reached; and would have held her longer, but with a little breathless laugh she released herself.

"My shoes are ruined," she remarked.

As they were of light grey suède, and the precipitous path they had traveled was a mixture of clay and limestone the ruin was palpable and very thorough. Dick surveyed them with compunction.

"I say, they're wet through! You must take them off at once. Get into the boat!"

"No, no!" She laughed again with more assurance. "I am not going to take them off. We couldn't dry them if I did, and I should never get them on again. Do you think we ought to get into the boat? Suppose the owner came along?"

"The owner? Lord Saltash, do you mean?" He scoffed at the idea. "Do you really imagine he would come within a hundred leagues of the place on such a day as this. No, he is probably many salt miles away in that ocean-going yacht of his. Lucky dog!"

"Oh, do you envy him?" she said.

He gave her a shrewd glance. "Not in the least. He is welcome to his yacht — and his Lady Jo — and all that is his."

"Dick!" She made a swift gesture of repudiation. "Please don't repeat that — scandal — again!"

He raised his brows with a faintly ironical smile. "Are you still giving her the benefit of the doubt?" he said. "I imagine no one else does."

The color went out of her face. She stood quite motionless, looking not at him but at a whirl of dancing gnats on the gold-flecked water beyond him.

"She went to Paris," she said, in the tone of one asserting a fact that no one could dispute.

"So did he," said Green. "The yacht went round to Bordeaux to pick him up afterwards. I understand that he was not alone."

She turned on him in sudden anger. "Why do you repeat this horrible gossip? Where do you hear it?"

He held out his hand to her. "Juliet, I repeat it, because I want you to know — you have got to know — that she is unworthy of your friendship, and — you shall never touch pitch with my consent. I have heard it from various sources, — from Ashcott, from the agent here, Bishop, and others. My dear, you have always known her for a heartless flirt. You broke with her because she jilted the man she was about to marry. Now that she has gone to another man, surely you have done with her!"

He spoke without anger, but with a force and authority that carried far more weight. Juliet's indignation passed. But she did not touch the outstretched hand, and in a moment he bent and took hers.

"Now I've made you furious," he said.

She looked at him somewhat piteously, assaying a smile with the lips that trembled. "No, I am not furious. Only — when you talk like that you make me — rather uneasy. You see, Lady Jo and I have always been — birds of a feather."

"Don't," he said, and suddenly gripped her hand so that she gasped with pain. "Oh, did I hurt you, sweetheart? Forgive me. But I can't have you talk like that — couple yourself with that woman whose main amusement for years has been to break as many hearts as she could capture. Forget her, darling! Promise me you will! Come! We're not going to let her spoil this perfect day."

He was drawing her to him, but she sought to resist him, and even when his arms were close about her she did not wholly yield. He held her to him, but he did not press for a full surrender.

And — perhaps because of his forbearance — she presently lifted her face to his and clung to him with all her quivering strength. "Just for today, Dick!" she whispered tremulously. "Just for today!"

Their lips met upon the words. And, "Forever and ever!" he made passionate answer, as he held her to his heart.

Chapter II

SALTASH

The sunshine was no less bright or the day less full of summer warmth when they floated out upon the lake a little later. But Juliet's mood had changed. She leaned back on Dick's coat in the stern of the boat, drifting her fingers through the rippling water with a thoughtful face. Once or twice she only nodded when Dick spoke to her, and he, bending to his sculls, soon fell silent, content to watch her while the golden minutes passed.

The lake was long and narrow, surrounded by woodland trees with colored water-lilies floating here and there upon its surface — a fairy spot, mysterious, green as emerald. The music of the band sounded distant here, almost like the echoes of another world. They reached the middle of the lake, and Dick suffered his sculls to rest upon the water, sending feathery splashes from their tips that spread in widening circles all around them.

As if in answer to an unspoken word, Juliet's eyes came up to his. She faintly smiled. "Have you brought that woodland pipe of yours?" she asked.

He smiled back at her. "No, I am keeping that for another occasion."

She lifted her straight brows interrogatively, without speaking.

He answered her still smiling, but with that in his voice that brought the warm color to her face. "For the day when we go away, together, sweetheart, and don't come back."

Her eyes sank before his, but in a moment or two she lifted them again, meeting his look with something of an effort. "I wonder, Dick," she said slowly, "I wonder if we ever shall."

He leaned towards her. "Are you daring me to run away with you?"

She shook her head. "I should probably turn into something very hideous if you did, and that would be — rather terrible for both of us."

"That's a parable, is it?" He was still looking at her keenly, earnestly.

She made a little gesture of remonstrance, as if his regard were too much for her. "You can take it as you please. But as I have no intention of running away with you, perhaps it is beside the point."

He laughed with a hint of mastery. "Our intentions on that subject may not be the same. I'll back mine against yours any day."

She smiled at his words though her color mounted higher. After a moment she sat up, and laid a hand upon his knee. "Dick, you're getting too managing — much. I suppose it's the schoolmaster part of you. I daresay you find it gets you the upper hand with a good many, but — it won't with me."

His hand was on hers in an instant, she thrilled to the electricity of his touch. "No — no!" he said. "That's just the soul of me, darling, leaping all the obstacles to reach and hold you. You're not going to tell me you have no use for that?"

"But you promised to be patient," she said.

"Well, I will be. I am. Don't look so serious! What have I done?"

His eyes challenged her to laughter, and she laughed, though somewhat uncertainly. "Nothing — yet, Dick. But — I don't feel at all sure of you today. You make me think of a faun of the woods. I haven't the least idea what you will do next."

"What a mercy I've got you safe in the boat!" he said. "I didn't know you were so shy. What shall I do to reassure you?"

His hand moved up her wrist with the words, softly pushing up the lacy sleeve, till it found the bend of the elbow, when he stooped and kissed the delicate blue veins, closely with lips that lingered.

Then, his head still bent low, very tenderly he spoke. "Don't be afraid of my love, sweetheart! Let it be your — defense!"

She was sitting very still in his hold save that every fiber of her throbbed at the touch of his lips. But in a moment she moved, touched his shoulder, his neck, with fingers that trembled, finally smoothed the close black hair.

"Why did you make me love you?" she said, and uttered a sharp sigh that caught her unawares.

He laughed as he raised his head. "Poor darling! You didn't want to, did you? Hard lines! I believe it's upset all your plans for the future."

"It has," she said. "At least — it threatens to!"

"What a shame!" He spoke commiseratingly. "And what were your plans — if it isn't impertinent of me to ask?"

She smiled faintly. "Well, marriage certainly wasn't one of them. And I'm not sure that it is now. I feel like the girl in *Marionettes* — Cynthia Paramount — who said she didn't think any women ought to marry until she had been engaged at least six times."

"That little beast!" Dick sat up suddenly and returned to his sculls.

"Juliet, why did you read that book? I told you not to."

Her smile deepened though her eyes were grave. She clasped her fingers about her knees. "My dear Dick, that's why. It didn't hurt me like *The Valley of Dry Bones.* In fact I was feeling so nice and superior when I read it that I rather enjoyed it."

Dick sent the boat through the water with a long stroke. His face was stern. After a moment Juliet looked at him. "Are you cross with me because I read it, Dick?"

His face softened instantly. "With you! What an idea!"

"With the man who wrote it then?" she suggested. "He exasperates me intensely. He has such a maddeningly clear vision, and he is so inevitably right."

"And yet you persist in reading him!" Dick's voice had a faintly mocking note.

"And yet I persist in reading him. You see, I am a woman, Dick. I haven't your lordly faculty for ignoring the people I most dislike. I detest Dene Strange, but I can't overlook him. No one can. I think his character studies are quite marvelous. That girl and her endless flirtations, and then — when the real thing comes to her at last — that unspeakable man of iron refusing to take her because she had jilted another man, ruining both their lives for the sake of his own rigid code! He didn't deserve her in any case. She was too good for him with all her faults." Juliet paused, studying her lover's face attentively. "I hope you're not that sort of man, Dick," she said.

He met her eyes. "Why do you say that?"

"Because there's a high priestly expression about your mouth that rather looks as if you might be. Please don't tell me if you are because it will spoil all my pleasure! Give me a cigarette instead and let's enjoy ourselves!"

"You'll find the case in my coat behind," he said. "But, Juliet, though I wouldn't spoil your pleasure for the world, I must say one thing. If a woman engages herself to a man, I consider she is bound in honor to fulfill her engagement — unless he sets her free. If she is an honorable woman, she will never free herself without his consent. I hold that sort of engagement to be a debt of honor — as sacred as the marriage vow itself."

"Even though she realizes that she is going to make a mistake?" said Juliet, beginning to search the coat.

"Whatever the circumstances," he said. "An engagement can only be broken by mutual consent. Otherwise, the very word becomes a farce. I have no sympathy with jilts of either sex. I think they ought to be kicked out of decent society."

Juliet found the cigarettes and looked up with a smile. "I think you and Dene Strange ought to collaborate," she said. "You would soon put this naughty world to rights between you. Now open your mouth and shut your eyes, and if you're very good I'll light it for you!"

There was in her tone, despite its playfulness, a delicate finality that told him plainly that she had no intention of pursuing the subject further, and, curiously, the man's heart smote him for a moment. He felt as if in some fashion wholly inexplicable he had hurt her.

"You're not vexed with me, sweetheart?" he said.

She looked at him still smiling, but her look, her smile, were more of a veil than a revelation. "With you! What an idea!" she said, softly mocking.

"Ah, don't!" he said. "I'm not like that, Juliet!"

She held up the cigarette. "Quite ready? Ah, Dick! Don't — don't upset the boat!"

For the sculls floated loose again in the rowlocks. He had her by the wrists, the arms, the shoulders. He had her, suddenly and very closely, against his heart. He covered her face with his kisses, so that she gasped and gasped for breath, half-laughing, half-dismayed.

"Dick, how — how disgraceful of you! Dick, you mustn't! Someone — someone will see us!"

"Let them!" he said, grimly reckless. "You brought it on yourself. How dare you tell me I'm like a high priest? How dare you, Juliet?"

"I daren't," she assured him, her hand against his mouth, restraining him. "I never will again. You're much more like the great god Pan. There, now do be good! Please be good! I am sure someone is watching us. I can feel it in my bones. You're flinging my reputation to the little fishes. Please, Dick — darling, — please!"

He held the appealing hand and kissed it very tenderly. "I can't resist that," he said. "So now we're quits, are we? And no one any the worse. Juliet, you'll have to marry me soon."

She drew away from his arms, still panting a little. Her face was burning. "Now we'll go back," she said. "You're very unmanageable today. I shall not come out with you again for a long time."

"Yes — yes, you will!" he urged. "I shouldn't be so unmanageable if I weren't so — starved."

She laughed rather shakily. "You're absurd and extravagant. Please row back now, Dick! Mr. and Mrs. Fielding will be wondering where we are."

"Let 'em wonder!" said Dick.

Nevertheless, moved by something in her voice or face, he turned the boat and began to row back to the little landing-stage. Juliet rescued the cigarettes from the floor, and presently placed one between his lips and lighted it for him. But her eyes did not meet his during the process, and her hand was not wholly steady. She leaned back in the stern and smoked her own cigarette afterwards in almost unbroken silence.

"Don't you want a water-lily?" Dick said to her once as they drew near a patch.

She shook her head. "No, don't disturb them! They're happier where they are."

"Impossible!" he protested. "When they might be with you!"

She raised her eyes to his then, and looked at him very steadily. "No, that doesn't follow, Dick," she said.

"I think it does," he said. "Never mind if you don't agree! Tell me when you are coming to sing at one of my Saturday night concerts at High Shale!"

"Oh, I don't know, Dick." She looked momentarily embarrassed. "You know we are going away very soon, don't you?"

"Where to?" he said.

"I don't know. Either Wales or the North. Mrs. Fielding needs a change, and I —"

"You're coming back?" he said.

"I suppose so — some time. Why?" She looked at him questioningly.

He leaned forward, his black eyes unswervingly upon her. "Because — if you don't — I shall come after you," he said, with iron determination.

She laughed a little. "Pray don't look so grim! I probably shall come back all in good time. I will let you know if I don't, anyway."

"You promise?" he said.

"Of course I promise." She flicked her cigarette-ash into the water. "I won't disappear without letting you know first."

"Without letting me know where to find you," he said.

She glanced over his shoulder as if measuring the distance between the skiff and the landing-stage. "No, I don't promise that. It wouldn't be fair. But you will be able to trace me by Columbus. He will certainly accompany the cat's-meat cart wherever it goes. Oh, Dick! There's someone there — waiting for us!"

He also threw a look behind him. "Shall I put her about? I don't see anyone, but if you wish it —"

"No, no, I don't! Row straight in! There is someone there, and you'll have to apologize. I knew we were being watched."

Juliet sat upright with a flushed face.

Dick began to laugh. "Dear, dear! How tragic! Never mind, darling! I daresay it's no one more important than a keeper, and we will see if we can enlist his sympathy."

He pulled a few swift strokes and the skiff glided up to the little landing-stage. He shipped the sculls, and held to the woodwork with one hand.

"Will you get ashore, dear, and I'll tie up. There's no one here, you see."

"No one that matters," said a laughing voice above him, and suddenly a man in a white yachting-suit, slim, dark, with a monkeylike activity of movement, stepped out from the spreading shadow of a beech.

"Hullo!" exclaimed Dick, startled.

"Hullo, sir! Delighted to meet you. Madam, will you take my hand? Ah — *et tu, Juliette!* Delighted to meet you also."

He was bowing with one hand extended, the other on his heart. Juliet, still seated in the stern of the boat, had gone suddenly white to the lips.

She gasped a little, and in a moment forced a laugh that somehow sounded desperate. "Why, it is Charles Rex!" she said.

Dick's eyes came swiftly to her. "Who? Lord Saltash, isn't it? I thought so." His look flashed back to the man above him with something of a challenge. "You know this lady then?"

Two eyes — one black, one grey — looked down into his, answering the challenge with gay inconsequence. "Sir, I have that inestimable privilege. *Juliette,* will you not accept my hand?"

Juliet's hand came upwards a little uncertainly, then, as he grasped it, she stood up in the boat. "This is indeed a surprise," she said, and again involuntarily she gasped. "Rumor had it that you were a hundred miles away at least."

"Rumor!" laughed Lord Saltash. "How oft hath rumor played havoc with my name! Not an unpleasant surprise, I trust?"

He handed her ashore, laughing on a note of mockery. Charles Burchester, Lord Saltash, said to be of royal descent, possessed in no small degree the charm not untempered with wickedness of his reputed ancestor. His friends had dubbed him "the merry monarch" long since, but Juliet had found a more dignified appellation for him which those who knew him best had immediately adopted. He had become Charles Rex from the day she had first bestowed the title upon him. Somehow, in all his varying — sometimes amazing — moods, it suited him.

She stood with him on the little wooden landing-stage, her hand still in his, and the color coming back into her face. "But of course not!" she said in answer to his light words, laughing still a trifle breathlessly. "If you will promise not to prosecute us for trespassing!"

"Mais, Juliette!" He bent over her hand. "You could not trespass if you tried!" he declared gallantly. "And the cavalier with you — may I not

have the honor of an introduction?"

He knew how to jest with grace in an awkward moment. Dick realized that, as, having secured the boat, he presented himself for Juliet's low-spoken introduction.

"Mr. Green — Lord Saltash!"

Saltash extended a hand, his odd eyes full of quizzical amusement. "I've heard your name before, I think. And I believe I've seen you somewhere too. Ah, yes! It's coming back! You are the Orpheus who plays the flute to the wild beasts at High Shale. I've been wanting to meet you. I listened to you from my car one night, and — on my soul — I nearly wept!"

Dick smiled with a touch of cynicism. "Miss Moore was listening that night too," he said.

"Yes," Juliet said quickly. "I was there."

Saltash looked at her questioningly for a moment, then his look returned to Dick. "I am the friend who never tells," he observed. "So it was — Miss Moore — you were playing to, was it? Ah, *Juliette!*" He threw her a sudden smile. "I would I could play like that!"

She uttered her soft, low laugh. "No; you have quite enough accomplishments, *mon ami.* Now, if you don't mind, I think we had better walk back and find Mr. and Mrs. Fielding. Perhaps you know — or again perhaps you don't — they live at Shale Court. And I am with them — as Mrs. Fielding's companion. I —" she hesitated momentarily — "have left Lady Jo."

"Oh, I know that," said Saltash. "I've missed you badly. We all have. When are you coming back to us?"

"I don't know," said Juliet.

He gave her one of his humorous looks. "Next week — some time — never?"

She opened her sun-shade absently. "Probably," she said.

"Rather hard on Lady Jo, what?" he suggested. "Don't you miss her at all?"

"No," said Juliet. "I can't — honestly — say I do."

"Oh, let us be honest at all costs!" he said. "Do you know what Lady Jo is doing now?"

Juliet hesitated an instant, as if the subject were distasteful to her. "I can guess," she said somewhat distantly.

"I'll bet you can't," said Saltash, with a twist of the eyebrows that was oddly characteristic of him. "So I'll tell you. She's running in an obstacle race, and — to be quite, quite honest — I don't think she's going to win."

There was a moment's pause. Then the man on Juliet's other side spoke, briefly and with decision. "Miss Moore is no longer interested in Lady Joanna Farringmore's doings. Their friendship is at an end."

Juliet made a slight gesture of remonstrance, but she spoke no word in contradiction.

A gleam of malice danced in Saltash's eyes; it was like the turn of a rapier in a practiced hand. "Most wise and proper!" he said. *"Juliette,* I always admired your discretion."

"You were always very kind, Charles Rex," she made grave reply.

Chapter III

THE PRICE

*T*hey went back up the winding glen, and as they went Lord Saltash talked, superbly at his ease, of the doings of the past few weeks, "since you and that naughty Lady Jo dropped out," as he expressed it to Juliet. He had just recently been to Paris, had motored across France, had just returned by sea from Bordeaux in his yacht, the *Night Moth.*

"Landed today — forgot this unspeakable flower-show — had to put in to get her cleaned up for Cowes — though it's quite possible I shan't go near Cowes when all's said and done. She's quite seaworthy, warranted not to kick in a gale. If anyone wanted her for a cruise — she's about the best thing going."

They reached the shrubbery to be nearly deafened by the band.

"Come through the gardens!" said Saltash, with a shudder. "We must get out of this somehow."

"But my people!" objected Juliet.

"Oh, Mr. Green will go and find them, won't you, Mr. Green?" Saltash turned a disarming smile upon him.

But Green looked straight back without a smile. "Miss Moore is under my escort," he observed. "If she agrees, I think we had better go together."

"And do you agree, *Juliette?"* enquired Saltash with interest.

Juliet met the mocking eyes with a smile that was certainly unintentional. "They may be in the Castle," she said. "I know they meant to go."

"Good!" he ejaculated. "Then come to the Castle! I will get you tea in my own secret den if such a thing is to be had — tea or a cocktail, *ma Juliette!*"

"Will you lead the way?" said Juliet, and for a second — only a second — her hand pressed Dick's arm with a quick, confidential pressure that was not without its appeal. "We always follow Charles Rex!" she said.

Saltash chuckled. Plainly the adventure amused him.

They entered the trim gardens, escaping thankfully from the wandering crowd of sight-seers. Saltash led the way with a certain unconscious arrogance of bearing. Somehow, his ugliness notwithstanding, he fitted his surroundings perfectly, save that the white yachting-suit ought to have been fashioned of satin, and a sword should have dangled at his side. The old stone turrets that towered above the blazing parterres gleamed in the hot sunlight — a mediaeval castle of romance.

"What a glorious old place!" said Juliet.

He turned to her. "You have never seen it before?"

"Never," she answered.

He made her a bow that was slightly foreign. There was French blood in his veins. "I give you welcome, *maladi,*" he said, "I and my poor castle are all yours to command."

He made a gallant figure there on his stone terrace. The girl's eyes shone a little, but they turned almost immediately to the other man at her side.

"Beautiful, isn't it, Dick?" she said.

He met her look, and she was conscious of a chill. She had never seen him look so aloof, so cynical. "A temple of delight!" he said.

His manner offended her. She turned deliberately away from him. And again Lord Saltash chuckled, as though at some secret joke.

They entered by a narrow door at the head of a flight of steps. "This at least is private," declared Saltash, as he took a key from an inner pocket.

"Does no one ever come in here when you are away?" Juliet asked.

"Not by this entrance," he said. "There is another into the Castle itself which is known to a few. It leads into the music room whence Mr. Green will be able to start upon his search."

He threw a mischievous glance at Green who met it with a look so direct, and so unswerving that the odd eyes blinked and turned away.

But curiously a spirit of perversity seemed to have entered into Juliet. She also looked at Dick. "I wish you would go and find them," she said. "I know they will be wondering where we are."

His brows went up. She thought he was going to refuse. And then quite suddenly he yielded. "Certainly if you wish it!" he said. "And when they are found?"

"Oh, dump them in the great hall!" said Saltash. "To be left till called for!"

"Charles!" protested Juliet.

He grinned at her — a wicked, monkeyish grin, and threw open the door, disclosing a steep and winding stone stair.

"Will you be pleased to enter!" he said, in the tone of one issuing a royal command.

But she hung for a moment, looking back with a strange wistfulness at the man she was leaving. The imprisoned air came out into the hot sunshine like a cold vapor. She shivered a little.

"Dick!" she said.

He stopped at the foot of the outside steps looking up at her. His eyes were extremely bright, and something within her shrank from their straight regard. It conveyed possession, dominance; almost it conveyed a menace.

"When you have found them, come and — tell me!" she said.

He lifted his hat to her with punctilious courtesy, and turned away. "I will," he said.

"That's a masterful sort of person," observed Saltash, as they mounted the dimly-lit turret stair. "What does he do for a living?"

Juliet hesitated, conscious of a strong repugnance to discuss her lover with this man from her old world whom, strangely, at that moment, she felt that she knew so infinitely better. But she could not withhold an answer to so ordinary a question. Moreover Saltash could be imperious when he chose, and she knew instinctively that it was not wise to cross him.

"By profession," she said slowly at length, "he is — a village school-master."

Saltash's laugh stung, though it was exactly what she had expected. But he qualified it the next moment with careless generosity.

"Quite a presentable cavalier, *ma Juliette!* And a fixed occupation is something of an advantage at times, *n'est-ce-pas? — Je t'aime, tu l'aime!* And how soon do you ride away? Or is that question premature?"

Juliet's face burned in the dimness, but she was in front of him and thankfully aware that he could not see it. "I am not answering anymore questions, Charles," she said. "Now that you have got me into your ogre's castle, you must be — kind."

"I will be kindness itself," he assured her. "You know I am the soul of hospitality. All I have is yours."

The narrow stair ended at a small stone landing on which was a door. Juliet stepped aside as she reached it, and waited for her host. "It's rather like a prison," she said.

"You won't think so when you get through that door," he said. "By Jove! To think that I've actually got you — you of all people! — here in my stronghold! Do you realize that without my permission you can't possibly get out again?"

Juliet's laugh was absolutely spontaneous. She faced him in that narrow space with the poise and confidence of a queen. The light from a window that pierced the wall above shone down upon her. In that moment she was endowed with an extraordinary beauty that was more of being, of personality, than of feature.

"It is exactly this that I have played for, Charles Rex," she said. "You hold all the cards, *mon ami.* But — the game is mine."

"How so?" He was looking at her curiously, a dancing demon in his eyes.

She put out her hand to him, and as he took it, sank to the stone floor in a superb curtsy. "Because I claim your gracious protection, my lord the king. I ask your royal favor."

He lifted her hand to his lips as she rose. "You are — as ever — quite irresistible, *ma Juliette,*" he smiled. "But — do you really contemplate marrying this fortunate young man? Because there are limits — even to my generosity. I am not sure that I can permit that."

Her eyes looked straight into his. "You can do — anything you choose to do, Charles Rex," she said; "except one thing."

He made a grimace at her. "I am king in my own castle anyway," he observed, watching her. "And you are at my mercy."

"It is your mercy that I am waiting for," she said, a faint smile at the corners of her lips.

"Ah!" he said, stood a moment longer, contemplating her, then turned abruptly and flung open the door against which he stood.

It led into a winding passage of such a totally different character from the stone staircase they had just mounted that Juliet stood gazing down it for some seconds before she obeyed his mute gesture to pass through. It was thickly carpeted, deadening all sound, and the walls were hung with some heavy material, in the color of old oak. It was lighted by three long perpendicular slits of windows, let into a twelve-foot thickness of wall. Juliet had a glimpse of many pine trees as she passed them.

The passage ended in heavy curtains of the same dark-brown material. She stopped and looked at her companion.

"What is it?" he said, with a laugh. "Are you afraid of my inner sanctuary?"

He parted the curtains, disclosing a tall oak door. She saw no latch upon it, but his hand went up behind the curtain, and she heard the click of a spring. In a moment the tall door opened before her.

"Go in!" he said easily.

She entered a strange room, oak-paneled, shaped like a cone, lighted only by a glass dome in the roof. It was the most curious chamber she had ever seen. She trod on a tiger-skin as she entered, and noted that the floor was covered with them. There was no chair anywhere, only a long, deep couch, also draped with tiger-skins. Tiger faces glared at her from all directions. She heard the door click behind her and turning realized that it had disappeared in the oak paneling against which her host was standing.

He laughed at her quizzically, "I believe you are frightened."

She looked around her, seeing no exit anywhere. "It is just the sort of freak apartment I should expect you to delight in," she said.

"You wouldn't have come if you had known, would you?" he said, a faint note of jeering in his voice.

"Of course I should!" said Juliet.

"Of course!" he mocked. "I am such a peculiarly safe person, am I not? Every member of your charming sex trusts me instinctively."

She turned and faced him. "Don't be ridiculous, Charles! You see, I happen to know you."

He looked at her with something of the air of a monkey that contemplates snatching some forbidden thing. "Why did you run away?" he said.

She hesitated. "That's a hard question, isn't it?"

"Oh, don't mind me!" he said. "I don't flatter myself I was the cause."

Her dark brows were slightly drawn. "No, you were not," she said. "It was just — it was Lady Jo herself, Charlie. No one else."

"Ah!" His goblin smile flashed out at her. "Poor erring Lady Jo! Don't be too hard on her! She has her points."

She laid her hand quickly on his arm. "Don't try to defend her! She is quite despicable. I have done with her."

His hand was instantly on hers. He laughed into her eyes. "I'll wager you have a lingering fellow-feeling for her even yet."

"Not since she was reported to have run away with you," countered Juliet.

He laughed aloud. "Ah! She forfeited your sympathy there, did she? Mais, Juliette —" his voice sank suddenly upon a caressing note, "there are few women to whom I could not give happiness — for a time."

"I know," said Juliet, and drew her hand away. "That is why we all admire you so. But even you, most potent Charles, couldn't satisfy a woman who was wanting — someone else."

"You don't think I could make her forget?" he said.

She shook her head, smiling. "When the real thing comes along, all shams must go overboard. It's the rule of the game."

"And this is the real thing?" he questioned.

She made a little gesture as of one who accepts the inevitable. *"Je le crois bien,"* she said softly.

Lord Saltash made a grimace. "And I am to give you up without a thought to this bounder?"

"You would," she replied gently, "if I were yours to give."

"If you were Lady Jo for instance?" he suggested.

"Exactly. If I were Lady Jo." She looked at him with the faint smile still at her lips. "It won't cost you much to be generous, Charles," she said.

"How do you know what it costs?" He frowned at her suddenly. "You'll accuse me of being benevolent next. But I'm not benevolent, and I'm not going to be. I might be to Lady Jo, but not to you, *ma chérie,* — never to you!" His grin burst through his frown. "Come! Sit down! I'll get you a drink."

She turned to the deep settee, and sank down among tigerskins with a sigh. He opened a cupboard in the paneling of the wall, and there followed the chink of glasses and the cheery buzz of a siphon. In a few moments he came to her with a tall glass in his hand containing a frothy drink. "Look here, *Juliette!*" he said. "Come to France with me in the *Night Moth,* and we'll find Lady Jo!"

She accepted the drink and lay back without looking at him. "You always were an eccentric," she said. "I don't want to find Lady Jo."

He sat on the head of the settee at her elbow. "It's quite a fair offer," he said, as if she had not spoken. "You will — eventually — return from Paris, and no one will ever know. In these days a woman of the world pleases herself and is answerable to none. *Mais, Juliette!*" He reached down and coaxingly held her hand. *"Pourquoi pas?"*

She lifted her eyes slowly to his face. "I have told you," she said.

"You're not in earnest!" he protested.

She kept her look steadily upon him. "Charles Rex, I am in earnest."

His fingers clasped hers more closely. "But I can't allow it. We can't spare you. And you — yourself, *Juliette* — you will never endure life in a backwater. You will pine for the old days, the old friends, the old lovers, — as they will pine for you."

"No, never!" said Juliet firmly.

He leaned down to her. "I say you will. This is — a midsummer madness. This will pass."

She started slightly at his words. The sparkling liquid splashed over. She lifted the glass to her lips, and drank. When she ceased, he took it softly from her, and put it to his own. Then he set down the empty glass and slipped his arm behind her.

"*Juliette*, I am going to save you," he said, "from yourself."

She drew away from him. "Charles, I forbid that!"

She was breathing quickly but her voice was quiet. There was indomitable resolution in her eyes.

He paused, looking at her closely. "You deny — to me — what you were permitting with so much freedom barely half-an-hour ago to the village schoolmaster?" he said.

Her face flamed. "I have always denied you — that!" she said.

He smiled. "Times alter, Juliette. You are no longer in a position to deny me."

She kept her eyes upon him. "You mean I have trusted you too far?" she said, a deep throb in her voice. "I might have known!"

He shrugged his shoulders. "Life is a game of hazard, is it not? And you were always a daring player. But, Juliette, you cannot always win. This time the luck is against you."

She was silent. Very slowly her eyes left his. She drooped forward as she sat.

He leaned down to her again, his face oddly sympathetic. "After all, — you claimed my protection," he said.

She made a sudden movement. She turned sharply, almost blindly. She caught him by the shoulders. "Oh, Charles!" she said. "Charles Rex! Is there no mercy no honor — in you?"

There was a passion of supplication in her voice and action. As she held him he could have clasped her in his arms. But he did not. He sat motionless, looking at her, his expression still monkeylike, half-wicked, half-wistful.

"Well, you shouldn't tempt me, Juliette," he said. "It isn't fair to a miserable sinner. You were always the cherry just out of reach. Naturally, I'm inclined to snatch when I find I can."

Juliet was trembling, but she controlled her agitation.

"No, that isn't allowed," she said. "It isn't the game. And you never — seriously — wanted me either."

"But I'm never serious!" protested Saltash. "Neither are you. It's your one solid virtue."

"I am serious now," she said.

He looked at her quizzically. "Somehow it suits you. Well, listen, *Juliette!* I'll strike a bargain with you. When you are through with this, you will come with me for that cruise in the *Night Moth*. Come!

Promise!"

"But I am not — quite mad, Rex!" she said.

He lifted his hands to hers and lightly held them. "It is no madder a project than the one you are at present engaged upon. What? You won't? You defy me to do my worst?"

"No, I don't defy you," she said.

He flashed a smile at her. "How wise! But listen! It's a bargain all the same. You put me on my honor. I put you on yours. Go your own way! Pursue this bubble you call love! And when it bursts and your heart is broken — you will come back to me to have it mended. That is the price I put upon my mercy. I ask no pledge. It shall be — a debt of honor. We count that higher than a pledge."

"Ah!" Juliet said, and suppressed a sudden tremor.

He stood up, gallantly raising her as he did so. "And now we will go and look for your friends," he said. "Is all well, *ma chérie?* You look pale."

She forced herself to smile. "You are a preposterous person, Charles Rex," she said. "Yes, let us go!"

She turned with him towards the paneling, but she did not see by what trick he opened again the door by which they had entered. She only saw, with a wild leap of the heart, Dick Green, upright, virile, standing against the dark hangings of the passage beyond.

Chapter IV

KISMET

*H*e was breathing hard, as if he had been hurrying. He spoke to her exclusively, ignoring the man at her side.

"Will you come at once? Mrs. Fielding has been taken ill."

She started forward. "Dick! Where is she?"

"Downstairs." Briefly he answered her. "She collapsed in one of the tents. They brought her into the house. She is in the library."

Juliet hastened along the passage. Like Dick, she seemed no longer aware of Saltash's presence. He came behind, a speculative expression on his ugly face.

"Let me go first!" Dick said, as they reached the head of the winding stairs.

Juliet gave place to him without a word. They descended rapidly.

At the foot the door stood open to the terrace. They came again into the blazing sunshine, and here Juliet paused and looked back at Saltash.

He came to her side. "Don't look so alarmed! It's probably only the heat. Do you know the way to the library? Through that conservatory over there is the shortest cut. I suppose I may come with you? I may be of use."

"Of course!" said Juliet. "Thank you very much."

Dick barely glanced over his shoulder. He was already on his way.

They entered the Castle again by the conservatory that Saltash had indicated. It was a mass of flowers, but the public were evidently not admitted here, for it was empty. In the center a nymph hung over a marble basin under a tinkling fountain. They passed quickly by to an open glass door that led into the house. Here Dick stopped and drew back, looking at Juliet.

"I will wait here," he said.

She nodded and went swiftly past him into the room.

It was a dark apartment, book-lined, chill of atmosphere, with heavy, ancient furniture, and a sense of solitude more suggestive of some monastic dwelling than any ordinary habitation. The floor was of polished oak that shone with a somber luster.

Juliet paused for a moment involuntarily upon entering. It was as if a sinister hand had been laid upon her, arresting her. The gloom blinded her after the hot radiance outside. Then a voice — Fielding's voice — spoke to her, and she went forward gropingly.

He met her, took her urgently by the shoulder. "Thank heaven, you're here at last!" he said.

Looking at him, she saw him as a man suddenly stricken with age. His face was grey. He led her to a settee by the high oak fireplace, and there — white, inanimate as a waxen figure — she found Vera Fielding.

Fear pierced her, sharp as the thrust of a knife. She freed herself from Fielding's grip, and knelt beside the silent form. For many awful seconds she watched and listened, not breathing.

"Is she gone?" asked Fielding in a hoarse whisper at last.

She looked up at him. "Get brandy — hot bottles — quick! Send Dick — he's in the conservatory. No, stay! Send Saltash! He's there too. He'll know where to find things. Tell Dick to come here! Have you sent for a doctor?"

"There's been no one to send," he answered frantically. "Some man helped to bring her in here, but she didn't faint till after we got in, and then I couldn't leave her. He went off to look after the crowd going round the Castle."

"All right," Juliet said. "Lord Saltash will see to that. Ask them to come in!"

She was unfastening the filmy gown with steady fingers. Whatever the dread at her heart there was no sign of it apparent in her bearing. She moved without haste or agitation.

At a touch on her shoulder she looked up and saw Dick at her side. "Ah, there you are!" she said. "We want a doctor. Will you see to it? No doubt there's a telephone somewhere. Ask Lord Saltash!"

"In the gun-room," said Saltash. "Door next to this on the left. Name of Rossiter. Shall I see to it?"

"No — no," she said. "You get some brandy, please — at once!"

They obeyed her orders with promptitude. Dick went straight from the room. Saltash turned to the fireplace, and pressed an electric bell three times very emphatically.

Then he came to Juliet's side. "You ought to lay her flat, *Juliette.* I know this sort of seizure. Heart of course! My mother died of it."

"Help me to lift her!" said Juliet.

They raised her between them with infinite care and flattened the cushions beneath her. Then Saltash, his queer face full of the most earnest concern began to chafe one of the nerveless hands.

Fielding tramped ceaselessly up and down the room, his head on his chest. Every time he drew near his wife he glanced at her and swung away again, as one without hope.

After a brief interval the door opened to admit a silent footed butler bearing a tray. Saltash turned upon him swiftly.

"Brandy, Billings? That's right. And look here! Find Mrs. Parsons! Tell her a lady has been taken ill in the library! She had better get a bed ready, and have some boiling water handy. Anything else?" He looked at Juliet.

She shook her head. "No, nothing till the doctor comes. I hope he won't be long."

Saltash poured out some brandy. Fielding came to a standstill behind Juliet, and stood looking on.

"We won't lift her again," whispered Juliet. "Try a spoon!"

He gave it to her, and she slipped it between the white lips. But there was no sign of life, no attempt to swallow.

"She is dead!" said Fielding heavily.

Saltash glanced at him. "I think not," he said gently. "I'm nearly certain I felt her pulse move just now."

The door opened again, and Dick entered. He went straight to the squire, and put his arm round his bent shoulders. "There'll be a doctor here in ten minutes," he said.

Fielding seemed barely to hear the words. "Do you think she'll ever speak again, Dick?" he said.

"Please God she will, sir," said Dick very steadily.

He kept his arm round Fielding, and in a few moments succeeded in drawing him aside. He put him into a chair by the table, poured out some brandy and water, and made him drink it. Looking up a moment later, he found Saltash's odd eyes curiously upon him. He returned the look with a conscious sense of antagonism, but Saltash almost immediately turned away.

There followed what seemed an interminable space of waiting, during which no change of any sort was apparent in the silent figure on the settee. The blatant bray of the band still sounded in the distance with a flaunting gaiety almost intolerable to those who waited. Saltash frowned as he heard it, but he did not stir from Juliet's side.

Then, after an eternity of suspense, the somber-faced butler opened the door again and ushered in the doctor. Saltash went to meet him and brought him to the settee. Fielding got up and came forward.

Dick stood for a moment, then turned and went back to the conservatory, where a few seconds later Saltash joined him.

"I should like to burn that damn band alive!" he remarked as he did so.

Dick shrugged his shoulders and said nothing.

Again Saltash's eyes dwelt upon him with curiosity. "I want to know you," he said suddenly. "I hope you don't object?"

"I am vastly honored by your notice," said Dick.

Saltash nodded. "Well, don't be an ass about it! I am a most inoffensive person, I assure you. And it isn't my fault that I was on friendly terms with *Mademoiselle Juliette* before she forsook the world, etc., etc., and turned to you to fill the void. Do you flatter yourself you are going to marry her by any chance?"

A swift gleam shot up in Dick's eyes. He stiffened involuntarily. "That is a subject I cannot discuss — even with you," he said.

Saltash smiled good-humoredly. "Well, I expected that. But your courtship on the lake this afternoon was so delightfully ingenuous that I couldn't help wondering what your intentions were."

Dick's mouth became a simple hard line. He looked the other man up and down with lightning rapidity ere he replied with significance.

"My intentions, my lord, are — honorable."

Saltash bowed with his hand on his heart and open mockery in his eyes. *"La pauvre Juliette!* And have you told her yet? No, look here! Don't knock me down! There's no sense in taking offence at a joke you can't understand. And it would be bad manners to have a row, with that poor soul in there at death's door. Moreover, if you really want to marry the princess *Juliette,* it'll pay you to be friends with me."

"I doubt if anything would induce me to be that," said Dick curtly.

"Oh, really? What have I done? No, don't tell me! It would take too long. I am aware I'm a by-word for wickedness in these parts, heaven alone knows why. But at least I've never injured you." Saltash's smile was suddenly disarming again.

"Never had much opportunity, have you?" said Dick.

"No, but I've got one now — quite a good one. I could put an end to this little idyll of yours for instance without the smallest difficulty — if I felt that way."

"I don't believe you!" flashed Dick.

"No? Well, wait till I do it then!" There was amused tolerance in Saltash's rejoinder. "You'll pipe another tune then, I fancy."

"Shall I?" Dick said. He paused a moment, his eyes, extremely bright, fixed unwaveringly upon the swarthy face in front of him. "If I do — you'll dance to it!" he said with grim assurance.

Saltash smothered a laugh. "Well done, I say! You've scored a point at last! I was waiting for that. You'll like me better now, most worthy cavalier. I daren't suggest a drink under the circumstances, but I'll owe you one." He extended his hand with a royal air. "Will you shake?"

Dick held back. "Will you play the game?" he said.

Saltash grinned. "My own game? Certainly! I always do."

Dick's hand came out to him. Somehow he was hard to refuse. "A straight game?" he said.

Saltash's brows expressed amused surprise. "I always play straight — till I begin to lose, — chevalier," he said.

"And then — you cheat?" questioned Dick.

"Like the devil," laughed Saltash. "We all do that. Don't you?"

"No," Dick said briefly.

"You don't? You always put all your cards on the table? Come now! Do you?"

Dick hesitated, and Saltash's grin became more pronounced. "All right! You needn't answer," he said lightly. "Do you know I thought you weren't quite as simple as you appeared at first sight. Just as well perhaps. *Juliette's* cavalier mustn't be too rustic." He stopped to look at Dick appraisingly. "Yes, I'm glad on the whole that your intentions are honorable," he ended with a smile. "I rather doubt if you pull 'em off. But you may — you may."

He turned sharply with the words as if a hand had touched him and faced round upon Juliet as she came out on to the step.

Her face had an exhausted look, but she smiled faintly at the two men as she joined them.

"She is still living," she said. "The doctor gives just a shade of hope. But —" She looked at Saltash — "he absolutely forbids her being moved — at all. I hope it won't be a terrible inconvenience to you."

"It will be a privilege to serve you — or your friends — in any way," said Saltash.

"Thank you," she said. "I am sure Mr. Fielding will be very grateful to you. The doctor is going to send in a nurse. Of course I shall not leave her. She has come to depend upon me a good deal. And we thought of telephoning to her maid to bring everything necessary from Shale Court."

"Of course!" said Saltash kindly. "Look here, my dear! Don't for heaven's sake feel you've got to ask my permission for everything you do! Treat the place and everyone in it as your own!"

"Thank you," she said again. "Then, Charles, if you're sure you don't mind, I'll send for my dog as well."

"What! Christopher Columbus? You've got him with you, have you?" Saltash's smile lighted his dark face. "Lucky animal! Have him over by all means! I shall be delighted to see him."

"You are very kind," she said, and turned with a hint of embarrassment to Dick. "Mr. Fielding says that you will want to be getting back and there is no need to wait. Will you take the little car back to the Court?"

"Certainly," Dick said. "Would you care to give me a list of the things you want the maid to bring?"

"How kind of you!" she said, and hesitated a moment, looking at him. "But I think I needn't trouble you. Cox is very sensible. I can make her understand on the telephone."

He looked back at her, standing very straight. "In that case — I will go," he said. "Good-bye!"

She held out her hand to him. "I — shall see you again," she said, and there was almost a touch of pleading in her voice.

His fingers closed and held. "Yes," he said, and smiled into her eyes with the words — a smile in which determination and tenderness strangely mingled. "You will certainly see me again."

And with that he was gone, striding between the massed flowers without looking back.

"Exit Romeo!" murmured Saltash. "Enter — Kismet!"
But Juliet had already turned away.

Chapter V

THE DRIVING FORCE

*T*hat Saturday night concert at High Shale entailed a greater effort
on Dick's part than any that had preceded it. He forced himself to make
it a success, but when it was over he was conscious of an overwhelming
weariness that weighed him down like a physical burden.

He said good-night to the men, and prepared to depart with a feeling
that he was nearing the end of his endurance. It was not soothing to
nerves already on edge to be waylaid by Ashcott and made the unwilling
recipient of gloomy forebodings.

"We shan't hold 'em much longer," the manager said. "They're getting
badly out of hand. There's talk of sending a deputation to Lord Wilchester or — failing him — Ivor Yardley, the K.C. chap who is in with
him in this show."

"Yardley!" Dick uttered the name sharply.

"Yes, ever met him? He took over a directorship when he got engaged
to Lord Wilchester's sister — Lady Joanna Farringmore. They're rather
pinning their hopes on him, it seems. Do you know him at all?"

"I've met him — once," Dick said. "Went to him for advice — on a
matter of business."

"Any good?" asked Ashcott.

"Oh yes, shrewd enough. Hardest-headed man at the Bar, I believe. I
didn't know he was a director of this show. They won't get much out
of him."

"I fancy they're going to ask you to draw up a petition," said Ashcott.

"Me!" Dick turned on him in a sudden blaze of anger. "I'll see 'em
damned first!" he said.

Ashcott shrugged his shoulders. "It's your affair. You're the only man who has any influence with 'em. I'm sick of trying to keep the peace."

Dick checked his indignation. "Poor devils! They certainly have some cause for grievance, but I'm not going to draw up their ultimatum for them. I've no objection to speaking to Yardley or any other man on their behalf, but I'm hanged if I'll be regarded as their representative. They'll make a strike-leader of me next."

"Well, they're simmering," Ashcott said, as he prepared to depart. "They'll boil over before long. If they don't find a responsible representative they'll probably run amuck and get up to mischief."

"Oh, man, stop croaking!" Dick said with weary irritation and went away down the hill.

He took the cliff-path though the night was dark with storm-clouds. Somehow, instinctively, his feet led him thither. There were no nightingales singing now, and the gorse had long since faded in the fierce heat of summer. The sea lay leaden far below him, barely visible in the dimness. And there was no star in the sky.

Heavily he tramped over the ground where Juliet had lingered on that night of magic in the spring, and as he went, he told himself that he had lost her. Whatever the outcome of today's happenings, she would never be the same to him again. She had passed out of his reach. Her own world had claimed her again and there could be no return. He recalled the regret in her eyes at parting. Surely — most surely — she had known that that was the end. For her the midsummer madness was over, burned away like the glory of the gorse-bushes about him. With a conviction that was beyond all reason he knew that they had come to a parting of the ways.

And there was no bond between them, no chain but that which his love had forged. She had pleaded to retain her freedom, and now with bitter intuition he knew wherefore. She had always realized that to which he in his madness had been persistently blind. She had known that there were obstacles insurmountable between them and the happy consummation of their love. She had faced the fact that the glory would depart.

Again he felt the clinging of her arms as he had felt it only that afternoon. Again against his lips there rose her quivering whisper, "Just for today, Dick! Just for today!" Yes, she had known even then. Even then for her the glory had begun to fade.

He clenched his hands in sudden fierce rebellion. It was unbearable. He would not endure it. This stroke of destiny — he would fight it with all the strength of his manhood. He would overthrow this nameless barrier that had arisen between them. He would sacrifice all — all he had — to reach her. Somehow — whatever the struggle might cost — he would clasp her again, would hold her against all the world.

And then — like a poisoned arrow out of the darkness — another thought pierced him. What if she were indeed of those who loved for a space and passed smiling on? What if the fatal taint of the world from which she had come to him had touched her also, withering the heart in her, making true love a thing impossible? What if she had indeed been fashioned in the same mold as the worthless woman whom she sought to defend?

But that was unthinkable, intolerable. He flung the evil suggestion from him, but it left a burning wound behind. There was no escape from the fact that she was on terms of intimacy with the man with whom that woman's name had been shamefully associated. And — remembering the discomfiture she had betrayed at their meeting — he told himself bitterly that she would have given much to have concealed that intimacy had it been possible.

But here his loyalty cried out that he was wronging her. Juliet — his Juliet of the steadfast eyes and low, sincere voice — was surely incapable of double dealing! Whatever her life in the past had been, however frivolous, however artificial, it had been given to him — perhaps to him alone — to know her as she was. A great wave of self-reproach went over him. How had he dared to doubt her?

The sea moaned with a dreary sound along the shore. A few heavy drops of rain fell around him. Mechanically he quickened his pace. He came at length down the steep cliff-path to the gate that led to the village. And here to his surprise a shuffling footstep told him of the presence of another human being out in the desolate darkness. Dimly he discerned a bulky shape leaning against the rail.

He came up to it. "Robin!" he said sharply.

A low voice answered him in startled accents. "Oh, Dicky! I thought you were never coming!"

"What are you doing here?" Dick said.

He took the boy by the shoulder with the words and Robin cowered away.

"Don't be cross! Dicky, please don't be cross! I only came to look for you," he said with nervous incoherence. "I didn't mean to be out late. I couldn't help it. Don't be cross!"

But Dick was implacable. "You know you've no business out at this hour," he said. "I warned you last time — when you went to The Three Tuns —" He paused abruptly. "Have you been to The Three Tuns tonight?"

"No!" said Robin eagerly.

Dick's hand pressed upon him. "Is that the truth?"

Robin became incoherent again. "I only came to meet you. I didn't think you'd be so late. And it was so hot tonight. And my head ached." He broke off. "Dicky, you're hurting me!"

"You have told me a lie," Dick said.

Robin shrank at his tone. "How did you know?" he whispered awestruck.

Dick did not answer. He shifted his hold from Robin's shoulder to his arm and turned him about. Robin went with him, shuffling his feet and trembling.

Dick led him in grim silence down the path to the village-road, past the Ricketts' cottage, now in darkness, up the hill beyond that led to the school.

Robin went with him submissively enough, but he stumbled several times on the way. As they neared the end of the journey he began to talk again anxiously, propitiatingly.

"I didn't mean to go, Dicky, but I was so hot and thirsty. And I met Jack and I went in with him. There were a lot of fellows there and Jack treated me, but I didn't have very much. My head ached so, and I sat down in a corner and went to sleep till it was closing time. Then old Swag made me get out, so I came to wait for you. I didn't hit him or anything, Dicky. I was quite quiet all the while. So you won't be cross, will you, — not like last time?"

"I am going to punish you if that's what you mean," Dick said, as he opened the garden-gate.

Robin shrank again, shivering like a frightened dog. "But, Dicky, I only — I only —"

"Broke the rule and lied about it," his brother said uncompromisingly. "You know the punishment for that."

Robin attempted no further appeal. He went silently into the house and blundered up to his room. There was only one thing left to do, and that was to pay the penalty — of which Dick's wrath was infinitely the hardest part to bear.

He crouched down on the floor by the bed to wait. The light from the passage shone in through the half-open door and the great lamp at the lodge-gates of the Court opposite, which was kept burning all night, glared in at the unblinded window, but there was no light in the room. There was something almost malignant to Robin's mind about the searching brilliance of this lamp. He hid his eyes from it, huddling his face in the bed-clothes, listening intently the while for Dick's coming but hearing only the dull thumping of his own heart.

There was no one in the house except the two brothers. A woman came in every day from the village to do the work of the establishment.

Now that Jack had found quarters elsewhere there was not a great deal to be done since Robin was accustomed also to making himself useful in various ways. It occurred to him suddenly as he crouched there waiting that Dick had been too hurried to eat much supper before his departure for High Shale that evening. The thought had been in his brain before, but subsequent events had dislodged it. Now, with every nerve alert and pricking with suspense, it returned to him very forcibly. Dicky was hungry perhaps — or consumed with thirst, as he himself had been. And he would certainly go empty to bed unless he, Robin, plucked up courage to go down and wait upon him.

It needed considerable courage, for his instinct was always to hide when he had incurred Dick's anger. Judicial though it invariably was, it was the most terrible thing the world held for him. It shook him to the depths, and to go down and confront it again with the penalty still unpaid was for a long time more than he could calmly contemplate. But as the minutes crept on and still Dick did not come, it was gradually borne in upon him that this, and this alone, was the thing that must be done. It was his job, forced upon him by an inexorable fate. Dick would probably be much more angry with him for doing it, but somehow in a vague, unreasoning fashion he realized that it had got to be done.

Even then it took him a long time to screw himself up to the required pitch of nervous energy required. He ached for the sound of Dick's step on the stairs, but it did not come. And so at last he knew there was no help for it. Whatever the cost, he must fulfill the task that had been laid upon him.

With intense reluctance he uncovered his face, flinching from the stark glare of the lamp across the road, and dragged himself to his feet. It was difficult to move without noise, but he made elaborate efforts to do so. He reached the head of the stairs and hung there listening.

Had he heard a movement below he would have stumbled headlong back to cover, but no sound of any sort reached him. The compelling force urged him afresh. He gripped the stair-rail and crept downward like a stealthy baboon.

The stairs creaked alarmingly. More than once he paused, prepared for precipitate retreat, but still he heard no sound, and gradually a certain desperate hope came to him. Perhaps Dicky was asleep! Perhaps the power that drove him would be satisfied if he collected some things on a tray and left them in the little hall for Dicky to find when he finally came up! If this could be done — and he could get back safe to the sheltering darkness before he found out! He would not mind the subsequent caning, if only he need not meet Dicky face to face again beforehand. Dicky's eyes when they looked at him sternly were anguish to his soul. And they certainly would not hold any kindness for him until the punishment was over. So argued poor Robin's anxious brain as he reached the foot of the stairs and stood a moment under the lamp dimly burning there, summoning strength to creep past the open door of the dining room.

A candle was flickering on the table, so he was sure Dick must be there. Would he see him pass? Would he call him in? Robin's heart raced with terror at the thought. But no! The urging force drove him in sickening apprehension past the door, and still there was no sound.

He was at the kitchen-door at the end of the passage, his fingers fumbling at the latch when suddenly he remembered that he had no candle. There was no candle to be had! The only one available downstairs was the one Dick had taken into the dining room. He could not go upstairs again to get another. He had no matches wherewith to explore the kitchen. He stood struck motionless by this fresh problem.

But Dicky was doubtless asleep or he must have heard those creaking stairs! Then there was still a chance. He might creep into the room and take the candle without waking him. He was gaining confidence by the prolonged silence. Dicky must certainly be fast asleep.

With considerably greater steadiness than he had yet achieved he returned to the open door and peeped stealthily in.

Yes, Dick was there. He had flung himself down at the table on which he had set the candle, and he was lying across it with his head on his arms. Asleep of course! That could be the only explanation of such an attitude. Yet Robin in the act of advancing, stopped in sudden doubt with a scared backward movement, his eyes upon one of Dick's hands that was clenched convulsively and quivering as if he were in pain. It certainly did not look like the hand of a man asleep.

The next moment Robin's ungainly form had knocked against the door-handle and Dick was sitting upright looking at him. His face was grey, he looked unutterably tired, his mouth had the stark grimness of the man who endures, asking nothing of Fate.

"Hullo, boy!" he said. "Why aren't you in bed?" Then seeing Robin's unmistakably hangdog air, "Oh, I forgot! Go on upstairs! I'm coming."

Robin turned about like a kicked dog. But the driving force stopped him on the threshold. He stood a second or two, then turned again with a species of sullen courage.

"May I have the candle?" he said, not looking at Dick.

"What for?" said Dick. "Haven't you got one upstairs?"

Robin stood a moment or two debating with himself, then made a second movement to go. "All right. I'll fetch it."

"Wait a minute!" Dick's voice compelled. "What do you want a candle down here for?"

Robin backed against the doorpost with a kind of heavy defiance. "Want to get something — out of the kitchen," he muttered.

"What do you want to get?" said Dick.

Robin was silent, stubbornly, insistently silent, the fingers of one hand working with agitated activity.

"Robin!"

It was the voice of authority. He had to respond to it. He made a lumbering gesture towards the speaker, but his eyes remained obstinately lowered under the shag of hair that hung over his forehead.

Dick sat for a few seconds looking at him, then with a sudden sigh that caught him unawares he got up.

"What did you come down for? Tell me!" he said.

His tone was absolutely quiet, but something in his utterance or the sigh that preceded it — or possibly some swiftly-piercing light of intuition — seemed to send a galvanizing current through Robin. With clumsy impulsiveness he came to Dick and stood before him.

"I was going — to get you — something to eat," he said, speaking with tremendous effort. "You must be — pretty near starving — and I forgot." He paused to fling a nervous look upwards. "I thought you were asleep. I didn't know — or I wouldn't have done it. I — didn't mean to get in the way." His voice broke oddly. He began to tremble. "I'll go now," he said.

But Dick's hand came out, detaining him. "You came down to get me food?" he said.

"Yes," muttered Robin, with his head down. "Thought I'd — put it in the hall — so you'd find it — before you came up."

Dick stood silent for a space, looking at him. His eyes were very gentle and the grimness had gone from his mouth, but Robin could not see that. He stood humped and quivering, expectant of rebuke.

But he recognized the change when Dick spoke. "Thought you'd provide me with the necessary strength to hammer you, eh?" he said, and suddenly his arm went round the misshapen shoulders; he gave Robin a close squeeze. "Thanks, old chap," he said.

Robin looked up then. The adoring devotion of a dumb animal was in his eyes. He said nothing, being for the moment beyond words.

Dick let him go. A clock on the mantelpiece was striking twelve. "You get to bed, boy!" he said. "I don't want anything to eat, thanks all the same." He paused a moment, then held out his hand. "Good-night!"

It was tacit forgiveness for his offence, and as such Robin recognized it. Yet as he felt the kindly grasp his eyes filled with tears.

"I'm — I'm sorry, Dicky," he stammered.

"I'm sorry too," Dick said. "But that won't undo it. For heaven's sake, Robin, never lie to me again! There! Go to bed! I'm going myself as soon as I've had a smoke. Good-night!"

It was a definite dismissal, and Robin turned away and went stumblingly from the room.

His brother looked after him with a queer smile in his eyes. It was Juliet who had taught Robin to say he was sorry. He threw himself into an easy chair and lighted a pipe. Perhaps after all in his weariness he had exaggerated the whole matter. Perhaps — after all — she might yet find that she loved him enough to cast her own world aside. Recalling her last words to him, he told himself that he had been too quick to despair. For she loved him — she loved him! Not all the fashionable cynics her world contained could alter that fact.

A swift wave of exultation went through him, combating his despair. However heavy the odds, — however formidable the obstacles — he told himself he would win — he would win!

Going upstairs a little later, he was surprised to hear a low sound coming from Robin's room. He had thought the boy would have been in bed and asleep some time since. He stopped at the door to listen.

The next moment he opened it and quietly entered, for Robin was sobbing as if his heart would break.

There was no light in the room save that which shone from the park-gates opposite and the candle he himself carried. Robin was sunk in a heap against the bed still fully dressed. He gave a great start at his brother's coming, shrinking together in a fashion that seemed to make him smaller. His sobbing ceased on the instant. He became absolutely still, his clawlike hands rigidly gripped on the bedclothes, his face wholly hidden. He did not even breathe during the few tense seconds that Dick stood looking down at him. He might have been a creature carved in granite. Then Dick set down his candle, went to him, sat on the low bed, and pulled the shaggy head on to his knee.

"What's the matter, old chap?" he said.

All the tension went out of Robin at his touch. He clung to him in voiceless distress.

Dick's heart smote him. Why had he left the boy so long? He laid a very gentle hand upon him.

"Come, old chap!" he said. "Get a hold on yourself! What's it all about?"

Robin's shoulders heaved convulsively; his hold tightened. He murmured some inarticulate words.

Dick bent over him. "What, boy? What? I can't hear. You haven't been up to any mischief, have you? Robin, have you?" A sudden misgiving assailed him. "You haven't hurt anybody? Not Jack, for instance?"

"No," Robin said. But he added a moment later with a concentrated passion that sounded inexpressibly vindictive, "I hate him! I do hate him! I wish he was dead!"

"Why?" Dick said. "What has he been doing?"

But Robin burrowed lower and made no answer.

Dick sat for a space in silence, waiting for him to recover himself. He knew very well that he had good reason for his rooted dislike for Jack. It was useless to attempt any argument on that point. But when Robin had grown calmer, he returned to the charge very quietly but with determination.

"What has Jack been doing or saying? Tell me! I've got to know."

Robin stirred uneasily. "Don't want to tell you, Dicky," he said.

Dick's hand pressed a little upon him. "You must tell me," he said. "When did you meet him?"

Robin hesitated in obvious reluctance. "It was after supper," he said. "My head ached, and I went outside, and he came down the drive. And he — and he laughed about — about you coming home alone from Burchester, and said — said that your game was up anyhow. And I didn't know what he meant, Dicky —" Robin's arms suddenly clung closer — "but I got angry, because I hate him to talk about you. And I — I went for him, Dicky." His voice dropped on a shamed note, and he became silent.

"Well?" Dick said gravely. "What happened then?"

Very unwillingly Robin responded to his insistence. "He got hold of me — so that I couldn't hurt him — and then he said — he said —" A great sob rose in his throat choking his utterance.

"What did he say?"

There was a certain austerity in Dick's question. Robin shivered as it reached him.

With difficulty he struggled on. "Said that only — a fool — like me — could help knowing that — you hadn't — a chance — with any woman — so long as — so long as —" He choked again and sank into quivering silence.

Dick's hand found the rough head and patted it very tenderly. "But you're not fool enough to take what Jack says seriously, are you?" he said.

Robin stifled a sob. "He said that — afterwards," he whispered. "And he took me along to The Three Tuns — to make me forget it."

"You actually drank with him after that!" Dick said.

"I didn't know what I was doing, Dicky," he make apologetic answer. "It — knocked the wind out of me. You see, I — I'd never thought of that before."

He began to whimper again. Dick swallowed down something that tried to escape him.

"A bit of an ass, aren't you, Robin?" he said instead. "You know as well as I do that there isn't a word of truth in it. Anyhow — the woman I love — isn't — that sort of woman."

Robin shifted his position uneasily. There was that in the words that vaguely stirred him. Dick had never spoken in that strain before. Slowly, with a certain caution, he lifted his tear-stained face and peered up at his brother in the fitful candlelight.

"You do — want to marry Miss Moore then, Dicky?" he asked diffidently.

Dick looked straight back at him; his eyes shone with a somber gleam that came and went. For several seconds he sat silent, then very steadily he spoke.

"Yes, I want her all right, Robin, but there are some pretty big obstacles in the way. I may get over them — and I may not. Time will prove."

His lips closed upon the words, and became again a single hard line. His look went beyond Robin and grew fixed. The boy watched him dumbly with awed curiosity.

Suddenly Dick moved, gripped him by the shoulders and pulled him upwards. "There! Go to bed!" he said. "And don't take any notice of what Jack says for the future! Don't fight him either! Understand? Leave him alone!"

Robin blundered up obediently. Again there looked forth from his eyes the doglike worship which he kept for Dick alone. "I'll do — whatever you say, Dicky," he said earnestly. "I — I'd die for you — I would!" He spoke with immense effort, and all his heart was in the words.

Dick smiled at him quizzically. "Instead of which I only want you to show a little ordinary common or garden sense," he said. "Think you can do that for me?"

"I'll try, Dicky," he said humbly.

"Yes, all right. You try!" Dick said, and got up, more moved than he cared to show. He turned to go, but paused to light Robin's candle from his own. "And don't forget I'm — rather fond of you, my boy!" he said, with a brief smile over his shoulder as he went away.

No, Robin was not likely to forget that, seeing that Dick's love for him was his safeguard from all evil, and his love for Dick was the mainspring of his life. But — though his development was stunted and imperfect — there were certain facts of existence which he was beginning slowly but surely to grasp. And one of these — before but dimly suspected — he had realized fully tonight, a fact beyond all questioning learnt from Dick's own lips.

Dick's words: "The woman I love," had sunk deep — deep into his soul. And he knew with that intuition which cannot err that his love for Juliet was the greatest thing life held for him — or ever could hold again.

And the driving force gripped Robin's soul afresh as he lay wide-eyed to the smothering gloom of the night. Whatever happened — whoever suffered — Dicky must have his heart's desire.

Chapter VI

THE SISTER OF MERCY

*F*or five days after that burning afternoon of the flower-show Juliet scarcely left Vera Fielding's side. During those five days Vera lay at the point of death, and though her husband was constantly with her it was to Juliet that she clung through all the terrible phases of weakness, breathlessness, and pain that she passed. Through the dark nights — though a trained nurse was in attendance — it was Juliet's hand that held her up, Juliet's low calm voice that reassured her in the Valley of the Shadow through which she wandered. Often too spent for speech, her eyes would rest with a piteous, childlike pleading upon Juliet's quiet face, and — for Juliet at least — there was no resisting their entreaty. She laid all else aside and devoted herself body and soul to the tender care of the sick woman.

Edward Fielding regarded her with reverence and a deep affection that grew with every day that passed. She was always so gentle, so capable, so undismayed. He knew that her whole strength was bent to the task of saving Vera's life, and even when he most despaired he found himself leaning upon her, gathering courage from the resolute confidence with which she shouldered her burden.

"She never thinks of herself at all," he said once to Saltash between whom and himself a friendship wholly unavoidable on his part and also curiously pleasant had sprung up. "I suppose in her position of companion she has been more or less trained for this sort of thing. But her devotion is amazing. She is absolutely indispensable to my wife."

"*Juliette* seems to have found her vocation," observed Saltash with a lazy chuckle. "But no, I should not say that she was specially trained for this sort of thing, though certainly it seems to suit her passing well. All the same, you won't let her carry it too far, will you? Now that Mrs. Fielding is beginning to rally a little it might be a good opportunity to make her take a rest."

"Yes, you're right. She must rest," Fielding agreed. "She is so marvelous that one is apt to forget she must be nearly worn out."

It was the fifth day and Vera had certainly rallied. She lay in the somber old library, that had been turned into the most luxurious bedroom that Saltash's and Juliet's ingenuity could devise, listening to the tinkle of the water in the conservatory and watching Juliet who sat in a low chair by her side with a book in her lap ready to read her to sleep.

There was a couch in the conservatory itself on which sometimes on rare occasions Juliet would snatch a brief rest, leaving the nurse to watch. Columbus regarded this couch as his own particular property, but he always gave his beloved mistress an ardent welcome and squeezed himself into as small a compass as possible at the foot for her benefit. Otherwise, he occupied the middle with an arrogance of possession which none disputed. The door into the garden was always open, and Columbus was extremely happy, being of supremely independent habits and quite capable of trotting round to the kitchen premises of the castle for his daily portion without disturbing anyone en route. How he discovered the kitchen Juliet never knew. Doubtless his exploring faculty stood him in good stead. But his appearance there was absolutely regular and orderly, and he always returned to the conservatory when he had been fed with the bustling self-importance of one whose time was of value. He never entered the sick-room except on invitation, and he never raised his voice above a whisper when in the conservatory. It was quite evident that he fully grasped the situation and accommodated himself thereto. All he asked of life was to be near his beloved one, and the snuffle of his greeting whenever she joined him was ample testimony to the joy of his simple soul. Just to see her, just to hear her voice, just sometimes to kiss and be kissed, what more could any dog desire?

Certainly an occasional scamper after rabbits in the park made a salutary change, but Columbus was prudent and he never suffered himself to be drawn very far in pursuit. A sense of duty or expediency always brought him back before long to the couch in the conservatory to lie and watch, bright-eyed, for the only person who counted in his world.

He was watching for her now, but without much hope of her coming. She seldom left Vera's bedside in the afternoon for it was then, in the heat of the day, that she usually suffered most. But today she had been better. Today for the first time she was able to turn her head and smile and even to murmur a few sentences without distress. Her eyes dwelt upon Juliet's quiet face with a wistful affection. She had come to lean upon her strength with a child's dependence.

"Quite comfortable?" Juliet asked her gently.

"Quite," Vera made whispered reply. "But you — you look so tired."

Juliet smiled at her. "I dare say I shall fall asleep if you do," she said.

"You ought to have a long rest," said Vera, and then her heavy eyes brightened and went beyond her as her husband's tall figure came softly in from the conservatory.

He came to her side, stooped over her, and took her hand. Her fingers closed weakly about his.

"Send her to bed!" she whispered. "She is tired. You come instead!"

He bent and kissed her forehead with a tenderness that made her cling more closely. "Shall I do instead?" he asked her gently.

She offered him her lips though she was panting a little. "Yes, I want you. Make Juliet — go to bed!"

He turned to Juliet, his wife's hand still in his. All the hard lines were smoothed out of his face. There was something even pathetic about his smile.

"Will you go to bed, Juliet," he said in that new gentle voice of his, "and leave me in charge?"

She got up. "I will lie down in the conservatory," she said.

"No — no!" He put his free hand on her arm with a touch of his customary imperiousness. "That won't do. You're to go to bed properly — and sleep till you can't sleep any longer. Yes, that's an order, see?" He smiled again at her, his sudden transforming smile. "Be a good child and do as I tell you! Cox is within call. We'll certainly fetch you if we find we can't do without you."

Juliet's eyes went to Vera.

"Yes, she wants to get rid of you too," said the squire. "We're pining to be alone. No, we won't talk. We won't do anything we ought not, eh, Vera, my dear? Nurse will be getting up in another hour so we shan't have it to ourselves for long."

He had his way. He could be quite irresistible when he chose. Juliet found herself yielding without misgiving, though till then he had only been allowed at Vera's bedside for a few minutes at a time. Vera was certainly very much better that day, and she read in her eyes the desire to meet her husband's wishes. She paused to give him one or two directions regarding medicine, and then went quietly to the door of the conservatory.

Columbus sprang to greet her with a joy that convulsed him from head to tail, and she gathered him up in her arms and took him with her, passing back through the library in time to see the squire lay his face down upon the slender hand he held and kiss it.

In the great hall outside she found Saltash loitering. He came at once to meet her, and had taken Columbus from her before she realized his intention.

"He is too heavy for you, *ma chérie,*" he said, with his quizzing smile. "Lend him to me for this afternoon! He's getting disgracefully fat. I'll take him for a walk."

Relieved of Columbus' weight, she became suddenly and overpoweringly aware of a dwindling of her strength. She said no word, but her face must have betrayed her, for the next thing she knew was Saltash's arm like a coiled spring about her, impelling her towards the grand staircase.

"I'll take you to your room, *Juliette,*" he said. "You might miss the way by yourself. You're awfully tired, aren't you?"

It was absurd, but a curious desire to weep possessed her.

"Yes, I know," said Saltash, with his semi-comic tenderness. "Don't mind me! I knew you'd come to it sooner or later. You're not used to playing the sister of mercy are you, *ma mie,* though it becomes you — vastly well."

"Don't, Charles!" she murmured faintly.

"My dear, I mean no harm," he protested, firmly leading her upwards. "I am only — the friend in need."

She took him at his word though half against her will. He guided her up the branching staircase to the gallery above, bringing her finally to a tall oak door at the further end.

"Here is your chamber of sleep, *Juliette!* Now will you make me a promise?"

She left his supporting arm with an effort. "Well, what is it?"

"That you will go to bed in the proper and correct way and sleep till further notice," he said. "You can't go forever, believe me. And you need it."

He was looking at her with a softness of persuasion that sat so oddly on his mischievous monkey-face that in spite of herself, with quivering lips, she smiled.

"You're very good, Charles Rex," she said. "I wonder how much longer you will manage to keep it up."

He bowed low. "Just as long as I have your exemplary example before me," he said. "Who knows? We may both fling our caps over the windmill before we have done."

She shook her head, made as if she would enter the room, but paused. "You will take care of Columbus?" she said.

"Every care," he promised. "If I fail to bring him back to you intact you will never see my face again."

She had opened the door behind her, but still she paused. "Charles!"

Her voice held an unutterable appeal. A grin of sheer derision gleamed for a second in his eyes and vanished. "They ring up from the Court every day, *Juliette*. Presumably he gets the news by that channel. He has not troubled to obtain it in any other way."

"How could he?" Juliet said, but her face was paler than before; it had a grey look. "He is busy with his work all day long. What time has he for — other things?"

"Exactly, *ma chérie!* One would not expect it of him. Duty first — pleasure afterwards, is doubtless his motto. Very worthy — and very appropriate, for one of his profession. Unquestionably, it will become yours also — in time."

A faint, sad smile crossed Juliet's face. She made no response, and in a moment Saltash bent and swept up Columbus under his arm.

"*Adieu,* sister of mercy!" he said lightly. "I leave you to your dreams."

He went away along the gallery, and she entered the room and shut herself in.

For a second or two she stood quite motionless in the great luxurious apartment. Then slowly she went forward to the wide-flung window, and stood there, gazing blankly forth over the distant fir-clad park. He had said that he would see her again. It seemed so long ago. And all through this difficult time of strain and anxiety he had done nothing — nothing. She did not realize until that moment how much she had counted upon the memory of those last words of his.

Ah well! Perhaps — as Charles Rex hinted — it was better. Better to end it all thus, that midsummer madness of theirs that had already endured too long! They had lived such widely sundered lives. How could they ever have hoped ultimately to bridge the gulf between?

Charles was right. His shrewd perception realized that dwelling as they did in separate spheres they were bound to be fundamentally strangers to one another. Surely Dick himself had foreseen it long since down on that golden shore when first he had sought to dissuade her from going to the Court!

Her heart contracted at the memory. How sweet those early days had been! But the roses had faded, the nightingales had ceased to sing. It was all over now — all over. The dream was shattered, and she was weary unto death.

Chapter VII

THE SACRIFICE

"I expect it's one of them abscies again," said Mrs. Rickett sympathetically. "Have you been to the doctor about it, my dear?"

Robin, sitting heaped in the wooden armchair in her kitchen, looked at her with a smoldering glow in his eyes. "Don't like doctors," he muttered.

Mrs. Rickett sighed and went on with her ironing. "No more do I, Robin. But we can't always do without 'em. Have you told your brother now?"

Robin, sullenly rocking himself to and fro, made no reply for several seconds. Then very suddenly: "He asked me if I'd got a headache and I told him No," he flung out defiantly. "What's the good of bothering him? He can't do anything."

"The doctor might, you know," Mrs. Rickett ventured again, with a glance through the window at Freddy who had been sent out to amuse himself and was staggering with much perseverance in the wake of an elusive chicken. "It's wonderful what they can do nowadays to make things better."

"Don't want to be better," growled Robin.

She turned and looked at him in astonishment. "You didn't ought to say that, my dear," she said.

Again he raised his heavy eyes to hers and something she saw in them

— something she was quite at a loss to define — went straight to her heart.

"Robin, my dear, what's the matter?" she said. "Is there something that's troubling you?"

Again Robin was silent for a space. His eyes fell dully to the ground between his feet. At last, in a tone of muttered challenge, he spoke. "Don't want it to get better. Want it to end."

"Sakes alive!" said Mrs. Rickett, shocked. "You don't know what you're saying."

He did not contradict her or lift his eyes again, merely sat there like a hunched baboon, his head on his chest, his monstrous body slowly rocking.

There followed a lengthy silence. Mrs. Rickett ironed and folded, ironed and folded, with a practiced hand, still keeping an eye on the small chicken-chaser outside.

After several minutes, however, the boy's utter dejection of attitude moved her to attempt to divert his thoughts. "I wonder when our young lady will be coming to see us again," she said.

Robin uttered a queer sound in his throat; it was almost like the moan of an animal in pain. He said nothing.

She gave him an uneasy glance, but still kind-heartedly she persevered in her effort to lift him out of his depression. "She was always very friendly-like," she said. "You liked her, didn't you Robin?"

Robin shifted his position with a sharp movement as though he winced at some sudden dart of pain. "What should make her come back?" he said. "She'll stay away now she's gone."

"Oh, I expect we shall be seeing her again some day," said Mrs. Rickett, "when poor Mrs. Fielding is a bit stronger. She's busy now, but she'll come back, you'll see."

Again almost violently Robin moved in his chair. "She won't!" he flung out in a fierce undertone. "Tell you she won't!"

"How can you possibly know?" reasoned Mrs. Rickett.

"I do know," he said doggedly. "She won't come back, — anyhow not till —" his utterance trailed off into an unintelligible murmur in his throat and he became silent.

Mrs. Rickett shook out a small damp garment, and spread it upon the table with care. "I don't see how anyone is to say as she won't come back," she said. "Of course I know she's a lady born, but that don't prevent her making friends among humbler folk. She's talked of this place more than once as if she'd like to settle here."

"She won't then!" growled Robin. "She'll never do that, not while —."
Again he became inarticulate, muttering deeply in his throat like an

animal goaded to savagery.

Mrs. Rickett turned from her ironing to regard him. She had never found Robin hard to understand before, but there was something about him today which was wholly beyond her comprehension. He was like some wild creature that had received a cruel wound. Dumb resentment and fiery suffering seemed to mingle in his half uttered sentences. As he sat there, huddled forward with his hands pathetically clenched she thought she had never seen a more piteous sight.

"Lor', Robin, my dear!" she said. "What ever makes you know such a lot? Why shouldn't she come back then? Tell me that!"

He shook his shaggy head, but more in protest than refusal.

Mrs. Rickett bent down over him, her kindly red face full of the most motherly concern.

"What's troubling you, Robin?" she said. "You aren't — fretting for her, are you?"

He threw her one of his wild, furtive looks, and again in his eyes she caught a glimpse of something that deeply moved her. She laid a comforting hand on his shoulder.

"Is that it, lad? Are you wanting her? Ah, don't fret then — don't fret! She'll surely come back — some day."

The boy's face quivered. He looked down at his clenched hands, and at length jerkily, laboriously, he spoke, giving difficult and bitter utterance to the trouble that gnawed at his heart.

"It's — Dicky that wants her. But she won't come — she won't come — while I'm here." A sudden hard shiver went through him, he drew his breath through his set teeth, with a desperate sound. "No woman would," he said with hard despair.

And then abruptly, as if with speech his misery had become unendurable, he blundered to his feet with outflung arms, making the only outcry against fate that his poor stunted brain had ever accomplished. "It isn't fair!" he wailed. "It isn't right! I'm going to God — to tell Him so!"

He turned with the words, the impulse of the stricken creature urging him, and ignoring the remonstrance which Mrs. Rickett had barely begun he made headlong for the door, dragged it open, and was gone.

He went past his little playmate in the yard, shambling blindly for the open, deaf to the baby's cry of welcome, insensible to everything but the bitter burden of his pain. He slammed the gate behind him and set off at a lumbering run down the glaring road.

The evening sun smote full in his face as he went; but it might have been midnight, for he neither saw nor felt. Instinct alone guided him — the instinct of the wild creature, hunted by disaster, wounded to the heart, that must be alone with its agony and its fruitless strife against fate.

He went up the cliff-path, but he did not follow it far. Something drew him down the narrow cleft that led to the spot where first he had seen her lying on the shingle dreaming with her head upon her arm. He turned off the path to the place where he had crouched among the gorse-bushes and flung stones to scare her away, and stood there panting and gazing.

The memory of her, the gracious charm, the quick sympathy, went through him, pierced him. He caught his breath as though he listened for the beloved sound of her voice. She had not been really angry with him for the wantonness of those stones. She had been very ready with her forgiveness, her kindly offer of friendship. She had never been other than kind to him ever since. She had awakened in him the deepest, most humble gratitude and devotion. She had even once or twice shielded him from Dicky's never unjust wrath. And he had come to love her second only to Dicky who must forever hold the foremost place in his heart.

He had come to love her — and he stood between her and happiness. He did not reason the matter. He had small reasoning power. He recognized that Jack's brain was superior to his, and Jack had made known to him this monstrous thing. True, Dicky had denied it, but somehow that denial had not been so convincing as Jack's statement had been. The corrosive poison had already done its work, and there was no antidote. He knew that Dicky loved Juliet, knew it from his own lips. "The woman I love — the woman I love —" How often had the low-spoken words recurred to his memory! And Dicky was not happy. He had watched him narrowly ever since that night. Dicky was not really hopeful for the winning of his heart's desire. He had said there were many obstacles. What they were, Robin could but vaguely conjecture — save one! And that one stood out in the darkness of his soul, clear as a cross against the falling night. Dicky had no chance of winning any woman so long as he — the village idiot — the hideous abortion — stood in his way. That was the truth as he saw it — the bitter, unavoidable truth. O God, it wasn't fair — it wasn't fair!

The evening shadows were lengthening. The waves splashed softly against the fallen rocks forty to fifty feet below. They seemed to be calling to him. It was almost like a summons from far away — almost like a bugle-call heard in the mists of sleep. Somehow they soothed him, lessening the poignancy of his anguish, checking his wild rebellion, making him aware of a strangely comforting peace.

As if God had spoken and stilled his inarticulate protest, the futile agony of his striving died down. He began to be conscious vaguely that somewhere within his reach there lay a way of escape. He stared out over the silver-blue of the sea with strained and throbbing vision. The sun had gone down behind High Shale, and the quiet shadows stretched towards him. He had the feeling of a hunted man who has found sanctuary. Again, more calmly, his tired brain considered the problem that had driven him forth in such bitterness of soul.

There was Dicky — Dicky who loved him — whom he worshipped. Yes, certainly Dicky loved him. He had never questioned that. He was the only person in the world who had ever wanted him. But a deeper love, a deeper want, had entered Dicky's life with the coming of Juliet. He wanted her with a great heart-longing that Robin but dimly comprehended but of which he was keenly conscious, made wise by the sympathy that linked them. He knew — and this without any bitterness — that Dicky wanted Juliet as he had never wanted him. It was an overmastering yearning in Dicky's soul, and somehow — by some means — some sacrifice — it must be satisfied. Even Dicky, it seemed, would have to sacrifice something; for he could not have them both.

Yes, something would have to be sacrificed. Somehow this obstacle must be cleared out of Dicky's path. Juliet could not come to Dicky while he was there. He did not ask himself why this should be, but accepted it as fact. He then was the main obstacle to Dicky's happiness, to the fulfillment of his great desire. Then he must go. But whither? And leave Dicky — and leave Dicky!

Again for a spell the anguish woke within him, but it did not possess him so overwhelmingly as before. He had begun to seek for a way out, and though it was hard to find, the very act of seeking brought him comfort. His own misery no longer occupied the forefront of his poor groping brain.

He sat for a long, long time up there on the cliff while the shadows lengthened and the day slowly died, turning the matter over and over while the flame of sacrifice gradually kindled in the darkness of his soul.

It was probably the growth of many hours of not too coherent meditation — the solution of that problem; but it came upon him very suddenly at the last, almost like the swift wheeling of a flashlight over the calm night sea.

He had heard the church clock strike in the distance, and was turning to leave when that first vision of Juliet swooped back upon him — Juliet in her light linen dress springing up the path towards him. He saw her as she had stood there, leaving the path behind her, poised like a young goddess against the dazzling blue of the spring sky. Her face had been stern at first, but all the sternness had gone into an amazing kindness of compassion when her look had lighted upon him. She had not shrunk from him as shrank so many. And then — and then — he remembered the sudden fear, the sharp anxiety, that had succeeded that first look of pity.

He had been standing on the brink of the cliff as he had stood many a time before — as he stood now. That cliff had been the tragedy of his ruined life. And yet he loved it, had never known any fear of it. But she had been afraid for his sake. He had seen the fear leap into her eyes. And the memory of it came to him now as a revelation. He had found the way of escape at last!

The sea was crooning behind him over the half-buried rocks. He stood again on the brink with his poor worn face turned to the sky. He had come to the end of his reasoning. The tired brain had ceased to grapple with the cruel problem that had so tortured it. He knew now what he would do to help Dicky. And somehow the doing did not seem hard to him, somehow he did not feel afraid.

One step back and the cliff fell away behind him. Yet for a space he went neither forward nor back. It was as though he waited for a word of command, some signal for release. The first star was gleaming very far away like a lamp lighted in a distant city. His eyes found it and dwelt upon it with a wistful wonder. He had always loved the stars.

He was not angry or troubled anymore. All resentment, all turmoil, had died out of his heart forever. That strange peace had closed about him again, and the falling night held no terrors. Rather it seemed to spread wings of comfort above him. And always the crooning of the sea was like a voice that softly called him.

It came very suddenly at the last — the sign for which he waited. Someone had begun to mount the cliff-path, and — though he was out of sight — he heard a low, summoning whistle in the darkness. It was Dicky's whistle. He knew it well. Dicky was coming to look for him.

For a second every pulse — every nerve — leaped to answer that call. For a second he stood tense while that surging power within him sprang upwards, and in sheer amazing fire of sacrifice consumed the earthly impulse.

Then it was over. His arms went wide to the night. Without a cry, without a tremor, he flung himself backwards over the grassy edge.

The crooning sea and the overhanging cliff muffled the sound of his fall. And no one heard or saw — save God Who seeth all.

Chapter VIII

THE MESSAGE

*F*rom the day that Juliet relinquished her perpetual vigil, the improvement in Vera Fielding was almost uninterrupted. She recovered her strength very slowly, but her progress was marked by a happy certainty that none who saw her could question. She still leaned upon Juliet, but it was her husband alone who could call that deep content into her eyes which was gradually finding a permanent abiding-place in her heart. The nearness of death had done for them what no circumstance of life had ever accomplished. They had drawn very close together in its shadow, and as they gradually left it behind the tie still held them in a bond that had become sacred to them both. It was as if they had never really known each other till now.

All Vera's arrogance had vanished in her husband's presence, just as his curt imperiousness had given place to the winning dominance which he knew so well how to wield. "You'll do it for me," was one of his pet phrases, and he seldom uttered it in vain. She gave him the joyful sacrifice of love newly-awakened.

"I wonder if we shall go on like this when I'm well again," she said to him on an evening of rose-colored dusk in early August when he was sitting by her side with her long thin hand in his.

"Like what?" said Edward Fielding.

She smiled at him from her pillow. "Well, spoiling each other in this way. Will you never be overbearing and dictatorial? Shall I never be furious and hateful to you again?"

"I hope not," he said. "In fact, I think not."

He spoke very gravely. She stirred, and in a moment her other hand came out to him also. He clasped it closely. Her eyes were shining softly in the dusk.

"You are — so good to me, Edward — my darling," she said.

His head was bent over her hands. "Don't!" he muttered huskily.

Her fingers closed on his. "Edward, will you tell me something?" she whispered.

"I don't know," he said.

"Yes, but I want you to. I'd rather hear it from you. The doctors don't think I shall ever be fit for much again, do they?"

She spoke steadily, with a certain insistence. He looked up at her sharply, with something of a glare in his eyes.

"You're not going to die — whatever they say!" he declared in a fierce undertone.

"No — no, of course not!" She spoke soothingly, still smiling at him, for that barely checked ferocity of his sent rapture through her soul. "Do you suppose I'd be such an idiot as to go and die just when I'm beginning to enjoy life? I'm not the puny heroine of a lachrymose novel. I hope I've got more sense. No, dear, what I really meant was — was — am I ever going to be strong enough — woman enough — to give you — what you want so much?"

"Vera — my dear!" He leaned swiftly to her, his arm pillowed her head. "Do you suppose — do you really suppose — I'd let you jeopardize your sweet life — after this — after this?"

He was holding her closely to him, and though a little spasm of breathlessness went through her she gave herself to him with a pulsing gladness that thrilled her whole being. It was the happiest moment she had ever known.

"Oh, Edward," she said, "do you — do you really feel like that?"

His cheek was against her forehead. He did not speak for a few seconds. Then, with something of an effort, "Yes," he said. "It's like that with me now, my dear. I've been through — a good deal — these last days. Now I've got you back — please God, I'll keep you!"

She pressed her face against him. "Ah, but Edward, you know you've always wanted —"

"Oh, damn my wants!" he broke in impatiently. "I don't want anything but you now."

She raised her lips to kiss his neck. "That's the loveliest thing you ever said to me, darling," she said, with a throb in her voice. "I love being an invalid — with you to spoil me. But — if you'll promise — promise — promise — to love me quite as much — if I get well, I will get well — really well — for your sake."

Again she was panting. He felt it as he held her, and after a moment or two very tenderly he laid her back.

"God bless you, my dear!" he said. "You needn't be afraid. I've learnt my lesson, and I shan't forget it."

"The lesson of love!" she murmured, holding his hand against her thumping heart.

"Yes. Juliet began the teaching. A wonderful girl that. She seems to know everything. I wonder where she learnt it."

"She is wonderful," Vera agreed thoughtfully. "I sometimes think she has had a hard life. She says so little about herself."

"She has moved among a fairly rapid lot," observed the squire. "Lord Saltash is intimate enough to call her by her Christian name."

"Does he ever talk about her?" asked Vera, interested.

"Not much," said the squire.

"You think he is fond of her at all?"

"I don't know. He doesn't see much of her. I haven't quite got his measure yet. He isn't the sort of man I thought he was anyway."

"Then it wasn't true about Lady Joanna Farringmore?" questioned Vera.

Fielding hesitated. "I don't know," he said again. "I have a suspicion that that report was not entirely unfounded. But however that may be, she isn't with him now."

"You don't think she is — on board the yacht?" suggested Vera.

"No, I don't. The yacht is being done up for a voyage. A beautiful boat from all accounts. He is very proud of her. I am to go over her with him one of these days, when she's ready — which will be soon."

Vera uttered a short sigh. "I wish we'd get a yacht, Edward," she said.

"Do you? Why?" He was looking at her attentively, a smile in his eyes.

She colored faintly. "I don't know. It's just a fancy, I suppose — a sick fancy. But I believe I could get well much quicker if I went for a voyage like that."

"You'd be bored to death," said Fielding.

She looked at him through sudden tears. "Bored! With you!" she said.

He patted her cheek gently. "Wouldn't you be bored? Quite sure? Suppose we were to borrow that yacht, do you think you'd really like it?"

Her eyes shone through the tears. "Of course I should love it!" she said. "Is there — is there any chance of such a thing?"

"Every chance," said Fielding. "Saltash most kindly placed her, with the captain and crew, at my disposal only last night."

"Oh, Edward! How tremendously kind!" She looked at him with an eagerness that seemed to transform her. "But — but would you like it too? Wouldn't you — wouldn't you feel it was an awful waste of time?"

"Waste of time! With you!" smiled Fielding.

She lifted his hand with a shy movement and put it to her lips. "Edward — darling, you get dearer every day," she murmured. "What makes you so good to me?"

He leaned down and kissed her forehead. "I happen to have found out — quite by accident — that I love you, my dear," he said.

She smiled at him. "What a happy accident! Then we are really going for that voyage together? What about — Juliet?"

"Don't you want Juliet?" he said.

"Yes, if she would come. But I have a feeling — I don't know why — that she will not be with us very long. I should be sorry to part with her for we owe her so much. But — somehow she doesn't quite fit, does she? She would be much more suitable as — Lady Saltash for instance."

Fielding laughed. "Saltash isn't the only fish in the sea," he remarked.

"You are thinking of — Mr. Green?" she questioned, with slight hesitation before the name. "You know, Edward —" she broke off.

"Well, my dear?" he said.

She turned to him impulsively. "I'm sorry I've not been nicer about that young man. I'm going to try and like him better, just to please you. But, Edward, you wouldn't want Juliet to marry — that sort of man? You don't, do you?"

Fielding had stiffened almost imperceptibly. "It doesn't much matter what I want," he said, after a moment. "It doesn't rest with me. Neither Dick nor Juliet are likely to consult my feelings in the matter."

"I don't want her to throw herself away — like that," said Vera.

"I don't think you need be afraid," he said. "Juliet knows very well what she is about. And Dick — well Dick's fool enough to sacrifice the heart out of his body for the sake of that half-witted boy."

"How odd of him!" Vera said. "What a pity Robin ever lived to grow up!"

"He's been the ruin of Dick's life," the squire said forcibly. "He's thrown away every chance he ever had on account of Robin. He doesn't fit — if you like. He's absolutely out of his sphere and knows it. But he'll never change it while that boy lives. That's the infernal part of it. Nothing will move him." He stopped himself suddenly. "I mustn't excite you, my dear, and this is a subject upon which I feel very strongly. I can't expect you to sympathize because —" he smiled whimsically — "well, mainly because you don't understand. We had better talk of something else."

Vera was looking at him with a slight frown between her eyes. "I didn't mean to be — unsympathetic," she said, a faint quiver in her voice.

"Of course not! Of course not!" Hastily he sought to make amends. "I don't know how we got on the subject. You must forgive me, my dear. I believe I hear Juliet in the conservatory. We won't discuss this before her."

He would have risen, but she detained him. "Edward, just a moment!

I want to ask you something."

"Well?" Reluctantly he paused.

"I — only want to know," she spoke with some effort, "what there is about — Mr. Green that — that makes you so fond of him."

"Oh, that!" He stood hesitating. But there were certainly footsteps in the conservatory; he heard them with relief. "I'll tell you some other time, my dear," he said gently. "Here comes Juliet to turn me out!"

He turned to the window as she entered and greeted her with a smile. Vera was still clinging to his hand.

"May I come in?" said Juliet, stopping on the threshold.

"Yes, of course, come in!" Vera said. "We have been talking about you, Juliet. Will you come for a voyage with us in Lord Saltash's yacht?"

Juliet came slowly forward. Her face was pale. She was holding a letter in her hand. She looked from one to the other for a second or two in silence.

"Are you sure," she said, in her low quiet voice, "that you wouldn't rather go alone?"

"Not unless you would rather not come," said the squire.

"Thank you," she said. "May I — think about it?"

The squire was looking at her attentively. "What is the matter?" he said suddenly.

She met his look steadily, though he felt it to be with an effort. Then quietly she turned to Vera.

"I have just had a letter," she said, "from a friend who is in trouble. Do you think you can spare me — for a little while?"

Vera stretched a hand to her. "My dear Juliet, I am so sorry. Of course you shall go. What is it? What has happened?"

Juliet came to her, took and held the hand. "You are very kind," she said. "But I don't want you to be troubled too. There is no need. You are sure you will be all right without me?"

"You will come back to me?" Vera said.

"I will certainly come back," Juliet made steadfast answer, "even if I can't stay. But now that you are able to sit up, you will need me less. You will take care of her, Mr. Fielding?" looking up at him.

He nodded. "You may be sure of that — the utmost care. When must you go?"

He was still looking at her closely; his eyes deeply searching.

Juliet hesitated. "Do you think — tonight?" she said.

"Certainly. Then you will want a car. Have you told Lord Saltash?" He turned to the door.

"No, I have only just heard. I believe he has gone to town." Juliet gently laid down the hand she was holding. "I will come back," she said again, and followed him.

He drew the door closed behind them. They faced each other in the dimness of the hall. The squire's mouth was twitching uncontrollably. "Now, Juliet!" His voice had a ring of sternness; he put his hand on her shoulder, gripping unconsciously. "For heaven's sake —" he said — "out with it! It isn't — Dick?"

"No — Robin!" she said.

"Ah!" He drew a deep breath and straightened himself, his other hand over his eyes. Then in a moment he was looking at her again. His grip relaxed. "Forgive me!" he said. "Did I hurt you?"

She gave him a faint smile. "It doesn't matter. You understand, don't you? I must go — to Dick."

He nodded. "Yes — yes! Is the boy — dead?"

"No. It was a fall over the cliff. It happened last night. They didn't find him for hours. He is going fast. Jack brought me this." She glanced down at the letter in her hand.

He made a half-gesture to take it, checking himself sharply. "I beg your pardon, Juliet, I hardly know what I'm doing. It's from Dick, is it?"

Very quietly she gave it to him. "You may read it. You have a right to know," she said.

He gave her an odd look. "May I? Are you sure?"

"Read it!" she said.

He opened it. His fingers were trembling. She stood at his shoulder and read it with him. The words were few, containing the bald statement, but no summons.

The squire read them, breathing heavily. Suddenly he thrust his arm round Juliet and held her fast.

"Juliet! You'll be good to my boy — good to Dick?"

Her eyes met his. "That is why I am going to him," she said. She took the note and folded it, standing within the circle of his arm.

"I'd go to him myself — if I could," Fielding went on unevenly. "He'll feel this — damnably. He was simply devoted to that unfortunate boy."

"I know," said Juliet.

Again he put his hand to his eyes. "I've been a beast about Robin. Ask him to forgive me, Juliet! Tell him I'm awfully sorry, that I'll come as soon as I can get away. And if there's anything he wants — anything under the sun — he's to have it. See? Make him understand!"

"He will understand," Juliet said quietly.

He looked at her again. "Don't let him fret, Juliet!" he said urgently. "You'll comfort him, won't you? I know I'm always rating him, but he's such a good chap. You — you love him, don't you?"

"Yes," she said.

"God bless you for that!" he said earnestly. "I can't tell you what he is to me — can't explain. But — but —"

"I — understand," she said

"What?" He stared at her for a moment. "What — do you understand?"

"I know what he is to you," she said gently. "I have known — for a long time. Never mind how! Nobody told me. It just came to me one day."

"Ah!" Impulsively he broke in. "You see everything. I'm afraid of you, Juliet. But look here! You won't — you won't — make him suffer — for my sins?"

Her hand pressed his arm. "What am I?" she said. "Have I any right to judge anyone? Besides — oh, besides — do you think I could possibly go to him if I did not feel that nothing on earth matters now — except our love?"

She spoke with deep emotion. She was quivering from head to foot. He bent very low to kiss the hand upon his arm.

"And you will have your reward," he said huskily. "Don't forget — it's the only thing in life that really counts! There's nothing else — nothing else."

Juliet stood quite still looking down at the bent grey head. "I wonder," she said slowly, "I wonder — if Dick — in his heart — thinks the same!"

Chapter IX

THE ANSWER

*T*he August dusk had deepened into night when the open car from the Court pulled up at the schoolhouse gate. The school had closed for the summer holidays a day or two before. No lights shone in either building.

"Do you mind going in alone?" whispered Jack. "I can't show here. But I'll wait inside the park-gates to take you back."

"You needn't wait," Juliet said. "I shall spend the night at the Court — unless I am wanted here."

She descended with the words. She had never liked Jack Green, and she was thankful that the rapid journey was over. She heard him shoot up the drive as she went up the schoolhouse path.

In the dark little porch she hesitated. The silence was intense. Then, as she stood in uncertainty, from across the bare playground there came a call.

"Juliet!"

She turned swiftly. He was standing in the dark doorway of the school. The vague light of the rising moon gleamed deathly on his face. He did not move to meet her.

She went to him, reached out hands to him that he did not take, and clasped him by the shoulders. "Oh, you poor boy!"

His arms held her close for a moment or two, then they relaxed.

"I don't know why I sent for you," he said.

"You didn't send for me, Dick," she made gentle answer. "But I think you wanted me all the same."

He groaned. "Wanted you! I've — craved for you. You told the squire?"

"Yes. He said —"

He broke in upon her with fierce bitterness. "He was pleased of course! I knew he would be. That's why I couldn't send the message to him. It had to be you."

"Dick! Dick! He wasn't pleased! You don't know what you're saying. He was most terribly sorry." She put her arm through his with a very tender gesture. "Won't you take me inside and tell me all about it?" she said.

He gave a hard shudder. "I don't know if I can, Juliet. It's been — so awful. He suffered — so infernally. The doctor didn't want to give him morphia — said it would hasten the end." He stamped in a sort of impotent frenzy. "I stood over him and made him. It was just what I wanted to do. It was — it was — beyond endurance."

"Oh, my dear!" she said.

He put his hands over his face. "Juliet, — it was — hell!" he said brokenly. "When I wrote that note to you — I thought the worst was over. But it wasn't — it wasn't! He was past speaking — but his eyes — they kept imploring me to let him go. — O God, I'd given my soul to help him! And I could do — nothing — except see him die!"

Again a convulsive shudder caught him. Juliet's arms went around him. She held his head against her breast.

"It's over now," she whispered. "Thank God for that!"

He leaned upon her for a space. "Yes, it's over. At least he died in peace," he said, and drew a hard, quivering breath. Then he stood up again. "Juliet, I'm so sorry. Come inside! I'll light the lamp. I couldn't stand that empty house — with only my boy's dead body in it. Mrs. Rickett has been there, but she's gone now." He turned and pushed open the door. "Wait a minute while I light up!"

She did not wait, but followed him closely, and stood beside him while he lighted a lamp on the wall. He turned from doing so and smiled at her, and she saw that though his face was ghastly, he was his own master again.

"How did you get here?" he said. "Who took the note? The doctor promised to get it delivered."

"Jack brought it," she said. "I came back with him."

"Jack!" His brows drew together suddenly. She saw his black eyes gleam. For a moment he said nothing further. Then: "If — Jack comes anywhere near me tonight, I shall kill him!" he said very quietly.

"Dick!" she said in amazement.

There was a certain awful intentness in his look. "I hold him responsible for this," he said.

She gazed at him, assailed by a swift wonder as to his sanity.

In a second he saw the doubt and replied to it, still with that deadly quietness that seemed to her more terrible than violence. "I know what I am saying. He is — directly responsible. My boy died for my sake, because he believed what Jack told him — that no woman would ever consent to marry me while he lived."

"Oh, Dick! You don't mean — he did it — on purpose!" Juliet's voice was quick with pain. "Dick, surely — surely — it wasn't that! You are making a mistake!"

"No. It is no mistake," he said, with somber conviction. "I know it. Mrs. Rickett knows it too. It's been preying on his mind ever since. He hasn't been well. He's suffered with his head a good deal lately. He —" He stopped himself. "There's no need to distress you over this. Thank you for coming. I didn't really expect you. Is he — is Jack — waiting to take you back?"

"No," said Juliet quietly.

His brows went up. "You are sleeping at the Court? I'll take you there."

"I'm not going yet, Dick," she said gently, "unless you turn me out."

His face quivered unexpectedly. He turned from her. "There's — nothing to wait for," he said.

But Juliet stood motionless. Her eyes went down the long bare room with its empty forms and ink-splashed desks. She thought it the most desolate place she had ever seen.

After an interval of blank silence Dick spoke again. "Don't you stay! I'm not myself tonight. I can't — think. It was awfully good of you to come. But don't — stay!"

"Dick!" she said.

At sound of her voice he turned. His eyes looked at her out of such a depth of misery as pierced her to the heart. She saw his hands clench against his sides. "O my God!" he said under his breath.

"Dick!" she said again very earnestly. "Don't send me away! Let me help you!"

"You can't," he said. "You've been too good to me — already."

"You wouldn't say that to me if I were — your wife," she said.

He flinched sharply. "Juliet! Don't torture me! I've had — as much as I can stand tonight."

She held out her hand to him with a gesture superbly simple. "My dear, I will marry you tomorrow if you will have me," she said.

He stood for a long second staring at her. Then she saw his face change and harden. The ascetic look that she had noticed long ago came over it like a mask.

"No!" he said. "No!"

Again he turned from her. He went away up the long room, the bare boards echoing to the tramp of his feet with a dull and hopeless sound. He came to a stand before the writing-table at the further end, and from there he spoke to her, his words brief, as it were edged with steel.

"Can you imagine how Cain felt when he said that his punishment was greater than he could bear? That's how I feel tonight. I am like Cain. Whatever I touch is cursed."

The words startled her. Again for a second she wondered if the suffering through which he had passed had affected his brain. But she felt no fear. She kept her purpose before her, clear and steadfast as a beacon shining in the dark.

"You are not like Cain," she said. "And even if you were, do you think I should love you any the less?"

He made a desperate gesture. "Would you love me if I were a murderer?" he said.

"I love you — whatever you are," she made unfaltering reply.

He turned upon her, almost like an animal at bay. "I am — a murderer, Juliet!" he said, a terrible fire in his eyes.

In spite of herself she flinched, so awful was his look. "Dick, what do you mean?"

He flung out a hand as if to keep her from him though she had not moved. "I will tell you what I mean, and then — you will go. On the night Robin was born, — I killed his father!"

"Dick!" she said.

He went on rapidly. "I was a boy at the time, but I had a man's purpose. My mother was dying. They sent me to fetch him. I loathed the man. So did she. He was at The Three Tuns — drinking. I hung about till he came out. He was blind drunk, and the night was dark. He took the wrong path that led to the cliff, and I let him go. In the morning they found him on the rocks, dead. I might have saved him. I didn't. I went back to my mother, and stayed with her — till she died."

"Oh Dick — my dear!" she said.

He stood stiffly facing her. "I never repented. I'd do the same again now — or worse, to such a man as that. He was a brute beast. But — I suppose God doesn't allow these things. Anyway, I've been punished — pretty heavily. I got fond of the boy. He was the only thing left to care for. He took the place of everything else. And now — because of a damnable lie —" Something seemed to rise in his throat, he paused, struggling with himself, finally went on jerkily, with difficulty. "One more thing — you'd better know. It'll help you to — forget me. The man I killed was not my own father — except in name. My mother refused to marry the man she loved because she thought it would injure his career — his people threatened to disown him. She gave herself instead to — the scoundrel whose name I bear — just to set him free."

Again he stopped. Juliet had moved. She was coming up the long room to him, not quickly, but with purpose. He stood, still facing her, his breathing short and hard.

Quietly, with that regal bearing that was so supremely her own, she drew near. And her eyes were shining with a light that made her beautiful. She reached him and stood before him.

"Dick," she said, "I am not like your mother. I've been fighting against it, but it's too strong for me. I have got to marry — the man I love."

He made an impotent gesture, and she saw that he was trembling.

She stood a moment, then reached out, took his arms, and drew them gently round her. "Are you still trying to send me away?" she said. "Because — it's stronger than both of us, Dick — and I'm not going — I'm not going!"

He looked into the shining, steadfast eyes, and suddenly the desperate strain was over. His resistance snapped. "God forgive me!" he said under his breath, and caught her passionately close.

There was that in his hold — perhaps because of the fullness of her surrender — that had never been before, — something flaming, something fiercely electric, in his swift acceptance of her. As he clasped her, she felt the wild throbbing of his heart like the pulsing force of a racing engine. He kissed her, and in his kiss there was more than the lover's adoration. It held the demand and mastery of matehood. By it he claimed and sealed her for his own.

When his hold relaxed, she made no effort to withdraw herself. She leaned against him gasping a little, but her eyes — with the glory yet shining in them — were still raised to his.

"So that's settled, is it?" she said, with a quivering smile. "You are quite sure, Dick?"

His hands were clasped behind her. His look had a certain burning quality as if he challenged all the world for her possession.

"What am I to say to you, Juliet?" he said, his words low, deeply vibrant. "I can't deny — my other self — can I?"

"I don't know," she said. "You were very near it, weren't you? I thought you had — all these weeks."

"Ah!" His brows contracted. "Will you forgive me, Juliet? I've had — an infernal time."

"Yes. I know," she said gently.

"No, dear, you don't know. How could you? Your life hasn't been one perpetual struggle against overwhelming odds like mine." He paused. "Look here, darling! I'm rather a fool tonight. I can't explain things. But you've been very wonderful to me. You've lighted a torch in the dark. I kept away because — it didn't seem fair to you to do anything else. You were back in your own inner circle, and I was miles outside. And you never wanted to be bound. When I saw you with — Lord Saltash — I knew why."

"My dear!" she said. "You didn't imagine I was in love with Saltash surely!"

"No — no!" he said. "I knew you weren't. And yet — somehow — I felt you were nearer to his world than mine. I realized it more and more as the days went on. And my boy was ill — I couldn't leave him. Juliet —" a hint of entreaty crept into his voice — "I can't explain. But somehow here on my own ground it's — different. I feel you belong to me here. I know I can win and hold you. But there — there — you are — leagues and leagues above me — far out of reach."

"Oh, Dick!" she said. "I thought you had more sense! Don't you realize — yet — that your world is the world I want to be in? I want to forget that other world — just to blot it out of my life — if only you will make that possible."

"If I will!" he said, with a deep breath. And then suddenly he took her face between his hands, looking closely into her eyes. "Don't you care about — all the horrible things I've told you?" he said. "Does it make no difference at all to you?"

She was still smiling — a tremendous smile. "It doesn't seem much like it, does it?" she said. "I'm not such a saint myself, Dick. Moreover, I knew about — some things — before I came."

"What things?" he said.

She made a very winning gesture towards him. "Don't think me a Paul Pry, dear! But I couldn't help knowing — ages ago — what made the squire — so fond of you."

"Juliet!" He gazed at her. "How on earth did you find out?"

She colored deeply under his look. "You — are rather alike — in some ways," she said. "It was partly that and partly being — well, rather interested in you, I suppose. And Mrs. Rickett told me as much of your family history as she knew before I ever met you. So, you see, I didn't have much to fill in."

"And still it makes no difference?" he said.

She shook her head. "None whatever. I'm just glad for your sake that the man you hated so was not your father. But I think you go rather far, Dick, when you say you killed him."

The hard onyx glitter shone again in his eyes. "No, it was not an exaggeration," he said. "I was a murderer that night. I meant him to go to his death. When he was dead I was glad. He had tortured the only being I loved on earth. I believed he was my father for quite a long time after — till the squire came home, and I told him the whole story. Then — in an impulsive moment — he told me the truth. He cared about my mother's death — cared badly. They would have been married by that time if her husband hadn't turned up again. It was two lives spoilt."

"And what about yours?" she said.

"Mine!" He smiled rather bitterly. "Well, I've never expected much of life. I've stuck to my independence and been satisfied with that. He'd have bossed my destiny if I'd have let him. But I wouldn't. I was cussed on that point, though if it hadn't been for Robin, I shouldn't have bothered. I stayed on here for the boy's sake. He wouldn't have been happy anywhere else. Well," he uttered a weary sigh, "that chapter's closed."

She pressed his arm. "Dick, we might never have met but for that."

"Oh, we might have met," he said. "But — you'd probably have detested me — under any other circumstances."

She smiled at him with a touch of wistfulness. "And you me, Dick. Neither of us would have looked below the surface if we'd met in the general hurly-burly. We shouldn't have had time. So we have a good deal to be thankful for, haven't we?"

He drew her to him again. The desperate misery had passed from his face, but he looked worn out. "What on earth should I do without you?" he said.

"I don't know, dear," she answered tenderly. "I hope you are not going to try any longer, are you?"

His lips were near her own. "Juliet, will you stay — within reach — till after the funeral?"

"Yes," she breathed.

"And then — then — will you — marry me?" His whisper was even lower than hers. The man's whole being pulsed in the words.

Her arms went round his neck. "I will, dearest."

His breath came quickly. "And if — if — later — you come upon some things that hurt you — things you don't understand — will you remember how I've been handicapped — and — forgive me?"

Her eyes looked straight up to his. They held a shadowy smile. "Dick, — I was just going — to say that — to you!"

He pressed her to his heart. "Ah, my Juliet!" he said. "Could anything matter to us — anything on earth — except our love?"

In the deep silence her lips answered his. There was no further need for words.

PART IV

Chapter I

THE FREE GIFT

"*I*'m not quite sure that I call this fair play," said Saltash with a comical twist of the eyebrows. "I didn't expect all these developments in so short a time."

"There are no further rules to this game," said Juliet, squeezing Columbus around his sturdy shoulders as he sat on the bench beside her. "Whoever wins — or loses — no one has any right to complain."

She spoke without agitation, but her face was flushed, and there was something about the clasp of her arm that made Columbus look up with earnest affection.

"If that's so," said Saltash, "I can withdraw my protection without compunction."

She smiled. "No doubt you can, most puissant Rex! But it really wouldn't answer your purpose. You've nothing to gain by treachery to a friend, and it would give you a horrid taste afterwards."

He made a face at her. "That's your point of view. And what am I to say when I meet Muff and all the rest of the clan again?"

She gave a slight shrug. "Do you think it matters? They are much too busy chasing after their own affairs to give me a second thought. If I were Lady Jo, they might be interested — for half-an-hour — not a minute longer."

Saltash made a mocking sound. "I know one person whose interest would last a bit longer than that — if you were Lady Jo."

"Indeed?" said Juliet.

"Yes — indeed, *ma Juliette!* I met him the other day at the Club before I went North, and it may interest you to know that he is determined to find her — and marry her — or perish in the attempt."

"It doesn't interest me in the least," said Juliet.

"No? Hard-hearted as ever!" Saltash's grin was one of sheer mischief. "Well, he seemed to share the popular belief that I know where the elusive Lady Jo is to be found. I really can't think what I've done to deserve such a reputation. I was put through a pretty stiff cross-examination, I can tell you."

"I have no doubt you were more than equal to it," said Juliet.

Saltash broke into a laugh. "It was such a skillful fencing-match that I imagine we left off much as we began. But I don't flatter myself that I am cleared of suspicion. In fact it wouldn't surprise me at all to find I was being shadowed — not for the first time in my disreputable career."

"I wonder when you will marry and turn respectable," said Juliet.

He made an appalling grimace. "Follow your pious example? May heaven forbid!"

She looked at him, faintly smiling. "Wait till the real thing comes to you, Charles Rex! You won't feel so superior then."

"Do you know how old I am?" said Saltash.

"Thirty-five," said Juliet idly.

Again his brows went up. "How on earth do you know these things off-hand?"

Her grey eyes were quizzical. "You are quite young enough yet to be happy — if only the right woman turns up."

He leaned back in his chair, his hands behind his head, and contemplated her with a criticism that lasted several seconds. His dark face wore its funny, monkeyish look of regret, half-wistful and half-feigned.

"I wish —" he said suddenly — "I wish I'd come down here when you first began to rusticate."

"Why?" said Juliet, with her level eyes upon him.

He laughed and sprang abruptly to his feet. *"Quien sabe?* I might have turned rustic too — pious also, my *Juliette!* Think of it! Life isn't fair to me. Why am I condemned always to ride the desert alone?"

"Mainly because you ride too hard," said Juliet. "None but you can keep up the pace. Ah!" She turned her head quickly, and the swift color flooded her face.

"Ah!" mocked Saltash softly, watching her. "Is it Romeo's step that I hear?"

Columbus wagged his tail in welcome as Dick Green came round the corner of the Ricketts' cottage and walked down under the apple trees to join them. He greeted Saltash with the quiet self-assurance of a man who treads his own ground. There was no hint of hostility in his bearing.

"I've been expecting you," he said coolly.

"Have you?" said Saltash, a gleam of malicious humor in his eyes. "I thought there was something of the conquering hero about you. I have come — naturally — to congratulate you on your conquest."

"Thank you," said Dick, and seated himself on the bench beside Juliet and Columbus. "That is very magnanimous of you."

"It is," agreed Saltash. "But if I had known what was in the wind I might have carried it still further and offered you Burchester Castle for the honeymoon."

"How kind of you!" said Juliet. "But we prefer cottages to castles, don't we, Dick? We might have had the Court. The squire very kindly suggested it. But we like this best — till our own house is in order."

"Still rusticating!" commented Saltash. "I should have thought your passion for that would have been satisfied by this time. I seem to have got out of touch with you all during my stay in Scotland. I never meant to go there this year, but I got lured away by Muff and his crowd. Mighty poor sport on the whole. I've often wished myself back. But I pictured you far away on the Night Moth with Mr. and Mrs. Fielding, and myself bored to extinction in my empty castle. And so I hung on. I certainly never expected you to get married in my absence, ma Juliette. That was the unkindest cut of all. Why didn't you write and tell me?"

"I didn't even know where you were," said Juliet. "You disappeared without warning. We expected you back at any time."

"Bad excuses every one of 'em!" said Saltash. "You know you wanted to get it over before I came back. Very rash of you both, but it's your funeral, not mine. Is this all the honeymoon you're going to have?"

Juliet laughed a little. "Well, my dear Rex, it doesn't much matter where you are so long as you are happy. We spend a good deal of our time on the sea and in it. We also go motoring in the squire's little car. And we superintend the decorating of our house. At the same time Dick is within reach of the miners who are being rather tiresome, so everyone — except the miners — is satisfied."

"Oh, those infernal miners!" said Saltash, and looked at Dick. "How long do you think you are going to keep them in hand?"

"I can't say," said Dick somewhat briefly. "I don't advise Lord Wilchester or any of his people to come down here till something has been done to settle them."

Saltash laughed. "Oh, Muff won't come near. You needn't be afraid of that. He's deer-stalking in the Highlands. He's a great believer in leaving things to settle themselves."

"Is he?" said Dick grimly. "Well, they may do that in a fashion he won't care for before he's much older."

"Are you organizing a strike?" suggested Saltash, a wicked gleam of humor in his eyes.

Dick's eyes flashed in answer. "I am not!" he said. "But — I'm damned if they haven't some reason for striking — if he cares as little as that!"

"How often do you tell 'em so?" said Saltash.

Juliet's hand slipped quietly from Columbus's head to Dick's arm. "May I have a cigarette, please?" she said.

He turned to her immediately and his fire died down. He offered her his cigarette-case in silence.

Juliet took one, faintly smiling. "Do you know," she said to Saltash, "it was Dick's cigarettes that first attracted me to him? When I landed on this desert island, I had only three left. He came to the rescue — most nobly, and has kept me supplied ever since. I don't know where he gets them from, but they are the best I ever tasted."

"He probably smuggles 'em," said Saltash, offering her a match.

"No, I don't," said Dick, rather shortly. "I get them from a man in town. A fellow I once met — Ivor Yardley, the K. C. — first introduced me to them. I get them through his secretary who has some sort of interest in the trade."

A sudden silence fell. Juliet's cigarette remained poised in the act of kindling, but no smoke came from her lips. She had the look of one who listens with almost painful intentness.

The flame of the lighted match licked Saltash's fingers, and he dropped it. "Pardon my clumsiness! Let's try again! So you know Yardley, do you?" He flung the words at Dick. "Quite the coming man in his profession. Rather a brute in some ways, cold-blooded as a fish and wily as a serpent, but interesting — distinctly interesting. When did you meet him?"

"Early this year. I consulted him on a matter of business. I have no private acquaintance with him." Dick was looking straight at Saltash with a certain hardness of contempt in his face. "You evidently are on terms of intimacy with him."

"Oh, quite!" said Saltash readily. "He knows me — almost as well as you do. And I know him — even better. I was saying to *Juliette* just now that I believe he shares the general impression that I have got Lady Jo Farringmore somewhere up my sleeve. She did the rabbit trick, you know, a week or two before the wedding, and because I was to have been the best man I somehow got the blame. Wonder if he'd have blamed you if you'd been there!"

Dick stiffened. "I think not," he said.

"Not disreputable enough?" laughed Saltash.

"Not nearly," said Juliet, coming out of her silence. "Dick has rather strong opinions on this subject, Charles, so please don't be flippant about it! Will you give me another match?"

He held one for her, his eyebrows cocked at a comical angle, open derision in the odd eyes beneath them. Then, her cigarette kindled, he sprang up in his abrupt fashion.

"I'm going. Thanks for putting up with me for so long. I had to come and see you, Juliette. You are one of the very few capable of appreciating me at my full value."

"I hope you will come again," she said.

He bowed low over her hand. "If I can ever serve you in any way," he said, "I hope you will give me the privilege. Farewell, most estimable Romeo! You may yet live to greet me as a friend."

He was gone with the words with the suddenness of a monkey swinging off a bough, leaving behind him a silence so marked that the fall of an unripe apple from the tree immediately above them caused Columbus to start and jump from his perch to investigate.

Then Juliet, very quiet of mien and level of brow, got up and went to Dick who had risen at the departure of the visitor. She put her hand through his arm and held it closely.

"You are not to be unkind to my friends, Richard," she said. "It is the one thing I can't allow."

He looked at her with some sternness, but his free hand closed at once upon hers. "I hate to think of you on terms of intimacy with that bounder," he said.

She smiled a little. "I know you do. But you are prejudiced. I can't give up an old friend — even for you, Dick."

He squeezed her hand. "Have you got many friends like that, Juliet?"

She flushed. "No. He is the only one I have, and —"

"And?" he said, as she stopped.

She laid her cheek with a very loving gesture against his shoulder. "Ah, don't throw stones!" she pleaded gently. "There are so few of us without sin."

His arm was about her in a moment, all his hardness vanished. "My own girl!" he said.

She held his hand in both her own. "Do you know — sometimes — I lie awake at night and wonder — and wonder — whether you would have thought of me — if you had known me in the old days?"

"Is that it?" he said very tenderly. "And you thought I was sleeping like a hog and didn't know?"

She laughed rather tremulously, her face turned from him. "It isn't always possible to bury the past, is it, however hard we try? I hope you'll make allowances for that, Dick, if ever I shock your sense of propriety."

"I shall make allowances," he said, "because you are the one and only woman I worship — or have ever worshipped — and I can't see you in any other light."

"How dear of you, Dicky!" she murmured. "And how rash!"

"Am I such an unutterable prig?" he said. "I feel myself that I have got extra fastidious since knowing you."

She laughed at that, and after a moment turned with impulsive sweetness and put her cigarette between his lips. "You're not a prig, darling. You are just an honorable and upright gentleman whom I am very proud to belong to and with whom I always feel I have got to be on my best behavior. What have you been doing all this time? I should have come to look for you if Saltash hadn't turned up."

Dick's brows were slightly drawn. "I've been talking to Jack," he said.

"Jack!" She opened her eyes. "Dick! I hope you haven't been quarreling!"

He smiled at her anxious face, though somewhat grimly. "My dear, I don't quarrel with people like Jack. I came upon him at the school. I don't know why he was hanging round there. He certainly didn't mean me to catch him. But as I did so, I took the opportunity for a straight talk — with the result that he leaves this place tomorrow — for good."

"My dear Dick! What will the squire say?"

"I can manage the squire," said Dick briefly.

She smiled and passed on. "And Jack? What will he do?"

"I don't know and I don't care. He's the sort of animal to land on his feet whichever way he falls. Anyhow, he's going, and I never want to speak or hear of him again." Dick's thin lips came together in a hard, compelling line.

"Are you never going to forgive him?" said Juliet.

His eyes had a stony glitter. "It's hardly a matter for forgiveness," he said. "When anyone has done you an irreparable injury the only thing left is to try and forget it and the person responsible for it as quickly as possible. I don't thirst for his blood or anything of that kind. I simply want to be rid of him — and to wipe all memory of him out of my life."

"Do you always want to do that with the people who injure you?" said Juliet.

He looked at her, caught by something in her tone. "Yes, I think so. Why?"

"Oh, never mind why!" she said, with a faint laugh that sounded oddly passionate. "I just want to find out what sort of man you are, that's all."

She would have turned away from him with the words, but he held her with a certain dominance. "No, Juliet! Wait! Tell me — isn't it reasonable to want to get free of anyone who wrongs you — to shake him off, kick him off if necessary, — anyway, to have done with him?"

"I haven't said it was unreasonable," she said, but she was trembling as she spoke and her face was averted.

"Look at me!" he said. "What? Am I such a monster as all that? Juliet,

— my dear, don't be silly! What are you afraid of? Surely not of me!"

She turned her face to him with a quivering smile. "No! I won't be silly, Dick," she said. "I'll try to take you as I find you and — make the best of you. But, to be quite honest, I am rather afraid of the hard side of you. It is so very uncompromising. If I ever come up against it — I believe I shall run away!"

"Not you!" he said, trying to look into the soft, down-cast eyes. "Or if you do you'll come back again by the next train to see how I am bearing up. I've got you, Juliet!" He lifted her hand, displaying it exultantly, closely clasped in his. "And what I have — I hold!"

"How clever of you!" said Juliet, and with a swift lithe movement freed herself.

His arms went round her in a flash. "I'll make you pay for that!" he vowed. "How dare you, Juliet? How dare you?"

She resisted him for a second, or two, holding him from her, half-mocking, half in earnest. Then, as his hold tightened, encompassing her, she submitted with a low laugh, yielding herself afresh to him under the old apple tree, in full and throbbing surrender to his love.

But when at last his hold relaxed, when he had made her pay, she took his hand and pressed a deep, deep kiss into his palm. "That is — a free gift, Dicky," she said. "And it is worth more than all the having and holding in the world."

Chapter II

FRIENDSHIP

*I*t was on a misty evening of autumn that Vera Fielding entered her husband's house once more like a bride returning from her wedding-trip. There was something of the petted air of a bride about her as she came in on the squire's arm throwing her greetings right and left to the assembled servants, and certainly there was in her eyes more of the shining happiness of a bride than they had ever held before. Her face was flushed with a pretty eagerness, and the petulant lines about her mouth were far less apparent than of old. Her laugh had a gay spontaneous ring, and though her voice still had a slightly arrogant inflection it was not without softer notes when she addressed the squire.

"I feel as if we had been away for years and years," she said to him, as they stood together before the blazing fire in the drawing room. "Isn't it strange, Edward? Only three months in reality, and such a difference!"

He was lifting the heavy coat from her shoulders, but she turned with it impulsively and caught him round the neck.

"My dear!" he said, and clasped her coat and all.

"It is going to last, isn't it?" she said, her breath coming quickly. "You promised — you promised — to love me just as much if I got well!"

He kissed her with reassuring tenderness. "Yes, my girl, yes! It's going to last all right. We're going to make a happy home of it, you and I."

She clung to him for a few seconds, then broke away with a little laugh. "You'll have to hunt this winter, Edward. You're getting stout."

"And shoot too," said the squire. "There promises to be plenty of birds. We'd better have a party if you feel up to it."

She looked at him with kindling eyes. "I'm up to anything. I should love it. Do you think Lord Saltash would come?"

"We must certainly ask him," said, the squire. "But you're not to work too hard, mind! That's an order. Let people look after themselves'"

"I'll get Juliet to come and help me," she said. "She must have lots of spare time. By the way, they'll be here to dine in another hour. I must go and dress."

"Have some tea first!" he said. "They won't mind waiting."

She slipped her hand through his arm. "Come and have it upstairs! It really is late. We'll have a cozy time together afterwards — when they're gone."

He smiled upon her indulgently. They had grown very near to one another during their cruise in the *Night Moth.* To him also their homecoming held something of bridal gladness. He had never seen her so glowing with happiness before. The love that shone in her eyes whenever they met his own stirred him to the depths. He had never deemed her capable of such affection in the old days. It had changed his whole world.

They went upstairs together closely linked. They entered Vera's room from which she imperiously dismissed her maid. They sat down on the couch beside the fire.

"Do you remember that awful day when we quarreled about Dick Green?" said Vera suddenly.

He kept her hand in his. "Don't!" he said. "Don't remind me of it!"

Her laugh had in it a thrill that was like a caress. "Wasn't I a pig, Edward? And weren't you a tyrant? I haven't seen you in one of your royal rages since. I always rather admired them, you know."

"I know you hated me," he said, "and I'm not surprised."

She made a face at him. "Silly! I didn't. I thought you the finest monster I had ever seen. So you were — quite magnificent." She put up a hand and stroked his iron-grey hair. "Well, we shan't quarrel about young Green anymore," she said.

"I wonder," said the squire, not looking at her.

"I don't." She spoke with confidence. "I'm going to be tremendously nice to him — not for Juliet's sake — for yours."

"Thank you, my dear," he said, with an odd humility of utterance that came strangely from him. "I shall appreciate your kindness. As you know — I am very fond of Dick."

"You were going to tell me why once," she said.

He took her hand and held it for a moment. "I will tell you tonight," he said.

The maid came in again with a tea-tray, and they had no further intimate talk. The squire became restless and walked about the room while he drank his cup. When he had finished, he went away to his own, and Vera was left to dress.

Her maid was still putting the final touches when there came a low knock at the door. She turned sharply from her mirror.

"Is that you, Juliet? Come in! Come in!"

Quietly the door opened, and Juliet entered.

"My dear!" said Vera, and met her impulsively in the middle of the room.

"I had to come up," Juliet said. "I hope you don't mind, but neither Dick nor I can manage to feel like ordinary guests in this house."

She was smiling as she spoke. The white scarf was thrown back from her hair. The gracious womanliness of her struck Vera afresh with its charm.

She held her and looked at her. "My dear Juliet, it does me good to see you. How is Dick? And how is Columbus?"

"They are both downstairs," Juliet said, "and one is working too hard and the other not hard enough. I had to bring dear Christopher. You don't mind?"

"Of course not, my dear. I would have sent him a special invitation if I had thought. Come and take off your coat! We got in rather late or I should have been downstairs to receive you."

"Tell me how you are!" Juliet said. "I don't believe I have ever seen you looking so well."

"I haven't felt so well for years," Vera declared. "But I have promised Edward all the same to go up to town and see his pet doctor and make sure that the cure is complete. Personally I am quite sure. But Edward is such a dear old fusser. He won't be satisfied with appearances."

She laughed on an indulgent note, and Juliet smiled in sympathy.

"Well, you've given him good cause for that, haven't you? And you enjoyed the cruise? I am so glad you had good weather."

"It was gorgeous," said Vera. "I must write and tell Lord Saltash. He has given me the time of my life. Have you seen anything of him by the way?"

"Only once," said Juliet. "He came over to congratulate us. But that is some time ago. He may be at the other end of the world by this time."

"No, I think not," Vera said. "I believe he is in England. Was he — at all upset by your marriage, Juliet?"

Juliet laughed a little. "Oh, not in the least. He keeps his heart in a very air-tight compartment I assure you. I have never had the faintest glimpse of it."

"But you are fond of him," said Vera shrewdly.

"Oh yes, quite fond of him," Juliet's eyes had a kindly softness. "I have never yet met the woman who wasn't fond of Charles Rex," she said.

"Does — your husband like him?" asked Vera.

Juliet shook her head quizzically. "No. Husbands don't as a rule."

"Something of a poacher?" questioned Vera.

"Oh, not really. Not since he grew up. I believe he was very giddy in his youth, and then a girl he really cared for disappointed him. So the story runs. I can't vouch for the truth of it, or even whether he ever seriously cared for her. But he has certainly never been in earnest since."

"What about Lady Joanna Farringmore?" said Vera suddenly.

Juliet was standing before the fire. She bent slightly, the warm glow softly tingling her white neck. "I should have thought that old fable might have died a natural death by this time," she said.

Vera gave her a sharp look. There was not actual distaste in Juliet's tone, yet in some fashion it conveyed the impression that the subject was one which she had no desire to discuss.

Vera abandoned it forthwith. "Suppose we go downstairs," she said.

They went down to find Dick and Columbus patiently waiting in the hall. Vera's greeting was brief but not lacking in warmth. The thought of Juliet married to the schoolmaster had ceased to provoke her indignation. She even admitted to herself that in different surroundings Dick might have proved himself to possess a certain attraction. She believed he was clever in an intellectual sense, and she believed it was by this quality that he had captivated Juliet. The fiery force of the man, his almost fierce enthusiasms, she had never even seen.

But she was immediately aware of a subtle and secret link between the two as they all met together in the genial glow of the fire. Dick's eyes that flashed for a second to Juliet and instantly left her, told her very clearly that no words were needed to establish communion between them. They were in close sympathy.

She gave Dick a warmer welcome than she had ever extended to him before, and found in the instant response of his smile some reason for wonder at her previous dislike. Perhaps contact with Juliet had helped to banish the satire to which in the old days she had so strongly objected. Or perhaps — but this possibility did not occur to her — he sensed a cordiality in the atmosphere which had never been present before.

When the squire came down they were all chatting amicably round the fire, and he smiled swift approval upon his wife ere he turned to greet his guests.

"Hullo, Dick!" he said, as their hands met. "Still running the same old show?"

"For the present, sir," said Dick.

They had not met since the occasion of Dick's and Juliet's marriage when the squire had come over immediately before the sailing of the *Night Moth* to be present, and to give her away. He had been very kind to them both during the brief hour that he had spent with them, and the memory of it still lingered warmly in Juliet's heart. She had grown very fond of the squire.

There were no awkward moments during that dinner which was more like a family gathering than Juliet had thought possible. The change in Vera amazed her. She was like a traveler who after long and weary journeying in shady places had come suddenly into bright sunshine. And she was younger, more ardent, more alive, than Juliet had ever seen her.

The same change was visible, though not so noticeable, in the squire. He too had come into the sun, but he trod more warily as one who — though content with the present — was by no means certain that the fair weather would last. His manner to his wife displayed a charming blend of tenderness and self-restraint; yet in some fashion he held his own with her, and once, meeting Juliet's eyes, he smiled in a way that reminded her of the day on which she had dared to give him advice as to the best means of securing happiness.

Dick was apparently in good spirits that night, and he was plainly at his ease. Having taken his cue from his hostess, he devoted himself in a large measure to her entertainment, and all went smoothly between them. When she and Juliet left the table she gave him a smiling invitation to come and play to them.

"I haven't brought the old banjo," he said, "but I'll make my wife sing. She is going to help me this winter at the Club concerts."

"Brave Juliet!" said Vera, as she went out. "I wouldn't face that crowd of roughs for a king's ransom."

"She has nothing to be afraid of," said Dick with quick confidence. "I wouldn't let her do it if there were any danger."

"They seem to be in an ugly mood just now," said the squire.

"Yes, I know." Dick turned back to him, closing the door. "But, taken the right way, they are still manageable. There is just a chance that we may keep them in hand if that fellow Ivor Yardley can be induced to see reason. The rest of the Wilchester crew don't care a damn, but he has more brains. I'm counting on him."

"How are you going to get hold of him?" questioned Fielding.

"I suppose I must go up to town some week-end. I haven't told Juliet yet. Unlike the average woman, she seems to have a holy hatred of London and all its ways. So I presume she will stay behind."

"Perhaps we could get him down here," suggested the squire.

Dick gave him a swift look. "I've thought of that," he said.

"Well?" said Fielding.

Dick hesitated for a moment. "I'm not sure that I want him," he said. "He and Saltash are friends for one thing. And there are besides — various reasons."

"You don't like Saltash?" said the squire.

Dick laughed a little. "I don't hate him — though I feel as if I ought to. He's a queer fish. I don't trust him."

"You're jealous!" said Fielding.

Dick nodded. "Very likely. He has an uncanny attraction for women. I wanted to kick him the last time we met."

"And what did Juliet say?"

"Oh, Juliet read me a lecture and told me I wasn't to. But I think the less we see of each other the better — if I am to keep on my best behavior, that is."

"It's a good thing someone can manage you," remarked Fielding. "Juliet is a wonderful peacemaker. But even she couldn't keep you from coming to loggerheads with Jack apparently. What was that fight about?"

Dirk's brows contracted. "It wasn't a fight, sir," he said shortly. "I've never fought Jack in my life. He did an infernal thing, and I made him quit, that's all."

"What did he do?" asked the squire. Then as Dick made a gesture of refusal: "Damn it, man, he was in my employment anyway! I've a right to know why he cleared out."

Dick pushed back his chair abruptly and rose. He turned his back on the squire while he poked the blazing logs with his foot. Then: "Yes, you've a perfect right to know," he said, speaking jerkily, his head bent. "And of course I always meant to tell you. It won't appeal to you in the least. But Juliet understands — at least in part. He was responsible for — my boy's death. That's why I made him go."

It was the first time that he had voluntarily spoken of Robin since the day that he and Juliet had followed him to his grave. He brought out the words now with tremendous effort, and having spoken he ceased to kick at the fire and became absolutely still.

The squire sat at the table, staring at him. For some seconds the silence continued, then irritably he broke it.

"Well? Go on, man! That isn't the whole of the story. What do you mean by — responsible? He didn't shove him over the cliff, I suppose?"

"No," Dick said. "He didn't do that. I almost wish he had. It would have been somehow — more endurable."

Again he became silent, and suddenly to the squire sitting frowning at the table there came a flash of intuition that told him he could not continue. He got up sharply, went to Dick, still frowning, and laid an impulsive arm across his shoulders.

"I'm sorry, my lad," he said.

Dick made a slight movement as if the caress were not wholly welcome, but after a moment he reached up and grasped the squire's hand.

"It hit me pretty hard," he said in a low voice, not lifting his hand. "Juliet just made it bearable. I shall get over it, of course. But — I never want to see Jack again."

Again for a space he stopped, then with a sudden fierce impatience jerked on.

"You may remember saying to me once — no; a hundred times over — that I should never get anywhere so long as I kept my boy with me — never find success — or happiness — never marry — all that sort of rot. It was rot. I always knew it was. I've proved it. She would have come to me in any case. And as for success — it doesn't depend on things of that sort. I've proved that too. But he — Jack — got hold of the same infernal parrot-cry. Oh, I'm sorry, sir," he glanced upwards for a second with working lips. "I can't dress this up in polite language. Jack said to my boy Robin what you had said to me. And he — believed it — and so — made an end."

He drew his breath hard between his teeth and straightened himself, putting Fielding's arm quietly from his.

"Good God!" said Fielding. "But the boy was mad! He never was normal. You can't say —"

"Oh, no, sir." With grim bitterness Dick interrupted. "He just took the shortest way out, that's all. He wasn't mad."

"Committed suicide!" ejaculated the squire.

Dick's hands were clenched. "Do you call it that," he said, "when a man lays down his life for his friends?"

He turned away with the words as if he could endure no more, and walked to the end of the room.

Fielding stood and watched him dumbly, more moved than he cared to show. At length, as Dick remained standing before a bookcase in heavy silence, he spoke, his tone an odd mixture of peremptoriness and persuasion.

"Dick!"

Dick jerked his head without turning or speaking.

"Are you blaming me for this?" the squire asked.

Dick turned. His face was pale, his eyes fiercely bright. "You, sir! Do you think I'd have sat at your table if I did?"

"I don't know," the squire said somberly. "You're fond of telling me I have no claim on you, but I have — for all that. There is a bond between us that you can't get away from, however hard you try. You think I can't understand your feelings in this matter, that I'm too sordid in my views to realize how hard you've been hit. You think I'm only pleased to know that you're free from your burden, at last, eh, Dick, and that your trouble doesn't count with me? Think I've never had any of my own perhaps?"

He spoke with a half-smile, but there was that in his voice that made Dick come swiftly back to him down the long room; nor did he pause when he reached him. His hand went through the squire's arm and gripped it hard.

"I'm — awfully sorry, sir," he said. "If you understand — you'll forgive me."

"I do understand, Dick," the squire said with great kindness. "I know I've been hard on you about that poor boy. I'm infernally sorry for the whole wretched business. But — as you say — you'll get over it. You've got Juliet."

"Yes, thank God!" Dick said. "I don't know how I should endure life without her. She's all I have."

The squire's face contracted a little. "No one else, Dick?" he said.

Dick glanced up. "And you, sir," he amended with a smile. "I'm afraid I'm rather apt to take you for granted. I suppose that's the bond you spoke of. I haven't — you know I haven't — the least desire to get away from it."

"Thank you," Fielding said, and stifled a sigh. "Life has been pretty damnable to us both, Dick. We might have been — we ought to have been — much more to each other."

"There's no tie more enduring than friendship," said Dick quickly. "You and I are friends — always will be."

Fielding's eyes had a misty look. "The best of friends, Dick lad," he said. "But will — friendship — give me the right to offer you help without putting up your pride? I don't want to order your life for you, but you can't go on with this village *domino* business much longer. You were made for better things."

"Oh, that!" Dick said, and laughed. "Yes, I'm going to chuck that — but not just at once. Listen, sir! I have a reason. I'll tell you what it is, but not now, not yet. As to accepting help from you, I'd do that tomorrow if I needed it, but I don't. I've no pride left where you are concerned. You're much too good to me and I'm much too grateful. Is that quite clear?"

He gave the squire a straight and very friendly look, then wheeled round swiftly at the opening of the door.

They were standing side by side as Vera threw it impatiently wide. She stood a second on the threshold staring at them. Then: "Are you never coming in?" she said. "I thought — I thought —" she stammered suddenly and turned white. "Edward!" she said, and went back a step as if something had frightened her.

Dick instantly went forward to her. "Yes, Mrs. Fielding. We're coming now," he said. "Awfully sorry to have kept you waiting. We've had things to talk about, but we've just about done. You're coming, aren't you, sir? Take my arm, I say! You look tired."

He offered and she accepted almost instinctively. Her hand trembled on his arm as they left the room, and he suddenly and very impulsively laid his own upon it.

It was a protective impulse that moved him, but a moment later he adjusted the position by asking a favor of her — for the first time in the whole of their acquaintance.

"Mrs. Fielding, please, after today — give me the privilege of numbering myself among your friends!"

She looked at him oddly, seeking to cover her agitation with a quivering assumption of her old arrogance. But something in his face deterred her. It was not this man's way to solicit favors, and somehow, since he had humbled himself to ask, she had it not in her to refuse.

"Very well, Dick," she said, faintly smiling. "I grant you that."

"Thank you," he said, and gently released her hand.

It was the swiftest and one of the most complete victories of his life.

Chapter III

CONFESSION

*I*t was nearly two hours later that Vera sitting alone before her fire turned with a slight start at the sound of her husband's step in the room beyond. She was wearing a pale silk dressing gown and her hair hung in a single plait over her shoulder, giving her a curiously girlish look. The slimness of her figure as she leaned among the cushions accentuated the fragility which her recent illness had stamped upon her. Her eyes were ringed with purple, and they had a startled expression that the sound of the squire's step served to intensify. At the soft turning of the handle she made a movement that was almost of shrinking. And when he entered she looked up at him with a small pinched smile from which all pleasure was wholly absent.

He was still in evening dress, and the subdued light falling upon him gave him the look of a man still scarcely past his prime. He stood for a moment, erect and handsome, before he quietly closed the door behind him and moved forward.

"Still up?" he said.

Again at his approach she made a more pronounced movement of shrinking. "But, I've been waiting for you," she said rather hopelessly.

He came to her, stood looking down at her, the old bitter frown struggling with a more kindly expression on his face. He was obviously waiting for something with no pleasant sense of anticipation.

But Vera did not speak. She only sat drawn together, her fingers locked and her eyes downcast. She was using her utmost strength to keep herself in hand.

"Well?" he said at length, a faint ring of irritation in his voice, "Have you nothing to say to me now I have come?"

Her lips quivered a little. "I don't think — there is anything to be said," she said. "I knew — I felt — it was too good to last."

"It's over then, is it?" he said, the bitterness gaining the upper hand because of the misery at his heart. "The indiscretions of my youth have placed me finally beyond the pale. Is that it?"

She gripped her hands together a little more tightly. "I think you have been — you are — rather cruel," she said, her voice very low. "If you had only — told me!"

He made a gesture of exasperation. "My dear girl, for heaven's sake, look at the thing fairly if you can! How long have I known you well enough to let you into my secrets? How long have you been up to hearing them? I meant to tell you — as you know. I've been on the verge of it more than once. It wasn't cowardice that held me back. It was consideration for you."

She glanced at him momentarily. "I see," she said in that small quivering voice of hers that told so little of the wild tumult within her.

"Well?" he said harshly. "And that is my condemnation, is it? Henceforth I am to be thrust outside — a sinner beyond redemption. Is that it?"

Her eyelids fluttered nervously, but she did not raise them again. She leaned instead towards the fire. Her shoulders were bent. She looked crushed, as if her vitality were gone, and yet so slender, so young, in her thin wrap. He clinched his hands with a sharp intake of the breath, and his frown deepened.

"So you won't speak to me?" he said. "It's beyond words, is it? It's to be an insurmountable obstacle to happiness for the rest of our lives? We go back to the old damnable existence we've led for so long! Or perhaps —" his voice hardened — "perhaps you think we should be better apart? Perhaps you would prefer to leave me?"

She flinched at that — flinched as if he had struck her — and then suddenly she lifted her white face to his, showing him such an anguish of suffering as he had not suspected.

"Oh, Edward," she said, "why did this have to happen? We were so happy before."

That pierced him — the utter desolation of her — the pain that was too deep for reproach. He bent to her, all the bitterness gone from his face.

"My dear," he said in a voice that shook, "can't you see how I loathe myself — for hurting you — like this?"

And then suddenly — so suddenly that neither knew exactly how it happened — they were linked together. She was clinging to him with a rush of piteous tears, and he was kneeling beside her, holding her fast pressed against his heart, murmuring over her brokenly, passionately, such words of tenderness as she had never heard from him before. When in the end she lifted her face to kiss him, it was wet with tears other than her own, and somehow that fact did more to ease her own distress than any consolation he could find to offer.

She slipped her arm about his neck and pressed her cheek to his. "I'm thankful I know," she told him tremulously. "Oh, Edward darling, don't — don't keep anything from me ever again! If I'd only known sooner, things might have been so different. I feel as if I have never known you till now."

"Have you forgiven me?" he said, his grey head bent.

She turned her lips again to his. "My dear, of course — of course!" And in a lower voice, "Will you — tell me about her? Did she mean very much to you?"

His arm tightened about her. "My darling, it's nearly twenty-three years ago that she died. Yes, I loved her. But I've never wanted her back. Her life was such an inferno." He paused a moment, then as she was silent went on more steadily. "She was eighteen and I was twenty-two when it began. I was home for a summer vacation, and she had just come to help her aunt as infant teacher at the school. All the men were wild about her, but she had no use for any of 'em till I come along. We met along the shore or on the cliffs. We met constantly. We loved each other like mad. It got beyond all reason — all restraint. We didn't look ahead, either of us. We were young, and it was so infernally sweet. I'm not offering any excuse — only telling you the simple truth. You won't understand of course."

She pressed closer to him. "Why shouldn't I understand?"

He leaned his head against her. "God bless you, my dear! You're very good to me — far better than I deserve. I was a blackguard, I know. But I never meant to let her down. That was almost as much her doing as mine — poor little soul! We were found out at last, and there was a fearful row with my people. I wanted to take her away then and there, and marry her. But she wouldn't hear of it — neither would her aunt — a hard, proud woman! I didn't know then — no one knew — that she was expecting a child, or I'd have defied 'em all. Instead, she urged and entreated me to go away for a few weeks — give her time to think, she said. I hoped even then that she would give in and come to me. But the next thing I knew, she was married to a brute called Green — skipper of a filthy little cargo-steamer, who had been after her for some time. She went with him on one or two short voyages. Heaven knows what she endured in that time. Then the baby was born — Dick. They called him a seven-months child. But I knew — I guessed at once. One day I met her — told her so. I saw then — in part — what her life was like. She was terrified — said Green would kill her if he ever found out. The man was a great hulking bully — a drunkard perpetually on shore. He used to beat her as it was. She implored me not to come up against him, and — for her sake alone — I never did. Then — it was nearly a year after — he went off on a voyage and didn't come back. The boat was reported lost with all hands. I think everyone rejoiced so far as he was concerned. She went back to work at the school, supporting herself and the child. I never induced her to accept any help from me, but gradually, as the years went on and my uncle died and I became my own master, I got into the position of intimate friend. I was allowed to interfere a bit in Dick's destinies. But for a long, long while she permitted no more than that. I don't know exactly what made me stick to her. I used to go away, but I always came back. I couldn't give her up. And at last — twelve years after Green's disappearance — I won her over. She promised to marry me. The very day afterwards, that scoundrel Green came back! And her martyrdom began again."

"Oh, Edward, my dear!" Vera's hand went up to his face, stroking, caressing. The suppressed misery of his voice was almost more than she could bear. "How you suffered!" she whispered.

He was silent for a moment or two, controlling himself. "It's over now," he said then. "Thank God, it's a long time over! She died — less than a year after — when Jack and Robin were born. Her husband fell over the cliff on the same night in a fit of drunkenness and was killed. That's all the story. You know the rest. I'm sorry — I'm very sorry — I hadn't the decency to tell you before we married."

"You — needn't be sorry, dear," she said very gently.

He looked at her. "Do you mean that, Vera? Do you mean it makes no difference to you?"

She met his eyes with a shining tenderness in her own that gave her a womanliness which he had never seen in her before. "No," she said, "I don't mean that. I mean that I'm glad nothing happened to — to prevent my marrying you. I mean — that I love you ten times more for telling me now."

He gathered her impulsively close in his arms, kissing her with lips that trembled. "My own girl! My own generous wife! I'll make up to you," he vowed. "I'll give you such love as you've never dreamed of. I've been a brute to you often — often. But that's over. I'll make you happy now — if it kills me!"

She laughed softly, with a quivering exultation, between his kisses. "That wouldn't make me happy in the least. And I don't think you will find it so hard as that either. You've begun already — quite nicely. Now that we understand each other, we can never make really serious mistakes again."

Thereafter, they sat and talked in the firelight for a long time, closely, intimately, as friends united after a long separation. And in that talk the last barrier between them crumbled away, and a bond that was very sacred took its place.

In the end the striking of the clock above them awoke Vera to the lateness of the hour. "My dear Edward, it's tomorrow morning already! Wouldn't it be a good idea to go to bed?"

"Of course," he said. "You must be half dead. Thoughtless brute that I am!" He let her go out of his arms at last, but in a moment paused, looking at her with an odd wistfulness. "You're sure you've forgiven me? Sure you won't think it over and find you've made a mistake?"

Her hands were on his shoulders. Her eyes looked straight into his. "I am quite sure," she said.

He began to smile. "What makes you so generous, I wonder? I never thought you had it in you."

She leaned towards him, a great glow on her face which made her wonderful in his sight. "Oh, my dear," she said, "I never had before. But I can afford to be generous now. What does the past matter when I know that the present and the future are all my own?"

His smile passed. He met her look steadfastly. "As long as I live," he said, "so shall it be."

And the kiss that passed between them was as the sealing of a vow.

Chapter IV
COUNSEL

Juliet and Columbus sat in a sheltered nook on the shore and gazed thoughtfully out to sea. It was a warm morning after a night of tempest, and the beach was strewn with seaweed after an unusually high tide.

Columbus sat with a puckered brow. In his heart he wanted to be pottering about among these ocean treasures which had a peculiar fascination for his doggy soul. But a greater call was upon him, keeping him where he was. Though she had not uttered one word to detain him, he had a strong conviction that his mistress wanted him, and so, stolidly, he remained beside her, his sharp little eyes flashing to and fro, sometimes watching the great waves riding in, sometimes following the curving flight of a sea-gull, sometimes fixed in immensely dignified contemplation upon the quivering tip of his nose. His nostrils worked perpetually. The air was teeming with interesting scents; but not one of them could lure him from his mistress's side while he sensed her need of him. His body might be fat and bulging, but his spirit was a thing of keen perceptions and ardent, burning devotion, capable of denying every impulse save the love that was its mainspring.

Juliet was certainly very thoughtful that day. She also was watching the waves, but the wide brow was slightly drawn and the grey eyes were not so serene as usual. She had the look of one wrestling with a difficult problem. The roar of the sea was all about her, blotting out every other sound, even the calling of the gulls. Her arm encircled Columbus who was pressed solicitously close to her side. They had been sitting so, almost without moving, for over half-an-hour.

Suddenly Columbus turned his head sharply, and a growl, swelled through him. Juliet looked round, and in a moment she had started to her feet. A man's figure, lithe and spare, with something of a monkey's agility of movement, was coming to her over the stones. They met in a shelving hollow of shingle that had been washed by the sea.

"Oh, Charles!" she said impulsively. "It is good of you to come!"

He glanced around him as he clasped her hand, his ugly face brimming with mischief. "It is rather — considering the risk I run. I trust your irascible husband is well out of the way?"

She laughed, though not very heartily. "Yes, he has gone to town. I didn't want him to. I wish I had stopped him."

He looked at her shrewdly. "You've got an attack of nerves," he observed.

She still sought to smile — though the attempt was a poor one. "To be quite honest — I am rather frightened."

"Frightened!" He pushed a sudden arm around her, looking comical and tender in the same moment. "And so you sent for me! Then it's Ho for the *Night Moth*, and when shall we start?"

She gave him a small push as half-hearted as her laugh had been. "Don't talk rubbish, please, Charles — if you don't mind! I don't see myself going on the *Night Moth* with the sea like that; do you?"

"Depends," he said quizzically. "You might be persuaded if the devil were behind you."

"What! In your company!" Her laugh was more normal this time; she gave his arm a kindly touch and put it from her.

"But I'm as meek as a lamb," protested Saltash.

She met his look with friendly eyes. "Yes, I know — a lamb in wolf's clothing — rather a frisky lamb, Charles, but comparatively harmless. If I hadn't realized that — I shouldn't have asked you to come."

"I like your qualification," he said. "With whom do I compare thus favorably? The redoubtable Dick?"

The color came swiftly into her face and he laughed, derisively but not unkindly.

"It's a new thing for me — this sort of job. Are you sure my lamblike qualities will carry me through? Do you know, dear, I've never seen you look so amazing sweet in all my life before? I never knew you could bloom like this. It's positively dangerous."

He regarded her critically, his head on one side, an ardor half-mocking, half-genuine, in his eyes.

Juliet uttered a sigh. "I feel a careworn old hag," she said. "My own fault of course. Things are in a nice muddle, and I don't know which way to turn."

"One slip from the path of rectitude!" mocked Saltash. "Alas, how fatal this may prove!"

She looked away from him. "Do you always jeer at your friends when they are in trouble?" she said somewhat wearily.

"Always," said Saltash promptly. "It helps 'em to find their feet — like lighting the fire when the chimney-sweep's boy got stuck in the chimney. It's a priceless remedy, my *Juliette*. Nothing like it."

"I shall begin to hate you directly," remarked Juliet with her wan smile.

He laughed, not without complacence. "Do you good to try. You won't succeed. No one ever does. I gather the main trouble is that Dick has gone to town when you didn't want him to. Husbands are like that sometimes, you know. Are you afraid he won't come back — or that he will?"

"He will come back — today," she said. "You know — or perhaps you don't know — there is going to be a concert tonight for the miners. He is going to talk to them afterwards. He has gone up today to see — Ivor Yardley."

"What ho!" said Saltash. "This is interesting. And what does he hope to get out of him?"

"I don't know," she said. "I had no idea who he was going to see till yesterday evening. Mr. Ashcott came in and they were talking, and the name came out. I am not sure that he wanted me to know — though I don't know why I think so."

"And so you sent me an S.O.S.!" said Saltash. "I am indeed honored!"

She turned towards him very winningly, very appealingly. "Charles Rex, I sent for you because I want a friend — so very badly. My happiness is in the balance. Don't you understand?"

Her deep voice throbbed with feeling. He stretched out a hand to her with a quick, responsive gesture that somehow belied the imp of mischief in his eyes. *"Bien, ma Juliette!* I am here!" he said.

"Thank you," she said very earnestly. "I knew I could count on you — that you would not withdraw your protection when once you had offered it."

"Would you like my advice as well?" he questioned.

She met his quizzing look with her frank eyes. "What is your advice?" she said.

He held her hand in his. "You haven't forgotten, have you, the sole condition on which I extended my protection to you? No. I thought not. We won't discuss it. The time is not yet ripe. And, as you say, the *Night Moth* in this weather, though safe, might not be a very comfortable abiding-place. But — don't forget she is quite safe, my *Juliette!* I should like you to remember that."

He spoke with a strange emphasis that must in some fashion have conveyed more than his actual words, for quite suddenly her throat worked with a sharp spasm of emotion. She put up her hand instinctively to hide it.

"Thank you," she said. "If I need — a city of refuge — I shall know which way to turn. Now for your advice!"

"My advice!" He was looking at her with those odd, unstable eyes of his that ever barred the way to his inner being. "It depends a little on the condition of your heart — that. When it comes to this in an obstacle race, there are three courses open to you. Either you refuse the jump and drop out — which is usually the safest thing to do. Or you take the thing at full gallop and clear it before you know where you are. Or you go at it with a weak heart and come to grief. I don't advise the last anyway. It's so futile — as well as being beastly humiliating."

She smiled at him. "Thank you, Charles! A very illuminating parable! Well, I don't contemplate the first — as you know. I must have a try at the second. And if I smash, — it's horribly difficult, you know — I may smash —" Sudden anguish looked at him out of her eyes, and a hard shiver went through her as she turned away. "Oh, Charles!" she said. "Why did I ever come to this place?"

He made a frightful grimace that was somehow sympathetic and

shrugged his shoulders. "If you smash, my dearly-beloved, your faithful
comrade will have the priceless privilege of picking up the pieces. Why
you came here is another matter. I have sometimes dared to wonder if
the proximity of my poor castle — No? Not that? Ah, well then, it must
be that our destinies are guided by the same star. To my mind that is an
even more thrilling reflection than the other. Think of it, my *Juliette*,
you and I — helplessly kicking like flies in the cream-jug — being drawn
to one another, irresistibly and in spite of ourselves, even leaving some
of our legs behind us in the desperate struggle to be calm and reasonable
and quite — quite moral! And then a sudden violent storm in the
cream-jug, and we are flung into each other's unwilling arms where we
cling for safety till the crack of doom when all the milk is spilt! It's no
use fighting the stars, you know. It really isn't. The only rational course
is to make the stars fight for you."

He peered round at her to see how she was taking his foolery; and in
a moment impulsively she wheeled back, the distress banished from her
face, the old steadfast courage in its place.

"Oh, Charles, thou king of clowns!" she said. "What a weird com-
forter you are!"

"King of philosophers you mean!" he retorted. "It's taken me a long
while to achieve my wisdom. I don't often throw my pearls about in
this reckless fashion."

She laughed. "How dare you say that to me? But I suppose I ought
to be humbly grateful. I am as a matter of fact intensely so."

"Oh, no!" he said. "Not that — from you!"

His eyes dwelt upon her with a sort of humorous tenderness; she met
them without embarrassment. "You've done me good, Charles," she said.
"Somehow I knew you would — knew I could count on you. You will
go on standing by?"

He executed a deep bow, his hand upon his heart. *"Maintenant et
toujours, ma Juliette!"* he assured her gallantly. "But don't forget the moral
of my parable! When you jump — jump high!"

She nodded thoughtfully. "No, I shan't forget. You're a good friend,
Charles Rex."

"I may be," said Saltash enigmatically.

Chapter V

THE THUNDERBOLT

*J*uliet lunched at the Court in Dick's absence. They thought her somewhat graver and quieter than usual, but there was a gentle aloofness about her that checked all intimate enquiry.

"You are not feeling anxious about the miners?" Vera asked her once.

To which Juliet replied, "Oh no! Not in the least. Dick has such a wonderful influence over the men. They would never do any brawling with him there."

"He has no business to drag you into it all the same," said the squire.

She looked at him, faintly smiling. "Do you imagine for one moment that I would stay behind? Besides, there is really no danger. His only fear is possible friction between the miners and the fishermen. They never have loved each other, and in their present mood it wouldn't take much to set the miners alight."

"I'd let 'em burn!" said the squire.

"They have some cause for grievance," she urged. "At least Dick thinks so."

"Well, and who hasn't, I should like to know?" he returned with warmth. "How many people are there in the world who don't feel that if they had their rights they'd be a good deal better off in one respect or another than they are? But there's no sense in trying to stop the world going round on that account. That's always the way with these miner chaps. What's the rest of the community matter so long as they get all they want? They're not sportsmen. They hit below the belt every time."

"That's just it," Juliet said. "Dick is trying to teach them to be sportsmen."

"Oh, Dick!" said the squire. "He'd reform the world if he could. But he's wasting his time. They won't be satisfied till they've had their fling. Lord Wilchester is a wise man to keep out of the way till it's over."

"I'm afraid I don't agree with you there," Juliet said, flushing a little. "He might at least hear what they have to say. But they can't get hold of him. He is abroad."

"But Yardley is left," said the squire. "I suppose he has power to act."

"Perhaps," she said, the moment's animation passing. "But it is Wilchester's business — not his. He shirks his duty."

"I notice you never have a good word for any of the Farringmore family," said the squire quizzically.

She shook her head. "They are all so selfish. It's the family failing, I'm afraid."

"You don't share it anyhow," said Vera.

"Ah! You don't know me," said Juliet.

They went for a long motor-ride when the meal was over, but at the end of it, it seemed to Vera that they had talked solely of her affairs throughout. She knew Juliet's quiet reticence of old and made no attempt to pierce it. But, thinking it over later, it seemed to her that there was something more than her usual reserve behind it, and a vague sense of uneasiness awoke within her. She wondered if Juliet were happy.

They had tea on their return, but Juliet would not stay any later. She must be back, she said, to meet Dick and be sure that the supper was ready in good time. So, regretfully, still with that inexplicable feeling of doubt upon her, Vera let her go.

Just at the last she detained her for a moment to say with an effort that was plainly no light one, "Juliet, don't forget I am here if — if you ever need a friend!"

And then Juliet surprised her by a sudden, close embrace and a low-spoken, "I shall never forget you — or your goodness to me."

But a second later she was gone, and Vera was left to wonder.

As for Juliet, she hastened away as one in a fever to escape, yet before she reached the end of the avenue her feet moved as if weighted with chains.

A mist was creeping up from the sea and through it there came the long call of a distant siren. The waves were no longer roaring along the shore. The sound of them came muffled and vague, and she knew that the storm had gone down.

There was something very desolate in that atmosphere of dimmed sight and muted sound. It was barely sunset, but the chill of the dying year was in the air. The thought came to her, suddenly and very poignantly, of that wonderful night of spring, when she had first wandered along the cliff with the scent of the gorse-bushes rising like incense all around her, when she had first heard that magic, flutelike call of youth and love. A deep and passionate emotion filled and overfilled her heart with the memory. As she went up the little path to the school-house, her face was wet with tears.

Dick had not returned, and she went into the little dining room and busied herself with laying the cloth for supper. Their only indoor servant — a young village girl — was out that evening, but she could hear Mrs. Rickett who often came up to help moving about the kitchen. She did not feel in the mood for the good woman's chatter and delayed going in her direction as long as possible.

So it came about that, pausing for a few moments at the window before doing so, she heard the click of the gate and saw the old postman coming up the path.

He moved slowly and with some difficulty, being heavily laden as well as bowed with age and rheumatism. She went quickly to the outer door, and, accompanied by the growling Columbus, moved to meet him.

"Evening, ma'am! Here's a parcel for you!" the old man said. "It's books, and it's all come to bits, but I don't think as I've dropped any of 'em. You'd best let me bring 'em straight in for I'm all fixed up with 'em now, and they'll only scatter if you tries to take 'em."

She led the way within, commiserating him on the weight of his burden which he thumped down without ceremony on the white cloth that she had just spread. The parcel was certainly badly damaged, and books in white covers began to slide out of it the moment they were released.

"I'll leave you to sort 'em, ma'am," he said airily. "Daresay as they're not much the worse. Schoolmaster's truck I've no doubt. If there was fewer books in the world, the postman would have an easier life than what he does and no one much worse off than they be now — except the clever folks as writes 'em! Well, I'll be getting along to the Court, ma'am, and I wish you a very good-night."

He stumped away, and in the failing evening light Juliet began to gather up the confusion he had left behind. She found it was not a collection of paper-backed school-books as she had at first imagined, and since the contents of the parcel were very thoroughly scattered she glanced at them with idle curiosity as she laid them together.

Then with a sudden violent start she picked up one of the volumes and looked at it closely. The title stood out with arresting clearness on the white paper jacket: *Gold of the Desert* by *Dene Strange*. Author of *The Valley of Dry Bones, Marionettes*, etc.

She caught her breath. Something sprang up within her — something that clamored grotesque and incoherent things. Her heart was beating so fast that it seemed continuous like the dull roar of the sea. The volumes were all alike — all copies of one book.

A sheet of paper fluttered from the one she held. She snatched at it with a curious desperation — as though, sinking in deep waters, she clutched at a straw.

Author's Copies — With Compliments, were the words that stood out before her widening gaze. She remained as one transfixed, staring at them. It was as if a thunderbolt had fallen in the quiet room. . . .

It must have been many minutes later that she came to herself and found herself huddled in a chair by the table, shivering from head to foot. She was conscious of a horrible feeling of sickness, and her heart was beating slowly, with thick, uneven strokes.

The room was growing dark. The chill desolation of the world outside seemed to have followed her in. She could not remember that she had ever felt so deadly cold before. She could not keep her teeth from chattering.

Something moved close to her, and she realized what had roused her. Columbus was standing up by her side, his forepaws against her, his grizzled nose nudging her arm. She stirred stiffly, and put the arm about him.

"Oh — Christopher!" she said, and gasped as if she had not breathed for a long time. "Oh — Christopher!"

He leaned up against her, stretching his warm tongue to reach her cheek, his whole body wriggling with gushing solicitude under her hand.

She looked down at him with the dazed eyes of one who has received a stunning blow. "I don't know what we shall do, my doggie," she said.

And then very suddenly she was on her feet, tense, palpitating, her head turned to listen. The gate had clicked again, and someone was coming up the path.

It was Dick, and he moved with the step of an eager man, reached the door, opened it, and entered. She heard him in the passage, heard his tread upon the threshold, heard his voice greeting her.

"Hullo, darling! All alone in the dark? I've had a beast of a day away from you."

His hands reached out and clasped her. She was actually in his arms before she found her voice.

"Dick! Dick! Please! I want to speak to you," she said.

He clasped her close. His lips pressed hers, stopping all utterance for a while with a mastery that would not be held in check. She could not resist him, but there was no rapture in her yielding. His love was like a flame about her, but she was cold — cold as ice. Suddenly, with his face against her neck, he spoke: "What's the matter, Juliet?"

She quivered in response, made an attempt to release herself, felt his arms tighten, and was still. "I have — found out — something," she said, her voice very low.

"What is it?" he said.

She did not answer. A great impulse arose in her to wrench herself from him, to thrust him back but she could not. She stood — a prisoner — in his hold.

He waited a moment, still with his face bent over her, his lips close to her neck. "Is it anything that — matters?" he asked.

She felt his arms drawing her and quivered again like a trapped bird. "Yes," she whispered.

"Very much?"

"Yes," she said again.

"Then you are angry with me," he said.

She was silent.

He pressed her suddenly very close. "Juliet, you don't hate me, do you?"

She caught her breath with a sob that sounded painfully hard and dry. "I — couldn't have married you — if I had known," she said.

He started a little and lifted his head. "As bad as that!" he said.

For a space there was silence between them while his eyes dwelt somberly upon the litter of books upon the table, and still his arms enfolded her though he did not hold her close. When at last she made as if she would release herself, he still would not let her go.

"Will you listen to me?" he said. "Give me a hearing — just for a minute? You have forgiven so much in me that is really bad that I can't feel this last to be — quite unpardonable. Juliet, I haven't really wronged you. You have got a false impression of the man who wrote those books. It's a prejudice which I have promised myself to overcome. But I must have time. Will you defer judgment — for my sake — till you have read this latest book, written when you first came into my life? Will you — Juliet, will you have patience till I have proved myself?"

She shivered as she stood. "You don't know — what you have done," she said.

He made a quick gesture of protest. "Yes, I do know. I know quite well. I have hurt you, deceived you. But hear my defense anyway! I never meant to marry you in the first place without telling you, but I always wanted you to read this book of mine first. It's different from the others. I wanted you to see the difference. But then I got carried away as you know. I loved you so tremendously. I couldn't hold myself in. Then — when you came to me in my misery — it was all up with me, and I fell. I couldn't tell you then, Juliet, I wasn't ready for you to know. So I waited — till the book could be published and you could read it. I am infernally sorry you found out like this. I wanted you — so badly — to read it with an open mind. And now — whichever way you look at it —

you certainly won't do that."

There was a whimsical note in his voice despite its obvious sincerity as he ended, and Juliet winced as she heard it, and in a moment with resolution freed herself from his hold.

She did it in silence, but there was that in the action that deeply wounded him. He stood motionless, looking at her, a glitter of sternness in his eyes.

"Juliet," he said after a moment, "you are not treating this matter reasonably. I admit I tricked you; but my love for you was my excuse. And those books of mine — especially the one I didn't want you to read — were never intended for such as you."

She looked back at him with a kind of frozen wonder. "Then who were they meant for?" she said.

He made a slight movement of impatience. "You know. You know very well. They were meant for the people whom you yourself despise — the crowd you broke away from — men and women like the Farring-mores who live for nothing but their own beastly pleasures and don't care the toss of a halfpenny for anyone else under the sun."

She went back against the table and stood there, supporting herself while she still faced him. "You forget —" she said, her voice very low, — "I think you forget — that they are my people — I belong to them!"

"No, you don't!" he flung back almost fiercely. "You belong to me!"

A great shiver went through her. She clenched her hands to repress it. "I don't see," she said, "how I can — possibly — stay with you — after this."

"What?" He strode forward and caught her by the shoulders. She was aware of a sudden hot blaze of anger in him that made her think of the squire. He held her in a grip that was merciless. "Do you know what you are saying?" he asked.

She tried to hold him from her, but he pressed her to him with a dominance that would not brook resistance.

"Do you?" he said. "Do you?"

His face was terrible. She felt the hard hammer of his heart against her own, and a sense of struggling against overwhelming odds came upon her.

She bowed her head against his shoulder. "Oh, Dick!" she said. "It is you — who — don't — know!"

His hold did not relax, and for a space he said no word, but stood breathing deeply as a man who faces some deadly peril.

He spoke at length, and in his voice was something she had never heard before — something from which she shrank uncontrollably, as the victim shrinks from the branding-iron.

"And so you think you can leave me — as lightly as Lady Joanna Farringmore left that man I went to see today?"

She lifted her head with a gasp. "No!" she said. "Oh, no! Not — like that!"

His eyes pierced her with their appalling brightness. "No, not quite like that," he said, with awful grimness. "There is a difference. An engaged woman can cut the cable and be free without assistance. A married woman needs a lover to help her!"

She shrank afresh from the scorching cynicism of his words. "Dick!" she said. "Have I asked for — freedom?"

"You had better not ask!" he flashed back. "You have gone too far already. I tell you, Juliet, when you gave yourself to me it was irrevocable. There's no going back now. You have got to put up with me — whatever the cost."

"Ah!" she whispered.

"Listen!" he said. "This thing is going to make no difference between us — no difference whatever. You cared for me enough to marry me, and I am the same man now that I was then. The man you have conjured up in your own mind as the writer of those books is nothing to me — or to you now. I am the man who wrote them — and you belong to me. And if you leave me — well, I shall follow you — and bring you back."

His lips closed implacably upon the words; he held her as though challenging her to free herself. But Juliet neither moved nor spoke. She stood absolutely passive in his hold, waiting in utter silence.

He waited also, trying to read her face in the dimness, but seeing only a pale still mask.

At last: "You understand me?" he said.

She bent her head. "Yes — I understand."

He stood for a moment longer, then abruptly his hold tightened upon her. She lifted her face then sharply, resisting him almost instinctively, and in that instant his passion burst its bonds. He crushed her to him with sudden mastery, and, so compelling, he kissed her hotly, possessively, dominatingly, holding her lips with his own, till she strained against him no longer, but hung, burning and quivering, at his mercy.

Then at length very slowly he put her down into the chair from which she had risen at his entrance, and released her. She leaned upon the table, trembling, her hands covering her face. And he stood behind her, breathing heavily, saying no word.

So for a space they remained in darkness and silence, till the brisk opening of the kitchen-door brought them back to the small things of life.

Dick moved. "Go upstairs!" he said, under his breath.

She stirred and rose unsteadily. He put out a hand to help her. She did not take it, did not seem even to see it.

Gropingly, she turned to the door, went out slowly, still as if feeling her way, reached the narrow stairs and went up them, clutching at the rail.

He followed her to the foot and stood there watching her. As she reached the top he heard her sob.

An impulse caught him to follow her, to take her again — but how differently! — into his arms, — to soothe her, to comfort her, to win her back to him. But sternly he put it from him. She had got to learn her lesson, to realize her obligations, — she who talked so readily of leaving him! And for what?

A wave of hot blood rose to his forehead, and he clenched his hands. He went back into the room, knowing that he could not trust himself.

When Mrs. Rickett entered with a lamp a few moments later, he was gathering up the litter of books and paper from the table, his face white and sternly set. He gave her a brief word of greeting, and went across to the school with his burden.

Chapter VI

COALS OF FIRE

*I*t was nearly half-an-hour later that Mrs. Rickett ascended the stairs and knocked at Juliet's door.

"Supper's been in this long time," she called. "And Mr. Green's still over at the school."

There was a brief pause, then Juliet's quiet movement in the room. She opened the door and met her on the threshold.

"Why, you haven't got a light!" said Mrs. Rickett. "Is there anything the matter, ma'am? Aren't you well?"

"Yes, quite, thank you," Juliet said in her slow gentle voice. "I am afraid I forgot the time. I will put on my hat before I come down."

Mrs. Rickett's eyes regarded her shrewdly for a moment or two, then looked away. "Shall I fetch you a candle?" she said.

Juliet turned back into the room. "I have one, thank you. Perhaps you wouldn't mind going to find Mr. Green while I dress."

Mrs. Rickett hastened away, and Juliet lighted her candle and surveyed herself for a second, standing motionless before the glass.

Several minutes later she descended the stairs and went quietly into the dining room. She was wearing a large-brimmed hat that shadowed her face.

Dick, standing by the mantelpiece, waiting for her, gave her a hard and piercing look as she entered.

"I am sorry I am late," she said.

He moved abruptly as if somehow the conventional words had an edge. He drew out a chair for her. "I am afraid there isn't a great deal of time," he said.

She sat down with a murmured word of thanks. He took his place, facing her, very pale, but absolutely his own master. He served her silently, and she made some pretence of eating, keeping her head bent, feeding Columbus surreptitiously as he sat by her side.

Her plate was empty when at length very resolutely she looked up and spoke. "Dick, I want you to understand one thing. I did not open that parcel of yours. It was open when it came."

Instantly his eyes were upon her with merciless directness. "I gathered that," he said.

She met his look unflinchingly, but her next words came with an effort. "Then you can't — with justice — blame me for surprising your secret."

"I don't," he said.

"And yet —" She made a slight gesture of remonstrance, as if the piercing brightness of his eyes were more than she could bear.

He pushed back his chair and rose. He came to her as she sat, bent over her, his hand on her shoulder, and looked at her intently.

"Juliet," he said, "I don't like you with that stuff on your face. It isn't — you."

She kept her face steadily upturned, enduring his look with no sign of shrinking. "You are meeting — the real me — for the first time — tonight," she said.

His mouth curved cynically. "I think not. I have never worshipped at the shrine of a painted goddess."

Something rose in her throat and she put up a hand to hide it. "I doubt if — Dene Strange — was ever capable of worshipping anything," she said.

His hand closed upon her. "Does that mean that you hate him more than you love me?" he said.

A faint quiver crossed her face. She passed the question by. "Do you remember — Cynthia Paramount — your heroine?" she said. "The woman you dissected so cleverly — stripped to the naked soul — and exposed to public ridicule? You were terribly merciless, weren't you, Dick? You didn't expect — some day — to find yourself married — to that sort of woman."

His face hardened. "In what way do you resemble her?" he said. "I have never seen it yet."

"Can't you see it — now?" she returned, lifting her face more fully to the light.

He was silent for several seconds, looking at her. Then very suddenly his attitude changed. He knelt down by her side and spoke, urgently, passionately.

"Juliet — for God's sake — let us remember what we are to each other — and put the rest away!"

His arm encircled her. He would have drawn her close, but she held back with a sharp sound that was almost a cry of pain.

"Dick, wait — wait a moment! You don't know — don't understand! Ah, wait — please wait! Take your arm away — just for a moment — please — just for a moment! I have something to tell you, but I can't say it like this. I can't — I can't! Ah! What is that?"

She broke off, gasping, almost fighting for breath, as the sudden rush and hoot of a car sounded at the gate.

Dick got to his feet. His face was white. "Are you expecting someone?" he said.

She clasped her hands tightly upon her breast to still her agitation. "No, I'm not expecting — anyone. But — but — someone — has come."

"Evidently," said Dick.

He turned towards the door, but in a moment she had sprung up, reaching it before him. "Dick, if it is Saltash —"

"Why should it be Saltash?" he said, with that in his voice that arrested her as compelling as if he had laid a hand upon her.

She faced him standing at the door, striving desperately for self-control. "It may be Saltash," she said, speaking more quietly. "I saw him this morning, and he knows about the concert tonight. Dick —" she caught her breath involuntarily — "Dick, why do you look at me like that?"

He made a curious jerky movement — as if he strove against invisible bonds. "So," he said, "you are expecting him!"

She stiffened at his words. "I have told you I am expecting no one, but that is no reason why Saltash should not come."

For a second he looked at her with something that was near akin to contempt in his eyes, then suddenly an awful flame leapt up in them consuming all beside. He took a swift step forward, and caught her between his hands.

"Juliet!" he said sternly. "Stop this trifling! What are you hiding from me? What is it you were trying to tell me just now?"

She shrank from the fire of his look. "I can't tell you now, Dick. It's impossible. Dick, you are hurting me!"

He spoke between his teeth. "I've got to know! Tell me now!"

Someone was knocking a careless tattoo upon the outer door. Juliet turned her head sharply, but she kept her eyes upon her husband's face.

"No, Dick," she said after a moment, and with the words something of her customary quiet courage came back to her. "I can't — possibly — tell you now. Do this one thing for me — wait till tonight!"

"And then?" he said.

"I promise that you shall know — everything — then," she said. "Please — give me till then!"

There was earnest entreaty in her voice, but she had subdued her agitation. She met the scorching intensity of his look with eyes that never wavered, and in spite of himself he was swayed by her steadfastness.

"Very well," he said, and set her free. "Till tonight!"

She turned from him in silence and opened the door. He stood motionless, with hands clenched at his sides, and watched her.

She went down the passage without haste and reached the outer door. She opened it without fumbling, and in a moment Saltash's debonair accents came to him.

"Ah, *Juliette!* You are ready? Has your good husband got back yet? Ah, there you are, sir! I have called to offer you and *madame* a lift. I am going your way."

He came sauntering up the passage with the royal assurance characteristic of him, and held out his hand to Dick with malicious cordiality.

"I come as a friend, Romeo. Do you know you're very late? Have you only just got back?"

Juliet's eyes were upon Dick. She saw his momentary hesitation before he took the proffered hand.

Saltash saw it also and grinned appreciatively. "Well, what news? What did Yardley have to say?"

"I didn't see him," Dick said briefly.

"No? How was that?"

Dick shrugged his shoulders. "Merely because he wasn't there. I can't tell you why, for I don't know. I waited about all day — to no purpose."

"Drew a blank!" commented Saltash. "No wonder you're feeling a bit savage! What are you going to do now?"

Dick faced him, grimly uncommunicative. "Oh, talk, I suppose. What else?"

"And you're taking Juliet?" pursued Saltash.

"Have you any objection?" said Dick sharply.

"None," said Saltash smoothly. "She is your wife, not mine — perhaps fortunately for her." He threw a gay glance at Juliet. "Are you ready, *ma chère?* Come along, *mon ami!* It will amuse me to hear you — talk."

Juliet went upstairs to fetch her cloak, and Dick took his coat from the peg in the hall, and began to put it on. Saltash watched him with careless amiability.

"Are you going to be there tonight then?" Dick asked him suddenly.

"I am proposing to give myself that pleasure," he returned. "That is, of course, if you on your part have no objection."

Dick's black eyes surveyed him keenly. "I am quite capable of protecting my wife single-handed," he said. "Not that there will be any need."

Saltash executed a smiling bow. "I am delighted to hear you say so. Have you got a cigarette to spare?"

Dick took out his case and held it to him. Saltash helped himself, the smile still twitching the corners of his mouth.

"Thanks," he said lightly. "So you have no anxieties about tonight!"

"None," said Dick.

"You think the men will come to heel?"

"They haven't broken away yet," Dick reminded him curtly.

Saltash raised his eyes suddenly. "When they do — what then?" he said.

"What do you mean?" said Dick.

He laughed mischievously. "I suppose you know that you are credited with being at their head?"

Dick, in the act of striking a match, paused. He looked at the other man with raised brows. "At their head?" he questioned. "What do you mean?"

Without the smallest change of countenance Saltash enlightened him. "As strike-leader, agitator, and so on. You have achieved an enviable reputation by your philanthropy. Didn't you know?"

Dick struck the match with an absolutely steady hand, and held it to his cigarette. "I did not," he said.

Saltash puffed at the cigarette, peering at him curiously through the smoke. "Which may account for your failure to find Ivor Yardley," he suggested after a moment.

"In what way?" said Dick.

Saltash straightened himself. "I imagine he is not a great believer in — philanthropy," he said.

Dick's eyes shone with an ominous glitter. "From my point of view these insinuations are not worth considering," he said, "though no doubt it has given you a vast amount of enjoyment to fabricate them."

"I!" said Saltash.

"You!" said Dick.

There was a moment's silence, then Saltash began to laugh. "My dear chap, you don't really think that! You'd like to — but you can't!"

Dick looked at him, thin-lipped, uncompromising, silent.

"You actually do?" questioned Saltash. "You really think I care a twopenny damn what anybody thinks about you or anyone else under the sun? I say, don't be an ass. Green, whatever else you are! It's too tiring for all concerned. If you really want to know who is responsible —"

"Well?" said Dick.

"Well," Saltash sent a cloud of smoke upwards, "look a bit nearer home, man! Haven't you got — a brother somewhere?"

Dick gave a sudden start. "I have not!" he said sternly.

Saltash nodded. "Ah! Well, I imagine Yardley knows him if you don't. He is the traitor in the camp, and he's out to trip you if he can." He laughed again with careless humor. "I don't know why I should give you the tip. It is not my custom to heap coals of fire. Pray excuse them on this occasion! I suppose you are quite determined to take *Juliette* to the meeting tonight?"

"I am quite determined to go," said Juliet quietly, as she came down the stairs. "Will you have anything, Charles? No? Then let us start! It is getting late. You are driving yourself?"

He threw open the door for her with a deep bow. "I always drive myself, *Juliette*, and — I always get there," he said.

Her faint laugh floated back to Dick as he followed them out.

Chapter VII

FLIGHT

*I*t was a dumb and sullen crowd that Dick Green faced that night in the great barn on the slope of High Shale.

A rough platform had been erected at one end of the place and this, with the deal table and lamp and one or two chairs, was all that went to the furnishing of his assembly-room. The men stood in a close crowd like herded cattle, and the atmosphere of the place was heavy with the reek of humanity and coarse tobacco smoke. There was a door at each end, but the night was still and dark and there was little air beyond the vague chill of a creeping sea-mist.

Dick, entering at the door at the platform end of the building instead of passing straight up through the crowd as was his custom, was aware of a curious influence at work from the first moment — an influence adverse if not directly hostile that reached him he knew not how. He heard a vague murmur as Juliet and Saltash followed him, and sharply he turned and drew Juliet to his side. In that instant he realized that she was the only woman in the place.

He faced the crowd, his hand upon her arm. "Well, men," he said, his words clean-cut and ready, "so you've left your wives behind, have you? I on the contrary have brought mine, and she has promised to give you a song."

The mutter died. Some youths at the back started applause, which spread, though somewhat half-heartedly, through the crowd, and for a space the ugly feeling died down.

"We'll get to business," said Dick, and took out his banjo.

The concert began, Ashcott came up on to the platform and under cover of Dick's jangling ragtime spoke in a low voice and urgently to Saltash.

The latter heard him with a laugh and a careless grimace, but a little later he leaned towards Juliet who sat behind the table and touched her unobtrusively. She looked round at him almost with reluctance, and he whispered to her in rapid French.

She listened to him with raised brows, and then shook her head with a smile. "No, of course not! I am going to sing to them directly. I am here to help — not to make things worse."

He shrugged his shoulders and said no more. In a few minutes Dick's cheery banjo thrummed into silence and he turned round.

"Are you ready?" he said to Juliet.

She rose and came forward, tall and graceful, bearing the unmistakable stamp of high-breeding in every delicate movement. She might have been on the platform of a London concert-hall as she faced her audience under the shadowing hat.

They stared at her open-mouthed, spellbound, awed by the quiet dignity of her. And in the hush that fell before her, Juliet began to sing.

Her voice was low, highly trained, exquisitely soft. She sang an old English ballad with a throbbing sweetness that held her hearers with its charm. And behind her Dick leaned against the table with his banjo and very softly accompanied her.

His face was in shadow also as he bent over the instrument. Not once throughout the song did he look up.

When she ended, there came that involuntary pause which is the highest tribute that can be paid by any audience, and then such a thunder of applause as shook the building. Saltash stepped forward to hand her back to her chair, but the men in front of her yelled so hoarse a protest that, laughing, he retired.

And Juliet sang again and again, thrilling the rough crowd as Dick had never thrilled them, choosing such old-world melodies as reach the hearts of all. Saltash watched her with keen appreciation on his ugly face. He was an accomplished musician himself. But Dick with his banjo, though he responded unerringly to every shade of feeling in the beautiful voice, never raised his head.

It was he who at last came forward and led Juliet back to her chair, but by that time the temper of the men had completely changed. They shouted good-humored comments to him and bandied jokes among themselves. The whole atmosphere of the place had altered. The heavy sullenness had passed like a thundercloud, and Ashcott no longer smoked his pipe in the doorway with an air of gloomy foreboding.

Dick laid aside his banjo and came to the front of the platform. There was absolute confidence in his bearing, a vital strength that imparted a mastery that yet was largely compounded of comradeship.

He began to speak without effort — as a man speaks to his friends.

"I have something to say to you chaps," he said, "and I hope you will hear me out fairly, even though it may not be the sort of thing you like to listen to. I think you know that I care a good deal about your welfare, and I am doing my level best to secure a decent future for you. I haven't accomplished very much at present, but I'm sticking to it, and I believe I shall win out some day. It won't be my fault if I don't, and I hope it won't be yours. What?" as a murmur broke out in the background. "Oh, shut up, please, till I've done, then if anyone wants to talk he shall have his chance. It might be your fault if I failed because I'm counting on you to back me up in a legal and orderly way. And if you don't, well, I'm knocked out for good and all. For I'm no strike-leader, and any man who strikes can go to blazes so far as I'm concerned. I wouldn't lift a finger to stop him going or to get him out when there; in fact it's the best place for him. No, boys, listen! Wait till I've done! A strike is a deadly thing. It's like a spreading poison in this country, and the beastly root of it is just selfishness. It will choke the very life out of the nation if it isn't stopped. It's a weapon that no self-respecting man should smirch his hands with. I know very well there are heaps of reforms needed, heaps of abuses to be stopped, but you don't cure evil with evil. You're only feeding the monster that will devour you in the end, and you're feeding him with human sacrifice moreover. Have you ever thought of that? And another thing! Do you ever look ahead — right ahead — beyond your own personal wants and grievances? Do you ever ask yourselves if strikes and violence are going to bring forth justice and equity? Do you ever work the thing out to its proper values — see it as it really is? This continual striving for money, for power, — this over-throwing of all established control — do you call it a fight for liberty by any chance? I tell you, men, that it's a struggle for the most hideous slavery that ever disfigured this earth. This perpetual fight for self will end in self-destruction. It always does. It's the law of creation. The thing that strikes rebounds upon the striker. The man who deliberately injures another injures himself tenfold more seriously. Isn't there something in the Bible about he who takes the sword perishes with the sword? That's justice — God's justice — and there's no getting away from that. You can overthrow every institution that was ever made, but you will never set up in its place a Government that will bring again the order you have destroyed. You can pull the Empire to pieces with dissensions and conspiracies, but — once down — you will never build it up again.

"Grievances? Yes, of course you have grievances — heaps of 'em. Who hasn't. And you've a right to try for better conditions. But in heaven's name, don't strike for them! Don't turn the whole world upside down because you want something you can't get! Be sportsmen and play a decent game! Stick to the rules and you may win! I tell you I'm fighting for you — I'm fighting hard. And I shan't rest so long as I have a decent crowd to fight for. But if you're going to follow the rotten example of the fellows who sacrifice the whole community to their own beastly greed — who strike like a herd of sheep because a few damned traitors urge 'em to it — who fling duty and honor to the winds on the chance of grabbing a little worldly advantage — in short, if you're not going to observe the rules of the game, I've done with the whole show.

"That's the position, men, and I want you to get hold of it, see it as it really is. Nothing on this earth worth having was ever gained by disloyalty. Think it out for yourselves! Don't be led by the nose by a parcel of agitators! Give the matter your own sane and deliberate thought! Form your own conclusions! Throw off this tyranny of other men's notions, and be free! If only every man in the kingdom would take this line and think for himself instead of giving his blind allegiance to a power that is out to ruin the nation, there would pretty soon be such a strike against strikes as would kill 'em outright. They're a hindrance to civilization and a curse to the world at large. They are selfishness incarnate and a stumbling-block to all national progress. And if there's any pride of race in you, any sense of an Englishman's honor, any desire for the nation's welfare (which is at a pretty low ebb just now) join with me and do your level best to cast out this evil thing!"

He ended as he had begun with clear and spontaneous appeal to the higher instincts of his hearers. He knew them well, knew their weakness and their strength; and he knew his own power over them and wielded it with unfailing confidence.

The hard-breathing silence that succeeded his words dismayed him not at all. He waited quite calmly for the question he had checked at the outset.

It came very gruffly from a burly miner immediately in front of him. "It's all very well," the man said. "But how are we to get our rights any other way?"

"Oh, you'll get 'em all right," Dick made answer. "This isn't an age of serfdom. You won't be downtrodden to that extent. You stick to your guns and have a little patience! Things are not standing still. State your grievances — if they're bad enough — and then give the owners a chance! But don't forget that there's got to be give and take between you! If you want fair play and consideration from the owners, you must give them the same. Don't forget that you sink or swim together! If you ruin them you ruin yourselves. Disloyalty means disruption, all the world over. So play the game like men!"

It was at this point that Ashcott touched him on the shoulder with a muttered word that made him turn sharply.

"What? Who?"

"Mr. Ivor Yardley!" the manager muttered uneasily. "He's waiting to speak to you — says he'll address the men if you'll allow him. Think it's safe?"

Dick frowned. "Of course it's safe! Where is he? Wait! I'll speak to him first. I'll get my wife to sing again while I do it." He turned round to Juliet sitting at the table behind him and bent to speak to her. "Can you give them another song — to fill in time? I've got to speak to a man outside." His eyes traveled swiftly on the words to the open doorway where a tall man, wearing a motor-mask and a leather coat, stood waiting.

Juliet's look followed his. She stood up quickly. "Dick! Who is it?"

Something in her voice brought his eyes back to her in sudden close scrutiny. For that instant he forgot the crowd of men and the need of the moment, forgot the man who waited in the background whom he had desired so urgently to see, forgot the whole world in the wide-eyed terror of her look.

Instinctively he stretched an arm behind her, but in the same moment Saltash came swiftly forward to her other side, and it was Saltash who spoke with the quick, intimate reassurance of the trusted friend.

"It's all right, *Juliette.* I'm here to take care of you. Give them one more song, won't you? Afterwards, if you've had enough of it, I'll take you back."

She turned her face towards him and away from Dick whose arm fell from her unheeded; but her gaze did not leave the figure that stood waiting in the dim doorway, upright, grim as Fate, watching her with eyes she could not see.

"Don't be afraid!" urged Saltash in his rapid whisper. "Anyhow, don't show it! I'll see you through."

"Are you ready?" said Dick on her other side.

His voice was absolutely steady, but it fell with an icy ring, and a great quiver went through her. She made a blind gesture towards Saltash, and in an instant his hand gripped her elbow.

"Can't you do it?" he said. "Are you going to drop out?"

She recovered herself sharply, as though something in his words had pierced her pride. The next moment very quietly she turned back to Dick.

"I am quite ready," she said.

He took her hand without a word, and led her forward. Someone raised a cheer for her, and in a second a shout of applause thundered to the rafters.

Dick smiled a brief smile of gratitude, and lifted a hand for silence. Then, as it fell, he stepped back.

And Juliet stood alone before the rough crowd.

Those who saw her in that moment never forgot her. Tall and slender, with that unconsciously regal mien of hers that marked her with so indelible a stamp, she stood and faced the men below her. But no song rose to her lips, and those who were nearest to her thought that she was trembling.

And then suddenly she began to speak in a full, quiet voice that penetrated the deep hush with a bell-like clearness.

"Men," she said, "it is very kind of you to cheer me, but you will never do it again. I have something to tell you. I don't know in the least how you will take it, but I hope you will manage to forgive me if you possibly can. Mr. Green is your friend, and he knows nothing about it, so you will acquit him of all blame. The deception is mine alone. I deceived him, too. I know you all hate the Farringmores, and I daresay you have reason. You have never spoken to any of them face to face, before, because they haven't cared enough to come near you. But — you can do so tonight if you wish. Men, I am — Lord Wilchester's sister. I was — Joanna Farringmore."

She ceased to speak with a little gesture of the hands that was quite involuntary and oddly pathetic, but she did not turn away from her audience. Throughout the deep silence that followed that amazing confession she stood quite straight and still, waiting, her face to the throng. A man was standing immediately behind her and she was aware of him, knew without turning that it was Saltash; but the one being in all the crowded place for whose voice or touch in that moment she would have given all that she had neither spoke nor moved. And her brave heart died within her. If he had only given some sign!

A hoarse murmur broke out at the back of the great barn, spreading like a wave on the sea. But ere it reached the men in front who stood sullenly dumb, staring upwards, Saltash's hand closed upon Juliet's arm, drawing her back.

"After that, *ma chère*," he said lightly into her ear, "you would be wise to follow the line of least resistance."

She responded to his touch almost mechanically. The murmur was swelling to a roar, but she scarcely heard it. She yielded to the hand that guided, hardly knowing what she did.

As Saltash led her to the back of the platform she had a glimpse of Dick's face white as death, with lips hard-set and stern as she had never seen them, and a glitter in his eyes that made her think of onyx. He passed her by without a glance, going forward to quell the rising storm as if she had not been there.

The man in the leather coat was with him. He had taken off his mask, and he paused before Juliet — a cynical smile playing about his face. It was a face of iron mastery, of pitiless self-assertion. The eyes were as points of steel.

He bent towards her and spoke. "I thought I should find you sooner or later, Lady Jo. I trust you have enjoyed your game — even if you have lost your winnings!"

She spoke no word in answer, but she made a slight, barely perceptible movement towards the man whose hand upheld her.

And Yardley laughed — an edged laugh that was inexpressibly cruel.

"Oh, go to the devil!" said Saltash with sudden fire. "It's where you belong!"

Yardley's cold eyes gleamed with icy humor. *"Eh tu, Brute!"* he said with sneering lips. "I wish you — joy!"

He passed on. Saltash's arm went round Juliet like a coiled spring. He impelled her unresisting to the door. Her hand rested on his shoulder as she stepped down from the platform. She went with him as one in a dream.

The air smote chill as they left the heated atmosphere, and a great shiver went through her.

She stood still for a moment, listening. The tumult had died down. A man's voice — Dick's voice — clear and very steady, was speaking.

"Come away!" said Saltash in her ear.

But yet she lingered in the darkness. "He will be safe?" she said.

"Of course he will be safe! They treat him like a god. Come away!"

His arm was urging her. She yielded, shivering.

He hurried her up the slope to the place where he had left his car. It stood at the side of the rough road that led to High Shale Point.

They reached it. Juliet was gasping for breath. The sea-mist was like rain in their faces.

"Get in!" he said.

She obeyed, sinking down with a vague thankfulness, conscious of great weakness.

But as he cranked the engine and she felt the throb of movement, she sat up quickly.

"Charles, what am I doing? Where are you taking me?"

He came round to her and his hands clasped hers for a moment in a grip that was warm and close. He did not speak at once.

Then, lightly, "I don't know what you'll do afterwards, *ma Juliette,*" he said. "But you are coming with me now!"

She caught her breath as if she would utter some protest, but something checked her — perhaps it was the memory of Dick's face as she had last seen it, stony, grimly averted, uncompromisingly stern. She gripped his hands in answer, but she did not speak a word. And so they sped away together into the dark.

Chapter VIII

OUT OF THE NIGHT

It was very late that night, and the sea-mist had turned to a drifting rain when the squire sitting reading in his library at the Court was startled by a sudden tapping upon the window behind him.

So unexpected was the sound in the absolute stillness that he started with some violence and nearly knocked over the reading-lamp at his elbow. Then sharply and frowning he arose. He reached the window and fumbled at the blind; but failing to find the cord dragged it impatiently aside and peered through the glass.

"Who is it? What do you want?"

A face he knew, but so drawn and deathly that for the moment it seemed almost unfamiliar, peered back at him. In a second he had the window unfastened and flung wide.

"Dick! In heaven's name, boy, — what's the matter?"

Dick was over the sill in a single bound. He stood up and faced the squire, bare-headed, drenched with rain, his eyes burning with a terrible fire.

"I have come for my wife," he said.

"Your wife! Juliet!" The squire stared at him as if he thought him demented. "Why, she left ages ago, man, — soon after tea!"

"Yes, yes, I know," Dick said. He spoke rapidly, but with decision. "But she came back here an hour or two ago. You are giving her shelter. Saltash brought her — or no — she probably came alone."

"You are mad!" said Fielding, and turned to shut the window. "She hasn't been near since she left this evening."

"Wait!" Dick's hand shot out and caught his arm, restraining him.

"Do you swear to me that you don't know, where she is?"

The squire stood still, looking full and hard into the face so near his own; and so looking, he realized, what he had not grasped before, that it was the face of a man in torture. The savage grip on his arm told the same story. The fiery eyes that stared at him out of the death-white countenance had the awful look of a man who sees his last hope shattered.

Impulsively he laid his free hand upon him. "Dick — Dick, old chap, — what's all this? Of course I don't know where she is! Do you think I'd lie to you?"

"Then I've lost her!" Dick said, and with the words some inner vital spring seemed to snap within him. He flung up; his arms, freeing himself with a wild gesture. "My God, she has gone — gone with that scoundrel!"

"Saltash?" said the squire sharply.

"Yes. Saltash!" He ground the name between his teeth. "Does that surprise you so very much? Don't you know the sort of infernal blackguard he is?"

The squire turned again to shut the window. "Damn it, Dick! I don't believe a word of it," he said with vigor. "Get your wind and have a drink, and let's hear the whole story! Have you and Juliet been quarreling?"

Dick ignored his words as if he had not spoken. "You needn't shut the window," he said. "I'm going again. I'm going now."

It was the squire's turn to assert himself, and he seized it. He shut the window with a bang. "You are not, Dick! Don't be a fool! Sit down! Do you hear? Sit down! You're not going yet — not till you've told me the whole trouble. So you can make up your mind to that!"

Dick looked at him for a moment as if he were on the verge of fierce resistance, but Fielding's answering look held such unmistakable resolution that after the briefest pause he turned aside.

"I'm sorry, sir," he said, and tramped heavily across to the hearth. "Put up with me if you can! God knows I'm up against it hard enough tonight."

He rested his arms on the mantelpiece and laid his head down upon them, and so stood motionless, in utter silence.

The squire came to him in a few seconds with a glass in his hand. "Here you are, Dick! This is what you're wanting. Swallow it before you talk anymore!"

Dick reached out in silence and took the glass. Then he stood up and drank, keeping his face averted.

Fielding waited till at last, without turning, he spoke. "I've always known it might come to this, but I never realized why. I suppose anyone but a blind fool would have seen through it long ago."

"What are you talking about?" said the squire. "I'm utterly in the dark, remember."

Dick's hands were clenched. "I'm talking of Juliet and — Saltash. I've always known there was some sort of understanding between them. He flaunted it in my face whenever we met. But I trusted her — I trusted her." The words were like a muffled cry rising from the depths of the man's wrung soul.

"Sit down!" said the squire gruffly, and taking him by the shoulders pushed him into the chair from which he himself had so lately risen.

Dick yielded, with the submission of utter despair, his black head bowed against the table.

Fielding stooped over him, still holding him. "Now, boy, now! Don't let yourself go! Tell me — try and tell me!"

Dick drew a hard breath. "You'll think I'm mad, sir. I thought I was myself at first. But it's true — it must be true. I heard it from her own lips. Juliet — my wife — my wife — is — was — Lady Joanna Farringmore!"

"Great heavens!" said the squire. "Dick, are you sure?"

"Yes, quite sure. She was caught — caught by Yardley at the meeting tonight. She couldn't escape — so she told the truth — told the whole crowd — and then bolted — bolted with Saltash."

"Great heavens!" said the squire again. "But — what was Saltash doing there?"

"Oh, he came to protect her. He knew — or guessed — there was something in the wind. He came to support her. I know now. He's the subtlest devil that ever was made."

"But why on earth — why on earth did she ever come here?" questioned Fielding.

"She was hiding from Yardley of course. He's a cold vindictive brute, and I suppose — I suppose she was afraid of him, and came to me — came to me — for refuge." Dick was speaking through his hands. "That's how he regards it himself. She was always playing fast and loose till she got engaged to him. It was just the fashion in that set. But he — I imagine no one ever played with him before. He swears — swears he'll make her suffer for it yet."

"Pooh!" said Fielding. "How does he propose to do that? She's your wife anyhow."

"My wife — yes." Slowly Dick raised his head, stared for a space in front of him, then grimly rose. "My wife — as you say, sir. And I am going to find her — now."

"I'm coming with you," said Fielding.

"No, sir, no!" Dick looked at him with a tight-lipped smile that was somehow terrible. "Don't do that! You won't want to be — a witness against me."

"Pooh!" said the squire again. "I may be of use to you before it comes to that. But before we start let me tell you one thing, Dick! She married you because she loved you — for no other reason."

A sharp spasm contracted Dick's hard features; he set his lips and said nothing.

"That's the truth," the squire proceeded, watching him. "And you know it. She might have bolted with Saltash before if she had wanted to. She had ample opportunity."

Dick's hands clenched at his sides, but still he said nothing.

"She loved you," the squire said again. "Lady Jo — or no Lady Jo — she loved you. It wasn't make-believe. She was fairly caught — against her will possibly — but still caught. She's run away from you now — run away with another man — because she couldn't stay and face you. Is that convincing proof, do you think, that she has ceased to love you? It wouldn't convince me."

Dick's clenched hands were beating impotently against his sides. "I — can't say, sir," he said, between his set teeth.

The squire moved impulsively, laid a hand on his shoulder. "Dick, I've seen a good deal — suffered a good deal — in my time; enough to know the real thing when I see it. She's loved you as long as she's known you, and it's been the same with you. You're not going to deny that? You can't deny it!"

Dick made a quick gesture of protest. For a moment the tortured soul of the man looked out of his eyes. "Does that make it any better?" he said harshly.

"In my opinion, yes." Fielding spoke with decision. "She may have taken refuge with Saltash, but that doesn't prove anything — except that the poor girl had no one else to turn to. You had failed her — or anyhow you didn't offer to stand by."

"I couldn't!" The words came jerkily, as if wrung from him by main force. "For one thing — the men were out of hand, and it was as much as I could do to hold them. She told them, I tell you — stood up and told them straight out — who she was. And they loathe the whole crowd. It was madness."

"Pretty sublime madness!" commented the squire. "And then Saltash took her away. Was that it?"

"Yes." Dick spoke with intense bitterness. "It was the chance he was waiting for. Of course he seized it. Any blackguard would."

"But you thought she might have come here?" pursued the squire.

"I thought it possible, yes. I told Yardley it was so. He of course sneered at the bare idea. I nearly choked him for it. But I might have known he was right. She wouldn't risk — my following her. She wanted to be — free."

"Why? Is she afraid of you then?" Fielding's voice was stern.

Dick threw up his head with the action of a goaded animal. "Yes."

"Then you've given her some reason?"

"Yes. I have given her reason!" Fiercely he flung the words. "You want to know — you shall know! This evening she found out something about me which even you don't know yet — something that made her hate me. I was going to tell her some day, but the time hadn't come. She said if she had known of it she would never have married me. I didn't realize then — how could I? — how hard it hit her. And I made her understand that having married me — it was irrevocable. That was why she ran away with Saltash. She didn't — trust me — any longer."

"But, my good fellow, what in heaven's name is this awful thing that even I don't know?" demanded the squire. "Don't tell me there has ever been any damn trouble with another woman!"

"No — no!" Dick broke into a laugh that was inexpressibly painful to hear. "There has never been any other woman for me. What do I care for women? Do you think because I've made a blasted fool of myself over one woman that I —"

"Shut up, Dick!" Curtly the squire checked him. "You're not to say it — even to me. Tell me this other thing about yourself — the thing I don't know!"

"Oh, that! That's nothing, sir, nothing — at least you won't think it so. It's only that during the past few years some books have been published by one named Dene Strange that have attracted attention in certain quarters."

"I've read 'em all," said the squire. "Well?"

"I wrote them," said Dick; "that's all."

"You!" Fielding stared. "You, Dick!"

"Yes, I. I meant to have told you, but so long as my boy lived, my job seemed to be here, so I kept it to myself. And then — when she came — she told me she hated the man who wrote those books for being cynical — and merciless. So I wrote another to make her change her mind about me before she knew. It is only just published. And she found out before she read it. That's all," Dick said again with the shadow of a smile. "She found out this evening. It was a shock to her — naturally. It's been a succession of obstacles all through — a perpetual struggle against odds. Well, it's over. At least we know what we're up against now. There will be no more illusions of any sort from today on." He paused, stood a moment as if bracing himself, then turned. "Well, I'm going, sir. Come if you really must, but — I don't advise it."

"I am coming," said the squire briefly. His hand went from Dick's shoulder to his arm and gave it a hard squeeze. "Confound you! What do you take me for?" he said.

Dick's hand came swiftly to his. "I take you for the best friend a man ever had, sir," he said.

"Pooh!" said the squire.

Chapter IX

THE FREE PARDON

*T*en minutes later they went down the dripping avenue in the squire's little car. The drifting fog made an inky blackness of the night, and progress was very slow under the trees.

"We should be quicker walking," said Dick impatiently.

"It'll be better when we reach the open road," said Fielding, frowning at the darkness.

The light at the lodge-gates flung a wide glare through the mist, and he steered for it with more assurance. They passed through and turned into the road.

And here the squire pulled up with a jerk, for immediately in front of them another light shone.

"What the devil is that, Dick?"

"It's another car," said Dick and jumped out. "Hullo, there! Anything the matter?" he called.

"Damnation, yes!" answered a voice. "I've run into this infernal wall and damaged my radiator. Lost my mascot, too, damn it! Sort of thing that always happens when you're in a hurry."

"Who is it?" said Dick sharply.

He was standing almost touching the car, but he could not see the speaker who seemed to be bent and hunting for something on the ground.

A sound that was curiously like a chuckle answered him out of the darkness, but no reply came in words.

Dick stood motionless. "Saltash!" he said incredulously. "Is it Saltash?"

"Why shouldn't it be Saltash?" said a voice that laughed. "Thank you, Romeo? Come and help me out of this damn fix! Oh, I'm fed up with playing benevolent fool. It gives me indigestion. Curse this fog! Afraid I've knocked a few chips off your beastly wall. Ah! Here's the mascot! Now perhaps my infernal luck will turn! What are you keeping so quiet about? Aren't you pleased to see me? Not that you can — but that's a detail."

"Are you — alone?" Dick said, an odd tremor in his voice.

"Of course I'm alone! What did you expect? No, no, my Romeo, I may be a fool, but I'm not quite such a three-times-distilled imbecile as that amounts to. Have you got a gun there?"

"No!" Dick's voice sounded half-strangled, as though he fought against some oppression that threatened to overwhelm him. "What have you come back for? Tell me that!"

"I'll tell you anything you like," said Saltash generously; "including what I think of you, if you will help me to shove this thing into a more convenient locality and then take me in and give me a drink."

"You'd better get the car up the drive here," came Fielding's voice out of the darkness. "You can see more or less what you're doing under the lamp. Wait while I get my own out of the way!"

"Excellent!" said Saltash. "I'm immensely grateful to you, sir, for not smashing me up. What, Romeo? Did I hear you say you wished he had? I didn't? Then I must have sensed battle, murder and sudden death in your silence."

But whatever Dick's silence expressed he refused stubbornly to break it. When the squire had maneuvered his car out of the way, he lent his help to pushing Saltash's across the road and up the drive into safety, but he did not utter a single word throughout the performance.

"A thousand thanks!" gibed Saltash. "Now for the great reckoning! I say, you will give me a drink, won't you, before you send me to my account? The villain always has a drink first. He's entitled to that, at least."

Again Fielding's voice came through Dick's silence. "Yes, come up to the schoolhouse!" he said. "We can't talk here. Have you got the key, Dick? Ah, that's right."

He found Dick and thrust a hand through his arm, leading him, stiffly unresponsive, across the road.

At the gate Dick stopped and spoke. "Let him go in front!" he said.

"With pleasure," laughed Saltash. "I'm lucky to have met you here. I was wondering how I should manage to break in."

He went up the path before them with his careless tread, and waited whistling while Dick opened the door.

The lamp in the little hall was burning low, but it shone upon his ugly face as he entered, and showed him the only one of the three who felt at ease. With royal assurance he turned to Dick.

"Well? Have you got a table and pistols for two? Great Scott, man! You look like a death-mask! Come along and let's get it over! Then perhaps you'll feel better."

Dick stood upright by Fielding's side, listening to the taunting words with a face that was indeed like a death-mask — save for the eyes that glowed vividly, terribly, with something of a tigerish glare.

He spoke at last with deadly quietness through lips that did not seem to move. "Where have you taken my wife?"

"Oh, she's quite safe," said Saltash; and smiled with a foxlike flash of teeth. "I am taking every care of her. You need have no anxiety about that."

"I asked — where you had taken her," Dick said, his words low and distinct, wholly without emotion.

Saltash's odd eyes began to gleam. "I heard you, *mon ami*. But since the lady is under my protection at the present moment, I am not prepared to answer that question off-hand — or even at all, until I am satisfied as to the kindness — or otherwise — of your intentions. When I give my protection to anyone — I give it."

"Is that what you came back to say?" said Dick, still without stirring hand or feature.

"By no means," said Saltash airily. "I didn't come to see you at all. I came — to fetch Columbus!"

He turned with the words, hearing a low whine at the door behind him, and opening it released the dog who ran out with eager searching. Saltash stooped to fondle him.

Something that was like an electric thrill went through Dick. He took a sudden step forward.

"Damn you!" he said, and gripped Saltash by the collar. "Tell me where she is! Do you hear? Tell me!"

Saltash straightened himself with a lightning movement. They looked into each other's eyes for several tense seconds. Then, though no word has passed between them, Dick's hand fell.

"That's better," said Saltash. "You're getting quite civil. Look here, my bully boy! I'll tell you something — and you'd better listen carefully, for there's a hidden meaning to it. You're the biggest ass that ever trod this earth. There!"

He put up a hand to his crumpled collar and straightened it, still with his eyes upon Dick's face.

"Got that?" he asked abruptly. "Well, then, I'll tell you something else. I've got a revolver in my pocket. I put it there in case the miners needed any persuasion, but you shall have it to shoot me with — and no doubt Mr. Fielding will kindly turn his back while you do it — if you will answer — honestly — one question I should like to put to you first. Is it a deal?"

Dick was breathing quickly. He stood close to Saltash, urged by a deadly enmity and still on the verge of violence, but restrained by something about the other man's attitude that he could not have defined.

"Well?" he said curtly at length. "What do you want to know?"

Saltash's lips twisted in a faintly sardonic smile. "Just one thing," he said. "Don't speak in a hurry, for a good deal depends upon it! If some kind friend — like myself for instance — had come to you, say, the night before your wedding and told you that you were about to marry Lady Jo Farringmore, would you have gone ahead with it — or not?"

He asked the question with a certain wariness, as a player who stakes more on a move than he would care to lose. The glint of the gambler shone in his curious eyes. His right hand was thrust into his pocket.

Fielding was watching that right hand narrowly, but Dick's look, grim and unwavering, never left his opponent's face.

"Why do you want to know?" he demanded.

Saltash's smile deepened, became a grimace, and vanished.

"I will tell you when you have answered me," he said. "But whatever you say will be used against you, — mind that!"

"What do you mean?" Dick said.

"Never mind what I mean! Just answer me! Answer me now! Would you have married her under those circumstances? Or would you — have thrown her over — to me?"

Dick's eyes blazed. "You damn blackguard! Of course I should have married her!"

"You are sure of that?" Saltash said.

"Damn you — yes!" With terrific force Dick answered him. He stood like an animal ready to spring, goaded to the end of his endurance, yet waiting — waiting for something, he knew not what.

If Saltash had smiled then he would have been upon him in an instant. But Saltash did not smile. He knew the exact value of the situation, and he handled it with a sure touch. With absolute gravity he took his hand from his pocket.

Fielding took a swift step forward, but with an odd twist of the brows Saltash reassured him. He held out a revolver to Dick on the palm of his hand.

"Here you are!" he said. "It's fully loaded. If you want to shoot a friend, you'll never have a better chance. Mr. Fielding, will you kindly look the other way?"

Dead silence followed his words. The lamplight flickered on Dick's face, throwing into strong relief every set grim feature. His lips were tightly compressed — a single straight line across his stern face. His eyes never varied; they were almost unbearably bright. They held Saltash's with a tensity of purpose that was greater than any display of physical force. It was as if the two were locked in silent combat.

It lasted for many seconds, that mute and motionless duel, then very suddenly from a wholly unexpected quarter there came an interruption. Columbus, sensing trouble, pushed his stout person between the two men and leapt whining upon Dick, pawing at him imploringly with almost human entreaty.

It put an end to the tension. Dick looked down involuntarily and meeting the dog's beseeching eyes, relaxed in spite of himself. Saltash uttered a curt laugh and returned the revolver to his pocket.

"That settles that," he observed. "Columbus, my acknowledgments — though I am quite well aware that your eloquent appeal is not made on my behalf! You know what the little beggar is asking for, don't you?"

Dick laid a soothing hand on the grizzled head. "All right, Columbus!" he said.

Saltash's smile leapt out again. "Oh, it's all right, is it? I am to have a free pardon then for boosting you over your last fence?"

Again Dick's eyes came to him, and a very faint, remote smile shone in them for an instant in answer. Then, very steadily, without a word, he held out his hand.

Saltash's came to meet it. They looked each other again in the eyes — but with a difference. Then Saltash began to laugh.

"Go to her, my cavalier! You'll find her — waiting — on the *Night Moth.*"

"Waiting?" Dick said.

"For Columbus," said Saltash with his most derisive grin, and tossed Dick's hand away.

Chapter X

THE LAST FENCE

A chill breeze sprang up in the dark of the early morning and blew the drifting fog away. The stars came out one by one till the whole sky shone and quivered as if it had been pricked by a million glittering spear-points. The tide turned with a swelling sound that was like a vast harmony, formless, without melody, immense. And in the state-cabin of the *Night Moth*, the woman who had knelt for hours by the velvet couch lifted her face to the open port-hole and shivered.

She had cast her hat down beside her, and the cold night-wind that yet had a faint hint of the dawn in it ruffled the soft hair about her temples. Her face was dead-white, drawn with unspeakable weariness, with piteous lines about the eyes that only long watching can bring. She looked hopeless, beaten.

The shaded light that gleamed down upon her from the cabin-roof seemed somehow to hurt her, for after a second or two she leaned to one side without rising from her knees and switched it off. Then with her hands tightly clasped, she gazed out over the dim, starlit sea. The mystery of it, the calm, the purity, closed round her like a dream. She gazed forth into the great waste of rippling waters, her chin upon her hands.

Softly the yacht lifted and sank again to the gentle swell. The wild waves of a few hours before had sunk away. It was a world at peace. But there was no peace in the eyes that dwelt upon that wonderful night scene. They were still with the stillness of despair.

The cold air blew round her and again she shivered as one chilled to the heart, but she made no move to pick up the cloak that had fallen from her shoulders. She only knelt there with her face to the sea, staring out in dumb misery as one in whom all hope is quenched.

From somewhere on shore there came the sound of a clock striking the hour in clear bell-like notes. One, two, three! And then silence, with the murmur and splash of the rising tide spreading all around.

And then suddenly out of the utter quietness there came a sound — the scuttle of scampering feet and an eager whining at the door behind her. It stabbed like a needle through her lethargy. In a moment she was on her feet.

The door burst in upon her as she opened it, and immediately she was sprung upon and almost borne backwards by the wriggling, ecstatic figure of Columbus. He flung himself into her arms with yelps of extravagant joy, as if they had been parted for months instead of hours, and when, somewhat overwhelmed with this onslaught, she sat down with him on the couch, he scrambled all over her, licking wildly whatever part of her his tongue could reach.

It took some time for his rapturous greetings to subside, but finally he dropped upon the couch beside her, pressed to her, temporarily exhausted, but still wriggling spasmodically whenever her hand moved upon him. And then Juliet, for some odd reason that she could not have explained, found herself crying in the darkness as she had not cried all through that night of anguish.

Columbus was deeply concerned. He crept closer to her, pawed at her gently, stood up and licked her hair. But she wept on helplessly for many seconds with her hands over her face.

It was Columbus who told her by a sudden change of attitude that someone had entered at the open door and was standing close to her in the dark. She started upright very swiftly as the dog jumped down to welcome the intruder. Vaguely through the dimness she saw a figure and leapt to her feet, her hands tight clasped upon her racing heart.

"Charles! Why have you come here?"

There was an instant of stillness, then a swift movement and a man's arms caught her as she stood and she was a prisoner.

She made a wild struggle for freedom. "No — no!" she panted. "Let me go!"

But he held her fast, — so fast that she gasped and gasped for breath, — saying no word, only holding her, till suddenly she cried out sharply and her resistance broke.

She hid her face against him. "You!" she said. "You!"

He held her yet in silence for a space, and through the silence she heard the beat of his heart; quick and hard, as if he had been running a race. Then over her bowed head he spoke, his voice deep, vibrant, seeming to hold back some inner leaping force.

"Didn't I tell you I should follow you — and bring you back?"

She shrank at his words. "I can't come — I can't come!" she said.

"You will come, Juliet," he said quietly.

"No — no!" She lifted her head in sudden passionate protest. "Not to be tortured! I can't face it! Before God I would rather — I would rather — die!"

He answered her with flame that leaped to hers. "And don't you think I would rather die than let you go?"

"Ah!" she said, and no more; for the fierce possession of his hold checked all remonstrance.

She sought to hide her face again, but he would not suffer it, and in the end with an anguished sound she ceased to battle with him and sank down in utter weakness in his hold.

He lifted her then, but he did not kiss her. He found the sofa and laid her down upon it. Then she heard him feeling along the wall for the switch.

She reached out a quivering hand and pressed it, then as the light glowed she turned from him, covering her eyes from his look. He stood for a few seconds gazing down at her, almost as if at a loss.

And while he so stood, there arose a sudden deep throbbing that mingled with the splash of water, and the yacht ceased to rise and fall and thrilled into movement.

Juliet gave a great start. "Dick! What are they doing? Oh, stop them — stop them!"

He stooped and caught her outflung hands. His eyes looked deeply into hers. "They are obeying — my orders," he said.

"Yours?" She gazed up at him incredulously, shivering all over as if in an ague.

His face told her nothing. It was implacable, granitelike, save for the eyes, and from those she shrank uncontrollably as though they pierced her.

"Yes, mine," he said somberly. "I have — something to teach you, Juliet — something that you can only learn — alone with me. And till you have learnt it, there will be no going back."

She bent her head to avoid the unwavering directness of his look. "You — are going to hurt me — punish me," she said under her breath.

His hands still held hers, and strangely there was something sustaining as well as relentless in their grasp.

"It may hurt you," he said. "I don't feel I know you well enough to judge. As to punishing you —" he paused a moment — "well, I think you have punished yourself enough already."

Again a great tremor went through her, — a tremor that ended in a sob. She bent her head a little lower to hide her tears. But they fell upon his hands and she could not check them. Her throat worked convulsively, resisting all her efforts and self-control. She became suddenly blinded and overwhelmed by bitter weeping.

"Ah, Juliet — Juliet!" he said, and went down on his knees before her, folding her closely, closely to his breast . . .

It seemed to her a very long time later that she found herself lying exhausted against the sofa-cushions, feeling his arm still about her and poignantly conscious of his touch. His other hand was pressed upon her forehead, and her tears had ceased. She could not remember that he had spoken a single word since he had taken her into his arms, neither had he kissed her, but all her fear of him was gone.

Through the open port-hole there came to her the swish of water, and she heard the throb and roar of the engines like the sound of a distant train in a tunnel. Moved by a deep impulse that came straight from her soul, she took the hand that lay upon her brow and drew it downwards first to her lips, holding it there with closed eyes while she kissed it, then softly to her heart while she turned her eyes to his.

"Oh, Dick," she said, "are you sure — are you quite sure — that — that — I am worth keeping?"

"I am quite sure I am going to keep you," he answered very steadily.

Her two hands closed fast upon his. "Not — not as a prisoner?" she whispered, wanly smiling.

"Yes, a prisoner," he said, not without a certain grimness, "that is, until you have learnt your lesson."

"What lesson?" she asked him wonderingly.

"That you can't do without me," he said, a note of challenge in his voice.

Something in his look hurt her. She freed one hand and laid it pleadingly, caressingly, against his neck. "Oh, Dicky," she said, "try to understand!"

His face changed a little, and she thought his mouth quivered ever so slightly as he said. "It's now or never, Juliet. If I don't come to a perfect understanding with you tonight, we shall be strangers for the rest of our lives."

She shivered at the finality of his words, but they gave her light. "I have hurt you — horribly!" she said.

He was silent.

She pressed herself to him with a sudden passionate gesture. "Dick — my husband — will you forgive me — can you forgive me — before you understand?"

Her eyes implored him, yet just for a second he hesitated. Then very swiftly he gathered her closely, closely against his heart, and kissed her pleading, upturned face over and over. "Yes!" he said. "Yes!"

She clung to him with all her quivering strength. "I love you, darling! I love you, — only — only — you!" she whispered brokenly. "You believe that?"

"Yes," he said again between his kisses.

"And if I tried to do without you it was only because — only because — I loved you so," she faltered on. "Your anger is just — the end of the world for me, Dick. I can't face it. It tears my very self."

"My darling! My own love!" he said.

"And then — and then — I had such an awful doubt of you, Dicky. I thought your love was dead, and I thought — and I thought I couldn't hope to hold you — after that. I'd got to free you somehow. Oh, Dicky, what agony love can be!"

"Hush, darling, hush!" he said.

She lay in his arms, her eyes looking straight up to his. "I never meant to do it, dear, — never meant to win your love in the first place. I always knew I wasn't worthy of it. I think I told you so. Dicky, listen! I've had a horrid life. My mother was divorced when Muff and I were youngsters at school. My father died only a year after, and no one ever cared what happened to us after that. We had an aunt — Lady Beatrice Farringmore — and she launched me in society when I left school. But she never cared — she never cared. She was far too busy with her own concerns. I just went with the crowd and pleased myself. No one ever took anything seriously in our set. It was just a mad rush of gaiety from morning till night. We were like a lot of empty-headed, mischievous children, horribly selfish of course, but not meaning any harm — at least not most of us. Everyone had a nickname. It was the fashion. It was Saltash who first called me Juliet. He said I was so tragically in earnest — which was really not true in those days. And I called him Charles Rex."

She paused, for Dick's arms had tightened about her.

"Go on!" he said, in a low voice. "I suppose he — made love to you, did he?"

"Everyone did that," she said. "He was just a specimen of the rest — except that I always somehow knew he had more heart. It was just a game with us all. It used to frighten me rather at first till — till I got used to it. When I was quite young I had rather a bitter lesson. I began to care for a man who I thought was in earnest, and I found he wasn't. After that, I never needed another. I played the game with the rest. Sometimes I hurt people, but I didn't care. I always said it was their fault for being taken in."

"That doesn't sound like you," he said.

"That was me," she returned, with a touch of recklessness, "till I read that first book of yours — *The Valley of Dry Bones*. That brought me up short. It shocked me horribly. You cut very deep, Dicky. I'm carrying the scars still."

He bent without words and set his lips to her forehead, keeping them there in mute caress while she went on.

"I had just begun to play with Ivor Yardley. He was my latest catch, and — I was rather proud of him. He didn't trouble to pursue many women. And then — after reading that book — I felt so evil, so unspeakably ashamed, that, when I knew he was really in earnest, I didn't throw him off like the rest. I accepted him."

She shuddered suddenly and twined her arm about her husband's neck.

"Dicky, I — went through hell — after that. I tried — I tried very hard — to be honorable — to keep my word. But — when the time drew near — I simply couldn't. He always knew — he must have known — I didn't love him. But he just wanted me, and he didn't care. And so — almost at the last moment — I let him down — I ran away. And, oh, Dicky, the peace of this place after all that misery and turmoil! You can't imagine what it was like. It was heaven. And I thought — I thought it was going to be quite easy to be good!"

"And then I came and upset it all," murmured Dick, with his lips against her hair.

Her hold tightened. "It's been one perpetual struggle against appalling odds ever since," she said. "If it hadn't been for — Robin — I should never have married you."

"Yes, you would," he said quietly. "That was meant. I've realized that since."

"I am not sure," she said. "If you hadn't been so miserable, I should have told you the truth. You wouldn't have married me then."

"Yes, I should," he said.

She drew a little away to look into his face. "Dick, are you sure of that?"

"I am quite sure," he said, and faintly smiled. "It's just because I am sure, that I am with you now — instead of Saltash. It was his own test."

Her eyes met his unflinching. "Dick, you believe that Saltash and I are just — friends?"

"I believe it," he said.

"And you are not angry with him?"

"No." He spoke with slight effort. "I am — grateful to him."

"But you don't like him?" she said.

He hesitated momentarily. "Do you?"

"Yes, of course." Her brows contracted a little. "I can't help it. I always have," she said rather wistfully.

He bent abruptly and kissed them. "All right, darling. So do I," he said.

She smiled at him, clinging closely. "Dicky, that's the most generous thing you ever did!"

"Oh, I can afford to be generous," he said, "now that I know your secrets and you know mine. Will you tell me something else now, Juliet?"

"Yes, dear," she whispered.

He laid his cheek against hers. "I was going to tell you my secret when you had read that last book of mine. When were you going to tell me yours?"

"Oh, Dicky!" she said in some confusion, and hid her face against his neck.

"No, tell me!" he said. "I want to know."

But Juliet only clung a little faster to him and buried her face a little deeper.

"Weren't you ever going to tell me?" he said, after a moment.

"Oh, yes — some time," she murmured from his breast.

"Well, when?" he persisted. "Just — any time?"

"No, dear, of course not!" A muffled sound that was half-sob and half-laugh came with the words.

Dick waited for a space, and then very gently began to feel for the hidden face. She tried to resist him, then, finding he would not be resisted, she took his hand and pressed it over her eyes, holding it as a shield between them.

"Won't you tell me?" he said.

She trembled a little in his hold. "That — that — is another secret, Dicky," she said very softly.

"Mayn't I — share it, sweetheart?" he said.

She uncovered her eyes with a little tremulous laugh, and lifted them to his. "Oh, I'm a coward, Dicky, a horrid coward. I thought — I thought I would tell you everything when — when you were holding your son in your arms. I thought you would have to — forgive me then."

"Oh, Juliet — Juliet!" he said, and tried to smile in answer, but could not. His lips quivered suddenly, and he laid his head down upon her breast.

And so, with her arms around him and the warm throbbing of her heart against his face, he came to the perfect understanding.

They saw the morning break through a silver mist, standing side by side on deck with the water sweeping snow-white from their keel.

Juliet, within the circle of her husband's arm, looked up and broke the silence with a sigh and a smile.

"Good morning, Romeo! And now that I've learnt my lesson, hadn't we better be going home?"

He kissed her, and drew her cloak more closely round her. "Do you want to go home?" he said.

She looked at him with a whimsical frown. "Well, I think I am at home wherever you are. But you are such a busy man. You can't be spared."

"They've got to spare me for today," he said.

"Ah! And tomorrow?"

"Tomorrow too, Juliet. I'm giving up my work at Little Shale."

"But you can't give it up at a moment's notice," she said.

"The squire is managing it. They can close the school for a week anyway. Then he can find a substitute."

Juliet pondered this. Then, "Let's go back till the end of the term, Dicky!" she said.

He looked at her. "You want to, my Lady Joanna?"

She shook her head at him. "You're not to call me that. Yes, I'd like to go back and finish there, but only as your wife — nothing else."

"My lady wife!" he said, patting her cheek.

She leaned her head against his shoulder. "Yes, and there are the miners to settle. Do you think they'll ever be friends with me, Dick?"

"Of course they will," he said. "By the way, Juliet, I've a piece of news for you. You know what Yardley came for?"

"No, I don't," she said, looking momentarily startled.

His hand reassured her. "No, not for you, darling. He didn't expect to find you. No, he came because he had been told — by Jack, if you want to know — that I was doing the work of an agitator among the men."

"Dick!" she said, with quick indignation. "How dared he?"

His touch restrained her. "It doesn't matter. He came to see for himself, and he knows better now. He told me after the meeting that I could take over his share of the concern if I liked. And I took him at his word then and there. I've got some money put by, and the squire can put up the rest. Do you think your brother will mind?"

"Muff!" she said. "Oh no! He never minds anything."

"I'll buy him out too then some day, and we'll make that mine a going concern, Juliet. I'll teach those men to use their brains instead of being led by these infernal revolutionists. They shall learn that those who fight for themselves alone never get there. I'll teach 'em the rules of the game. They shall learn to be sportsmen."

Juliet's eyes were shining. "Bravo, Dick!" she said softly.

He met her look. "You'll have to help me, sweetheart," he said.

She gave him her hands. "I will help you in all that you do, Dick," she said.

It was at this point that Columbus, who had been sitting a little apart with his back turned, got up, shook himself vigorously as if to give warning of his approach, and went to Juliet.

He set his paws against her with a loud pathetic yawn.

She bent over him. "Oh, poor Columbus! He's so bored! Do you want to go home, my Christopher?"

"Poor chap!" said Dick. "It is rather hard to be dragged away on someone else's honeymoon whether you want to or not. Had enough of it, eh? Think it's high time we took the missis home?"

Columbus snuffled into his hand, and wagged himself from the tail upwards.

Juliet put her arms round him and kissed him. "Dear old fellow, of course he does! He thinks we are just the silliest people alive. Perhaps — from some points of view — we are."

Columbus said nothing, but he surveyed them both with a look of twinkling humor, and then smothered a laugh with a sneeze.

THE END

CPSIA information can be obtained at www.ICGtesting.com
Printed in the USA
BVOW02s1022091213

338591BV00001B/147/P

9 781606 642153